The Killing

Daniel Faust, Book Five

by Craig Schaefer

Craig Schaefer / Demimonde Books
2328 E. Lincoln Hwy, #238
New Lenox, IL 60451-9533
www.craigschaeferbooks.com

Publisher's Note: This is a work of fiction. Names, characters, places, and incidents are a product of the author's imagination. Locales and public names are sometimes used for atmospheric purposes. Any resemblance to actual people, living or dead, or to businesses, companies, events, institutions, or locales is completely coincidental.

Cover Design by James T. Egan of Bookfly Design LLC.
Author Photo ©2014 by Karen Forsythe Photography
Craig Schaefer / The Killing Floor Blues — 1st ed.
ISBN 978-0-9961927-3-6

Prologue

Fleiss cradled the folder to the chest of her gray wool blazer like it was a sleeping rattlesnake. The glass elevator chimed, its cage shuddering as it soared up to the penthouse floor. Her final destination.

The door opened onto a window-walled antechamber done up with burnt-orange trim and beech furniture. A young woman—her dress an identical shade of orange—rose from behind the reception desk.

"Welcome to Northlight, Ms. Fleiss," she chirped. "Did you have a good flight?"

Fleiss ignored the pleasantries. She slipped off her mirrored sunglasses as she strode toward the tall double doors at the opposite end of the waiting room, her heels clicking on the hardwood floor.

"May I see him?"

The receptionist waved her hand, still flashing a thousand-watt smile, and the doors swung open onto darkness.

No windows in the penthouse. The doors glided shut behind her, sealing her inside, plunging her into shadow.

That was fine. Fleiss could see in the dark.

Behind a curving desk, a figure sat silently in the gloom. A man built of shadow and fog, a living negative scratched onto the film of the world. He idly shuffled a worn-out pack of tarot cards. He'd flip a few cards onto the desk, study them for a moment, then shuffle them back in and try again.

His head lifted, tilting Fleiss's way, and he flashed gleaming, perfectly white teeth.

"My darling," the Smile said. "Now what was so important you had to come all the way here just to see me? I hope you're bringing me happy news."

"My lord." She dropped into a nervous half bow. "We may have a problem. I just received the latest surveillance data from our seers."

She set her folder on the desk between them.

"They believe—" She paused, swallowing hard. "They believe the Paladin was in Las Vegas. Recently."

He didn't reply at first. Ghostly fingers opened the folder, leafing through pages of hand-typed transcripts.

"*Was,*" he finally echoed, his voice gone cold.

"By the time they picked up the trace, it was too late. They only caught the faintest scent. They don't even know if it's a man or a woman this time around—"

"The Paladin is a woman," the Smile spat. "It is *always* a *woman.* Do me a favor, love: go down to the laboratory, pick out the weakest seer, and put a bullet in his head. Then give the others a pay bonus. See if that encourages them to work more diligently."

"There's something else," Fleiss said.

"Of course there is. Continue."

"There was some sort of occult-underworld gathering in Chicago. A poker tournament. They think at least one of our enemies was there, but that's not the problem. Daniel Faust was in Vegas at the same time as the Paladin. And we know he was at that tournament in Chicago, too. It could be a coincidence, but—"

"But there are no coincidences. First rule of magic, I've been told. You're *certain* Faust is nothing but a penny-ante street mage?"

Fleiss nodded vigorously. "I've swapped him into the Play, making him take the Thief's place. I couldn't have done that if he was one of...one of *your* kind, my lord. It wouldn't have worked.

My concern is that he's being manipulated by outside forces. A rogue pawn."

The Smile shuffled his cards and tossed one down, letting it flutter to the desk. The Fool. Then another. The Wheel of Fortune.

"I would like, with your permission," Fleiss said, "to hedge our bets."

"I'm listening."

Fleiss touched the desk with her fingertips. She eyed the cards as the Smile scooped them up again.

"All the Play actually *requires* is that the Thief—or in this case, Daniel Faust—be imprisoned, suffer, and die. We've already achieved the first condition just by snaring him in our trap. While I have no doubt that the ordeals ahead will get the rest of the job done to your satisfaction, I could arrange to send in a pair of contractors with concealed weapons. They'll ensure we get the ending we need."

"You mean to say," the Smile asked, "that you want to guarantee the fulfillment of a sacred prophecy by *cheating?*"

She bowed her head.

"I meant no offense, my lord."

He stood—*flowed* up from his desk, a serpentine coil of darkness mimicking a man's shape. He glided against her, three hands stroking the small of her back, two cold mouths tasting the skin of her neck as she rolled her head back and gasped.

"I approve," he murmured. "Do it."

"Anything for you, my lord," Fleiss whispered. "I worship your shadow. I revere the ground you walk upon."

He chuckled, slowly pulling away. His smoky outline billowing.

"I know," he said. "I created you that way. And soon I'll be back to my old glory. I've been stretching my muscles a bit. Reminding myself what I'm capable of. Not much I can do beyond this paltry tower, but it keeps me entertained. Now go. Kill Faust for me. Fulfill what is written."

Behind her, the penthouse doors swung open. Fleiss bowed and took her leave. She strode through the sapphire-blue lobby, her heels muffled on the thin gray carpeting. The receptionist, his suit the same shade of blue as the walls, rose from behind his desk.

"Thank you for coming, Ms. Fleiss," he said with a smile. "Have a safe flight home."

1.

I woke to the grind of a school bus engine and the stench of diesel exhaust. *No,* I thought, looking out at the Mojave Desert through a mesh of reinforced steel, *not a school bus.*

My head pounded like a five-tequila hangover and my mouth was dry as a cotton ball. I tried to rub my forehead. Chains rattled. My hand jerked short.

Shackles. A heavy leather belt was locked around my waist. A belt over a dingy orange jumpsuit. Chains ran to the cuffs on my wrists and ankles.

"...the fuck am I?" I muttered. The guy sitting next to me had *Emilie* tattooed down his neck in flowing calligraphy. He gave me the side-eye.

"Transfer bus, man. Goin' to the Iceberg. Eisenberg Correctional."

Now I was wide awake. We rode near the back of a packed bus, two men in jumpsuits and chains to each dirt-brown vinyl bench. Up front, a Department of Correctional Officer held a shotgun like he thought he was in a cowboy movie.

"What? That's a prison."

He looked at me like I'd sprouted a second head. "Uh-huh. You were expecting Disney World?"

"I was expecting *county.* I just got busted an hour ago. I should be in jail waiting for—"

No. Not an hour ago. It all flooded back to me at once: the setup, getting caught red-handed with a dead drug dealer and a gun one bullet short. Hauled in by Las Vegas Metro. Trying to convince Harmony Black that the Chicago Outfit's pet shape-shifter had framed me for murder.

It had *just happened*. I knew it just happened. So why was the high-noon sun burning down at least twelve hours later, and why couldn't I remember anything that had happened in between then and now?

"There's been a mistake," I told the guy. "I can't be going to prison. I haven't even had a bail hearing yet, let alone a trial."

He shook his head, giving me a gap-toothed smile.

"Man, most dudes just insist they're innocent and leave it at that. You're really going the extra mile."

I stared out the window, though the mesh, looking out over the desolation. Nothing here but rocks, cactus and sand, stretching out to the horizon line. Then the bus turned, the two-lane highway bending hard left, and I got a glimpse of our final destination.

Beehives. Those were what I thought of when the towers loomed up ahead, boiling like a mirage in the dry desert air. Three giant beehives, fat cones of drab beige concrete dotted with tiny windows that caught the sunlight and flashed like diamonds.

"Bigger than it looks," my neighbor told me. "Had a buddy who did a nickel in there. He says most of it's *under*ground."

I wouldn't know. The hardest time I'd ever done was a three-day stint in a county jail, if you didn't count my stretch in a halfway house for wayward youth. I'd always held that the most important skill in any career criminal's resume was "not getting caught."

At the moment, that wasn't working out so well for me.

Two rings of fencing stood between us and the prison, fifteen feet high and topped with razor-sharp concertina wire. A bright orange sign on the outer ring screamed "This Fence Is Electrified at All Times," next to a cartoon silhouette of a skeleton hit by a lightning bolt. The bus slowed to a stop and waited. A horn blared, twice, and the outer gate slowly rolled open.

As we stopped again, between the two gates, guards circled the bus. One held a huge black mastiff on a lead, while the other inspected the bus's undercarriage with a mirror on a telescoping rod. They were some kind of private security outfit, not state Correctional Officers, wearing crisp navy blue uniforms and belts loaded for bear: sleek black automatics on one hip, canisters of pepper spray on the other.

Satisfied, the guard with the mirror rapped on the bus door and waved us on. The second gate rolled open, grinding on its wheels, and my stomach roiled like I'd just gulped down an entire bottle of hot sauce. This was wrong, this was all wrong, and I wanted to run until my legs gave out.

I looked out the window, up to the towers that dotted the fence line. Polished windows gave each crow's nest a three hundred and sixty degree view of the action, and every guard on point wore a military-grade sniper rifle slung over one shoulder.

I hadn't even gotten off the bus yet, and I was already counting all the ways to die.

"On your feet!" shouted the officer up front as the bus came to its final stop. "You will exit the bus single file. You will follow the white line into the processing building. You will not speak."

I was bad at following orders. I got up and joined the slow line off the bus, shuffle-stopping every few feet until I got close enough to catch the officer's eye.

"Excuse me," I said, "I need to talk to somebody in charge. There's been a mistake—"

"You *will* exit the bus." His fingers tightened around the shotgun barrel. "You will *not* speak."

No point arguing with a brick wall. Especially not a brick wall with a gun. I stepped off the bus, my sneakers—*no, not my sneakers,* I thought, looking down at the ratty white track shoes—touching down on dusty gravel. Autumn had washed over the desert, casting the sky in a gloomy haze but not doing a thing to temper the gritty heat.

Two more guards stood at the edge of a long white line painted on the gravel, next to a gray plastic barrel. They unlocked my shackles and belt, tossing them into the barrel. I rubbed my wrists as I walked the line and smeared a bead of sweat on my forehead. I didn't feel any freer.

The white-line highway ran between two walls of fencing, an open yard on either side where inmates did pull-ups on chin bars, played chess, walked, and shot the breeze. Mostly, though, they watched. Casually glancing to my left and right, I saw more cons watching me than guards. They were casual about it, too, but I knew when I was being sized up.

Just ahead of me, my seatmate said softly, "Don't make eye contact, bro. Don't wanna start shit 'til you get the lay of the land."

It was good advice. I kept my mouth shut and my eyes open. I wasn't planning on moving in, anyway; as soon as I got the ear of somebody in charge, he'd figure out the mix-up and I'd be on the first bus out of here. I was already working on my exit strategy.

My lawyer, J.T. Perkins, was a demon in the legal arena—and everywhere else, for that matter. He'd make sure I'd be granted bail. I'd walk out of jail and *keep* walking. Just take Caitlin and go.

Vegas was over. Nicky Agnelli was on the run, his empire in ruins. Jennifer would have to run, too, just in case Nicky decided to try his luck at turning state's evidence. The Chicago Outfit had won. That stung, but all I cared about was breathing free air. Maybe I could pack up my whole crew: take Corman and Bentley, Jennifer and Mama Margaux, and escape to someplace without an extradition treaty. Find a white-sand beach on the edge of paradise with crystal-clear water and frosty piña coladas all day long. Early retirement.

The fantasy kept my feet moving. Reality waited on the other side of a reinforced steel door, inside a lobby that reminded me of a DMV. Whirring, overtaxed fans pushed stagnant air around, and we followed the white line across a grimy linoleum floor.

"Head of the line, *halt!*" a basso voice shouted. The voice's owner had a head like a block of granite, with a broad lantern jaw and a flattop buzz cut. He walked up and down the line, taking time to give each and every one of us the stink eye.

"My name is Correctional Officer Jablonski," he bellowed, puffing out his chest. "You will address me as Correctional Officer Jablonski, or you will address me as sir. I do not know where you came from, and I do not care. You are now in *my* house, and so long as you are living under my roof and eating my food, you will obey my rules. The first rule is to keep your toes *on* that white line."

"Asshole thinks he's a drill sergeant," my seatmate muttered next to me.

Jablonski's head snapped on a swivel. He was up in the con's face in a heartbeat, leaning in so close I could smell the liver and onions on his breath. "*What* did you say, prisoner?"

He held up his hands in a nervous apology. "Nothing, man, nothing. Sorry."

Jablonski stared him down, daring him to open his mouth again. I held my breath. The convict cast his gaze to the floor. Satisfied, Jablonski slowly turned away.

The baton slid from his holster so fast I barely saw it coming. My seatmate didn't see it at all. Jablonski spun around, whipping the baton across his head with a deafening crack. Blood spattered the shoulder of my jumpsuit as the convict dropped like a sack of rocks, dribbling a trickle of crimson across the white line.

Fight or flight. My heart pounded, mainlining on a sudden speed pump of raw adrenaline. How many guards in the lobby? Six? Seven. Too many guns. No chance to fight, no chance to run. And while I wasn't up on the latest in prison administration policies, I was pretty goddamn sure what I'd just witnessed was illegal as all hell. I swallowed it down, bottling the fear, standing still as a statue and digging my nails into my palms to keep my hands from shaking. Same as the other convicts.

"Take this joker to the hole," Jablonski told a nearby guard. "Write it up. Prisoner was reaching for my weapon. Self-defense."

They dragged him off by his wrists. I felt like I had a chicken bone lodged in my throat.

"Excuse me," I said, my voice coming out softer than I wanted it to. "Correctional Officer Jablonski. Sir."

His gaze swung my way, steady and harsh as a spotlight.

"I think there's been a mistake," I said. "I'm supposed to be in county, waiting for a bail hearing."

"What's your name, prisoner?"

"Faust. Daniel Faust."

He waved over a guard with a sheaf of papers on a stainless-steel clipboard. His finger slid down a list of names, his lips moving as he read silently.

He rapped the clipboard, twice. Then he looked my way. His voice low, on the edge of a growl.

"Do you enjoy wasting people's time, prisoner? Let me phrase that a different way. Do I *look* like somebody whose time you should be wasting?"

"No," I said, bracing myself. "Sir."

His hand eased toward his baton.

On the street, I'd know what to do. Throw the first punch, and make it a good one. Get inside his reach and beat him down before he knew what hit him. If we were alone, away from witnesses, whip out some magical firepower. On the street, I could have handled Correctional Officer Jablonski.

We were a long way from the street. And I realized, feeling the eyes of every guard in the room burning into me, I didn't *have* any options. Jablonski could do whatever he wanted to me, and all I could do was take it.

Helpless. I'd learned what it meant to be helpless as a child growing up in my father's house. And I'd dedicated most of my life to making damn sure I'd never feel that way again.

But here I was.

2.

J ablonski's hand hovered over the hilt of his baton. Then, slowly, it eased back.

"Let's go," he called out, turning away from me and addressing the entire line. "Processing time. Strip down."

Guards slid big cardboard boxes down the line. Grumbling as loudly as they dared, the convicts undressed like they were in the locker room at the neighborhood gym. I didn't like it, but I didn't see any other option. I kicked off my shoes and socks, tossing them into the nearest box, and unbuttoned the orange jumpsuit. I blinked as I tugged it down.

Tighty-whities? I thought. *Those weren't my sneakers, and this sure as hell isn't my underwear. Whose clothes are these, and where did I get them?* That gap of missing time, night to noon, kept gnawing at the back of my mind as I stripped down.

I stood with my bare toes on the line and tried to ignore that I was stark naked. At least I wasn't alone. The inked-up skin around me must have kept a tattoo parlor in business for a year.

"As I come to you," Jablonski bellowed, "you will squat with your knees spread, lift your scrotum, and cough. If I suspect you are attempting to smuggle contraband into my house, you will be dealt with *most* severely. Am I understood?"

I didn't join the tepid chorus of "yes, sirs." I just waited my turn, squatted down at his feet, and completed my part of the humiliating ritual before he moved on to the next man. A sullen silence felt like my only defense. A cardboard shield is still a shield if that's all you've got.

"Lice?" Jablonski called out. Another guard walked the line with an industrial-sized bottle of green, goopy liquid. "Not in *my* house. You will thoroughly rub the disinfectant into your scalp and pubic hair, assuming you are old enough to grow any."

Two pumps of the goop squirted into my cupped hands, ice cold and vaguely tingling. I massaged it into my hair and tried to think of white-sand beaches.

At least the next step was a change of clothes. One by one, guards dropped a neatly folded bundle into each waiting prisoner's arms. Eisenberg Correctional's uniform was military tan. I ended up with a button-down shirt and trousers—the pants one size too large, the shirt one size too small—an undershirt, socks, underwear, and beige canvas shoes with cracked rubber soles. I was just happy to be dressed again. They marched us up the hall, where a pair of inmates stood beside antique barber chairs.

"Just a little off the top," I told him when it was my turn in the chair.

"Funny guy," he said, firing up his electric clippers.

Stroke by shrill, whining stroke, I watched the remnants of a twenty-dollar haircut tumble to the floor. As he ushered me out of the chair and waved over the next prisoner in line, I caught a glimpse of myself in the mirror. Crude buzz cut, prison fatigues, and a haunted look in my eyes.

I looked just like everybody else.

The guard with the clipboard, a thin guy with peach fuzz for a mustache, surveyed the room. "Prisoners! When your name is called, step forward. Bachman, MacGillis, Posner, Faust!"

I approached in a cluster with the other three, and he lined us up in front of him.

"I'm Correctional Officer Emerson," he said, handing the first prisoner a long envelope and working his way down the line as he spoke. "You four are being housed in Hive C. These envelopes contain your admissions paperwork, orientation and rules, commissary and deposit information. You will be evaluated for work assignments tomorrow morn—"

He paused in front of me. No more envelopes on the clipboard.

"Damnit," he sighed. "I'd like to go just one shift without a paperwork screwup. All right, Faust, just get situated in your cell and we'll send someone with your file once the front office finds it. Don't worry, this happens every day."

"I'm not even supposed to be here," I told him, but I knew I was wasting my breath.

"If I had a nickel for every time I heard that." He rolled his eyes. "All right, men, listen up. For better or for worse, you're here now, and Hive C is your new home for the duration. Do your time, follow the rules, and we'll get along just fine. And just in case you're having unhealthy thoughts, here's a fact you should take to heart: Eisenberg Correctional was built in 1997. In this institution's history, there have been *zero* successful escapes. You will not be the first."

*　*　*

From the outside I'd seen the great concrete hives rising up from the desert waste. Now, on the inside, I realized that was exactly what they were: hives for human beings.

Cells ringed the conical base. Above it, a second tier, slightly overhanging the first and slightly smaller. Then another, and another, floor after floor. *Not a hive after all*, I thought, *a warehouse. And a damn big one.* A guard tower stood at the heart of the hive, connected by steel mesh walkways to the outer tiers at various levels. Warped one-way glass covered the shaft of the tower, reflecting back at the cells like the mirrors in a carnival funhouse. At the top, where the tower flared outward like a mushroom cloud, guards with sniper rifles kept watch from their perch.

"Observe that red line," Emerson told us, gesturing to the ring of red paint that circled the base of the tower. "If you cross that line, or attempt to enter the tower, you will be killed."

A sign plastered to the mirrored wall, just left of the guards' key-carded doorway, read "*NO WARNING SHOTS WILL BE FIRED.*"

I was feeling the warning shots from the gallery floor, myself. The open space around the tower was a free-for-all, prisoners milling around or sitting at round plastic tables with bench seats, some playing cards or flipping dominoes. I'd felt watched from the yard outside, but now that scrutiny was as focused and hot as a surgical laser.

It wasn't like the movies. There weren't any catcalls; nobody threw anything—not even a harsh word—but my quiet sense of apprehension grew worse with each passing glance. I knew the score: regardless of what Correctional Officer Jablonski wanted to believe, this was *their* house. And I wasn't invited.

"Faust," Emerson said, pointing up. "Your cell is two-thirty-two. Go up those stairs, hang a left."

As he gave the other newcomers their cell numbers, I realized what little safety I'd felt was long gone. Emerson wasn't here to protect me; he was here to process me into the system. Now I was processed and forgotten.

I walked into the mix, alone.

Chin up, I thought, coaching myself. *Eyes front. Don't walk too fast. If they smell fear on you, you're finished. You don't care about any of this. Repeat that until you believe it. You just don't care.*

Nobody reacted to me, nobody said a word. I was a ghost. A ghost with a hundred pairs of eyes following his every move.

I wasn't prepared for the stench. Air didn't flow through the hive so much as hang there like a pair of dirty sweat socks. It smelled like body odor and stale piss and food from a dead refrigerator. More than anything, it reminded me of the monkey house at a zoo. I climbed up to the second tier and went looking for my new cage.

They squeezed a lot of furniture into a space not much bigger than Caitlin's closet. Two narrow beds, one on each side, with beige blankets that matched my uniform, a stainless-steel sink, a toilet and a mirror, a narrow desk, and a pair of wall-mounted cabinets with sliding doors. My cell already had an occupant. He lay back on one bed and paged through a dog-eared paperback of John-Paul Sartre's *No Exit*.

"'Hell is other people,'" I quoted, leaning against the open cell door.

He lowered the book, tapped the pages, and smiled. He was maybe in his late forties, a little pudgy, with a wiry salt-and-pepper beard and cheap prescription glasses.

"Indeed it is," he said. "Ever seen the play?"

"I've only read it."

"Reading about hell," he said, swinging his legs around and sitting up, "makes me feel better about being here. It reminds me that there's always someplace worse you can go. I'm Paul, by the way."

"Daniel." I shook his hand. "I'm apparently your new roommate."

"I already like you better than the last one. *His* ideal use for a book was hollowing one out to hide contraband. Not much of a conversationalist."

"Well," I said, "don't get too used to me. I'm not supposed to be here."

Paul smirked. "Because you're innocent, right? Everybody here is innocent. Well, except for me. I'm the only guilty man in the whole place. You know anybody in here?"

"Not a soul. Mind giving me the lay of the land?"

He gestured to the opposite bunk, and I took a seat. The mattress was thinner than my index finger, layered over a slab of concrete.

"Here's the high points," Paul said. "First off, we just got off lockdown a couple of days ago, so tensions are running high. A couple of bangers brought their outside beefs in with them. That's a big no-no, but it happens. This is a black-on-brown deal, we're staying out of it, so do yourself a favor and keep strictly to the white corner of the yard until it all gets sorted out."

"Gotta tell ya," I said, "I'm not really big on the whole racial segregation deal."

Paul snorted and pushed up a sleeve. "Hey, you see a swastika on my arm? Outside of those Aryan Brotherhood assholes—and stay clear of them, because they're high *and* crazy—it isn't a racist thing. Just a race thing."

"Not real clear on the difference."

"It's not about hate. It's about having a group of people around who'll watch your back when the shit starts to fly. We all wear the same uniform, so what's that leave us? Skin. Each color polices their own, and the shot-callers try to keep the peace. Keep in mind that whites are outnumbered five to one in here. Bad odds for a lone wolf."

"So run with a pack," I said. "Noted. What else?"

"Watch the guards. Emerson, Emerson's okay—he just started working here, too new to pick up bad habits—but the rest of them..." He shook his head. "Never be alone with a guard if you can help it, and don't try to get familiar. All you'll do is end up on their radar, and you don't want that."

"I already met Jablonski in processing."

"Jablonski's a sadist," Paul said, frowning. "Worse, he's a stone killer. Likes to sit up in that tower and masturbate with a sniper rifle in his free hand, that's what I think."

"I saw him beat the crap out of a guy for nothing. How do they get away with that?"

Paul leaned over on his cot, glancing out the open cell door and up toward the top of the guard tower.

"You aren't just a ward of the state, my friend. The Iceberg is a *private* prison. Corporate owned and taxpayer financed. The guards aren't members of the state union, and they don't answer to anybody but the bean counters at Rehabilitation Dynamics. On that note? Stay out of the bathrooms on tier three."

"Yeah? Why's that?"

Paul shot another glance toward the open cell door. "Worst-kept secret in Hive C: the security camera in there's been broken for a month, and either nobody's bothered calling in a repair order or the bean counters don't want to pay for a new one. The guards only poke their heads in once a day. That place is Grand Central Station when it comes to dirty business."

A snaggletoothed con with a head like a bullet loomed in the doorway. He jerked his thumb my way and looked at Paul.

"He ain't seen Brisco yet."

"Brisco's the shot-caller for the whites in here," Paul told me. "You should go talk to him, introduce yourself. It's a respect thing. Respect is *very* important in here."

I stood up and stretched. Moving, but taking my time.

"Well," I said, "seeing as I've got an escort and everything, let's go meet the man in charge."

3.

Bullethead led me down to the floor of the hive. Inmates got out of our way, and fast. It was a calculated action, though; gazes flicked the other way, or it was suddenly time to wave and walk over to someone on the far side of the lockup, any excuse to suddenly be elsewhere. Everybody wanted to keep out of Bullethead's path, but nobody wanted to look like they were doing it because of him.

The man of the hour sat at a round plastic table, throwing down cards from a losing hand. He wore a permanent scowl, and he'd stripped down to his undershirt to show off muscles like steel cables under sleeves of cheap prison ink. I didn't need an introduction to know he was the shot-caller. The way all conversation died when we walked up to the table, and the way the four other players looked his way, told me all I needed to know.

"Brisco, I presume," I said, nodding his way.

He looked down at my empty hands. "That's right. Where's your jacket?"

"Jacket?"

His buddies had a snicker at that. Brisco sighed and laid his palms flat on the table.

"Your papers."

"They lost 'em," I said. "Emerson said he'd send them over as soon as the office got it sorted out."

They didn't like the sound of that. I wasn't sure what I'd said wrong, but there wasn't a friendly face at the table. They didn't invite me to sit down, either.

"Listen, fish." Brisco's eyes went hard. "I need to know who you are, and where you've been. And jackets don't lie. Now sometimes, just sometimes, we get new arrivals who think they can hide their tracks. Like rapists. People who rape kids, even."

He left it at that, tossing me the verbal ball. I locked eyes with him. I knew I was standing in a minefield. Worse, the mines had been planted according to a specific list of rules, and nobody had bothered giving me a copy. The last thing I wanted was a fight with Brisco, and going on the offensive could buy me more trouble than I could handle. At the same time, backing down felt like a bad, bad idea.

"If somebody said that about me," I replied, taking it slow, "they'd better be ready to back that up with some proof, or there's going to be more than harsh words between us."

He shrugged one shoulder.

"My boy Zap," Brisco said, "he's a trustee. He's allowed up in the front offices, and it's real easy for him to snag a few minutes of computer time. Now, when this conversation's over, he's gonna go check you out. So I ask you: is there anything in your jacket you wanna tell me about? Because if you man up and tell it straight, right here, right now, it'll go a lot easier than if Zap finds something I don't like."

I thought about a fervent denial, but in the end I just shrugged right back at him. "Let him look."

Everyone at the table turned to Brisco. He rapped his fingers on the fallen cards and nodded. "Okay," he said, "we can do it that way. Probably wanna go back up to your cell."

I obliged him. *This is bad*, I thought, climbing up the stairs. I didn't have a jacket because I wasn't even supposed to be in prison. What would Brisco's guy say when a database search came up empty? This place ran on rules. Rigid, unbending rules, the kind that get enforced with a shiv in the kidneys. I didn't think

Brisco was the type of guy who'd be happy with an unknown factor in his house.

Paul glanced up from his book as I walked in. "I need to talk to the warden," I told him.

"Jesus," he said, setting the paperback in his lap. "What'd you do?"

"Like I said, I'm not supposed to be here. The guards won't listen. I've got to go higher up the food chain."

Paul waved a hand. "You don't want that kind of attention. Look, just take it easy. Tomorrow you'll get a work assignment. Earn a little money and you can use the pay phones, get in touch with your lawyer."

"When do we get paid?"

Paul's lips moved as he ran the numbers in his head. "Next...Thursday. But pay's monthly, and there's a one-month delay for new arrivals—"

"A month? Paul, I can *not* be in here for a month."

He laughed, but there wasn't a speck of humor in it.

"You can't do a month? Friend, I've been here for eight years. Trust me. You can do a month."

How long before people start looking for me, I wondered. By now, Jennifer would know about her dead pot dealer. Once the cops started scouring Vegas looking for Nicky, *everybody* would know something was up. And then there was Caitlin. I'd been on my way to see her last night before I walked into the Chicago Outfit's trap; she'd be hunting for me already.

I slowed my breathing, willing my muscles to unclench, fighting panic. I had people on the outside. My people, my family. And once they discovered I was lost somewhere in the penal system, they'd raise hell to find me.

I almost wanted to smile. Daniel Faust, victim of the worst computer glitch in history.

Except that didn't explain my twelve hours of missing memory.

"Look," Paul said, "just get right with Brisco, keep your head down, and take it one day at a time. The days go faster than you think once you get used to being here."

"And don't drop the soap, right?"

Paul snorted. "It's not like on TV. I'm not saying *nobody* ever gets raped in here, but that's usually a revenge thing, not a sex thing. If somebody wants to get off and their right hand isn't doing the trick, there are plenty of ways to get that taken care of with a willing partner. Willing and enthusiastic, if you've got trade goods."

"Trade goods?"

"Commissary's got all the comforts of home, or at least a halfway decent 7-Eleven. Expensive, though, and unless you've got family on the outside and they're willing to put money on your account, you've gotta shop with the wages from your work detail."

"How much does that pay?" I asked him.

"Thirty cents an hour."

I arched one eyebrow.

"I know," Paul said, "right? But I'll tell you something: after you spend five hours mopping floors so you can afford a Hershey bar, that is the *finest* damn Hershey bar you will ever taste. Most of these guys, they don't have anybody on the outside, so they don't have much to shop with. You can get a lot of bang for your buck if you're willing to trade what you've got and help them out a little. Lots of us have side hustles. Like Sully, three cells down, he brews prison wine. The stuff smells like dog puke, but it'll get you higher than—"

He fell silent. Brisco's shadow loomed in the doorway, flanked by two dead-eyed bruisers. Nobody had a smile for me.

Brisco held an envelope in his calloused hands.

"Paul," he said softly, "let us have the room for a minute, would you please? Need a word with your bunkmate."

"Sure, okay," Paul said, nodding uncertainly as he made himself scarce.

Brisco and his boys came into the cell. Blocking the only way out.

"My boy found your paperwork," Brisco said. "Checked you out."

I stood up. Squared my shoulders.

"Yeah? Interesting reading?"

He glanced down at the envelope, then back at me. There was something in his eyes I couldn't quite read. Something anxious, like his world just went into a spin and he was still sorting out why.

He held out the envelope.

"Jesus, man, why did you think you had to *hide* that from us?" He looked to the thug on his left. "This guy, do you believe this? He's a for-real, no-bullshit *contract killer*. He's a fucking hit man for Nicky Agnelli."

I let out a sigh of relief. They'd found my real paperwork. Great. One step closer to getting this mess sorted, and one step closer to my bail hearing. Which I would gladly post a bond for—five minutes before fleeing the country.

"Well," I said, improvising, "I didn't want to come off like I was bragging or anything. And they really did lose my paperwork."

"It's all there," Brisco said. "And hey, something else."

He nodded to the guy on his right, who dropped a plastic shopping bag at the foot of my bunk. I peeked inside and found a cornucopia of goodies. Instant soup packets, powdered hot chocolate, a couple of candy bars, and mini bags of potato chips.

"It's how we welcome all the new guys," Brisco explained, "since it'll be a month before you'll be able to get anything at the commissary on your own. That should tide you over. Keep in mind, you'll be expected to contribute to the next one. Everybody pays it forward."

"I appreciate that," I said and offered him my hand. He had a grip like a bear trap.

"Come on down once you get settled in," he said, "and I'll introduce you around."

They left me alone with the goodies and the envelope. I sat back down and leafed through it, skipping the rules and regulations and heading straight for my rap sheet. It was nestled at the back, folded and printed on lime-green paper.

Then I started to read, and the entire world fell out from under me.

I read it a second time, then a third, as if the words might change. As if I was somehow misunderstanding them, and one more reading would make everything clear. As if it would make what I was reading any less insane. My eyes started skipping over the page, picking up words here and there.

...Murder, First Degree, one count

Racketeering, two counts

Criminal Conspiracy, four...

"No," I whispered.

...Daniel Faust stands convicted on all counts and sentenced to life in prison without possibility of parole.

The page buckled in my hands. In the top corner, I read the date.

I hadn't lost twelve hours of memory.

I'd lost four months.

4.

This wasn't Chicago's work. No, the Outfit had framed me for murder, pretty as a picture, but they couldn't have wiped the memories of my trial. They didn't have that kind of magical juice. And even if they could, why do it in the first place? The end result—getting me out of the picture while they laid siege to Las Vegas—was the same.

And where was my crew? There was no way they would have let me rot behind bars for four months. If the trial had been going that badly, Caitlin would have torn the county jail apart with her bare hands to get me out.

Assuming she wanted to, the traitor in the back of my mind piped up. The one who'd listened when Nadine told me that Caitlin was only using me. That once she was done with me, she'd throw me away.

No. *No.* I believed in Caitlin. And even in the worst-case scenario I could imagine, even if she'd turned her back on me, the rest of my family would still come to the rescue.

So where were they?

I struggled to think back, walking through the events of four months ago—or in my muddled mind, the last few days. There'd been the botched heist at Damien Ecko's jewelry store, the underground poker tournament, then handing off that Aztec dagger and finding out my "client" was really a hostage in his own mansion. I'd flown home to Vegas and got the call from the Outfit's rakshasa imitating Jennifer's voice, and walked right into their—

Wait. Back it up.

The store robbery. We'd worn monster masks because it was mid-September and Halloween stores were sprouting up like weeds in strip malls across the suburbs. That would make it January now.

So why did it still feel like late summer when I got off the prison bus? A hot, dusty day. Not that we often got a white Christmas in the Mojave Desert, but there was still a difference between September and January temperatures. The weather felt *exactly* the way it had when I'd flown back to Vegas.

I stepped outside and glanced into the next cell. A human skeleton with a conga line of needle marks running down his arm slouched on his bunk, staring at a magazine.

"Hey," I said, "you know what the date is?"

"Seventeenth," he told me.

"Yeah, but what month?"

He arched an eyebrow at me. "September."

I went back to my bunk.

I was busted in September. Sentenced four months later. But it was still September. Yesterday was the sixteenth. I'd flown home on the sixteenth. Gotten busted on the sixteenth. Then I spent four months in the legal system. In one day.

Sudden pain flared behind my eyes and inside my nostrils, a fire raging in my sinuses. I squeezed my eyes shut and pinched the bridge of my nose until it passed.

I read the date on the paperwork again. But now it wasn't a date at all. It was a blur, a blob of ink that shifted and squirmed. A liar unmasked, its hold on my mind broken.

It was a con. None of it had happened. Somebody, somehow, had thrown me behind bars with a mix of bogus paperwork and magical mind-hacking. How, I didn't know, but that was secondary to my real problem.

As far as the state was concerned, I would spend the rest of my life in this cell.

Unless I could prove otherwise. How far did the setup go? If

I found the judge who supposedly oversaw my trial, would she remember sentencing me? Hell, all I had to do was match the trial transcript to my arrest report, and that would *prove* the trial couldn't have possibly taken place. More than ever, I needed to get the ear of somebody in authority, somebody with the pull to—

"New guy."

I looked up, jolted from my thoughts. I had a visitor. A visitor the size of a professional wrestler, showing off the kind of muscles you only get with vigorous and enthusiastic steroid abuse.

"I'm Simms," he said, sounding friendly enough. There was something in his eyes, though, a predatory edge he couldn't hide.

"Faust," I told him.

"Thought I should introduce myself. See, I handle security for this tier."

"Security," I echoed, my voice flat.

"Yeah, I mean, it's a prison, right? Lotta bad guys around here. Some of these lifers, they've got nothing to lose. They'll take everything you've got and shank you just for kicks. You need a buddy, somebody to watch your back."

"I thought that was Brisco's job."

He flinched just a little at the mention of Brisco's name. Guess he hoped he'd catch the new guy before I learned the lay of the land. Didn't slow down his sales pitch, though. He was too single-minded for that.

"Nah, forget him. Look, know how many whites are living on this level? *Six.* On the whole tier. If a riot pops off, you think Brisco and his boys are gonna run down from tier five and save you? Not happening. But me, I'm just two cells away." He nodded to the left. "And I'll take care of you."

"For a price," I said.

"Sure. You scratch my back, I scratch yours, right? That's the American way. You give me, say, ten percent of your commissary goods, and I'll make sure nobody messes with you."

He came closer. Glanced down at the plastic bag at the foot of my bunk and nudged it with the toe of his canvas shoe.

"Case in point. This? This is just unsafe. Some big guy could walk in here right now and rip you off, take *all* your stuff. But if you sign up for my protection plan, I'll only take half, and we can be buddies."

"Half?" I asked. "What happened to ten percent?"

"First-day sign-up fee."

It wasn't hard to read between the lines. Simms was running a by-the-books extortion scam, and from the tension in his voice he was about ten seconds from escalating to the hard sell. The kind that, out in the civilian world, usually involves smashing up a store and doing some property damage to make a point.

In here, the only thing I had worth smashing up was *me*.

I weighed my options. Back down? Let him rob me? Not happening. Once word spread that I'd bent over for Simms, I could expect a parade of thugs outside my cell door, lining up to take the rest of my stuff and whatever else they wanted. I strongly doubted Simms's "protection" would be worth a bent nickel. That left me with one option. And facing down a guy at least a hundred pounds heavier and a foot taller than me while I didn't have a weapon or any of my magical gear didn't leave much doubt about the outcome.

The knowledge that I was probably about to get my ass kicked left me oddly tranquil. Pain was inevitable. Death wasn't. Once I accepted I was about to pick a fight and lose, I could focus on strategy.

What did I need? To get rid of Simms and show everybody else I wasn't afraid to brawl. That meant a change of venue.

"Well, that sounds reasonable," I said, leaning forward on my bunk as if to reach for the bag.

Then I shot to my feet with no warning, barreling toward him in a sprinter's launch and throwing my shoulder into his chest. It felt like hitting a slab of beef. He staggered back a step, grunting, then grabbed me in a clinch and swung me around. The cell bars rattled as I slammed against them, pain rocketing through my skull and shoulders. His fist hit my gut like a pile driver.

"Come on," he said, clenching my shoulder as he pulled his free hand back for another punch. "Don't be stupid. Just give it up—"

I turned my head and bit down on his hand as hard as I could, teeth breaking skin and grinding bone. It tasted like chewing into a rotten steak. He yelped, jerking his hand away, and I spat blood onto the cell floor. He was off-balance for a second, but I didn't press the attack. Instead I slipped to one side and took a running leap backward, throwing myself out of the cell and onto the tier walkway.

My back hit the walkway handrail as if Simms was the one who had thrown me, my arms flinging against the steel railing like a boxer on the ropes. I took a deep breath.

"*You're fucking dead,*" I roared at the top of my lungs. The dramatic cell exit had drawn a few eyes. Now *everybody* was watching. Heads popped out of cell doors all along the tier like woodchucks on Groundhog Day, and the crowds on the floor above leaned over the railing to get a view.

If Simms were smart, he would have cut his losses and backed down. He wasn't smart. Balling his bloody hand into a fist, he charged. He hit me like a freight train, his weight pulling me down to the walkway floor, both of us tumbling and throwing wild punches.

His fist cracked across my left eye, cut my eyebrow, and blotted out my vision in a trickle of blood. I kicked at him, couldn't connect, and he hammered my face again. My ears rang, a klaxon that wavered from one eardrum to the other, warbling across my brain. No, the alarm was real, as real as the boots thundering toward us from the tower walkway.

I looked up as they hit us with the pepper spray.

A torrent of bright orange foam splashed across my face, setting my eyes on fire. It felt like I'd just stuffed a fistful of hot peppers in my mouth and started chewing, the burn choking my nostrils and streaming down my throat, washing out my entire world in white-hot pain. They hauled Simms off me and pulled me back by my armpits, but all I could do was sputter and choke and claw at the foam on my face, smearing it in deeper.

I was worse than blind as the guards dragged me off, but I could hear the other inmates. Cheering, catcalling, hammering on cell bars and hooting. They'd gotten an unexpected show to liven up their afternoon, and they liked what they saw.

I had, I presumed, made my point.

5.

*L*ancaster read the brass nameplate on the warden's desk. A miniature Nevada state flag framed it on one side. On the other, Texas.

The warden was a big man with expansive body language and a powder-blue suit. When he spoke, eyeing me across his immaculately clean desk, he had a genteel Southern manner about him. He made me think of smoke and old hickory.

"I'd like to say that you set a record, son, getting into a fight less than two hours after arriving at my facility. I'd dearly like to say that."

My manacled hands sat idly in my lap, chained to a belt like I'd worn on the prison bus. They'd rinsed my eyes and slapped tiny bandages on the cuts on my eyebrow and cheek. I ached, mostly. My back throbbed, my face felt like a tenderized steak, and my ribs stung if I poked them. So I stopped poking them.

"What's the record?" I asked.

"Thirty-seven seconds. I watched the security camera footage and timed it with a stopwatch, for posterity's sake."

His office was plush, with a carpet that matched his suit and neo-Victorian furniture. A shrink's office, or a lawyer's maybe. We might have been standing in the heart of a prison, but the warden didn't skimp on comfort.

"That's the problem with criminals," I told him. "They tend to commit crimes."

I glanced back. A pair of stone-faced guards flanked the doorway, eyeing me like a roach that just scurried out from under their refrigerator.

"And yet, it is my sworn duty—as bequeathed upon me by God, the great state of Nevada, and the shareholders of Rehabilitation Dynamics of America—to impose some measure of order and safety upon this forlorn place. You are not making my job any easier, son."

"I'm not in the habit of looking for trouble," I lied.

The door opened. A prisoner came in—no shackles, toting a plastic bucket full of cleaning supplies. *One of the trustees*, I thought, *maybe the one Brisco had check me out*. He paused in the doorway, looking to Lancaster.

"Window cleaning, boss?"

"Go on." Lancaster gave him a nod. As the trustee shuffled across the office and sprayed the window down with blue cleaning fluid from a squirt bottle, the warden turned back to me. "I understand that sometimes fights are one-sided things. For example, in your case. This other man, Simms?"

My cheek ached. "It wasn't all that one-sided. I got a few good punches in."

Lancaster let out a polite chuckle. "What I mean is you may not have had a choice. I've gotten several reports that Simms is shaking down the weaker inmates. Extorting food and money. Is that what happened? Did he try to rob you?"

Over by the window, the trustee took his time wiping the glass clean. He wasn't being thorough; he was being slow. Making sure he didn't leave the office before he heard what I had to say.

If I told Lancaster what he wanted to hear, I might have a shot at winning him over. Maybe I could get him to dig up my case files and prove I didn't belong in here. Then again, every word that came out of my mouth would go straight to Brisco's ear. If there was one absolute, unbreakable rule of the underworld, written in blood and stone, it was this: *don't snitch*. Acting like I wanted Lancaster to solve my problem with Simms would make me look weak, and I couldn't afford that reputation if I wanted to survive long enough to escape.

"No," I told him, hating the words but saying them anyway. "It was me. I started the fight. Simms was just minding his own business."

Lancaster knitted his brows. "Minding his own business. In your cell."

"What can I say?" I shrugged. "He made a wrong turn and got lost. In his defense, all the cells look the same. Easy mistake to make."

"And you got the sudden notion to attack a man twice your size...why, exactly?"

"That's what the movies all say to do."

He tilted his forehead my way. "Pardon?"

"Prison movies. They all say that you're supposed to find the biggest, baddest guy in the yard and pick a fight on your first day." I paused as if reflecting. "Did...did the movies lie to me? That's the problem, warden. My brain's been corrupted by violent media and rock music."

Lancaster sighed. "While I'm certain it has, I find your explanation a bit far-fetched. Are you afraid of reprisal? Just tell us what really happened. We can protect you from Simms."

"I started the fight," I repeated.

The trustee finished. The window gleamed.

"All done here, boss," he said as he slunk out the door.

Lancaster folded his hands on the desk. "Normally, we have several means of addressing inmate-on-inmate violence. Loss of privileges. Time in administrative segregation. Criminal charges and additional years on your sentence. And if I truly believed you started that fight, we'd be pursuing one or several of those corrective measures. As it happens, I don't. But if you insist on refusing our protection, I just hope that the next time we speak, it isn't in the infirmary."

*   *   *

The prison yard made me think of a carton of Neapolitan ice

cream. Instead of strawberry, chocolate, and vanilla, the yard split along racial lines, but the invisible border between each color was just as real.

I didn't like it, but then again, I didn't like Neapolitan ice cream either.

The setup wasn't too shabby. A couple of weight sets alongside a jogging track, picnic benches here and there, a few two-seater tables with chessboards set into the plastic tabletops. I could imagine I was on a college campus, if it weren't for the fences, the gun towers, and the razor wire.

Paul walked the track, smoking a cigarette, keeping to himself. He gave me a wave and I wandered over. He shook his head at me.

"Wow. You just jump right in with both fists, don't you? Gonna have a beauty of a shiner there, too."

I touched the skin under my eye and winced. Puffy and raw.

"Well, shit," I told him, falling into step as we walked along the oval track, "there goes my modeling career. Hey, read something for me?"

I tugged the last sheet of my paperwork from my pocket, folded into a neat square, and unfurled it.

"They have a literacy class here, meets every Tuesday." Paul reached for the page. "You should look into that."

"Here," I said, tapping the corner of the sheet. The dates still blurred in my vision, like newsprint smudging under a gob of liquid soap. "How much time passed between my arrest and landing in here?"

"You tell me. You lived it."

"Humor me. What does it say?"

Paul shrugged. "Four months, give or take?"

I tapped another line. "When was I brought into custody?"

"September sixteenth."

"And what day is today?"

"The seventeenth," Paul said. "Why? What's the big deal?"

"Paul, how could four months have passed between yesterday and today?"

He blinked. Squinted at me.

"It...didn't. That doesn't make sense." Suddenly on edge, he pressed the page back into my hand. "I don't do riddles."

"Not a riddle. How could I have been tried and convicted if I was just arrested—"

He held up a hand, grimacing like he felt a migraine coming on. "Please, drop it, okay? My head is killing me."

This was bad. I'd hoped that whoever was behind all this, screwing with my memory and my sense of time, had kept it localized to me and anyone involved with putting me behind bars. I'd never met Paul before today, and even he couldn't push his brain through the teeth of this trap. Under normal circumstances, most people would assume a time discrepancy like that was a typo or a filing mistake, but that's not what was happening here. Anyone thinking about my trial just couldn't parse time at all. And thinking *too* hard earned them an instant burst of sinus pain, encouraging a change of subject.

How many people had been affected? The whole prison system?

The whole planet?

More important question: who had the power to weave a curse like that, and what had I done to piss them off?

Prince Sitri. This deal had his name written all over it. One of his little games, maybe: drop me in prison, bury me deep, and see if I could claw my way out. Exactly the kind of dick move he'd pull if he was bored enough, or if he wanted to make some kind of point.

And what if the point is "Caitlin isn't coming to help you"?

I shoved that thought into a mental box already cluttered with all the things that kept me up at night. Not a lot of room left in that box.

I was good at two things: leading my crew, and magic. Now my friends and family were on the far side of an electrified fence, and I couldn't work a ritual in a place with zero privacy and guards standing watch around the clock. If there was a better way to keep me caged, I couldn't think of one.

Despair started to creep around the edges of my mind, like lead weights tied to my wrists and ankles. I shoved that into the box, too.

Dig deeper, I told myself. *There's no such thing as a no-win situation. Think fast, fight hard, and breathe free air again. No matter what it takes.*

"Back in processing," I said to Paul, "Emerson told us that nobody's ever escaped from the Iceberg. That true?"

"No, but...well, sort of. It's compli—" He froze, eyes darting left. "Oh shit, hold on, here it comes."

I saw it too. Two guys from the black corner of the yard, shirts tied off around their waists, marching hard and fast with murder in their eyes. Coming up on a skinny Latino with a full-chest tattoo of the Virgin Mary, all on his own by the chess tables. A lone gazelle, separated from the herd and blissfully unaware of the doom heading his way.

6.

"We've gotta do someth—" I started to say. Paul put his hand on my chest.

"No, we *don't*," he told me. "This is *prison*, okay? You want to survive this place? Here's the best advice you'll ever get: never get involved in other people's fights. That makes it *your* fight."

I wouldn't have gotten there in time anyway. I watched as one of the attackers looped his arm around their target's throat, hauling him back and off-balance. The other reached under his tied-off shirt and yanked out a shiv—a jagged spike of metal wired to a broom-handle hilt, cheap and nasty and built for violence. The blows rained down fast and frantic, punching the spike into the Latino's chest and stomach and mutilating his tattoo, turning the Virgin Mary into a murder victim. If he prayed to her, it didn't help him any.

A klaxon whined from the gun towers, shrill as fingernails on a blackboard and loud enough to set my teeth on edge. Paul dropped to his knees and hissed, "Down! Do exactly what I do!"

I followed his lead, kneeling on the jogging track and lacing my fingers behind my neck. Around us, from one side of the yard to the other, everyone—including the two assassins—was doing the same. The killer dropped his shiv and knelt down beside his victim's corpse, waiting patiently as the hive doors burst open and uniforms flooded the yard. The klaxon fell silent.

"Don't even breathe funny until they give the all clear," Paul warned in a low voice, "and if you've got an itchy nose, live with it. Seriously, I can see the tower behind you. Jablonski's up there and he's staring right at us."

"Us? Why? We had nothing to do with it."

"Rotten bastard's looking for an excuse to put a bullet in me. Which we are *not* going to give him today. Just stay calm and pretend you're a statue."

The assassins were hauled off in cuffs, their victim on a stretcher already dark with old bloodstains. The wave of guards fell back like a navy blue tide. Then the alarm honked, twice in sharp succession.

The inmates unlaced their hands and got back on their feet. Cigarettes lit up. A basketball thumped, game back underway. Like one of those old westerns where a bad guy gets gunned down in the saloon, life went right back to normal the second the body was dragged out of sight.

Except that it didn't. As I gazed across the yard, I caught a web of silent glances, shifting conversations, and furtive finger signs. A conversation happening all around me, riding on the arcane geometries of the prison grapevine, and I felt a shift in the wind.

"That," Paul said, following my gaze as he dug out a fresh cigarette, "is a problem. Smoke?"

"No, thanks. What's going on?"

"Remember how I said we were fresh out of lockdown?" Paul took a long, slow drag, exhaling thin gray smoke into the warm afternoon air. "Way I heard it, there's beef between the Cinco Calles and the Fine Upstanding Crew. It's a drug thing, some kind of Vegas turf battle. The Calles made peace with the Bishops, who *used* to be tight with the Crew, so you can imagine how well that went over."

I knew the Cinco Calles, by their reputation and their colors at least. They were in a partnership with my friend Jennifer, and they'd turned an abandoned tenement by the airport into an urban fortress. She hadn't told me about any turf battles, at least none that had progressed from shoving matches to bloodshed. Then again, if Nicky Agnelli was on the run or already in custody somewhere, all the gangs that used to pay him fealty would be looking to carve out their own little kingdoms.

Forget the Chicago Outfit. With Nicky gone, Vegas could tear itself apart *without* their help.

"Hear anything else from the outside?" I asked. "Any idea how bad it is on the streets right now?"

Paul shrugged. "Been in here for eight years. My grasp of current events is secondhand and sketchy at best."

"So what was that about Jablonski?"

He glanced back, craning his neck as we walked along the track.

"Thing you need to understand is Rehabilitation Dynamics of America pays their staff bottom dollar. I'm talking twenty percent less than *any* regular prison guard in the state, *and* they're not union. So you can imagine the kind of applicants they get."

"Washouts," I said. "The guys who couldn't qualify to work at Ely State."

"Right, or the ones too dumb or too sadistic to *keep* their jobs there. RDA doesn't care. Their job is to keep this place filled to capacity, so they get that sweet, sweet taxpayer funding, and run it as cheaply as possible. Now, when one of the hives—or better yet, all three—go into lockdown because of a gang violence problem, that's considered a high-hazard situation. Guard shifts double and run long."

"Overtime," I said.

"Overtime. And the 'high hazard' is watching a bunch of cons who are locked up tight in their cells. Safer shifts and a bigger paycheck for our just and valorous overseers."

"Which means," I said, sniffing out the scam, "the guards have an incentive to *promote* inmate violence. We kill each other, there's a lockdown, and they get paid more."

Paul snapped and pointed a finger gun my way. "Give that man a prize. And while a better-run prison would hire guards with, say, morals, character, and human decency, those aren't qualities that RDA screens for. If you can pee in a cup and you don't have a felony on your record, congratulations, you're hired. I say again, RDA doesn't care."

"So why were you worried about Jablonski in particular? Besides that he's an asshole, I mean."

Paul looked behind us again.

"The whites in Hive C don't want any part of this feud. Not our problem, not our fight. Well, that's just not enough mayhem for our dear *Correctional Officer* Jablonski. One of the Aryan Brotherhood heavies got released last month, so Jablonski spread a rumor about how they'd found a hit list in his cell with addresses for the families of the Upstanding Crew brothers on our tier."

"Hoping they'd lash out in reprisal."

"Exactly. I overheard him gloating about it to another guard. So I sent a line to Marcus, the shot-caller for the blacks, and convinced him to pow-wow with Brisco and one of the saner AB guys. Cooled everything down—and since those 'hits' on the outside never happened, in a few days everybody knew Jablonski was full of shit."

We rounded the curve of the track. Guards stood like sentinels up on the gun towers, afternoon sunlight painting their glasses the color of cheap tequila.

"And he knows you were the one who snipped the fuse."

"That's what I get for playing peacemaker. That said, having one pissed-off guard drawing a target on my back is still better than a race war."

A convict near the fence caught my eye. His hair did, anyway, a fluffed-out shock of white that reminded me of Albert Einstein. He looked sixty-something, wearing a hangdog expression on his deeply lined face as he stumbled along, kicking at the ground and mumbling to himself.

"What's his story?"

Paul followed my gaze. "Oh, the Prof? Guy's harmless. Totally nutty, lives in his own little world, but good psychiatric drugs just don't fit in RDA's budget."

"The Prof?"

"Short for professor, I think. Not sure what he's in for, but he's been here longer than anybody can remember." Paul paused, frowning. It was the same frown he'd made when I showed him the dates on my paperwork.

"What?"

"I'm...certain I was here when they brought him in," Paul said slowly, brow furrowed. "Could swear I remember Brisco pulling his jacket and checking him out. But I know he was here before me...forget it. Never mind, just ignore the poor guy. He's crazy."

Maybe so, I thought. *Then again, the way this day's been going so far, I'm not too sure about my sanity either.*

I needed to keep an eye on the Prof.

"Heads up, three o'clock." Paul lowered his voice. "Ray-Ray's coming."

Ray-Ray was the bullet-headed con who had led me to Brisco when I first arrived. He nodded his head over one broad shoulder, back toward the picnic benches by the hive wall.

"The man needs to see you."

Brisco sat flanked by his hangers-on. And Simms. There was another spot at the table, wide open just for me, but I didn't sit down. Until I knew which way the wind was blowing, I wanted to stay mobile.

"I've been told," Brisco said, his gaze swinging between me and Simms, "there was a problem on the tier earlier."

Simms didn't make eye contact with him. I did.

"No problem," I said. "I think we understand each other now."

"Is that right?" He looked at Simms. "Do you *understand each other now,* Simms?"

Simms shrugged and stared down at the table. Eloquent.

"Settle it up," Brisco told him.

Simms set a plastic bag on the table and shoved it my way. A couple of Hershey bars and a bag of potato chips nestled inside.

"It's fine," I said. "I don't need it."

"Faust," Brisco said. "When things are finished in here, they've gotta be *finished,* you understand? Lingering resentments, insults that don't scab over—these are the things that can get a man killed."

"I'm over it."

"We don't know that. And Simms is trying to make amends." Brisco gestured at the bag. "So settle it up, and make us all feel better."

I took the bag.

"Thanks," I told Simms. "We're cool."

He muttered something that sounded like a thank-you and gave Brisco a sheepish side-eye. I noticed a fresh bruise on his chin that I couldn't remember giving him.

"My boy Zap says the warden tried to get you to rat," Brisco said. "He says you didn't give an inch of ground."

I glanced around the table. Quiet faces, hard eyes, but the blanket hostility I'd first felt was ebbing away. Now I was more of a curiosity, a new dog at the pound. Maybe friendly, maybe the kind that might bite.

"What happened was between us," I said. "Simple as that."

Two of the guys in Brisco's entourage had my attention, as discreetly as I could manage. They were twitchier than junkies gone two days without a fix. I got the feeling they had something to say and didn't want an audience when they said it. So I walked away from the table and gave them plenty of lead if they felt like following me.

Sure enough, I turned around at the edge of the fence and there they were. Hovering ten feet back, locked in a silent argument. One wore the tattoo of a skeletal eagle on his meaty bicep, its black claws extended as it swooped in for the kill.

I knew that insignia. Blood Eagles. One-percenter outlaw bikers.

And I owed their boss a whole lot of money.

7.

"**Y**ou're Daniel Faust," one of the bikers said, like he wasn't so sure.

"That's what they tell me."

"Jaysus, man," the other said in a voice tinged with an Irish brogue, letting out a gasp of relief, "we thought you'd *never* get here. Did Winslow get you inside?"

Of all the greetings I'd expected from the Blood Eagles—a vicious stomping being first *and* last on the list—that wasn't one of them.

"To tell you the truth, I'm still working out how I got here."

"He told us you guys had a deal. I mean, the stories about you are true, right? You handle the...the weird stuff?"

The "weird stuff" being underworld code for, well, the *weird stuff*. In other words, my average Tuesday. It all came back to me as I remembered my last sit-down with Winslow. I'd been backed into a corner, going up against a fanatic half-demon cult called the Redemption Choir. I needed wheels and a gun. Winslow sold me both, at one hell of an inflated price, but at the time I wasn't in a position to argue.

He'd asked, then, if I thought I was "going inside." This was long before the Chicago situation, but I'd been facing a shaky firearms charge and Harmony Black's all-star cop coalition was dogging me all over Vegas.

"I've got a buddy inside right now," he'd told me. *"Friend of the MC. Needs a little help. Your kind of help."*

Then he'd laid out his terms. If I remained a free man, I owed him cash, and a lot of it. If I went behind bars, and I could help his buddy out, we'd be square. I had completely put the offer out of my mind. After all, no way I would end up in prison, right?

Right.

"Lucky for you," I said, "it looks like I might be stuck here for a few days. What's going on?"

"I'm Jake," the biker with the eagle tat said, then nodded at the Irishman, "and this is Westie."

We shook hands like gentlemen.

"I got transferred over from Ely with three other guys," Westie said. "Overcrowding, they said. That was three months ago. Today? I'm the only one left. We're getting whittled down, one by one."

"They're not the only ones," Jake added. "Two of my brothers got it, too. Two of the biggest badasses in the whole MC, gone just like that."

"When you say 'gone'..."

Westie took a deep breath. "It started with T-Bolt. My cellmate. One night, I wake up to hear the door rattling open. Then suddenly there's a big-ass flashlight in my face. Damn CRT bum-rushed us."

"Cell Reclamation Team," Jake explained. "Guards trained to go in if a con barricades himself in a cell. Riot shields, padded armor, and pepper spray. They work in teams of four."

Westie looked to the fence, his gaze distant.

"Yeah, but we sure as hell weren't starting a riot. We were *sleeping*. They keep the light in my eyes, tell me not to move a muscle if I don't want to eat a Taser, and they grab T-Bolt. And that was the last time I saw him. Have you met Zap? He's a trustee, got his fingers in all the warden's records. He checks it out, and get this: it was written up as a standard 'housing change order.' Says T-Bolt got moved to Hive B, with no reason given."

"Same deal with my brother Sledge," Jake said. "Got cut up in a scuffle with the Mexicans. Three measly stitches. Two nights later, guards grab him and hustle him out of the cell. Same paper-work, Zap said. Transfer to Hive B. I was awake, man. I saw them drag Sledge out. He had a *bag* on his head, like it's goddamn Guantanamo Bay in here."

I wasn't sure what all this had to do with me, but they had my attention. "So what's the word from Hive B?"

"There isn't one," Jake said. "Hive B's been in lockdown for a little over a year. The whole damn thing. No word in or out. Guards get rotated between hives, but they won't help."

"Did I hear you right?" I asked. "They've been keeping an entire wing of prisoners in their cells for over a *year*? Is that even legal?"

Westie spat into the dust. "Said it was because of a riot. Wasn't any damn riot. One day they just sealed it up like a tomb and that was that."

"It gets weirder," Jake said. "This has been happening like clockwork for a couple of months now. Once a week or so, middle of the night, CRT rolls in and one of us gets dragged off. I just spent a couple of days in Ad Seg after a fight. Down in the hole, my next-door neighbor came from Hive A. According to him, the exact same thing happened in *his* hive for about three months before it suddenly stopped."

"And started in up Hive C," I guessed. "Like they didn't want to snatch too many people from one place. Better to keep the panic down."

"That's right," Jake said.

"So what do you think this is all about?"

"You got me," he replied, "but...Winslow says you can *do* things. I mean, we all heard stories about that thing with his sis-ter..."

Jake shot a nervous glance over his shoulder. I noticed Brisco had his eye on the three of us. He still held court at his picnic table, surrounded by his entourage, but he couldn't help glancing our way.

"What does Brisco say about all this?"

"Nothing," Westie said, "and we're not supposed to talk about it either. He thinks if we make waves, it'll just make things worse."

Jake snorted. "Brisco's scared as shit. This isn't something he can deal with, and he knows it. And that makes him look weak. So he's playing ostrich, hoping the whole mess will just go away if he ignores it long enough."

Great, I thought. *So if I swoop in and start playing detective, it'll look like I'm trying to show him up. That doesn't bode well for my health.*

On the other hand, what choice did I have? Bad enough I was trapped in here, but now I could wake up with a bag over my head and a one-way transfer to a hive in permanent lockdown. Brisco might have felt safe sticking his head in the sand, but I was a little more proactive when it came to staying alive.

"All right," I said, "here's the deal. I'll check it out and see what I can learn about your missing friends. But as far as anybody knows, I turned you down flat. In fact, we never had this conversation. When Brisco or one of his guys asks—and they *are* gonna ask—you came over to talk about the debt I owe Winslow."

"A lot of these guys would sleep easier knowing you're on the job," Jake said.

"And I *wouldn't* sleep easier if Brisco thought I was making him look like a chump. I need to be discreet about this."

Easier said than done in a prison where guards were watching my every move. Guards who, according to Jake and Westie, were neck-deep in this whole mess. There were a hundred ways to die behind bars, and I kept discovering brand-new ones.

I went back to my cell. I needed what little privacy I could get to come up with a plan of attack. That didn't last long. The sound of a truncheon rapping against the bars jolted me from my thoughts.

"Faust," a guard at the cell door said, looking dead-eyed and bored. "You've got a visitor."

He walked me off the hive, down corridors of slab rock painted pea-soup green. I swallowed my excitement, breathed deep to slow my pounding heart, and took mental notes. We paused at two checkpoints along the way, waiting as he flashed his ID and a guard on the other side flipped a switch to make the gate rattle open.

I counted guards and guns. Studied the consoles we passed and whether they needed keys or cards to operate. Checked for mirrors, windows, and blind spots as I built up my mental map of Eisenberg Correctional.

Every iceberg has cracks. And every prison has a weakness. If I stayed sharp and kept my eyes open, I'd find my way out.

All that faded away, though, as we stopped beside a painted stencil reading "VISITOR CENTER" in big block letters. A visitor was a lifeline. A visitor meant my friends had found me.

A visitor was a taste of home.

I held out my arms in a T pose, and the guard patted me down from neck to toe. It was a thorough job, down to making me open my mouth and wriggle my tongue from side to side while he flashed a penlight across my tonsils. *At least it wasn't a strip search*, I figured. At that moment, it didn't matter. Anything to get me through that door.

The visitor center wasn't much to write home about. Just a stark white-walled lounge with a scattering of round tables and cheap folding chairs and a couple of vending machines humming in a corner alcove. A sign plastered to one wall screamed out the rules in two-inch-high letters.

1. *No physical contact.*
2. *No passing of materials between convict and visitors.*
3. *Only visitors may operate the vending machines.*
4. *No items from the vending machines may be taken back to the hives.*
5. *Visitations may be terminated at any time at the supervising officer's discretion.*

A few men sat spread out at the tables with heir visitors, talking in hushed tones. I saw wives, children, a toddler who had to be pulled back before she could clamber into her daddy's lap. Family.

Not my family, though. I glanced around, trying to spot my visitor, hope soaring. Then I saw her, flashing an eager smile my way.

"Well, hello, lover."

Nadine.

8.

My heart sank like a stone in the ocean, my lifeline cut.

Nadine extended a hand, beckoning me to a table in the back corner. Her blond bob gleamed like spun gold under the harsh fluorescent lights. She'd dressed for the occasion, wearing a stylish sweater with muted black and white stripes. Cute.

"You like?" she asked, following my gaze.

"You're behind the times," I said. "Cons mostly wear orange jumpsuits now."

"How...seventies of them. I think I'll pass."

As I came close, she reached for my hand. I barely had time to flinch before one of the officers—spread out along the walls like angry statues—stepped in.

"No physical contact," he barked.

She frowned and sat down. I pulled out a chair on the far side of the table. Nadine might have been the last person in the world I'd want to speak to under normal circumstances, but these weren't normal circumstances. And at this moment, any familiar face—even an enemy's—was a tiny comfort.

"In the 1930s," she murmured, "Henry Harlow conducted experiments on rhesus monkeys to study the effects of maternal and social deprivation. He subjected them to long-term isolation, denied them affection, even simple *touch*. The monkeys went quite mad. Primates need to be touched, regularly and with care, to stay healthy. It's ingrained in your brain chemistry."

"Why are you telling me this?"

"I'm just wondering how long *your* sanity will last." She held up a smooth, pale hand. "Can you feel it? That hungry crawling beneath your skin? The pain of knowing you'll never feel a tender touch upon your body again? Wouldn't you kill for the comfort of a gentle embrace, even *mine?* It must be torture."

I didn't answer. I turned my chair at an angle, looked at the wall, and fell into a sullen silence. I figured I'd wait until she had something useful to say.

"I came to your trial," she told me, "every single day."

"No. You *really* didn't." I paused. "But tell me the truth: do you actually remember a trial? How long has it been since we last saw each other?"

Her ruby lips pursed in a pout. "What kind of a question is that? You know when it was. The airport in Chicago. About four months ago."

Except it was yesterday, I thought, my hope draining like sand through a sieve. There had to be a way to break this curse, to force someone to see the blatant contradiction.

"Before they took your belongings away," Nadine said, "did you happen to open the envelope?"

The envelope. The ticking time bomb she'd dropped in my lap at O'Hare. Containing, allegedly, proof that Caitlin was out to stab me in the back. No, I hadn't opened it. I hadn't thrown it away either.

"Is that what you came here for?"

"No. I came here as an emissary of the Court of Night-Blooming Flowers. To show our respect and prove that we want you on our team."

"Oh?" I didn't buy it. "And how will you do that?"

"By saving your life."

She leaned as close as she dared, pitching her voice in a low whisper.

"This morning, one of my operatives was approached in hopes of hiring him for an assassination. *You* were the target."

"Me?" I touched my chest. "Did they know I'm in prison?"

"Absolutely. He was supposed to infiltrate, as a prisoner or a guard, and take you out from inside the walls. The one absolute criteria of your death was pain. You were meant to suffer, as grievously as possible, before you died."

I drummed my fingers on the table, thinking. That kind of hit had *revenge* written all over it. I could see the Chicago Outfit ordering up a kill like that, but why bother? They'd already gotten me thrown in prison. It'd be crueler to make me live out a life sentence.

Damien Ecko maybe? I'd ruined his business and run him out of Chicago with a bounty from two infernal courts on his head. He wanted me dead in the worst way, I had no doubt, but hiring a *living* hit man wasn't the necromancer's style. Besides, he'd never reach out to the Dead Roses for help. Nadine's crew were among the demons competing to hunt him down.

What about Angus Caine, Lauren Carmichael's mercenary captain? He'd gone into hiding along with what was left of Xerxes Security Solutions after Carmichael died. So had those two mad-scientist whackjobs on her payroll.

"Penny for your thoughts?" Nadine said.

"Just realizing," I told her, "that I really need to stop letting my enemies live. The second I get out of here, fixing that becomes priority one."

"Speaking of which—" She fell silent. A guard lazily patrolled past our table, taking the time to look her up and down like a butcher eyeing a prime slab of meat. She puffed her hair and smiled at him until he walked out of earshot. "Speaking of which, only say the word. We have a plan."

"We?"

"The Flowers, Daniel. Your new court. Join us. Swear fealty to Prince Malphas, and Royce and I will have you out of here before midnight. It's that simple."

"Caitlin might have something to say about that."

Nadine shook her head, putting on a wistfully sad face for me. I almost believed she felt bad.

"Oh, Daniel. Isn't it time to face the truth? She abandoned you. She went home to Prince Sitri's court the night you were arrested, and she never looked back. She never will. Your usefulness was at an end. She's probably already forgotten your name."

I had to fight to keep the smile off my face. I knew something Nadine didn't.

When I was in Chicago, getting ready to break into Damien Ecko's jewelry store, Caitlin was making preparations of her own. Prince Sitri had a gala planned. That meant Caitlin's job, as his right-hand woman, was going back to hell so she could stand next to his throne and look menacing while the nobles partied it up.

"I'm leaving Emma in charge while I'm gone," she had told me on the phone. *"She should be able to keep the wolves at bay for a few days."*

I never actually got in touch with Caitlin the night I came back to Vegas and got busted. If she'd had to leave early...that had to be it. Caitlin had left town all right, but only for the party. A party that, since only a day had really passed, was still in full swing.

That meant as soon as it was over, she'd be coming home to Vegas. And she'd be looking for me.

"That's a generous offer," I told Nadine, "but I have faith."

She frowned. "You don't get it. As long as you're in this prison, you're defenseless. My operative turned down the contract, but the client will keep looking until she finds someone who *will* kill you, and then what good will your 'faith' do you?"

"She?"

"A *human.*" Nadine wrinkled her nose. "Possibly a sorcerer of some pedigree. My operative was...unnerved by her presence. She called herself Mater Tantibus."

I scraped the rust off my Latin. "Mother of Nightmares?"

"Pretentious, right?"

Said the Grand Matriarch of the House of Dead Roses, I thought, but I was smart enough not to say that out loud. Instead I asked, "Anything else to go on? I've pissed off a lot of people, but this 'Mater Tantibus' isn't jogging my memory."

Nadine shrugged. "Curly black hair pinned in a bun, dark

skin, tailored suits and mirrored sunglasses—she had money. British accent, very clipped."

I leaned back in my chair and sighed. I knew exactly who wanted me dead.

"Fleiss."

"Hm?"

"Her real name, at least the name she gave me. 'Ms. Fleiss.' Her 'boss' commissioned me for a heist. Except, as far as I can tell, she was the one pulling his strings."

Normally, answers were a relief. This one just sprouted more questions. My business with Fleiss was over, and if she'd wanted to kill me, she—and Pachenko, her slab of imported muscle—had plenty of chances to do it before we parted ways. Kill me? Hell, she'd *paid* me and flown me home on her private jet. If I'd put together a list of all the people with a motive to send a hit man after me, she wouldn't have even made the top fifty.

"Do me a favor," I said. "I don't think my family knows I'm in here. Can you get word to—"

"I only do *favors* for members of my court." Nadine smiled sweetly. "And your 'family,' as you call them, can't help you now. Only we can."

A man in a fitted black pinstripe suit and an earpiece, looking like a Secret Service agent, approached our table and leaned in. As he did, I noticed two fingers were missing from his left hand. His right was a twisted blanket of faded burn scars that crept up his wrist and disappeared into his sleeve.

"Ma'am," he said, "we've just received word. Nyx has arrived in Talbot Cove. Her hunt is underway."

Nadine slid back her chair and rose, making a purring noise as she stretched her arms above her head.

"You'll have to excuse me, Daniel. My daughter is having a...recital of sorts, and I believe she's about to make me very proud. I'll come back in a couple of days to see how you're enjoying prison life. Maybe you'll have come to your senses by then. That is, of course, assuming you're still alive."

9.

C how time was seven o'clock. Another chance to fill in my mental map of Eisenberg Correctional. If I had my bearings right, the cavernous cafeteria squatted at the intersection of the hives, serving all three in staggered shifts. The concrete ramp on the way inside had a subtle slope, but that and the lack of windows in the dingy tile walls told me we'd gone underground.

The ceiling was unfinished, just girders and the occasional vent interspersed among harsh white industrial fluorescents. If the vents were for circulation, they weren't doing their job: the air was swampy, stagnant, stinking with the kind of wet sweat-sock odor that comes from packing five hundred men into a room built for three hundred and turning up the heat.

Any other time that would have killed my appetite, but my stomach growled in eager anticipation as I shuffled into the serving line. *After all, I haven't eaten in four months*, I thought. Black humor was about the only weapon I had left.

I felt like I was in high school again. I came away from the line with a gray plastic tray, paper plate, and three small dollops of food from a surly inmate's ladle. Dinner was watery mashed potatoes the color of a soap bar and what you might call creamed chicken and rice, if you were in the mood to be charitable and squinted a little.

I thought about eating beef Wellington at Gordon Ramsay's and sharing the sticky-toffee pudding dessert with Caitlin. Imperial Peking duck at Saffron East. Fat slices of pepperoni pie at

Secret Pizza. Hell, at that moment I would have killed for the greasy shrimp toast and a mai tai from Tiki Pete's.

That was when the reality of the situation hit me, a full-bore shotgun blast straight to my reptile brain. I was a prisoner here. I was a *convict*. And all the things I loved, all the things I dreamed about, were just that: dreams. Everything I couldn't have. For the rest of my life.

I swallowed down my sudden animal panic, pursing my lips into a taut line, and looked for a place to sit.

The cafeteria tables were more Neapolitan ice cream. Vanilla on the left. Paul caught my eye and waved me over, scooting to make a spot beside him.

"Welcome to Chez Eisenberg," he said, nodding across the table as I swung a leg over the bench and sat down. "You know Jake and Westie?"

"Yeah, we met in the yard. Hey, guys. Speaking of, remember our talk out there, Paul? You had started to say something about breakouts."

He dipped his plastic spoon in the chicken and rice, giving it a dubious sniff. "Huh? Oh, right. Okay, so it's not totally true. People *have* broken out of the Iceberg—"

"Lucky bastards," Westie grumbled.

"Wait for it. They have, maybe three or four times, but they either get caught or gunned down right after."

Paul pressed his spoon against his mashed potatoes, separating them into a pair of lumps and drawing a thin potato road between them. I sampled a mouthful of the chicken and rice and struggled to hold it down. The meat was half gelatin and half gristle, in a sauce that tasted like warm mayonnaise.

"This food is...not food," I said, chasing it with a swig of lukewarm water. "They seriously feed you this slop?"

"All meals meet a minimum caloric and nutritional standard," Paul said, engrossed in his potato sculpture building, "emphasis on *minimum*. Food budget's something like four bucks a day per prisoner."

"Now you know why people shank each other over commissary goods," Jake cast a cautious glance across the room. "And why aren't we on lockdown after that shit that popped off in the yard today? The blacks and browns are givin' each other snake eyes, and I've seen two guards so far with their fingers *on* their triggers."

"Probably hoping it gets worse," Westie said, following his gaze. "Hell, a full-on cafeteria riot? They could put the whole hive in lockdown for a *month*. Gotta get all that overtime in before Christmas shopping, right?"

I took a deep breath, steadying myself as much as I could manage, and stretched out my senses. Psychic tendrils, glistening in my second sight like purple sea anemones, drifted across the room. Touching brains, scooping up surface thoughts, sifting through emotions like panning for gold in a vat of sludge. Fear. So much fear. The kind of anxiety that turned a man feral. Anger, but that was mostly surface bluster. A crude dam to keep the terror from breaking loose.

The way I saw it, the cafeteria was a hair's breadth from going nuclear. One wrong move, one jostle or a second of eye contact with the wrong person, and blood would spill.

I wasn't sure what worried me more: standing at ground zero in the heart of a riot, or the idea of being locked in a cell for a month afterward.

"Okay," Paul told me, wagging his spoon at his mashed-potato map. "It's like this: we're in the middle of a desert."

"You don't say," Jake muttered.

"Nearest town is Aberdeen, thirty miles south. This two-lane road was built at the same time the prison was. Most of the guards, support staff, even the warden lives in Aberdeen. Interstate 80 brushes the edge of town, heading east and west. Those are pretty much your only travel options."

"So you need wheels to get out of here," I said, thinking it through. "You'll die on foot in the heat. And by the time you reach Aberdeen—"

Paul tapped the mashed-potato road with his spoon. "You got it. Total lockdown. All they have to do is put two roadblocks on I-80 and you aren't going *anywhere*. Most escapees either get caught at the roadblock or on the way there. Nobody's ever gotten farther than that."

"Why take the road at all?" Jake asked. "It's a desert. Just pick a direction and ride."

Paul shook his head. "It's not a *flat* desert. Sand dunes, drifts, rocks...yeah, you could do it in an ATV, easy—but only if you can see where you're going. Do it during the day, you'll stick out like a sore thumb. Helicopters'll spot you in seconds. Do it at night, without headlights, you'll end up in a wreck before you make it five miles."

"Why do you wanna know anyway?" Westie asked me.

I shrugged.

"I've got restaurant reservations. Don't want to be late."

*　*　*

After lights out, I rested on my back on the slab of concrete that passed for a bunk and tried to ignore the cold. The Iceberg earned its name after sunset. I imagined arctic wind whistling over a frozen tombstone. And there, under the snow and the permafrost, entombed I lay.

Thinking.

I'd already spent all the time I wanted behind bars. And the amount of time I wanted was zero. I was *leaving*, and I didn't care if I had to climb a mountain of corpses to do it.

Couldn't be reckless, though. While my reptile brain thrashed its tail against the back of my skull, kicking me into fight or flight, I clamped down hard and forced myself to think it through. Going off half-cocked would just get me shot or worse. I needed a plan.

So nobody had ever successfully escaped from Eisenberg Correctional. I was willing to bet they'd never had a prisoner like me, but then again, that was probably what every other would-be escapee thought before he ate a bullet. The prison, the town, the highway...I played around with my mental map for a while, floating possibility after possibility like helium balloons and shooting each one down.

That was fine, for now. A solo escape act was my last resort. If I could crack the curse around my imaginary "trial" and get somebody in authority to see I'd gone from arrest to prison in the blink of an eye, that would solve everything. The confusion would at least be enough to gum up the legal works. All I needed was a hearing, and then I'd be on my way to a country with no extradition treaty faster than you could say "bail money." If nothing else, worst-case scenario, they'd have to move me to a county jail until everything was sorted out.

It'd be a hell of a lot easier to break out of county.

Speaking of hell, Caitlin would be back to Vegas in a few days, and she wouldn't waste any time trying to track me down. Did I have that long, though? If Nadine was telling the truth—and I couldn't find a good reason to doubt her, much as I tried—I could expect a hired killer or two to come hunting for me. Soon. It was in my best interest to be long gone before that happened.

No, waiting for Caitlin to find me was too risky. I needed to take this bull by the horns and find a way to get word to the outside. I had a few thoughts in that direction, but my head kept coming around to Fleiss. I couldn't figure out why she wanted me dead—she and I were going to have a chat about that as soon as I got loose. For now, though, I was a sitting duck in here. I needed a weapon. Not a sharpened broom handle or a razor blade either. My kind of weapon.

No grimoires, no ritual tools, no herbs or oils, no privacy. Trying to do magic behind bars was like trying to build a nuke with a nine-volt battery and some chewing gum. Still, I knew one spell that would get me exactly what I needed.

A spell I'd only cast once in my entire life, for a damn good reason.

10.

Her name was Jenna Rearden, and she kept her hands clasped tight before her, like a penitent nun, to keep them from shaking. It wasn't me she was afraid of.

Not entirely me, anyway. This wasn't long after I'd broken company with Nicky Agnelli. A heist went bad, shook my confidence, threw me off my game. Instead of getting back on Nicky's payroll, I shifted gears and tried something new. I hung out my metaphorical shingle, offering vengeance for hire. Dirty deeds done at premium prices.

It was mostly curse work, though I passed myself off to my clients as a mundane "fixer" who could arrange convenient accidents for anyone who had done them wrong. Cheating spouse? Sexually harassing boss? Cross my palm with silver, and I could make your problems go away.

Then came Jenna. Young, mousy, freshly divorced with a six-year-old daughter. A daughter who had gone from vibrant and outgoing to sullen and stormy, a pattern that grew worse with every weekend visit to her father's house. Jenna got smart; she slipped a voice-activated recorder into her daughter's Hello Kitty knapsack. The audio told her everything she needed to know.

"My lawyer says there's no guarantee how much prison time he'll get," Jenna told me, "or if he'll get any at all. There are cases where men have...done this to their children and even kept *visitation rights*. I can't do it, Mr. Faust. I can't. I'll take her and run if I have to. I'll spend the rest of my life as a fugitive before I'll—"

I held up a hand. "You won't. Go home, and go about your business like it was any other day. I'll handle everything."

"How will I know when—"

"You'll know."

I didn't need to hear the audio, but I still listened. I listened to every cry and muffled whimper. All two hours of it. I needed the hatred, coursing through my veins like high-octane gasoline, to do what I did next.

Two days later, a noise complaint led the cops straight to Jenna's ex. He was sitting up in bed and screaming. Just staring into space and shrieking, endlessly, until his vocal cords tore and nothing but agonized wheezes gusted over his blood-flecked tongue. Last I'd checked, he was still in a padded cell at Napa State Hospital, under heavy sedation.

He'd be there for the rest of his life. Even if I wanted to, what I did to him couldn't be undone.

I wouldn't bring that kind of doom down on somebody's head under normal circumstances, unless they truly deserved it. These weren't normal circumstances, though, and a weapon was a weapon.

It was time to call upon the King of Worms.

* * *

I'd found the king's name in Bentley and Corman's back-room collection, a trail that slid in and out of history like a wisp of sulfur smoke. Here, a mention in a sixteenth-century French black magician's manual. There, a casual aside in a colonial witch hunter's diary. Puzzle pieces scattered across time, waiting for someone foolish enough to put them back together.

It was never quiet in prison. Even at midnight, even in the darkness, the hive was a cacophony of snoring, wheezing, coughing, whispering. Faint metal clanks and the sudden strangled sound of a sob muffled by a pillow. I pulled the paper-thin blanket aside and sat up in my bunk, crossing my legs and resting my upturned palms on my knees.

If I leaned forward and craned my neck, looking toward the

tower in the heart of the hive, I could make out shapes through the darkened windows at the top. A couple of guards stood watch, looking out over the tiers through the bug-eye glass of night-vision goggles.

I straightened my back and closed my eyes.

All magic starts with a breath. I inhaled for four seconds, held my breath for four seconds, exhaled for four seconds. Then again. And again, as my thoughts slipped into the background, taking the noise and the prison along with them. My heartbeat slowed with the clock, seconds squeezing by like drops of molasses through an hourglass.

It was dark behind my eyes, but I saw a light in the distance. A silver pinprick. I walked toward it.

A chant reverberated through my skull, half in my voice, half in a stranger's. A litany of ancient names. A warning in a language I didn't speak. Now I walked along a winding ribbon of tarnished pewter, inlaid with swirling Hebraic script reading *Malkhut, Yesod, Hod, Gevurah, Da'ath.*

The ribbon rose and twisted, taking me along with it. Plunging into worlds of shadow that billowed like black smoke. I wasn't in my cell. I wasn't not in my cell. I was in between.

The shadow in-between, I thought as the ribbon became a road.

In the darkness, looming up before me, was a throne. A throne eighty feet tall, a mountain of crumbling black basalt. The king who sat slumped upon that throne, a giant in moldering robes with a rusted crown upon his skeletal brow, had been dead since time began.

"I come as a pilgrim," I said, "with hands empty and cold."

My gifts are free, rasped the King of Worms in a voice that came from everywhere and nowhere.

"Decay is the fate of all life." I clasped my hands before me, giving the ritual response.

And madness is the fate of all sanity.

"I seek to spread your wisdom upon the flesh of the world once more."

This would please me. Come. Receive your sacrament.

Figures emerged from the shadows at the foot of the throne. Two of them shuffling toward me in spasmodic convulsions, walking with muscles gone stiff from rigor mortis. They were women, perhaps, wearing the habits of nuns but their garb adorned with crimson symbols from no earthly order. Empty eye sockets turned my way.

I stood my ground and counted my breaths. Four seconds in. Hold. Four seconds out.

The king's servants converged upon me. One shambled in a slow, painful circle, neck bones crackling as she kept her eyeless face trained upon mine. The other reached for me with one slender, rotting hand. Her flesh, what little remained of it, was a hive of maggots. No, some alien species *like* a maggot, with skin glistening, jet-black, and reflecting the pinprick light from distant stars.

The nun stroked my cheek, gentle, like a lover.

I didn't flinch.

The other nun laid her rotted hand upon my scalp and yanked my head back with ferocious strength as she pushed downward, forcing me to my knees with my face upturned.

The one before me reached up to her throat and plucked a single, squirming maggot-thing from her rotten skin. It twisted and writhed, pinned between thumb and forefinger, as she held it above my face. Panic welled up and I fought to keep my fear in check, holding very, very still as her hand came down.

I smelled mildew, and decay, and sweet rose water. Just before she dropped the maggot into my left nostril.

I lurched forward, eyes wide open, the vision torn away and the stench and sounds of the prison hammering my senses. Suddenly free and suddenly entombed. I clutched the thin blanket, pressing my face to the foot of my bunk, clenching my jaw until it ached. I could feel it, the alien *thing* inside my body, crawling up my sinuses and spreading a rash of pain like I'd just snorted chili powder. I felt the maggot squirm across the back of my eyeball, my vision blurring as it left a burning trail on its way to my brain.

I wanted to claw at my skin, rip out my eye, anything to get the damned thing *out*. All I could do was count my breaths and hold very still, clutching the blanket, waiting for the feeling to end.

But it didn't. The insect curled up on the skin of my brain—against all logic, against everything I knew about the human body, I could feel it there—and went to sleep. An unscratchable itch beneath my skull. A parasite made of cosmic filth.

It would only sleep for so long. I had two days, three at most, before it would start to *burrow*. It needed a warm, safe place, after all.

A warm, safe place to feed.

That was the number-one reason I'd only done this once before and hoped to never do it again. I had two days to pass the king's "gift" to another victim, or it would devour me alive from the inside out.

Nothing in this universe is ever really free.

11.

I slept, if you could call it sleep. A few fitful hours of tossing and turning on the quarter-inch mattress, waking up with my back aching and my eyelids sagging, more tired than when I'd laid down in the first place. And I could still feel the maggot, nesting inside my skull. Paul chuckled as he pushed himself up from his bunk.

"Don't worry, it gets easier," he said. "My first week, I couldn't sleep a wink. Eventually you just tune everything out. It's amazing what you can get used to when you don't have any other choice."

I didn't plan on being here long enough to get used to it.

The tiers showered in shifts, and we waited for the guards to pop our cell door, calling us out to stand along the railing in single file. We shuffled downstairs and through an access corridor, like the world's slowest conga line at the world's saddest party.

The movies had told me to expect a big, open room lined with shower nozzles, the space filled with milling naked bodies and the threat of violence. What I got instead was more like the showers in a college dorm. Individual stalls lined in white ceramic tile—with dingy plastic curtains, no less, though they didn't quite cover the entire opening. Stepping into that stall and pulling the curtain shut behind me was the closest thing I'd had to privacy since I arrived at the Iceberg. I let out a faint sigh of pleasure and luxuriated under the sputtering lukewarm spray, running my fingers over my scalp. I only had five minutes, but it was enough.

Outside, toweling off with my uniform folded on a long

wooden bench at my side, I got Paul's attention and nodded left. Two men stood with crossed arms outside a curtained stall, staring daggers at anyone who came within ten feet.

"What's up with that?" I asked.

"Like I said, usually don't have to worry about being raped in the showers," he told me, "but it's a *great* place to get stabbed. Sometimes guys trade off like that, two standing guard while one showers, to make sure nobody pulls anything funny. Heck, put up some commissary goods and you can hire your very own bodyguards. Bet you never thought a chocolate bar could save your life."

I had chocolate on the brain as we fell in line again down in the cafeteria. It was better than the watery scrambled eggs they were serving up, falling from the server's ladle to my paper plate in a messy *plop*.

"So when does Hive B eat?" I asked the server. "I only see A and C on the schedule."

"They don't. Lockdown means all the meals get delivered to their cells. We cook 'em up and send them all over on rolling carts for the guards to pass out."

"There a lot of guys in Hive B?"

He stared at me like I'd found his last nerve and planted my heel on it. Behind me, the line kept getting longer. I moved on.

The prisoners in Hive B were still eating, which meant they weren't dead. One possible explanation down, countless more to go.

The back of my neck prickled as I walked the aisle, looking for a place to sit. I caught glances out of the corner of my eye, mostly from the Latino wedge of the cafeteria. Hard, narrowed eyes and soft murmurs. I slipped into an open spot not far from Brisco.

"Might have a problem," he said, shooting a quick look over his shoulder.

Ray-Ray, sitting next to him, snorted over his eggs. "Yeah, and his fuckin' name is Jablonski."

"You may have felt," Brisco told me, "a little shade from our brown brothers over there being thrown your way."

"I noticed," I said.

"That's not by accident. *Someone* slipped a copy of your jacket to the browns' shot-caller, and he passed it on to the Cinco Calles. They know who you are."

"Not seeing a problem," I said. "They're tight with a friend of mine on the outside. She can smooth it."

Ray-Ray shook his head. "You're in here for icing one of their dealers, bro. They gotta do something about that. Mexican honor, you know?"

"I was framed. And I'm pretty sure they're Puerto Rican."

He furrowed his brow at me. "What's the difference?"

"Seems pretty clear Jablonski and his boys want to turn this black-brown feud into a three-way," Brisco said. "Get us all fighting so they can justify a hive-wide lockdown, sit on their asses, and collect overtime pay 'til Christmas. And you're the wedge."

"I can smooth it," I said again. "Point out a Calles big shot for me. I'll have a chat."

"Never point your finger at anybody in here," Brisco said. "That's a good way to die. But if you'll look a little more to your left—see the guy at the end of that table? Skinhead with a hooknose and the double-teardrop tat at the corner of his eye? That's Raymundo. Thinks he's Don Corleone, which he ain't, but he's hooked up with the Calles from end to end."

"End to end?"

"Yeah," Brisco said, "cradle to grave. Old-school gangster. Listen, Faust, you gotta understand something. I'm not letting my people get sucked into this fight. We're outnumbered, big time, and any kind of race-war-type-situation is going to end with a lot of my guys in the infirmary or the morgue. That's just how it is. We'll watch your back if we can..."

"But if it gets hot, I'm on my own." I stirred my plastic fork in the eggs, leaving a slug trail of yellow water on my plate. "Message received."

"Well we're not *giving* you to 'em." Brisco nodded at Ray-Ray. "Stay close. And Ray-Ray and Slanger'll watch your curtain while you shower. Just make sure to return the favor. Safety in numbers."

Safety in numbers was the first thing I had to shed out in the prison yard. I spotted Raymundo quick. He was over by the weight benches, shouting encouragement as one of his buddies lifted the equivalent of a small car on his barbell. Five guys in all, mostly shirtless and flashing calligraphic CC tattoos on their pecs or shoulder blades, one keeping a hard-eyed watch while the others pumped iron and joked around.

The joking stopped, dead cold, when I walked up alone.

The barbell rattled onto its rack and the weightlifter sat up, shooting a lethal glare. Everybody froze except for Raymundo. He went on the offensive, strutting up with his hands spread wide.

"Look at this," he said in a sibilant rasp. "You believe the balls on this *pendejo?* What's up, you in a *hurry* to die?"

I took a deep breath, locking eyes with him. Showing my open hands, keeping my tone light and my moves easy.

"I come in respect. I hear you've been told some falsehoods about me. I want to set the record straight, before the situation gets out of control."

"No, no." He wagged his finger. "There's no falsehoods. Jacket's a jacket, and we've seen yours."

"Sure. And who gave you that jacket? A guard who wants to set off a race war."

He shrugged. "So what if he does? Doesn't mean you didn't shoot Little Konnie."

Konstantin Floros, I thought. My alleged "victim," a low-level pot dealer on Jennifer's payroll.

"Floros wasn't even part of your set," I told him. "He didn't fly your flag. You don't have to go to war for him."

"He worked for our partnership. He was an earner. If we let you skate, that makes us look weak."

"Good news, then. I didn't kill him. You can get in touch with the outside, reach out to Jennifer. She's family. She'll tell you there's no way in hell I pulled the trigger on one of her guys."

Raymundo's bushy eyebrows fell into a straight line, sharp as the path of a bullet. He got inside my personal space.

"Jennifer?" he said. "What do you know about JJ?"

"Enough to know she'll vouch for me. I've known her longer than you have. We've been places together. We've seen things."

He thought that over. The scowl didn't leave his face, though.

"Can't call her," he said. "She ain't around right now."

"What do you mean?"

"I mean what I mean. She ain't around."

She's just hiding, I told myself, forcing my gut to unclench. *She heard about the cops going after Nicky, and she went underground to wait out the heat. She's smart. She's fine. She's safe.*

But with a turf war brewing, I couldn't know that. I couldn't know anything for certain—not until I got the hell out of here and fought my way back home.

"You should wait to talk to her before you do anything she might not like," I told Raymundo.

"Maybe," he replied.

That was all he had to say. I took one step backward, then another. He mirrored me. I didn't turn my back and walk away until I was well out of arm's reach, and even then I held my breath until I'd taken a good twenty steps. Nobody ran up on me from behind. I was safe.

This time.

I found Paul walking the oval track, sucking on a cigarette. He glanced my way.

"So how'd *that* go?"

"I'm still breathing."

"That bad, huh?"

"I've got to get word to the outside," I told him. "And without being listened in on. Anybody ever smuggle a cell phone in here?"

Paul flicked his cigarette to the track and snuffed it under the heel of his canvas shoe.

"Sure," he said, "pricey, though. Burner with an hour or two of call time on it can run you four, five hundred bucks in commissary credit. Oh, there's one other problem. In Hive C, there's really only one reliable supplier."

"Yeah? Who's that?"

Paul nodded back toward the weight benches.

"Raymundo. Wanna go back over there, ask if he'll talk business?"

"Shit."

Paul lit another cigarette. Offered it to me. I passed. He took a deep drag and looked up to the cloudless sky.

"You are so right, my friend," he said. "And we are all neck-deep in it."

As we walked, I could feel the alien maggot crawling across my brain. Writhing over gray meat, leaving a burning slug trail in its wake. How long, I wondered, before it would stop wriggling and start *chewing?* Swallowing down my revulsion, I took a walk, alone, along the fence line. I knew that wasn't safe, but I hoped I'd bought myself a little time with Raymundo and his boys. I needed a few quiet minutes to think.

Instead, I saw an unexpected arrival hobbling my way. The Prof. He goggled at me, eyes wide and bulging, coming closer in a limping shuffle-step like one of his legs was an inch longer than the other.

I stopped cold by the fence and waited for him.

"You," he said, sounding as perplexed as he looked, "are *not* the Thief."

"To the contrary. I'm a pretty damn good thief." I shrugged. "Current situation notwithstanding."

"You're not *the* Thief. You—you shouldn't be here."

"That's what I keep telling people."

He grabbed a handful of his wild snow-white mane, yanking it in frustration and squeezing his eyes shut.

"No," he snapped. "This is all wrong. He's telling the story wrong. *You aren't supposed to be here.* You...you need to talk to my sister. She can explain. Better than I can. I get...confused. My head is foggy."

"Hey, if they ever have an open visiting day, feel free to introduce me. I just don't think—"

"No. She can't come here. But you can talk to her from my cell."

I grabbed his shoulder.

"Are you telling me," I said, "that you've got a cell phone? Let me borrow it for five minutes, and I'll talk to anybody you want. Just one phone call, that's all I need."

His lips curled, and he gave me a slow, mad-eyed smile.

"Come with me."

12.

Back in Hive C, up on the fourth tier, I knew the Prof's cell before he led me inside. It was the one that glowed in my second sight.

The tiny chalk mark on the threshold was aflame with power. I didn't recognize the symbol, but I could taste its intent, like the memory of ginger on my tongue and the scent of sandalwood incense. A warding sigil. Three more dotted his cell, one for each wall, the white glyphs tucked into hard-to-spot places. While I counted sigils, he reached under his bunk and dragged out a plastic storage tub.

"You're a magician," I said, keeping my voice low.

He paused, turning his head to grin my way.

"No, magic is tricks and lies. I peddle the truth. Only truth, but nobody ever believes me."

The stench that roiled out when he popped the plastic lid, something like three-day-old roadkill on a hot Nevada highway, nearly knocked me flat. Prison wine. I recognized the makings of a crude still for fermentation, cobbled together with cast-off containers and plastic tubing.

"Problem is," he muttered, shuffling to his desk and picking up a dusty plastic cup, "nobody wants truth. It's a hard sell. I was a traveling salesman once, before I found my true vocation. Did you know that?"

"Buddy," I told him, "I don't even know your name."

He barked a delighted laugh.

"Buddy. My name is Buddy. My parents were avid fans of the blues, quite avid. Here, hold this cup."

I obliged him, but I wasn't sure why.

I thought the stench from the makeshift still couldn't get any worse. He took a Ziploc bag from the container, fat with viscous, strawberry-colored goop, and proved me wrong the second he opened it. I raised an eyebrow as he poured out three fingers of the nasty stuff, splattering into the cup.

"So, uh, what's in this, exactly?"

"This and that." He winked and sealed the bag back up. "Something old, something new, something borrowed, something blue. No, not blue. Pink."

"Thanks, but I'm really not thirsty. So about that phone—"

"I know, I know, you want to talk to your—" He paused, furrowing his brow and tilting his head. "Cait...Caitlin. And you're afraid for Jennifer, so very afraid, though you're trying to tell yourself everything's fine."

"I get it," I said, though I wasn't sure I did. "You're a psychic. A mind reader."

Buddy slapped the plastic cover over his improvised still, frowning as he waved a fluttery hand.

"I hear the machinery of the *universe*," he said. "So many thoughts, so many voices, crowding everything out of my head. They tried to put me on pills once. Just made it worse. Nothing stops the transmission. I'm Radio Free Buddy."

Poor guy. I'd seen the unlucky ones like him before. Natural talents who never got the training they needed. It was easy to dig too deep, push the senses too hard, and end up a burnout or a head case. *There but for the grace of Bentley and Corman go I*, I thought, thinking back to my own misspent youth.

Still, he could come in handy. It'd be easier to clear up the mystery of Hive B and get back in good graces with Winslow and his gang if Buddy had any talent for remote viewing.

"I don't have a phone," Buddy said, "but I have a *connection*.

My sister, she's singing out across the lines. You need to hear her. Drink."

I eyed the pink glop. I'd swallowed some pretty dubious concoctions in my day, either for occult purposes or just in the pursuit of a good time, but this was a little extreme even for me.

"Hey," I said, reaching to hand the cup back to him, "look, not that I don't appreciate the offer, but I'm going to take a pass—"

"Lauren Carmichael," he said.

That froze me.

"My sister," he said, squinting as if listening to a voice I couldn't hear, "says you think it's over. But you don't understand. Everything Lauren Carmichael did and all that she became, everything you *think* you stopped...it was nothing but a *side effect*."

I should have been able to put it all behind me. Lauren Carmichael was dead. I should know—I'd helped kill her. I'd put her, her followers, and her whole rotten legacy to the torch. I should have been able to sleep easy after that.

Sometimes, though.

Sometimes, if I heard her name, or if I was lying awake in the still hours of the night, I was suddenly right back there again—back in that place I never wanted to go.

Flat on my back on a blood-soaked carpet, paralyzed, my aura shredded, her hands on my body. Forcing her toxic energy inside me, one quivering inch at a time. Hearing her gasp of pleasure as she finished her work and let go.

I should have been strong enough to fight her off. I should have been strong enough, after it was all over, to shrug off the memory and let it go. And I hated that I couldn't. I hated that it was so easy to slip back to that place in my mind, feeling filthy and worthless all over again like it just happened yesterday.

I'd killed Lauren Carmichael, but I couldn't kill her ghost.

Maybe this would bring me one step closer.

"Buddy," I said, lifting the cup to my lips and trying to ignore the stench.

He looked at me, a question in his eyes.

"If this is a trick," I told him, "I *will* kill you. Understand that."

"No tricks." He nodded, his shock of hair bobbing. "No treats either, sorry. Only truth."

I held my nose and drank it down.

The slime tasted like a rotten animal carcass smells. It coated my tongue and got stuck in the back of my mouth, my gag reflex fighting me as I forced myself to swallow. Blood roared in my ears as the drink hit my stomach, the cell beginning to spin, the ground falling away from my feet and chunks of concrete raining down as the ceiling wrenched itself open to let in a stream of molten light.

Then I was gone.

* * *

Home again.

I stood in the middle of South Las Vegas Boulevard under a burning midday sun. Raw desert heat washed over me, stealing my breath, turning distant parked cars into mirages.

Not parked. Abandoned. Crashed. One of the busiest streets in the world was a graveyard of broken-down, rusted, and burned-out shells. Dead taxis and capsized rental cars. I stood alone in the wreckage.

The last living man in Las Vegas.

The Karnak, once a pyramid of glass thirty stories tall, was nothing but a shattered, twisted skeleton of steel girders burned black. Its closest neighbor, a resort built to look like a fantasy castle, had been through a siege: what walls remained were charred and half-battered to rubble. In the other direction, the Taipei Tower—Caitlin's home—stood skewed on blasted foundations and poised to fall.

A page from the *Las Vegas Sun* blew past my feet, carried on a stray gust of hot wind. I snatched at it, too slow, and only saw the single-word headline before the breeze carried it under the smoldering husk of a taxicab.

GOODBYE.

Rattling, squeaking wheels turned my head. A stoop-shouldered woman puttered up the sidewalk, her tangled hair poking out from under a dirty lace shawl, pushing a shopping cart piled high with empty cans and clutter. She stopped. As she raised her head, I realized she could pass for Buddy's twin.

"You aren't the Thief," she croaked.

"So I've been told."

"Then who are you?"

I took a step closer, showing her my open hands, trying to be reassuring. She didn't seem to be afraid of me, though.

"I'm Daniel Faust."

"I didn't ask your name," she said. "I asked *who are you?* Not the same question at all. A reasonably bright dog can learn his own name. Do you even know who you are?"

I gestured at the wreckage. "Is this the future?"

She snorted, waving a wrinkled hand at me.

"How could it be the future if it already happened? Don't think about past or present. Forget about time, boy, it won't help you. Think *sideways*. Look *closer*."

She pointed to my left, at the broken Ionic columns and flame-scorched steps. I looked up at the marquee and frowned.

"This is the Monaco," I told her. "I've been here a hundred times. So why does the sign say—"

"This isn't your home," she said. "It's mine. Call me Cassandra, if you're needing a name. Not the one I was born with, but it suits me these days."

Graffiti caught my eye, spattered across a leaning wall. A crescent curve like a sideways moon spray-painted in neon purple, lined with uneven squares. Chaos inside symmetry. It took me a minute to realize I was looking at a picture of smiling teeth.

"He's the man with the Cheshire smile," Cassandra said, following my gaze, "and rest assured, he is the reason you're here."

"Did he do all this?" I turned toward her.

"This?" She looked into the distance. Faint plumes of black smoke licked the cloudless sky. "This was only the beginning. Some people had a very good idea, though, my brother tells me.

They couldn't kill him, you see. He just keeps coming back. He'll *always* come back. So they trapped him. Snared him in a land of smoke, under a black sun. Sealed away and left to rot in the darkness."

Her words fired a memory in the back of my mind. My confrontation with Bob Payton, the rogue engineer who had conjured the smoke-faced men—the same creatures who nearly tricked Lauren Carmichael into triggering the apocalypse. He'd been giddy, telling me about the other realms he and his partners had plumbed.

"In our early work, we came across a world of absolute silence. An Earth stripped bare of resources, of life, of anything at all, crumbing under a cold and black sun. Lonely creatures walked the wastes, creatures born of entropy. The antithesis of life itself."

And he'd opened a doorway from that world to ours. Just for a minute.

"Unintended consequences," Cassandra said, her chapped lips spreading to flash a broken-toothed smile, "will fuck you raw, every time. Remember the old woman who swallowed the fly?"

"Cassandra, who is he? The man with the Cheshire smile. What's his real name?"

"I told you already, those are two different questions. And he plays with names. Sometimes he comes as a friend, sometimes a lover, always with a smile. Sometimes he plays at being a god, but that's all smoke and mirrors—"

"Please," I said, "tell me his name."

"I just *told* you his name, if you'd *listen*. He's the man with the red right hand, the unweaver, the unmaker. He's the last word on the last page of the last book, and he does *not* believe in happy endings." Cassandra raised her chin, her voice strident, echoing off the ruins. "He came here to test us, to judge us, and *we were found wanting.*"

She turned away. Her head sagged.

"We did everything wrong this time around. *Everything.* He barely had to lift a finger to win. Tragedy never visited the Paladin's doorstep, and she ended up a backwoods sheriff's deputy; that one needs pain to drive her ambition. The Scribe met his death at the bottom of a vodka bottle. The Witch never found her Knight; they're supposed to be unstoppable, united...but only for a little while. I could go on: the Thief, the Killer, all the others..."

She looked back toward me. Her eyes downcast.

"And as for the Prophet," she said with a bitter little laugh, "she was just an old bag lady with a shopping cart full of cans. And nobody listened to her until it was much, *much* too late."

13.

"**I**f you need a name to hang on his smile," Cassandra told me, "call him the Enemy. For that is his nature and his role to play."

I turned in a slow circle, staring up at the broken skyline, trying to wrap my head around the sheer scale of destruction. "And how do I stop him? How do I stop this from happening?"

"You don't. You can't."

I looked back at her. I blinked.

"I don't believe in no-win situations, Cassandra. There has to be a way—"

She held up a hand and shook her head, her tone almost gentle.

"The very fact that you're here, standing in the Thief's shoes, means the Enemy has already won. He's changing the rules. Perverting the natural order of things. I fear he's found a loophole."

"A loophole? In what?"

She strolled up the sidewalk, leaving her shopping cart behind, and waved for me to follow.

"A very, very long time ago, a time old as language itself—as old as wisdom —a story was told. A very *special* story. A mark was made upon the wheel of worlds. And so these souls return, again and again, cursed to play out their parts. Bound to meet their dooms or their triumphs, and woe to any mortal drawn into their tale. Only the Paladin, the chosen one, can defeat the Enemy."

She shook her head at me, smiling sadly.

"And you are *not* the chosen one, Daniel Faust. You're merely a man. Here by the grace of cosmic accident and bad luck. Your best hope is to scurry out of the way, like an ant dodging the footfalls of elephants."

I stopped in my tracks. I grabbed her arm and made her stop too, turning her toward me.

"I don't believe in 'chosen ones,'" I told her. "I don't believe in fate, and I sure as *fuck* don't believe in rolling over and dying when I can fight instead. *Tell me how to beat him.*"

She studied me for a long minute, looking deep in my eyes.

"Perhaps," she said, "all hope is not yet lost. I understand my twin is imprisoned. Another of the Enemy's machinations, no doubt."

"That's right."

"The Prophet's voice must be heard," she said. "For there to be the slimmest chance of success, his truth *must* reach the right ears. Will you be his liberator?"

"Wait," I said. "I thought you said *you* were the Prophet."

"I was, the last time around. But this story is over—this *world* is over—and the mantle is his to bear." She paused. "Mine to bear, technically."

"So you and Buddy...are the same person?"

She spread her hands. "What you're seeing has already come to pass. I'm told we met in the prison yard. Will meet, for me. Met, for you. See? Time complicates things. Throw out your clocks. Learn to think sideways, while you're liberating the Prophet's voice."

"Just to be clear on this: you're asking me to bust Buddy out of prison?"

She nodded, grave. I took a deep breath and let it out as a sigh.

"All right," I said. "I'll find a way. Somehow."

"But understand this: by whimsy or spite, the Enemy has swept you up into his grand design. If you thwart his plans, he *will* come for you. Your death will not be a merciful one."

"He'll have to find me first," I said. "I've got a little magic of my own."

She chuckled at me.

"And there you fail. You see, your magic can only change what things are. His magic can change *why* things are."

Thump.

The ground shook under our feet. A single, sharp jolt, and a booming sound that reverberated through the ruins. Then another.

Thump.

Cassandra sighed. She looked up to the shattered skyline.

"My final prophecy," she said. "I always knew I was going to die today."

Thump.

Then I glimpsed it. The shadow of a shape, just out of sight behind the leaning corpse of the Taipei Tower. The shape that slowly lurched forward, making the ground shiver with every thunderous step.

A shape at least thirty stories tall.

"Come on." I tugged at Cassandra's shoulder. "Come on, we have to *run*—"

"We?" Her voice was placid. Tired. Resigned. "I told you, this is my home, not yours. You're not even really here. You're just watching from afar. A voyeur at the end of the world next door."

She pulled her shoulder away.

"Now go," she said, turning her back on me. "I'm meant to die alone. We must all fulfill our part of the story. As we shall, again and again, until the last world dies and sets us free."

*   *   *

I lay on the concrete floor of Buddy's cell, flat on my back, head throbbing. Driblets of his foul concoction on my lips, the aftertaste coating my fuzzy tongue like a layer of paint. Empty plastic cup in my outstretched hand.

Buddy crouched over me, wide-eyed.

"I don't remember how I got here," I mumbled.

He offered me his hand. "The same way you left."

I got to my feet, legs wobbly, and spat into the stainless-steel toilet. It didn't help. Buddy took the cup from me and pressed a warm can of Coke into my hand. I popped the tab and chugged it down.

"Did she explain?" he asked.

I wiped my hand across the back of my mouth.

"Too damn little, but apparently you've got an important message to deliver." I gave him the side-eye. "Do you, uh, know what the message is, and where it goes?"

"I will." He tapped his ear. "The machinery of the universe will tell me. Radio Free Buddy is on the air, twenty-four seven."

"I don't suppose the 'machinery of the universe' has a plan for getting you out of here?"

He tilted his head, listening to voices I couldn't hear. Then he nodded, smiling bright.

"Yes," he said. "*You.*"

Everybody's a comedian.

Bad enough I had to find my own way out of the Iceberg, but now I had a tagalong. A tagalong who might be vital to saving the world. A world that, just an hour ago, I didn't even know was in danger.

That was assuming, of course, I could believe anything I'd just seen. Assuming that it wasn't some elaborate hallucination caused by an overdose of bad prison wine. For that matter, "Cassandra" might have been more lucid than Buddy, but she didn't seem much more sane.

Still, I couldn't deny what had happened to me. Somebody had carved me out of my life and shoved me inside a prison, thanks to a mind hex that affected not only me but, well, *everybody.* There was power, and then there was *power* on a scale I'd never seen before. Cassandra's claim that I'd been swapped out with "the Thief," whoever the hell that was, made as much sense as any theory I could come up with on my own.

Didn't explain why Fleiss wanted to take out a hit on me, but I'd solve one problem at a time.

Speaking of problems, my original plan—prove I never got a trial, post bail, and flee the country—had just gone down in flames. I could get myself out that way, but that'd mean leaving Buddy behind. There was only one way to save my skin and get Buddy where he needed to go.

A good old-fashioned prison break.

"Buddy," I said, "you and me, we've got a lot of work to do."

* * *

Funny thing was, I was okay with it. Trouble had a way of sharpening my senses, putting me on top of my game. And I had plenty of trouble to keep me occupied.

As evening fell, I found myself shuffling along in the chow line, chewing over the problem. It was better than chewing the food. I was so wrapped up in plotting that I almost missed the change in temperature. I was still catching dagger-sharp glares from the Cinco Calles and their buddies, but now they weren't the only ones. A few of the whites—some of Brisco's guys and a handful of strangers—gave me the side-eye and dropped into low murmurs as I walked by.

Westie cleared a seat at the table for me, but he didn't look up from his food.

"Tell me something good," I said, setting my tray down beside his.

"All out of good news, friend. Brisco spent most of the afternoon in deep consultation with a gentleman of the Latin persuasion. Word is, talks didn't go so well."

"The Calles want me that bad?"

"Far as they're concerned," he said, "every day you're breathin' their air is an unforgivable insult. The Calles are having some kinda leadership shake-up on the outside. Raymundo is up for parole in a few months. He puts you on ice, that's a feather in his cap once he rejoins his brethren in sunny Las Vegas."

I dragged a plastic fork along a gray lump of mashed potatoes. I didn't have much of an appetite.

"Makes sense," I said. "Killing me, and getting away with it, will make him look like a guy who can get things done. Somebody who isn't afraid to spill a little blood. What's Brisco think?"

Westie shrugged. "Brisco doesn't want a war. And his general course of action, when it comes to problems, is to do whatever makes said problem go away. As quietly as possible."

"You think he'll hand me over to the Calles?"

"Not a chance, friend. The prisoners who take this white-solidarity business seriously would skin him alive for it. But just because he's not handing you over..."

He let the thought trail off.

"Doesn't mean," I said, "he won't stand aside and let them take a shot at me. 'Oops, sorry, they shanked him when we weren't looking. It couldn't be helped.'"

Westie twisted his lips into a bitter smile.

"Now you're thinking right. Watch your arse, Dan. Raymundo will make a move on you, and soon—it's not *if*, it's *when*."

When I'd finished choking down dinner, I fell in with a ragged crowd of men heading back to Hive C. All my shade of pale, most of them Brisco's boys.

I'd never felt so alone in a crowd.

Back in my cell, I caught Paul up on current events. He sat on his bunk, a dog-eared paperback by Voltaire nestled in his lap, and sighed.

"You've got options," he said, "but ultimately it comes down to a choice of evils. There's voluntary segregation, for instance."

"Voluntary?"

Paul nodded. "Sure. Any prisoner who feels threatened has the right to request voluntary segregation."

"How's that work?"

"You know Ad Seg? The hole? Solitary confinement? That's where they stick you. Hell, you can do your whole sentence in solitary. Pros: you won't get stabbed. Cons: you'll probably go insane from the isolation."

"Not an option," I said. "What else have you got?"

"Kill him first? Not easy to pull off, considering Raymundo never rolls with less than three of his, er, 'homies' to play body-guard, but you seem like a resourceful gentleman. Of course, then the banger who takes his place will have to kill you to avenge Ray-mundo, and so on down the line." He wagged his paperback at me. "Vengeance is an endless cycle. Tragic, really."

That idea had some merit. Not sure how I'd pull it off, though. I set it on the back burner.

"Of course," Paul added, "you could also...not be here when the attack happens. Those questions you asked me about people breaking out of the Iceberg. Those weren't hypothetical, were they?"

I caught the glint in his eye.

"Paul?" I asked. "By any chance, would you be interested in getting out of here?"

"Hmm." He glanced at his bare wrist, as if checking an invis-ible watch. "Well, I've got nothing else to do for another...forty years or so. So yes, Daniel, yes I would."

"Forty more years? Christ, what'd you do?"

Paul smirked. "Less than you did, according to your rap sheet. But to answer your question, I'm a bad, bad man. A bad, bad man who made the mistake of trusting a public defender with a heavy caseload. I may have committed a tiny little murder, but there *are* such things as mitigating circumstances, you know?"

"If we do this, you'll be a fugitive for the rest of your life. You okay with that?"

He stretched his arms over his head and stifled a yawn.

"My wife divorced me. She's made it clear I'll never see my lit-tle girl again, and I'm *pretty* sure my tenure at the university's been revoked by now. It's not as if I have a whole lot from my old life to cling to. So. You have a plan?"

"I'm working on that," I told him.

Later, I lay awake in my bunk, staring at the eggshell paint on the wall and listening to the restless sounds of the prison after dark. They were less jarring than the night before, and it was that much easier to close my eyes and slip, if not into sleep, into an uneasy waking dream.

The alien maggot inside my skull, the gift from the King of Worms, squirmed across the meat of my brain. I could see it when I closed my eyes, its black, rubbery skin still reflecting the light from distant stars. Its hunger growing.

14.

I dreamed of Caitlin.

It wasn't a message, no mystic vision. Just a snatch of memory on repeat. Sitting at a plastic two-seater in the secret little pizza parlor at the Metropolitan, side by side, sharing Cokes and fat, greasy slices of pepperoni pizza. She flashed her smile my way and I felt...whole. Human. Warm inside.

Then I woke up to the clattering and shouts and stench of the cellblock. My new home. My new home for the rest of my life if I didn't start making moves.

I joined the line for the showers, letting myself be herded like a cow, hating how fast it became routine. Brisco's boys, Ray-Ray and Slanger, fell in on my left and right. I gave Ray-Ray a nod.

"Brisco wants us to cover you while you shower," he told me. "In case the Calles get stupid. Just do the same for us, okay?"

"Good deal," I said.

I stripped down, setting my folded clothes on a long wooden bench, and stepped into the narrow shower stall. The curtain hung short, and even with it pulled closed I could see my new bodyguards' feet outside, standing watch for me. For five minutes, at least, I could exhale and let my guard down.

I didn't, though.

Something was off. As the lukewarm water splashed across the stubble on my scalp and rolled down my naked back, I stretched out my psychic tendrils. A mind here, a mind there. Snatches of confusion, of sudden anxiety, adrenaline spiking.

Fewer minds than there should have been. And the ones I could touch were *leaving*.

I turned around in the stall and looked down to the curtain gap. Ray-Ray and Slanger were gone.

Here it comes, then, I thought.

In the moments before a confrontation—when you know it's going to be genuine kill-or-be-killed violence, no discussion, no debate—the world slows to a crawl. Time turns into an hourglass filled with molasses, the seconds dripping down one leaden echoing heartbeat at a time. Your vision narrows, the walls closing in around you.

I took a deep breath, living in that silent, eternal moment.

Then the curtain ripped open, and everything happened very, very fast.

He was shorter than me, Asian, cropped black hair, but my eyes were on his knife. Not prison junk. Carbon black steel, spec-ops style, and forged to carve skin like butter.

Pro, said the back of my brain while the rest of me went into overdrive, dodging to one side as he lunged at me. The blade stabbed empty air, one inch from my left shoulder. I grabbed his wrist, twisted, shoved him a step backward, and slammed his arm against the shower stall opening as hard as I could. His forearm met the white tile with a shotgun *crack* as a bone fractured. He grunted through gritted teeth, but he clung to the knife with a death grip.

He had a buddy with a blade of his own, dancing around outside the stall like a prizefighter waiting for his title shot. The stall was too small, and they could only come at me one at a time. My only edge. That, and the weapon they didn't know I had.

The first hitter grabbed his knife with both hands, using his good arm to push as he forced me back a step, my shoulder blades pressed to the cold tile. The tip of the knife inched toward my belly as the shower rained down, drenching us both and turning the world into a wet blur as the downpour washed over my eyes.

As I pushed his hands back, straining against him, the alien maggot in my skull writhed with excitement. I felt it crawling across the back of my eyeball. Then it squirmed its way through the gelatinous tissue and nestled inside.

The hitter got a bright idea. Suddenly he wasn't pushing, he was *pulling*, hauling me off-balance and sending me stumbling out of the shower stall. Out into the empty room, where they could both have a go at me. The second killer was eager, too eager. He took a wild swing, his knife slicing the air as I ducked, and he didn't have time to recover before I threw myself on top of him. We landed on the wooden bench, rolled, landed hard on the floor, almost nose to nose.

I saw a heartbeat of terror register on his face. Then it was too late.

The black maggot spat from my iris like a bullet. It left no wound in its wake, and it didn't leave a visible wound on him either. Not when it chewed its way into his eyeball, and not when it dug into his brain like a diamond-tipped drill.

He dropped his knife and clutched his face, shrieking, feet pounding the floor. The confusion bought me a precious second, just enough time to snatch up his fallen blade and jump back. I came up in a crouch as the first hitter, the one with the fractured arm, lunged at me. I grabbed my shirt from the bench and swung it like a whip, snapping it at his face. Then I darted in and slashed, shredding his shirt and drawing a thin red line from his nipple to his gut with the tip of the blade.

He broke and ran, cradling his arm. There were no alarms, no pounding of guards' booted feet, and the security camera in the corner hung as a mute and witness. Nobody was coming. The guards had been bought off or warned off. It was just me and the second hitter, pressing his palms to his eyes and screeching like a newborn baby as he thrashed on the floor.

A kinder man would have put him out of his misery. I wasn't that man. Besides, I needed to make a statement to the entire prison. He'd do. I toweled off, pocketed his knife, got dressed, and walked out of the shower room, letting the door shut on his terrorized wails.

*   *   *

Out in the yard, they were playing cards at Brisco's picnic table. Sounded like a raucous good time, at least until they saw me coming.

A metal detector checkpoint stood between the hive and the yard, so I'd stashed the knife in my cell before I came out to play. That was all right. By now, they'd have found the second hitter, and word spread fast on the prison grapevine. I waited just long enough in my cell, before heading outside, to make sure the story got around.

Fear was my best weapon.

Ray-Ray and Slanger found someplace else to be, fast. The others could tell something was up but looked more confused than anxious; they must not have been in on the hit. Brisco, he just turned into a statue, his eyes going marble-hard.

"Hey, Brisco," I said, "what's up? You look like you've seen a ghost."

He leaned back a little, shoulders tensing.

"Guys," he said, "need a minute here."

His buddies cleared off, orbiting the table at a respectful distance. I sat down across from Brisco. And stared, without saying another word.

He tugged at his collar like a suspect sweating it out under an interrogation-room lamp and looked everywhere but straight ahead.

"It wasn't...it wasn't anything personal," he finally said.

"Funny," I told him. "When somebody tries to screw somebody else over and fails hard? That's always the first thing out of their mouth. 'It was only business.' 'It wasn't personal.' Thing is, to the guy *getting* screwed? It's *always* personal."

"You—you don't understand." He wrung his hands on the table. "I'm trying to save *lives* here, man. The browns are itching to go to war, and it's all because of you and those fucking Calles. No you, no more problem."

"Except those hitters weren't CCs. For one thing, they were Asian. Korean, maybe. Second, they were genuine operators. Where'd they come from, Brisco?"

He looked up at me and shook his head. "Outside. Don't know. Didn't ask. They said they'd been hired to take you out, and they came in with fake jackets. I know they had some bent guards covering for 'em. They said...they said if I set the scene and pulled my protection away, they'd move in and seal the deal. They get what they want, my problem goes away, everybody's happy."

"Yeah. Everybody's happy, except for me." I rested my palms on the picnic table and locked eyes with him. "You can imagine I might have a slight problem with that."

He froze, a deer in headlights. When he opened his mouth again, his voice came out in a near whisper.

"That guy...that guy they pulled out of the showers. They're saying he doesn't have a scratch on him. But he was screaming like he was burning alive. Said it took horse tranquilizers to knock him out. The second he woke up...he just started screaming again."

"Yeah," I said. "That's what I heard, too."

"What did—" Now he did drop to a whisper, eyes flicking left and right before he finished the question. "What did you *do* to him, Faust?"

I leaned in and gave him the sweetest smile I could muster.

"I did what I do."

He swallowed hard.

"Seems to me," I said, "the other day, at this very table, you were explaining the danger of holding grudges in here. So tell me, Brisco...are you going to settle things up with me? Make it right? Or are we going to have a problem?"

"No, no problem." He shook his head, eyes going wide. "What...what would square us, do you think?"

"That's simple. Right now, unless a friendly guard already smuggled him out, there's a hit man with a broken arm hiding somewhere in this prison. I want you, and all your boys, to go on a scavenger hunt. Find him, and bring him to me, *alive*. He needs to answer some questions. You do that, and as far as I'm concerned, I can let bygones be bygones. Fair enough?"

"Yeah." He pushed himself up on shaky legs, waving a hand to call his entourage back. "And I mean it, it was nothing personal—"

I held up one hand. He stopped talking.

"Also," I said, "I want a cell phone."

15.

After I gave my new best friend his marching orders, I went looking for Jake and Westie. I found them over by the fence, sharing hits off a half-burnt cigarette.

"Hey," Jake said, "don't suppose you've got any smokes on you? We're down to the bottom of the pack."

"Sorry. Never picked up the habit. I figure it's best if there's at least *one* vice I don't indulge in."

Westie took a drag, passed the cigarette to Jake, and looked me up and down.

"You in one piece, friend? Heard some funny stories about the showers this morning. Stories where your name popped up."

"What can I say?" I shrugged. "I'm a popular guy. Been thinking about our problem, the Hive B thing."

Jake glanced at the cigarette stub between his fingers. Fingers that trembled just a bit.

"Yeah? All that thinking taking you anywhere in particular?"

"Yep." I nodded toward the fence and the endless plain of scrub and sand on the other side. "Out. Seems to me, if people are being snatched and taken away for possibly nefarious purposes, the best solution is to be far, far away from the guards doing the snatching. Wanna come with?"

Westie arched one bushy eyebrow. "A prison break? You takin' the piss?"

"I've got a bit of a contrarian nature," I said. "Tell me something's never been done before, or *can't* be done, and it just encourages me. Besides, I can't get used to this lifestyle. Don't like the accommodations, don't like the fashion, and I sure as hell don't care for the cuisine. So what do you say? If I can spring us, you in?"

They shared a quiet glance. A whole conversation passed between them without a word being said.

"Who else knows?" Jake asked. Cautious, but nibbling at the hook.

"Paul's on board. And, ah, we have to take Buddy."

"Buddy?"

"The Prof."

Jake tilted his head at me. Then he looked off to the left. I followed his gaze. Buddy sat at one of the chess tables, alone, having what looked like an animated conversation.

"He's talking to his chess pieces," Jake said.

"Yep. That he is."

"And...he's pausing, like he's hearing them talk back."

I shrugged. "Admittedly, he's more of a liability than an asset, but I gotta get him out of here. Favor for a friend."

Westie rubbed his chin. "Man's brain is fried. Paul's solid, though. Bit of an egghead, but we could use that. So a four-man crew. Plus the Prof. You got a plan up your sleeve?"

"I'm working on that."

Jake and Westie shared another silent conversation.

"Let us know when you've got something solid," Jake said. "And *if* the plan feels right...hell, man, I'm in. I hear Mexico's nice this time of year."

"Yeah, all right," Westie said. "I'm up for some beachside piña coladas. You let us know, Dan. We'll be waiting."

Back in the hive, out on the gallery floor, I caught movement in my peripheral vision. Another man cutting through the crowd, headed toward me on a collision course. I tensed up. Something must have shown in my eyes as I turned, because he froze in his tracks. It was Zap, Brisco's pet trustee.

"Hey, man, it's cool. I'm just playing delivery boy."

I showed him my open hands, and we both relaxed.

"Walk with me," he said.

He matched my stride, moving to stand on my left side, opposite the gun tower at the heart of the hive.

"Gonna put something in your left hand," he said in a low voice. "Keep it out of sight."

I felt the sleek plastic shell of a flip phone slide against my palm.

"This is major-league contraband," he warned me. "You're looking at a month in Ad Seg if you get caught with it. So don't get caught with it. And if you do get caught, I don't know you."

"You're a good man, Zap."

"Brisco's a good man. So, uh, are you gonna kill him?"

"Probably not," I told him, "but we'll see how things go. The day is still young."

My pulse raced as I climbed the metal stairs, rounded the tier catwalk, and headed straight for my cell. I had to force myself to slow my stride no matter how badly I wanted to run. One-way mirrors plastered the central tower like posters on a subway wall; it was impossible to tell if a guard was watching. Thinking fast, I opened the little storage cabinet, stood up the phone—a cheap prepaid burner with a scratched-up purple plastic shell—on a shelf, and leaned in close.

Perfect. At that angle, even if a guard spotted me, it'd look like I was just rummaging through my stuff. If I kept my head turned, they wouldn't even see my lips moving. I dialed a number I knew by heart, fingers trembling so bad I messed up and had to redial.

The phone purred once. Twice. Then a click.

"Thank you for calling the Scrivener's Nook," Bentley's reedy voice intoned. "How may I help you?"

I almost couldn't answer, the words catching in my strangled throat. So many things I'd taken for granted: freedom, money, the high life, and the Vegas lights. So many things I didn't appreciate until they were suddenly gone.

Family, most of all.

"Bentley, it's…it's me."

"Daniel! Where *are* you? We've been trying to visit you ever since the trial ended, but nobody seems to know anything. It's as if you vanished from the system."

"Because I was never *in* the system. It's a con, Bentley. The whole damn thing. I'm at Eisenberg Correctional. I—damn it, I've got so much to say, and I don't even know how much time I've got on this phone."

"Then say it in person. We're coming to see you, right now."

"I need you to get in touch with Jennifer," I said, the words flowing fast now like water from a spigot. "There's some trouble with her business partners. And also get word to—"

"In person," Bentley repeated. I heard a gruff voice in the background. "Yes, Cormie, it's Daniel. Daniel, we'll be there in a few hours. Stay strong, son."

The line went dead.

The minutes left weren't the problem, I realized. The phone's battery was down to half strength, and I doubted I'd get my hands on a charger in here. Once it died, there went my lifeline to the outside world. Still, my next call was just as urgent as the first.

"Southern Tropics Import-Export," said a nasal operator. "How may I direct your call?"

"Emma Loomis, please."

"I'm *so* sorry," she droned, though she didn't sound sorry at all. "Ms. Loomis is in meetings all day and can't be disturbed. If I could take your number—"

"Tell her it's Daniel Faust. I'm in a situation here, and I need her help."

"Certainly, sir. I'll give her that message as soon as she's done with her meetings for the day."

"No." I took a long, deep breath. It didn't help. "I mean, I need you to do it *now*."

"Oh, but that's quite impossible. She's in a meeting."

Southern Tropics was a front company, established to finance Prince Sitri's operations on Earth and provide cover for his agents.

I should have expected the head office of Hell Incorporated would have an unhelpful receptionist. *How does Caitlin deal with these people?* I thought. Then the answer came to me.

"I'm calling on hound business," I said. "And if you don't have Emma Loomis on this phone in the next sixty seconds, I will personally have you rolled in batter, boiled alive in cooking oil, and served in the company cafeteria as a tempura dish."

Dead silence.

Then the operator let out an exasperated *tsk*. "Well, that's *all* you had to say in the *first place*, sir. Please hold."

The hold music came on. Kenny G, playing saxophone.

"Daniel?" Emma said. "Where are you?"

"Hey, Emma. I'm in prison. Don't suppose you know when Caitlin's coming home?"

"You're in—wait, did you say *prison?*"

"Yeah, I imagine it's like hell, but the food's probably worse."

"Don't count on that," she said. "And speaking of, our prince's gala is...ongoing. These affairs tend to run long. There's allegedly quite the orgy going on. Which I am *missing*, having been left behind to tend the shop in everyone's absence."

"I'm sure your dedication is appreciated."

"Don't count on that either. As for Caitlin, I'm expecting she'll be back by tomorrow evening. Now, *why* are you in prison?"

The power bar on the phone drooped, shifting color from pale green to warning yellow.

"I don't know how long I'll have this phone," I told her, "but call Corman and Bentley tomorrow morning and they'll fill you in on everything. Can you get word to Caitlin?"

"I can try using the conduit. Even if I do, though, she won't be able to come home early, not without Prince Sitri's leave. Can you wait until tomorrow night?"

Good question. I'd used my one holdout weapon, the "gift" from the King of Worms, and I didn't dare ask for another. Not with my head still throbbing and one eye feeling raw every time I blinked. Not when I'd come that close to being its meal. I had the knife, but the metal detectors meant I couldn't get it out onto the yard, where I was most likely to get jumped. Meanwhile, Jennifer's gang buddies wanted me dead, Fleiss might send more assassins—at least one of whom, even with a broken wing, was still lurking around the prison—and I had little doubt Brisco would steer me into another ambush if he thought the second time would be the charm.

"Sure," I said. "No problem. Everything's just peachy."

16.

I hid the phone under my mattress, along with the knife. I'd be screwed if the guards decided to search my cell, but then again, it wasn't like they could add more years to my life sentence.

Then I waited.

I paced. I did push-ups against the eggshell-white wall. I hooked my feet on the end of my cot and did sit-ups until my stomach muscles burned. Killing the hours, one endless minute at a time. Christmas was never really a thing at my house when I was young—every dollar my old man earned went straight to the liquor store—but now I could imagine what it'd feel like to be a kid on Christmas morning, waiting until I could finally open my presents.

My present arrived in the form of a bored-looking guard coming to escort me to the visitor center. We didn't go straight there; two other prisoners on the tier had guests waiting, and he collected us all before marching us single file down the maze of corridors.

Once we arrived it took everything I had to keep from running over to Bentley and Corman, throwing my arms around them, and hugging them like a drowning man hugs a life preserver. As it was, all it took was Bentley's hand on my shoulder to draw a bark of "No physical contact" from one of the guards.

I bit back the urge to tell him where he could stick his rules. Instead, I sat down, took a deep breath, and tugged my folded rap sheet out of my pocket.

"You need to see this," I said. "But first, were you able to get hold of Jennifer?"

Bentley's brow furrowed. "Nobody's seen her. Her, Nicky, Nicky's, er, little helpers..."

"And your lawyer too," Corman muttered, "but we know why *that* shyster went into hiding. Caitlin told him she'd skin him alive if he lost your trial."

I unfolded the printout, smoothing it out on the table between us.

"I didn't have a trial."

"What do you mean?" Bentley asked. "Cormie and I were there, every single day."

I tapped the corner of the page where the words faded into a smeared blob. "What's this say? What day was I arrested?"

"September sixteenth," Corman replied.

"And what day is today?"

"The eighteenth."

"And how did four months pass between then and now?" I asked.

Bentley fished inside his vest, taking out a slim pair of bifocals. He slipped on the glasses, squinting at the page. Corman just frowned like he was trying to do long division in his head.

"Don't know what you mean," Corman said.

This wasn't working. I had to find some way of attacking the curse at its root. Pointing out the impossibility of the date didn't seem to dent it; the facts just slipped in one ear and out the other.

"Okay," I said, "you were both at the trial. Who was the first witness?"

"It was—" Bentley started. He looked at Corman, who blinked.

"I think it was one of the cops," Corman said. "Wasn't it? It was."

"It was," Bentley agreed. The momentary confusion on their faces ebbed away, replaced by absolute clarity. Clarity that only became stronger as they told me about the polite young officer, filling in each other's half-finished sentences and painting more and more details—more detail than anyone could possibly remember four months after the fact.

It's like a virus, I thought. *The damn curse is rooting itself deeper in their heads while I'm trying to purge it. Like a self-defense mechanism.*

I tried a second time, asking about the jury. Starting from halting reminiscences, over the course of five minutes they went on to completely "remember," and describe in photographic detail, all twelve jurors down to the color of their socks.

"Okay," I said, "let's try this. You both remember the last day of the trial?"

"Of course we do," Corman said. "What are you getting at anyway?"

I held up a finger. "One question. Not about the trial, not about the courtroom, just that day. That morning. I want you to tell me...what you had for breakfast."

"It was..." Bentley's voice trailed off, leaving a space as empty as the look in his eyes.

Corman just stared at me, uncertain.

"C'mon," I said. "It was the last day of the trial. I'm sure you can remember how you felt, the lawyers' summations, all of it, right? It was a big, big day for all of us. So tell me what you had for breakfast."

"I don't seem to recall," Bentley said. "Maybe my stomach was too upset to eat."

"How about dinner?" I asked.

Corman winced. He squeezed his eyes shut and rubbed a calloused knuckle against his forehead.

"Tell me anything about what happened *outside* the courtroom in the last four months," I said. "Anything you remember. Bentley, you read at least one book a week. What were the last five books you read? Who were the authors?"

Bentley touched his glasses with trembling fingertips, staring down at the rap sheet.

"Oh dear," was all he said.

"Corman, how's your fantasy football league going? You play every year. I've seen you obsess over your team's stats like it's a matter of life or death. So. You winning?"

Corman leaned his head back, taking a ragged breath. His eyelids snapped open.

"You see it now," I said.

"How did we not?" Bentley whispered, horrified. "You were arrested two days ago. I see it, plain as day, but just a moment ago I couldn't. I just *couldn't*. There was no trial, but I...I *remember* it. I was *there*."

Corman dragged the printout closer, his fingers rapping against the blurry text.

"Someone laid one hell of a whammy on us," he growled.

"Not just on you. On *everybody*. People I've never even *met* somehow lose the ability to understand a calendar the second my so-called 'trial' comes up."

"I'm not fond of the word 'impossible,'" Bentley said, "but if you'd asked me yesterday if such a thing could be done, I'd have dismissed it out of hand. Troubling. Very troubling."

"It gets worse," I said and gave them a rundown of my vision trip with Buddy and Cassandra. I left out the part about the assassins in the shower; they didn't need me piling any more worry on their shoulders.

"It appears—" Bentley fell abruptly silent as a guard strolled past our table. He waited, then spoke in a grave whisper. "It appears that what we require, first and foremost, is an *exit strategy*."

"You're reading my mind," I told him. "I've got some interested parties who might want to join in on the fun. What I'm going to need, on your end, is logistical support. Specifically a few books in your back-room collection."

Corman shook his head. "We can mail you a care package, but I gotta think everything gets searched and double-searched. They gonna let that through?"

I hadn't thought of that. Antique books of black magic probably weren't on the approved-items list. I could make do with just a few relevant pages once I knew exactly what I needed for the plan, but my gaze drifted to the big block-letter rules on the wall. *No passing of materials between convict and visitors.*

"But legal paperwork," I said, thinking out loud. "I have a right to that, don't I?"

Corman arched an eyebrow. "What's the angle, kiddo?"

"Still figuring that out. You're sure Perkins ran for the hills?"

"If he was subject to the same illusion we were," Bentley said, "then he fully believes he lost the case. Remembers it happening, even. I don't expect he'll show his face anytime soon."

A red-tinted light on the wall flashed and emitted a short, sharp electric buzz. Visiting hours were over.

"I'll call you," I said quickly, "and Emma Loomis—you remember her, from that whole Redemption Choir mess? She's going to get in touch with you first thing in the morning. Tell her everything I told you. She's trying to get a message to Caitlin."

We all rose together, plastic chairs squeaking on the tile floor.

"Watch your ass, kiddo," Corman told me, "and let us know once you've got a game plan."

"You'll know the second I do. Do me a favor: hit the books and see if you can find anything that resembles what Cassandra told me. It all sounded...archetypical. Like some weird-ass take on a tarot deck." I thought back, rattling off the names I could remember. "The Prophet, the Enemy, the Paladin...the Thief, the Witch and her Knight. I think she said it all originated in some kind of story. Maybe a fairy tale, I don't know. It's worth following up on."

Bentley held up a finger. "I'll see what I can dig up. Just one question: how did *you* break the curse?"

"Easy," I said. "C'mon, sentenced to life in prison? That's how I knew something was fishy. You would have moved heaven and earth to get me out of here."

Bentley smiled thinly, with a mischievous glint in his eye.

"You make the plan, son," he said, "and we'll warm up the bulldozers."

* * *

We hid in plain sight. Down on the open floor, in clear view of the central guard tower and surrounded by milling convicts, I commandeered a folding table and Westie bummed a deck of cards. Jake and Paul joined us, a perfect foursome for bridge. That was what we pretended to play, anyway—ignoring our hands and idly flipping cards to look busy—while we talked it out in low, furtive voices.

"Seems to me," I said, "the main road's a no-go. No guarantee we can get out without setting off an alarm, and if we do, we're sunk. The highway patrol will have roadblocks up on I-80 twenty minutes before we get there."

Westie shot a glance over his shoulder. "The desert, then? We'll stick out like a devil in church. Choppers'll run us down before we make it five miles."

"Not if we play it right. Paul, you said it could be done on an all-terrain vehicle. On my way to the visitor center, I saw a sign pointing toward the prison motor pool. Do the guards actually *have* an ATV?"

"I said it could be done," he murmured into his cards, "and I also said you'd be seen by day and crash by night. There *is* no 'right way.'"

"They got 'em, though," Jake said. "I work the garage detail. They've got dune buggies, two of 'em. Supposedly for rescue and retrieval, in case some prisoner's dumb enough to try to escape across the desert on foot, but mostly the guards just take 'em out to tear around and have fun after hours."

"And they can go the distance?" I asked.

"Hell yeah they can. They're Wildcat Sport XTs. Four-stroke engines, double A-arm suspension, front differential locks. Those babies can haul ass."

"Which isn't going to mean a thing," Paul said, "when you ram straight into a boulder in the dark. Or run off a ridge and flip over. And forget daytime—I don't care how fast they are, they're not faster than a helicopter."

"You work garage detail," I said. "So you have access to those buggies?"

Jake snorted and slapped a couple of cards on the table. "Yeah, to wash and wax. All the keys are in a lockbox up in a guard booth, and there's always at least one guy on duty, usually two. Might as well be sealed up in Fort Knox, for all the chance I'd have to snatch 'em. Garage detail mostly means cleaning the guards' personal vehicles. That and scrubbing sand off the transfer buses."

"So what're you thinking about?" Westie asked me.

I laid my cards down, spreading them out on the table.

"Our exit strategy," I said. "Here's how we're going to do it."

17.

"Jake," I said, "how late do the garage details run?"

He shrugged. "Depends on the day. Sometimes as late as five. We knock off just before the dinner bell rings."

My fingers danced over my cards, turning them, laying them out like a crude pasteboard map as I drew upon my memories of the walks to and from the visitor center.

"Here's the hive," I said, tickling the face of the jack of hearts, "and here's the exit checkpoint. From here you can reach the visitor center or, turning left on this corridor, head toward the motor pool."

"Yeah," Jake said, "there's another checkpoint at the end, though. Sealed gate, and the guard on the other side has to buzz you through."

"Speaking of guards," I said, "they don't have nearly enough of them. That's the flaw in their armor. One flaw, anyway. I just had a visitor; so did a couple of other guys. They sent one guard to walk us all there and back again. Is that common?"

"Sure." Westie nodded up toward the central tower. "They all want to play at being a badass sniper up in the towers. Prisoner-escort duty is shit work."

I tapped the card that stood in for the access hallway.

"That's how we do it. See, right around the end of visiting hours, while Jake's working in the motor pool, the rest of us are going to get visitors."

Paul shook his head. "Nobody's come to visit me in years."

"That's okay. I've got a bunch of friends on the outside. They'll be your friends, too. It won't matter anyway, because we won't be *going* to the visitor center."

Jake put the pieces together quick. "Four men against one guard."

"I figure you all heard about the dustup in the showers this morning," I said. "I took a knife off one of the hitters. Mean-looking mother of a blade, too, not some two-bit shank. Right here, at the hallway bend, that's where we do it. Convex mirrors here and here, but no camera coverage."

"You gonna carve him a new smile?" Westie asked.

I shook my head. "Not if I don't have to. A live hostage is more valuable than a corpse. I figure we introduce ourselves and 'convince' him to walk us over to the motor pool. If he can talk us through that checkpoint, we're halfway home. If not, I take his gun and *make* the checkpoint guard open up for us. Either way, once we're through, we bum-rush the place. Jake, you'll already be on the scene, so we'll need you to create a distraction. Something to draw the guards out of that booth with the keys, so we can jump them from behind."

Jake rubbed the thick stubble on his granite jaw. "Yeah, I can do that. I'm pretty good at causing a commotion. Now, those Wildcats are two-seaters. There's five of us, so somebody's gonna have to hang on tight to the back. Strap a couple of gas cans to each buggy, so we can go the distance...damn, I think this might actually work."

"Two problems," Paul said. "First, no matter which way we go, there are two ten-foot gates standing between us and freedom. One of which is electrified."

"We'll have hostages," Westie told him.

"Uh-uh. Getting through a checkpoint by threatening a hostage? That's one thing. But if we call up Warden Lancaster and tell him we've got his men, he won't open the gates for us. He'll lock the whole prison down and send in a 'rescue' team with orders to shoot us on sight." Paul tossed a card onto the table and scooped up another pair. "And I repeat, once again, you can't cross the desert in the dark. We won't make it five miles without headlights. *With* headlights, we get spotted by the choppers. Same outcome."

I glanced up to the tower. The shadows of men prowled behind the smoky glass, rifles slung over their shoulders. I thought back to my first night behind bars, watching them in the dark.

"After the hive goes into lockdown for the night," I said, "the tower guards put on night-vision goggles. Fancy gear. I figure, we get our hands on a couple of pairs, and whoever drives the Wild-cats—"

"Dibs," Jake said.

"—whoever drives," I repeated, "won't *need* headlights to see."

Paul nodded toward the span of open space around the tower, marked off by a fat stripe of red paint.

"You see that line?" he asked me. "That's not a joke. You take one step across it, even by accident, they *will* gun you down. I've seen it happen. How the hell are we going to get to the top of the tower, let alone steal two pairs of night-vision goggles?"

"That's my job," I said. "Opening the gate, too, that's on me. I just need to know if you're down for the rest."

Westie gave me a long, hard look. Taking my measure.

"I'm game—for my part of the job—but if you foul this up, we're all gonna be flatliners. You're sure you can pull this off, friend? Would you bet your life on it?"

"I *am* betting my life on it," I told him.

"I've heard things about you," Jake said. "Some of the shit Winslow's said when he's drunk...yeah, all right. If it was anybody else, I'd walk away. But if you say you can do it, you can do it. I'm in."

Paul looked down at the cards in his hands, like he was searching for some meaning there, or just a little good advice. His shoulders slumped.

"This is reckless, stupid, and probably going to get us all killed," he said with a sigh, "but maybe that's better than another forty years in this hellhole. Sure. What the hell. I'm in. What about the Prof? Are we sure he's up for it?"

"He'll be up for it," I said. "I think we're all in agreement that we go sooner rather than later, yes? It's going to take me a couple of days to get everything I need, so I say we do it the night after tomorrow. Two days between us and freedom. All in?"

Jake and Westie bumped fists. All in. I looked to Paul.

"I know this prison is run on a shoestring, but do they have any kind of a library?"

He shrugged. "If you can call it that."

"Do they have atlases? Maps?"

"They have some middle-school American history books," he told me. "Close enough?"

"It'll have to be. You're on navigation duty. 'Drive south until we hit the Mexican border' is a good idea in theory, but a lousy plan. I want you to figure out the best course to take. What roads we'll eventually cross over and which cities and towns we might pass close to on our way out of Nevada. Ideally, we'll want to find a remote spot close to the edge of civilization, dump the buggies, and steal fresh transportation to cover our tracks. Can you handle that?"

"I'm on it," Paul said.

"Good. Westie, we've got one checkpoint—and one metal detector—to pass through on our way out of the hive. Now, I know people manage to get shanks through there; I saw somebody get stabbed my first hour on the yard. How do they do it?"

"Easy as peaches," he said. "Lots of ways. Routine makes the guards sloppy. Case in point, I'm on cleaning detail most weeks. They give me an old wheeled rust bucket to slop water around in, and it sets off the detector every single time. They pat me down, but they don't give the bucket a second glance."

"So if you stash something in there," I said, "and rest your mop on top of it—"

"Like I said, easy."

"I need you to find a secure spot, right about here," I said, sliding my finger along the playing-card 'map,' "and arrange to be mopping the floor when the rest of us pass by with the guard. I'll give you the knife beforehand to smuggle through the metal detector. Is that doable?"

Westie pursed his lips, staring down at the cards. He tossed down his hand and crossed his arms over his chest.

"Aye. Got some ideas already."

"Jake," I said, "your part's obvious: the motor pool. Scope it out from end to end. I want guard numbers, rotation timing, layout, anything that'll give us an edge. And figure out a good distraction for when we make our play. We'll need to take control fast to keep anybody from radioing for help. We've got zero margin for error here."

"Can do," he said.

"And while you're all doing that, I'll work out the gate and the goggles." I gathered up the 'map,' shuffling the cards back into the deck. "When we get to Mexico, first round's on me."

We played cards for real after that, with nothing to wager but bragging rights. Anything to kill a little time. My head wasn't in the game; I was attacking the problem, trying to figure out what I could pull from my bag of tricks. My gaze kept drifting upward, to the tower and the maze of metal walkways that filled the hive like the strands of a steel spiderweb.

Emerson—the guard who'd brought me in from processing, the one Paul said hadn't been here long enough to pick up bad habits—strolled the upper walkways. It didn't take long to realize what was off about him, and another few minutes of casual observation confirmed it.

He wasn't watching the prisoners. He was watching the other guards.

I filed it away in the back of my mind, something to ponder—or not—once the real work was done. I'd taken the two biggest parts of this escape plan onto my shoulders, and it wasn't just *my* ass in the fire if I couldn't pull it off. While I played cards on autopilot, doing back-brain math and moves I'd learned by rote, my thoughts drifted back to older, happier times.

18.

I stared down at the card in my hand, the three of clubs with my signature scrawled across the face in black Sharpie. The exact same card I'd shuffled into the half deck in Bentley's hands not one minute earlier.

I was nineteen years old, and I was learning the basics.

"It's impossible," I said.

He shook his head with a smile, leaning back against the counter, and fanned the cards in his hands.

"It clearly just happened, so it can't be impossible," he said. "The magical arts require a certain shift in vocabulary. The question isn't, 'Is this possible?' The question is, 'What means can be undertaken to *make* it possible?'"

"I had half of the deck," I said slowly, puzzling it out, "and you had half of the deck. I saw you shuffle my card into your half. You never *touched* my half. I've had it in my hand the entire time. So...wait, was that *real* sorcery? Some kind of, I don't know, illusion spell?"

"Maybe it was sleight of hand, and maybe it was a spell. Does it matter?" Bentley asked.

I gaped at him. "Of course it matters."

"Why?"

"Because," I said with the sort of exasperation only a teenager can muster, "one's just a trick, and one's...you know...*magic*."

"And yet, the end result is exactly the same: the signed card ended up in your hands. If I need to dig a hole in the ground, does it matter if I use a shovel or my bare hands, as long as the hole gets dug?"

I relented, almost saying no—then I paused. I eagerly brandished the signed card, certain I'd caught my teacher in an obvious blunder.

"It does. Because it's not just the outcome that matters; one way is a heck of a lot more work than the other way. Why would anyone dig with their hands when they could use a shovel?"

"Precisely." His sly smile told me I was the one who had just been outmaneuvered. "Now then, observe and learn."

He took my cards, set the signed one facedown on the counter, and joined the deck back together. He shuffled, cut, and handed me half of the cards, then made sure I was watching as he slipped the signed card back into his half.

"The magician has two considerations in every challenge." He flipped his half of the deck over and fanned out the cards one by one, showing them to me. "One: what techniques can achieve your desired end? Two: if multiple approaches would work, which one is the most effective tool for the task?"

My card wasn't in his hands. He nodded at my half. I flipped the top card and stared down at my own signature. Again.

"Now what's more likely? That I engineered a spell to warp your perception, or that I simply relied"—he passed his open hand over my half of the deck, and my signed card vanished—"on skilled misdirection?"

Bentley held up his hand and snapped his fingers. As he did, the signed card flipped up from the cup of his palm with a flourish, caught between his thumb and forefinger.

I blinked at him. "Is *that* why you're making me learn card tricks before you teach me the real stuff? Because it's easier?"

"Easier, my ass," Corman grunted, lugging a cardboard box full of books from the back room. "Try doing the oil and water routine one-handed, *without* using real sorcery to help."

"Which you will be learning how to do eventually," Bentley told me.

"You know," I said, looking between them, "I *have* seen *The Karate Kid*. If this is building up to some wax-on, wax-off moment of Zen revelation—"

Bentley tapped one of his temples. "We're teaching you the most important foundational skill for a sorcerer. How to *think* like one. At its core, all magic—be it the real thing or stage tricks—is about misdirection."

"In other words," Corman said, "it's all bullshit. And so's ninety-eight percent of everything else in the world. People try to lie to you twenty times a day. Forty times, if you don't change the channel when commercials come on. Before you can pull a con on somebody else, you've gotta be able to spot when a grifter's pulling one on *you*."

I walked through Bentley's card trick in my memory, playing it out step by step. I knew I'd held the half deck tight between my fingers. No chance he'd slipped it in under my thumb without me feeling it. Yet I'd seen him, twice now, take my signed card and shuffle it into his—

I paused. Watching his hand in my mind's eye smoothly slip the card back into his deck. Facedown.

The corners of Bentley's eyes wrinkled with amusement as he watched me think it through. "What do I keep telling you, Daniel? Always question your assumptions."

"Every good con," Corman said, "feeds on the mark's assumptions. Let him do the hard work for you."

"My card," I said slowly, "couldn't have been slipped into my half of the deck after you gave it to me. Which means...you did it *before* you gave it to me. I saw you slip *a* card into your half, facedown, and I just assumed it was the one I signed. But you switched the signed card with a different one while you were cutting the deck, didn't you?"

Bentley gently applauded. "And the student is learning. This is exactly what I mean, Daniel. People build assumptions about the world around them in countless ways, every single day. It's a form of mental shorthand, and most of the time, it's a useful survival mechanism. There's nothing wrong with assuming, say, that gravity will tether you safely to the Earth, or that fire will burn so you shouldn't touch it. If you stopped to question everything around you, at every moment, you'd be paralyzed."

"But those same assumptions can bend you over a barrel." Corman tugged a couple of hardbound books with staid dust-covers from his carton and hunted for an open spot on the over-stuffed shelves. "Especially when real sorcery's in the mix. Eyes open, kiddo."

"Which brings us back to the question of tools," Bentley told me. "Any magician worthy of the name knows three ways, at minimum, to accomplish any given effect. Which methods you use, and in what combination, depend on the needs of the moment. Sometimes the best answer really *is* to weave an illusion spell. Or sometimes I can get the exact same result by palming a card and letting your imagination do the work for me. Digging with a shovel versus digging by hand."

"So," I asked, "how do I know which to use?"

"Practice. But first...you learn the moves." Bentley handed me the deck of cards. "Here. Your turn. I'll show you a few methods of moving a signed card into *my* hand."

My stomach growled. I eyed the cards dubiously.

"Couldn't we do this after lunch?"

"We will eat," he said with a soft chuckle, "once you've managed to slip a card past me."

*   *   *

Five years later, on the morning of my twenty-fourth birthday, I was sitting in a chair.

"Sitting" being relative, considering I was tied to it. And the chair was upside down, dangling by a rope from the sturdy light fixture in the dusty back room of the Scrivener's Nook. Lengths of chain wound like boa constrictors around my chest, wrists, and ankles, secured by combination padlocks.

"Hey, kiddo," Corman said, amiably munching on a slice of cake. "How's it going?"

"Hey, Corman. A little help here?"

He took a long look at me, shrugged, and scooped up another forkful of cake.

"Nope."

I wriggled against the loops binding my wrists. The motion made the chair slowly turn, twirling on its rope, and the blood rushed to do a dizzy conga in my brain.

"Seriously," I said, "this is impossible. I can't do it."

"Sure you can. Y'know, I saw Harry Blackstone Junior perform in Manhattan once. He did this exact same escape *plus* he was inside a burlap sack. Took him twelve minutes."

I squirmed, rocking the chair, sending it turning in the other direction.

"Not for nothing," Corman said, "but your birthday cake is *amazing*. Butter cream and French silk chocolate. That's the good stuff. You should come down from there and get some before it's all gone."

"Oh, *great* idea," I said. "I'll be right there."

"That's the spirit," he said with a smile.

As the door swung shut behind him, leaving me alone in the gloom, I realized my sarcasm might have misfired.

All right, I told myself, *first things first. Get a grip.*

I focused on my breathing. Deep and steady. Tuning out my anxiety, my fear of failure, all the distractions I didn't need. In their wake, new, positive thoughts flooded in to fill the gap. Ideas. Inspirations. My bag of tricks. Five years of learning everything from sleight of hand to eldritch conjurations.

I've exorcised a demon, I reminded myself, *and I've spoken to the Mourner of the Red Rocks and lived. Also, I play the meanest three-card monte on Fremont Street, and I can do the oil and water routine with one arm behind my back.*

Tied to a chair? I can handle this.

Like a magic trick, anxiety transformed into excitement. I attacked the problem from a fresh perspective. I wasn't tied to a chair. Individual *parts* of me were tied to a chair. Escape was a series of steps, a multilayered puzzle to be unraveled.

First, information, I thought. *Find out what I'm up against.*

I lifted my legs as much as I could, muscles straining. The combination padlock dangled down, giving me a good look at the faceplate. *Master Lock 1533*, I noted, thinking back over everything I'd been taught about how to crack a combination lock and that model in particular.

I curled my hands into a cup, flexing my arms as much as the chain binding me to the chair would allow. I slowly, sinuously writhed, slipping the bonds down a millimeter at a time, giving me more room to bend my elbows. Finally, the padlock on my wrist chains dropped into my hands. I'd have to crack it backward, by touch alone.

I didn't escape in twelve minutes. It took closer to three hours.

But that was a damn fine birthday cake.

19.

Joining the ragged, shuffling chow line in the dining hall, I tried to call on that same old confidence. It wasn't easy, not with a third of the room staring daggers at me—and any number of them carrying *real* daggers hidden under their shirts—but it felt good to have a plan in motion. I needed to figure out my end, but once that fell into place, freedom was just a few risky moves away.

Watching the stone-faced guards along the wall, fingers resting light on their triggers, I realized they might be my way in. According to Paul—and the general behavior from the guards I'd seen since I got here—the Iceberg's keepers were mired in incompetence and outright corruption. If I could find a guard with a weak spot and apply the right pressure, I wouldn't have to break into the tower to get those goggles: I could make him do it for me.

Not Emerson, though. I kept thinking back to his strange patrol on the catwalks, how he watched the other guards. Studied them. Something was all kinds of wrong about Emerson, but I couldn't put my finger on it.

As I took a seat at the far end of a table, the other convicts gave me space. Way too much space. Nobody made eye contact, much less casual conversation. Word spread fast. I guessed that by now everybody had heard about the ambush in the showers and how one of the assassins ended up. They didn't know what I'd done to him or how; they just knew that I'd done *something*. Something they didn't want any part of.

There was one big problem with using fear as a weapon: terrorize someone whose entire sense of self is invested in being the biggest badass on the block, and it can backfire. Hard. I cast a glance toward the Calles' table, where Raymundo and his boys were deep in a heated argument. I couldn't make out the words, but the body language was three degrees south of a full-on brawl.

I looked for too long. Raymundo locked eyes with me. Then he shot to his feet, curling his hands into stony fists. Quick hands tugged him back down, heads shaking wildly, raised voices halfway between appeasement and dread. He shook them off, slammed his palms down on the table, and took a deep breath.

I turned away, but I made sure to keep him in my peripheral vision until I was done eating. Just in case.

I hadn't seen Brisco or his entourage in the crowded hall, and I found out why soon enough. On my way back to the hive, he fell in beside me and spoke in a low murmur.

"Found your guy."

"You got him?"

"*Found* him. Cornered him. Little fucker's got a knife like something out of a Rambo movie. He's fast, too. Slashed Ray-Ray's arm open from his elbow to his pinky finger, made us fall back. He's pinned down, though. He ain't going anywhere 'til you say so."

"Where's he at?"

Brisco jerked his chin upward. "The bathrooms," he said, "on tier three."

*   *   *

Stay out of the bathrooms on tier three, Paul told me on my first day in the Iceberg. The security camera in there's been broken for a month, and either nobody's bothered calling in a repair order or the bean counters don't want to pay for a new one. The guards only poke their heads in once a day. That place is Grand Central Station when it comes to dirty business.

Great place for an ambush. Like if Brisco wanted to take another shot at me, for example. How many guys could he throw at me if he felt motivated enough? Five? Six? The second I stepped into that bathroom, I'd have nowhere to run and no hope of rescue.

I tried to never go into a room with only one exit. This whole prison was nothing *but* rooms with only one exit. Too many blind corners and too many ways to die. So I told Brisco I'd meet him up there, then stopped off at my cell.

I reached under my cot and curled my fingers around the hilt of the black carbon steel knife I'd taken off the other hitter. I slipped it under my waistband, the cold blade dangerously close to my hip.

Brisco and three of his hangers-on loitered outside the bathroom door, arms crossed and leaning against the dirty eggshell-white walls. Brisco jerked a meaty thumb toward the entrance.

"He's right in there."

As I approached the door, my heart thudded against my chest. I flexed and unflexed my fingers to keep the jitters away. Brisco's boys were close, too close, and it wouldn't take more than a moment to follow me inside and jump me from behind.

One hand drifted toward my hip. I worked a plan on the fly, the best one I could come up with. *First one to follow me inside gets cut,* I thought. *Five quick stabs, don't aim, don't stop to check your work, just stab until he goes down. Second one should be surprised, at least for a couple of seconds. That one, go for the vitals.*

They didn't follow me in, though, and the swinging door groaned shut at my back.

The bathroom was a janitor's nightmare, smeared with grime and human waste. Mirrors made from sheets of stainless steel stood hammered with dents, throwing off distorted funhouse reflections. One light was smashed; the other gave off a dim, flickering yellow glow and a hum that filled the room like droning flies.

Three toilet stalls. No doors on any of them. And no signs of life.

I slipped the knife from my waistband.

"I'm not looking for a fight," I said. "I just want to talk to you."

The only reply was the electric hum.

I inched forward, craning my neck to check the first stall. Empty. Sodden toilet paper clogged the filthy bowl, lapping over one side of the seat.

"We can still work this out."

Second stall. Empty.

I turned the knife in my grip and bent my knees, keeping limber. I wasn't any kind of a knife fighter, not like a real pro, but I knew the basics. It took a special kind of reptilian cold to work with a blade. Anybody could pull a trigger, killing from across the room or across the street, but getting in close and personal—embracing the bile and the blood like a natural-born butcher—was a kind of violence I never wanted to get too comfortable with.

Even I had my limits. Problem was, the guy I was maybe about to fight with—he didn't. And the most dangerous opponent in the world was the one backed into a corner.

I stopped just shy of the third stall and risked a quick glance to my right, toward the battered steel mirror. I was a distorted blur in the reflection—and so was he, standing a heartbeat away on the other side of the plastic partition.

"Tell me one thing," I said. "Love or money?"

"Meaning?" he replied. Only one word, but it dripped with loathing.

"You're no punk with a zip gun. You're the real thing. An operator. So. Do you get paid for your skills, or is this a passion project?"

He paused a moment.

"I charge ten thousand dollars per hit," he said. "Plus expenses."

"Good. You're a businessman. So am I. See, if you were doing this out of some...fanatic devotion to your boss, or maybe you just get off on it—well, we wouldn't be able to have a rational conversation, now would we? But we can. And we are."

He didn't reply. His blurry reflection crouched a little lower. I tightened the grip on my blade.

"I know you're good," I said, "real good. But I also know one of your arms is fractured. You've been running yourself ragged, hiding out, haven't had anything to eat…you've gotta be coasting on fumes by now. So if it comes down to dancing, you've got to know our odds are pretty even. I don't want to die tonight. Do you?"

"No," he said after he took a little while to think about it.

"Good. I like talking face-to-face, so I'm going to come a little closer. I'm not dropping my knife, and I don't expect you to drop yours. Let's just maybe not kill each other until we've run out of better ideas, okay?"

He fell silent.

I edged closer. He leaned back against the inner wall of the third stall, one arm cradled protectively to his chest, the other clutching my knife's twin. He eyed me like a rabid dog, but he didn't bite.

"I'm Daniel Faust," I said, "but I'm figuring you knew that, since you were sent to kill me. You got a name?"

"Kim," he spat.

"What's your first name?"

"*Mister.*"

"Okay." I held up my open hand, keeping my distance. "I'd like to say it's a pleasure to meet you, Mister Kim, but I think this day's been pretty shitty for both of us."

"What did you do to my partner?" The words sounded more like an accusation than a question.

"Whatever I had to, to survive. I'd apologize, but let's face it, you were both trying to carve me up like a turkey. Fleiss didn't warn you about what I was capable of, did she?"

One of his eyelids twitched.

"That's right," I said. "I know who sent you. What I don't know—and what I'm really interested in finding out—is why. Because last I checked, she and I were on amicable terms. That, and she had every chance to kill me a couple of days ago, but she didn't even try. Why the change of heart?"

"I," he seethed, "will tell you *nothing.*"

I glanced down at the knife in his hand and felt the weight of mine, the black steel cold against my palm.

"You wanted to know," I said, "about that thing I did to your partner. What is it, do you think? What could do that to a man, without leaving a mark on his skin? What could make him scream like that?"

I looked him dead in the eye.

"Because I can arrange a demonstration."

20.

I try not to bluff with an unloaded gun, but you work with what you have. Kim and I stared at each other, neither of us blinking, neither standing down.

He swallowed. The slightest hint of a nervous gulp.

"I don't ask for reasons," he said. "Not my business."

"So you'll murder anyone, as long as the money's green?"

Kim snorted. "How many men have you killed in the name of Nicky Agnelli's bank account? Don't act like you're better than me."

"You don't know the whole story."

"Don't presume you know mine."

"Fair enough," I said. "So Fleiss didn't say why she had it in for me?"

"No. But she wanted the job done as soon as possible. I normally take at least two weeks to prepare for a hit. Studying the target, securing the killing ground, preparing evac routes...no. She wanted you done *immediately*. And the more it hurt, the better." He frowned, as if jolted by a strange memory.

"She said something you didn't like. Something that threw you off-balance. What was it? C'mon, you can tell me. We're both pros here."

He shook his head. "That was odd, now that you mention it. I've had special requests like that, where the client wants me to take my time, really make the target suffer. But two things always go along with that. First, they always whine about the target and all the reasons they deserve to die slow. Even when I say I don't care, they've got to go on, and on, and on. *Justifying* themselves. She didn't."

"So she didn't act like she had a hate-on for me, but she still wanted me to suffer. What's the other thing?"

"They always want me to deliver some stupid *speech*. The target always has to know who sent me, and why they're about to die, and—" He shook his head. "It's ridiculous. And embarrassing."

"People have no respect for professionalism," I said.

"*Exactly.*" He waggled the tip of the knife at me, wincing as his fractured arm shifted an inch. "*You* get it. I'm trying to provide an efficient, skilled service, but no, they want me to stand there and *talk* the target to death, like I'm some kind of Saturday morning cartoon villain. Anyway, that was the other weird thing with Fleiss. No message."

"She didn't want me to know she sent you?"

"She didn't *care*. I even asked her, since she'd requested a slow death, and she just looked at me like she didn't understand the question. It was as if...you were important, but you weren't important. Like ordering your death was something on a to-do list, right between laundry and shopping."

"So she arranged for you to infiltrate the prison?"

He rolled his eyes. "Please. My partner and I did that ourselves. You aren't the first target we've killed in that shower. It's always been gang-related before, though. Oh. That was the other weird thing. We actually had a better plan, but she said no."

"Yeah? What was it?"

"Fake some transfer paperwork and make them move you," Kim said. "Plan was to ambush the bus on the road back to Aberdeen. We'd perch on the roadside with a concealed machine gun, wait for the bus to roll by, and open fire on full auto. Maybe lay a spike strip along the road. With the wheels blown, you'd be a sitting duck in there. Quick, easy, and no need for us to risk infiltrating the prison."

I tried not to shudder, thinking about how I woke up on the

bus to Eisenberg Correctional. Crammed in like sardines, wrists chained to waist-belts and prisoner chained to prisoner. A front-row seat for the meat grinder.

"Workable plan," I said, keeping my tone even. "She didn't like it?"

"She said it had to be done *here*." Kim shifted his shoulder, leaning on the stall divider. "You had to die on the prison grounds, no matter what. That was crucial."

Mister Kim might have known more about murder than me, but I was pretty sure I knew more about magic than him—and this had all the hallmarks of a spell. Bloodshed was a common part of ritual; so was pain, harnessed to raise ecstatic levels of power. And it had to be done here. My blood had to soak the floors of Eisenberg Correctional, nowhere else.

Kim hadn't been hired to assassinate me. He'd been hired to *sacrifice* me.

No chance this wasn't connected to Buddy somehow. He and his sister insisted I'd swapped places with "the Thief," whoever that was. *The very fact that you're here*, Cassandra had said, *standing in the Thief's shoes, means the Enemy has already won. He's changing the rules.*

The Enemy. The man with the Cheshire smile. I still didn't know who he was—or *what* he was—but I knew how I'd landed on his radar. Fleiss must be the connection. I'd pulled that heist in Chicago for her "boss," who turned out to be nothing but a puppet, a prisoner in his own mansion. If Fleiss was really working for the Enemy, that'd make me one hell of a convenient pawn.

By the rules of whatever game these people are playing, the Thief has to die in this prison, I thought. *But the smiling man doesn't want the Thief dead. So they pulled a substitution play. I take the hit, and the real Thief goes on his merry way.*

I bit back a surge of anger. It'd be one thing if this were personal. If I'd done something to cross the smiling man, if this were payback, at least I could understand it. But it wasn't even *about* me. I was just the unlucky bastard whose entire life got uprooted and rewritten, condemned to die behind bars so some other guy didn't have to. I was nothing but a living get-out-of-jail-free card.

It was an understatement to say this entire situation was out of my league. The kind of magic that changed *reality* was in play here. Mythical stuff, a ritual on a scope I couldn't begin to wrap my brain around. I was just a street sorcerer with a few nasty tricks.

Cassandra was right. I wasn't "the chosen one." I was only a man. A man who still had his wits, two good fists, and a burning desire to demonstrate what happened when people tried to play me. I'd start with handing the Enemy a double defeat: I wasn't going to die in here, and when I made my exit, Buddy was coming with me.

Then, once I was breathing free air again, Fleiss and I were going to have a nice long chat.

"So," Kim said softly as he slumped back, his face beaded with sweat, "what now?"

I had to think about that.

"You came in undercover, as a prisoner," I told him. "What's your exfiltration strategy? I imagine you're not going to serve out a full sentence."

He half smiled. "That's exactly the plan. My forged jacket was backdated, saying I've been in here for three years. My 'sentence' is almost up. First thing tomorrow, I walk out of here a free man. Easiest escape ever. That is...assuming."

"Assuming," I echoed. I looked down at his knife. I ran the pad of my thumb over the hilt of my own. "Assuming we can work this situation out. Don't suppose you could just tell her you killed me?"

Kim wrinkled his nose like he smelled something foul. "I never lie to a client. Besides, I take a job, I do the job."

I almost laughed. I'd said pretty much those exact same words to Caitlin when I agreed to pull the heist for Fleiss. I guess I had more in common with Kim than I thought.

"But you can't do *this* job," I said, "not without a very good chance of leaving in a body bag. You don't want this fight any more than I do. So...could you tell her you tried but never got the chance to seal the deal?"

He thought it over. "I'd...have to return her advance. And it would be bad for my reputation. I'm not known for failure."

"I'd call that the least-worst choice out of a handful of bad options."

"Maybe so." He sighed. "Maybe so. But don't imagine we have a truce. Once my arm heals, if she sends me after you again—"

"I'll expect you to try harder," I said. That put a tired smile on his face. "And I don't think that'll be a problem. Fleiss needs me to die behind bars. By the time you're ready for a rematch, I won't *be* behind bars."

"We'll see," he told me. "So how do you want to do this?"

I left first. Backing away, slowly, slipping out of reach before a wounded viper could bite. I didn't turn my back until my shoulders bumped the bathroom door. I hid my knife in my waistband, then stepped outside.

Brisco, still leaning against the wall, gave me a questioning look.

"He's gonna come out in a few minutes," I said. "Let him go. Situation's defused. He won't be a problem for anybody."

He blinked, from me to the door and back again.

"And how about you and me?"

"Listen," I told him. "I respect what you're trying to do. You don't want your people getting hurt in a war that's got nothing to do with you. I get that. Just like *you* need to get that coming after me again, even in a roundabout way, would be a very, very bad play. We on the same page here?"

"Yeah." He nodded, a little too quick. "Sure."

"I can't tell you what I'm planning, but I can give you my word: in two days, the Cinco Calles won't be after me anymore. No friction between the whites and the Latinos, nothing for the guards to use against you. Can you be cool for two days?"

He glanced to one side, thinking. Then he stuck out his hand. We shook on it.

A warning klaxon sounded five minutes before lights-out. Back in my cell, I kept my eyes on the door until the second klaxon sounded and it slowly rattled shut. I felt safer sleeping behind a locked and barred door, at least until Mister Kim left the prison tomorrow morning. I was pretty sure he'd keep his word and back off, but better safe than sorry. Or dead.

"Gonna miss this place," Paul said softly as the lights along the tier flickered out one by one.

"Really?"

"Hell no." He lay back on his cot. "You really think we can pull this off?"

"I like our chances. Besides, whatever happens, it beats the alternative."

Guards walked the shadowed tiers with penlights and clip-boards, running cell checks and making sure all the good little convicts were tucked in for the night. I got as comfortable as I could and shut my eyes, trying to relax. We had a lot of hard work ahead of us.

I wasn't sure what time it was when my eyes snapped open in the darkness. Something had roused me, a sound different from the distant clamor and clanking and snoring that filled the prison hive. My muscles tensed as my body jolted into high alert.

I caught motion in the corner of my eye. Paul, waving a frantic hand. He made eye contact, then pantomimed being asleep. I followed his lead, lying on my back, watching the cell door through eyes narrowed to slits.

Figures crept into view on the other side of the bars. Four men in black riot gear, two hefting Plexiglas shields. The strobe of a penlight gleamed across the cell. I shut my eyes completely and I did my best impression of a corpse as the white light washed over my face.

The CRT, Jake and Westie had called them. Cell Reclamation Team. The ones who came in the night, picking out prisoners to send to Hive B.

21.

"Cell two thirty-two," the guard with the penlight murmured. I heard paper rustle. "They're both on the list. Which one first?"

I tensed. The knife was under my cot. Could I get to it in time? They'd bum-rush us with the riot shields. Press in and force us down. Even if I could slip around, find an angle of attack, their armor looked bulky. Ceramic plates, I guessed. Good chance of turning a blade, unless I got lucky and found a weak spot.

I'd have to get lucky four times in a handful of heartbeats. In the dark, outnumbered and outgunned by men who did takedowns like this for a living. That was lottery-winner luck. No matter how I played it, I couldn't see a fight going my way.

I tensed up and got ready for one anyway. My hand crept under the blanket, snail slow, toward the edge of the cot.

"I want two thirty-four," growled another guard. "Bastard kicked me when we broke up that fight two days ago. My knee still hurts."

"Fine," the first said. I heard the penlight click. "These two'll keep until next time."

They crept away. I opened my eyes and looked over at Paul. He stared back from the shadows, petrified.

"Don't worry," I mouthed.

He pulled his blanket up over his shoulders and clutched it like a little kid afraid of the dark.

Not like we needed more motivation to escape, I thought, *but there it is.*

Everything happened at once. I heard the electric hum and rattling of a barred door two cells down. Then the quick, hard stampede of boots on concrete and a confused, sleepy shout of surprise cut short by the *crack* of a truncheon. Even with a black sack over his head, I recognized the bulky prisoner they dragged, shackled and squirming, past our cell door: Simms, who'd tried shaking me down on my first day. He shouted but his voice was muffled, like he had a gag in his mouth. One of the guards jabbed a stun gun into his kidney. He crashed to his knees, grunting; they hauled him back to his feet and kept moving.

Paul and I waited until they were long gone, and another ten minutes after that for good measure, before either of us said a word.

"You heard that, right?" he whispered.

"Day after tomorrow," I breathed. "Eyes on the prize, Paul. By the time they come for us, we'll be long gone."

That was the plan, anyway.

* * *

I drowsed more than slept, drifting in and out of anxious nightmares until the morning klaxon shrilled and our cell door rattled open. Brisco's boys covered me while I showered, and this time, they didn't vanish. Breakfast was another lump of cold, watery eggs and a charred, rock-hard wedge of something that might have been hash browns. I would have killed for a cup of espresso.

I met up with my makeshift crew out on the yard. Paul, Westie, Jake, and I walked in a ragged line along the jogging track, and they passed a cigarette back and forth while we talked.

"Knife's taken care of," Westie said. "Give it to me tomorrow morning. By the time we're ready to move, it'll be stashed safe halfway to the visitation center."

I nodded. "Good. I'm getting in touch with my people today, making sure we have 'visitors' lined up for each of us."

"Not sure about the route." Paul took a drag from the cigarette, clutching it in trembling fingers. He nearly dropped it passing it over to Jake. "I spent the morning in the library, pulling together whatever I could, but any maps I could scrounge up were either too vague to be helpful or ten years outdated."

"Don't worry," I told him. "We'll just have to play that part by ear. As long as we can make it to a good-sized town, ditch the buggies, and steal fresh rides and some civilian clothes, we'll be fine."

Jake put the cigarette to his lips, glancing over his shoulder as he exhaled a plume of gray smoke.

"Think I've got a diversion planned out. On my shift this afternoon, I'll move all the pieces into place." He handed Westie the cigarette. "Holy shit, we're really doing this, aren't we?"

Westie grinned. "First men to ever escape the Iceberg. Hell, I bet they'll make a movie about us. George Clooney might play me."

"You don't look anything like George Clooney," Jake said.

"Said *might*, not *would*. Don't piss on a man's dreams."

"*Shit*," Paul hissed. "We gotta split up. Don't look, but Jablonski's up on the guard tower behind us. He's watching."

Jake arched an eyebrow. "So? Fuck Jablonski. Let him watch."

"*You're* not the one who got him angry," Paul said. "We don't need attention, not from him, not right now. I'll see you guys later."

"Paul, c'mon—" Westie said, but Paul waved him off and stomped toward the picnic benches.

"He's tense," I said. "He's got reason to be. You heard they grabbed Simms last night?"

"Another poor bastard gone to Hive B," Westie said. "Everyone's heard. What of it?"

"We heard them talking. Our cell's next on their hit list. Only reason they didn't grab one of *us* last night is because one of the guards had a grudge against Simms."

Jake let out a long, low whistle. Westie offered me the cigarette. I was tempted, but I shook my head.

"Did they let on what they're taking people for?" Jake asked.

"Nope, but it's nothing good. All that matters right now is making sure we're long gone before their next shopping trip."

"Hold up." Jake's eyes narrowed. His head was on a swivel, glancing left and right. We slowed to a near stop.

"Aw, Christ," Westie muttered. "Apaches on the warpath."

I frowned at him. "What do you mean?"

"You ain't been here long enough to read the signs. All right, casual-like, take a peek over toward the weight benches."

Body language was the same book, inside prison and out. Raymundo and his crew were taut as steel coils compressed to the breaking point. That much I could see.

"Watch the blockers," Westie told me.

I figured he meant the men only pretending to work out, the ones who just happened to be standing in the line of sight from the guard towers, inching sideways to cover the convicts behind them.

The ones crouched in the scrub, digging with their hands.

Over at Brisco's table, his boys jumped up like ants boiling out of a kicked-over hive. Some ran for other patches of scrub; others walked fast, hands casually down by their waists but flashing finger signals like they were sending out an emergency telegraph in rapid-fire sign language. Silent panic washed over the yard, a dry tsunami of looming dread.

One of Raymundo's diggers came up from a crouch. The sunlight glinted off the steel spike in his hand.

The world froze, for just a heartbeat, under the Nevada sun. A single moment crystallized in time.

Then the crystal shattered.

A convict fell with a grunt, blitzed from the side, a shiv buried in his guts. Another went down under a pile of bodies, kicking and punching. The violence swirled around us, a siege in miniature as the Calles launched their attack, war-cries splitting the air. Jake, Westie, and I went shoulder-to-shoulder, forming a loose triangle.

"Where's Paul?" Jake shouted.

"By the picnic tables," I said. Then a wave of panic hit me. "Where's *Buddy?*"

Talking to his chess pieces. Oblivious to the world as a Calles with a shiv ran up on him from behind.

The air turned to molasses. I charged, too slow, trying to close the gap. "Hey, asshole," I shouted. "*I'm the one you want!*"

I lunged, throwing a wild punch, and he turned just in time for me to feel the cartilage of his nose splatter under my knuckles. He staggered back, but he wasn't alone; hands looped under my arms, grappling me and pinning me in place. They hauled me around, and the next thing I saw was Raymundo's fist slamming into my stomach like a pile driver, blasting the air from my lungs.

Raymundo held up his weapon—a razor blade wedged onto the end of an old toothbrush—so I could get a good look.

"Gonna bleed you like a pig, *cabron*," he snarled. He was too focused on me to see Jake coming in hot. The biker's fist cracked across the back of Raymundo's skull just as Westie tackled my grappler, all three of us crashing into a struggling pile in the dirt.

The tower alarms shrieked across the yard, reverberating with the blood roaring in my ears. I didn't know how long they'd been blaring, nothing but background noise for the brawl. Then a rifle shot boomed like a peal of graveyard thunder, and the brawl was over.

All across the yard, prisoners dropped to their knees and laced their fingers behind their heads. I pulled myself out of the tangle, rolled onto my belly in the dirt, and knelt up, struggling to catch my breath.

The hive doors burst open and uniforms filled the yard. All was silent but the groans of the injured, loaded up on stretchers and carted out one by one.

"This ain't over," Raymundo hissed, kneeling a few feet away.

"When Jennifer gets back," I said, "you are gonna owe me one hell of an apology."

"She ain't comin' back," he sneered.

I locked eyes with him. He gave me a bloody-toothed grin.

"What *exactly* do you mean by that?"

"Just sayin'. Word from the outside is JJ ain't in a position to call any shots, not anymore. Change in management. Pretty soon she ain't gonna be in a position to do *anything*."

I took a deep breath and struggled to keep my fingers laced behind my head. They wanted to be wrapped around his throat. They wanted it more than anything.

"Raymundo, I'm going to ask you a question. And I want you to consider it the most important question you've been asked in your entire life. *Where is Jennifer?*"

Two guards seized him from behind, hauling him to his feet and shackling him, while another scooped up his razor-blade toothbrush from the dirt.

"Take this one to solitary," the guard with the blade said. "Gang unit's gonna want a word with him."

"*Raymundo*," I shouted, "*where is she?*"

He just laughed as they dragged him away.

"Easy," Jake told me, "calm down, man. Don't give 'em an excuse to get trigger happy."

Westie hadn't said a word. His head was turned, gazing across the yard. His shoulders sagged.

"Aw, no," he whispered. "Damn it all. Damn it all to hell."

I followed his gaze.

We'd heard the rifle go off, the thunder that ended the fight. The last word of the argument. I just hadn't seen where the bullet landed.

Paul lay sprawled in the scrub, his beige uniform soaked with blood where his heart used to be. His eyes wide and glassy, staring up at the cloudless sky. A perfect kill shot.

Up on the tower catwalk, I saw Jablonski. Clutching his rifle and grinning like a big-game hunter who'd just bagged a rhino. Another guard strolled by and gave him a pat on the back.

22.

hey locked us down in the hive while the prison investiga-
tors worked to sort out the whole sorry mess. I paced my five
feet of freedom, trying to take a maelstrom of worries and turn
them into some kind of coherent plan.

Paul's tattered paperback, Sartre's *No Exit*, sat abandoned on
his bunk.

All I could think about was Jennifer. If Raymundo was telling
the truth, her alliance with the Calles had gone off the rails in the
worst way. I wouldn't have believed it—the last time I'd visited
their little urban fortress, it looked like a perfect match—but
things were different now. Nicky Agnelli had kept the reins of the
Vegas underworld in an iron grip for years; now with Nicky on the
run, nobody was running the show. No force in nature was dead-
lier than a power vacuum.

Anything could be happening out on the streets. All I knew
was my friend was in trouble, and I wasn't there to help her.

"Kite coming left!" shouted a voice from the cell next door.

An elaborately folded piece of paper flew through the bars of
my cell, with a length of dirty twine strung through a hole in the
corner of the packet. Kites were a prison version of a telegram:
you could get a message to any cell in the hive with
one—eventually. Since the lockdown kites had been flying fast
and furious, one passing my cell every five minutes or so. I
crouched and picked up the paper, reeling in the line.

The number 248 was scrawled in blue ballpoint on the outside of the fold. I gathered up all the twine—a good ten feet of it—and slid the paper back out through the bars before calling out "Kite coming left!"

Kneeling by the door with the twine in both hands, I gave it a good swing. The paper rustled as it flew, arcing almost out of sight but falling short of its next stop. I swung it back and forth, gathering momentum, and gave it more line this time. Now I felt a quick double tug, letting me know the prisoner on my left had caught the paper. I let go as the length of twine slithered away.

All right, I told myself, *focus. You can't do a damn thing if you're distracted in five different directions. Nothing's changed. The plan is the plan, which means I still need to figure out how I'm going to open that gate and get my hands on a pair of night-vision goggles.*

I was staring at Paul's empty bunk when the answer came to me.

Another kite swung through the cell door. I passed it along, then reached under my mattress and slid out the cell phone. The charge was in the deep amber now, twelve percent and dropping. I dialed fast.

"Scrivener's Nook. Whatcha need?" Corman's voice was a little touch of home. I wanted to cling to it with everything I had.

"Corman, it's me. Listen, I don't know how much time I've got left on this phone, but tomorrow's the big day. I'm going to give you a couple of names; we need a 'visitor' for each one of them, and they all need to show up at the prison a little after five p.m. Is that doable?"

"Sure thing, kiddo. What do they have to do when they get there?"

"Not a damn thing. We'll be taking a little detour on our way to the visitor center. There's one other thing I need. You've got a copy of Bruhn's *Ruminations on the Spirit* in your private collection, right?"

"Sure. It's an oldie and a goodie."

"I need the ritual for creating a Hand of Glory."

He paused. When he spoke again, I could hear the uncertainty in his voice.

"Kiddo," he said, "you do know what you need to make one of those, right? I mean, the basic ingredients?"

I looked over at Paul's empty bunk.

"Yeah. It's not a problem."

"If you say so. Sure, I've got the info, but how do I get it to you?"

"I've been thinking about that," I said. "Communications with my lawyer are privileged; the guards can't even listen in. I don't need the whole book, just the pertinent pages. If you can copy them and slip them inside a few sheets of legal paperwork, it'll be easy to smuggle it inside."

"You're forgetting one thing. Perkins took a powder, remember? He thinks your girlfriend's going to skin him alive for losing your trial. He's no dummy. He's probably halfway across the world by now."

"Been thinking about that too. I think we can find a stand-in. You know...the one in Denver."

Corman let out a grumbling *hrm*. "You sure about that, kiddo? Probably gonna cost you a favor or two."

"If it gets me out of here, it's worth it."

I glanced at the battery indicator. It had dropped another hair-thin notch and the readout had turned stoplight red.

"Gotta go, this phone's just about dead. I'll see you, okay? I'll see you tomorrow night."

"We'll have dinner ready. Anything you want, just name it."

A parade of gourmet cuisine marched through my mind's eye. I chuckled. "Y'know what? Honestly, I'd kill for a cheeseburger right now. A thick, medium-rare cheeseburger and Jack Daniels on ice."

"I'll fire up the grill. Hey, you be safe out there. We'll be waiting up for you."

I cradled the phone in my hands for a while after he hung up, not wanting to let it go. Then one of my neighbors called out,

"Kite coming right!" and I hid the phone away, ambling to the bars to pass along another message. This one, though, had my cell number on it.

I carefully unfurled the page. With no staples or tape, kite writers secured their "envelopes" with complex folds that reminded me of origami butterflies.

"Good news," it read, "heard some guards talking, pissed. Warden said 'no' on total lockdown, some peeps got punctured in that scrap but no casualties. We should have some 'free time' tomorrow hahaha. Raymundo and his buddies are all in the hole, so stay tight tonight + all is roses. We'll pour one out for Paul. Cheers from your pals in 431."

I grabbed a blue pen from Paul's tiny desk. Dents and furrows covered the cap, like a beaver had spent a few weeks gnawing on it. I crossed out my cell number on the back of the page and scribbled in 431.

"Salutations from 232," I wrote under the first message. "I'm lining up everything we need to arrange a fitting memorial for our fallen friend. I will need a little help from you both in the morning. No worries, I'll do the heavy lifting. Meanwhile I've been assured that well-wishers are coming to the visitor center to express their condolences, just as we'd hoped. All is well. D."

I mimicked the elaborate folds as best I could and sent the kite winging on its way back to Westie and Jake.

After that, there was nothing to do but wait.

Behind bars, time mocks you. You'll think an hour's gone by, but then you check the clock and realize your sentence is only five minutes shorter than the last time you looked. It was just me, my boredom, and a litany of fears, sealed behind iron bars painted eggshell white.

Thinking about Paul made me think about Jablonski. I didn't know Paul well, but I liked the guy. I liked him enough to want that score settled. I wouldn't endanger our escape plan to take a crack at Jablonski, but if the opportunity came up, I'd seize it.

And if not, I could always find out where he lived and come

back in a few months once the heat died down. Pay him a little visit after business hours.

Dinner came on wheeled carts and plastic trays shoved at us through foot-wide horizontal slats in the cell bars. Emerson, the new guy, was on zoo-feeding detail. "Room service?" I asked him as I took my tray. "Sir, there's been a mistake. I clearly ordered the filet mignon."

Emerson rolled his eyes. "Funny. I've only heard that line thirty times in the last hour."

"I'll get some new material," I told him. I set the tray down on the writing desk and gave it a dubious eye. My final dinner in prison was chipped beef in white gravy—at least I hoped it was chipped beef—a slice of burnt toast, and a ladleful of anemic green peas. I poked an experimental finger into the gravy. Ice cold.

My last dinner behind bars, I thought. *This time tomorrow, I'll be in the middle of a prison break.*

Then, freedom. Well, that or we'd all be dead.

No pressure.

*　*　*

Lights-out brought new anxiety. I knew my cell was next on the list for "transfers" to Hive B. Then again, they'd just taken Simms, and according to Jake and Westie, the abductions were always spaced out by days or weeks. Never twice in two nights.

That said, there was a first time for everything.

I tried to relax, but every metallic clang, every footfall on the catwalks, jolted me awake with a fresh rush of tension. Eventually, my body shut down from sheer exhaustion.

A faint whirring woke me up. Like the fluttering of a cockroach's wings, just beside my ear. The metallic hum dragged me from a dreamless sleep, and my fogged brain tried to place it—

Phone!

I rolled onto my side, digging under the thin mattress and tugging out the phone. It vibrated against my palm as I flipped it open and pinned it between the pillow and my ear to keep the glowing screen out of sight.

"Hello?" I whispered.

"Daniel! I just got back. What have they *done* to you?"

Caitlin's Scottish burr wrapped my heart in rose vines, from the bright red blooms to the prickling thorns. I wanted to sweep her up in my arms and hold her until the death of the world, but that just reminded me that I was trapped here, entombed in iron, separated from everyone I loved. I'd never been so happy to hear her voice. I'd never been so miserable.

"Cait," I said, my throat suddenly bone dry. "It's all right. I've got a plan—"

"It is *not* all right. It is the *last possible thing* from all right, and everyone who had any part in committing this insult is going to pay grievously for it. Bentley and Corman talked me out of tearing that place down with my bare hands, but I might just change my mind."

"I've got a plan," I told her again. "I'll be home tomorrow night, I promise."

She made a sound halfway between grumbling and purring.

"And then," she said, "we punish those responsible."

"Yeah, that might be tricky. I'll explain when I see you in person. Listen, Caitlin, I lo—"

The phone clicked and went dead. No battery.

"I love you," I whispered to the piece of dead plastic.

I didn't try to push away the longing, or the pain. I didn't try to distract myself from how I felt here: trapped, helpless, angry. I embraced it. Bathed in it and let it fuel me. Tomorrow night, I'd need every last bit of that pain to give me the strength to make it home alive.

23.

Lockdown lifted with the sunrise. Our cage doors rattled open on electric tracks, and shuffling sleepy lines formed for the showers and the cafeteria. The endless tedium of prison life back on its cycle.

Around nine, a guard came to fetch me. "Faust," he said, jerking his thumb over his shoulder, "your lawyer's here."

Legal consults weren't held in the visitor center. They got a special venue right next door, in a foursome of glass-walled booths flanking a corridor where a pair of guards lazily strolled back and forth. Clever setup: they could see everything, to watch for contraband or other funny business, but hear nothing.

J.T. Perkins waited for me in booth three, wearing his sharkskin suit and wolfish grin. His hair and his teeth were in a competition to see which could be more perfect. As the guard ushered me into the booth, Perkins shot up from his chair and pumped my hand.

"Mr. Faust," he said, "I can't tell you what a pleasure it is to be working with you again."

"Feeling's mutual," I replied.

The guard shut the windowed door behind him, sealing us in. Perkins gestured to the small interview table, and I took the chair on the opposite side.

Perkins sat down. Paper cup of coffee to his left, Louis Vuitton attaché case to his right. He ran his fingertips over the leather like a piano player warming up for an audition. With his back to the glass, the guards couldn't see his face.

His eyes turned tiger orange.

"So," Naavarasi said in her own voice, "what do you think? A superb imitation, no?"

I inclined my head. "You are a mistress of your art. None could dispute that. Thank you for coming."

Her ego properly fed, she smiled. "How could I resist? I would never refuse to help a friend in need. And you are clearly in need. Your face, it's bruised."

I touched the skin under my eye and winced. It was still raw from my fight with Simms.

"Welcoming committee," I told her. "I gave as good as I got. Mostly."

"And your hair." She tsked. "It's...stubble."

"Free haircut for all new guests. How could I refuse a bargain like that?"

"How were you captured in the first place? To be honest, Daniel, I expected better from you."

"I'm hoping you can shed some light on that. The Chicago Outfit's making a play for control of Las Vegas. As part of their opening salvo, they framed me for murder. Seems they've got a shape-shifter on their payroll, a rakshasi, like you." I paused. "Rakshasa? What's the word if it's male?"

Her orange eyes flared, as if tiny flames blossomed behind her pupils.

"Impossible," she said. "I am the last of my kind, the queen of a dead bloodline. Prince Malphas saw to that. And no child of mine would ever bend his knee to a *human*. You were evidently twice deceived."

"I know what I saw."

She laughed. "Foolish words from a man who should know better. I am a mistress of illusion, and you trade in tricks. Eyes *do* lie. You know this."

"I also know that I'm here because I got played by a shape-shifter *you* say doesn't exist. He walked me right into a police ambush."

Naavarasi cocked an eyebrow. "And? You had weapons, yes? Why didn't you just slay your way out, like a warrior should?"

"Because I'm not looking to gun down some poor beat cops who are just doing their jobs."

"You're a ruthless man," she said, shaking her head, "but not ruthless enough."

I leaned forward. Locking eyes with her.

"Not ruthless enough for *what?*"

"The future holds many possibilities. Why don't you let me train you, Daniel? Six months in my hands and you'd be a weapon, forged from fire and blood."

"A weapon in whose hands?"

"Caitlin's," she said with a tiny smile. "Of course."

"I'll take it under consideration. So. Did you bring something for me?"

"Maybe."

I had to tread carefully here. Naavarasi had—or at least I hoped she had—the ritual I needed to break free. If I pissed her off enough, she might leave in a huff and ruin the entire escape plan. On the other hand, if I let on how badly I needed those pages...well, the rakshasi queen was hard enough to deal with when she *didn't* have leverage on me.

"All right," I said, resting my palms on the table. "Are we negotiating?"

"Well, I did drop everything and fly here in the small hours of the morning, then drive for miles in the desert, just to help you. And I had a lovely conversation with those two older gentlemen—Bentley and Corman, was it?—in which I did my utmost to forget how they insulted me upon our first meeting—"

"You threatened to *eat* them after masquerading as my ex-girlfriend, remember?"

"And? Your point?"

"Sorry," I said. "Please, continue."

"My time is valuable, and I don't see any other means of acquiring what you desire, save through my aid. As such, I think I'm entitled to...five years of service."

"Are you entitled to make bad jokes? Because that's the worst one I've heard in ages." I rapped my knuckles on the table. "Five years? Get real. Did you really come all this way just to waste my time?"

"I knew you'd say no, but I thought you might make a counteroffer," she said. "With, say, *one* year of service?"

"Is that your new offer?"

"That's my *only* offer." Her orange eyes darkened. "One year of service in exchange for the ritual. Take it or leave it. Of course, if you leave it, I suppose I'll be visiting you here for the next few *decades*."

This was pretty much the worst-case scenario. She had me bent over a barrel, and she knew it. If I said yes and signed on the dotted line, there'd be no wriggling out of the deal. I'd be hers—lock, stock, and barrel—for a year of my life.

What kind of man would I be after a year under Naavarasi's thumb? I wasn't sure, and I didn't want to know. I needed to throw her off-balance, come up with an angle to make her *want* to help me.

"Well," I said, "I do have an alternative offer in the wings."

Her brow furrowed. "Alternative?"

"Mm-hm. You aren't my first visitor. Nadine came to see me."

"That...*creature*." Naavarasi scowled. "What did she offer you?"

"A way out. All I have to do is go to work for Prince Malphas. Nadine and Royce are standing by to bust me out of here the second I say yes."

She leaned back in her chair and laughed. "Oh, Daniel, you should stop trying to outwit me. It can't be done. You would never accept an arrangement like that. Cross lines in the cold war? Turn against *Caitlin*? You would die first."

"That was my first reaction too," I told her. "But then, after a couple of nights in here? Locked in, shivering in a cell in the dark and thinking about spending the rest of my life in this place? That offer gets more and more attractive. Besides, you're missing something."

"Enlighten me."

"You and I both know that you're smarter than Royce, smarter than Nadine. I'm pretty sure you're smarter than Malphas."

That made her smile. "Well...yes, of course I am, but what of it?"

"Any deal I work out with them, I'm pretty sure I can wriggle my way out of. Might take some doing, but I'll slip free eventually. A deal with *you* is ironclad. Like you said, I couldn't possibly outwit you."

"You do have a point." She steepled her fingers, thinking it through.

"Of course, until I do cut loose, that's bad news for whatever you've got planned. C'mon, Naavarasi. We both know you're looking to stick a dagger into Malphas's back. The only reason you haven't already defected to Prince Sitri's side is because you've got a plan in motion. Do you really want me working for Malphas, sniffing around, poking into things and generally making a mess?"

"You do have an amusing talent for causing chaos," she said. "It's more amusing when it's not directed at *me*. All right. Perhaps one year is an excessive demand. I'm not helping you for free, though. I need a favor to balance the scales."

"That's reasonable. What do you have in mind?"

She smiled, and I didn't like it. "The use of your talents. It's true, I do have certain wheels in motion. At some point—not now, but soon—I'll need a particular item. An item which does not belong to me."

"You want me to steal something," I said. "Okay, I'll bite. What's the score?"

"You'll have to allow me a bit of mystery, Daniel. If you knew my target before I was ready to strike, it could be...problematic for me. I assure you, this object is well within your ability to acquire. Do you fear that I'm deceiving you?"

I didn't fear it so much as *know* it with rock-solid certainty. Naavarasi had a fondness for trickery that bordered on the fetishistic. That said, I'd never known her to blatantly lie. She just chose her words with razor-sharp precision and spoke around the truth. A nasty suspicion occurred to me.

"And this item," I said, "does it belong to Prince Sitri? Or Caitlin?"

She chuckled. "Clever boy. That would land you in hot water, wouldn't it? But no. And if it helps to clarify, the item does not belong to any member of the Court of Jade Tears."

That was one potential snare eliminated. Only a few hundred possibilities to go. It was probably still a trap. Of *course* it was a trap. Even so, I wasn't seeing a whole lot of alternatives.

"All right," I said. "You've got yourself a deal."

24.

Naavarasi opened the attaché case, sliding out a blank piece of parchment and a green marbled fountain pen. As her palm slowly passed over the empty page, elegant calligraphy appeared in its wake. The jet-black ink blossomed like flowering vines, the rakshasi's thoughts made manifest.

"Cute trick," I said, pulling the parchment toward me and giving it a read. It was a contract, simple and to the point—and that bothered me. Nothing Naavarasi ever did was simple and to the point. It didn't take long to read between the lines.

"'Should the object not be delivered to Naavarasi by the deadline of her choosing,'" I read aloud, "'Daniel Faust's soul shall be forfeit'—oh, *come on*. You'll just say the deadline is five seconds after you give me the job."

Watching Naavarasi pout with J.T. Perkins's face was unsettling.

"I'm hurt that you think I'd be so obvious."

"You weren't. That clause was to distract me from the better-hidden one two lines down." I rapped my finger on the page. "The one that lets you redefine the definition of 'success' at will."

"Language...is a fluid thing."

I slid the parchment across the table, back toward her.

"How about this," I said. "We shake on it instead. You give me what I need, here and now, and when the time comes I'll return the favor. I give you my word."

She eyed me dubiously. "And what is your word worth?"

I had to think about that.

"Depends on who I'm talking to. For you? More than for a lot of other people. Remember, I've got a built-in incentive to help you out: you've got it in for Prince Malphas. So does Caitlin's boss. What makes you happy is probably going to make Prince Sitri happy, which makes Caitlin happy, and so on down the line."

As she reached across the table, her hand—*just* her hand—rippled like a mirage. The skin turned the color of burnt honey, fingers lengthened, nails grew and flourished with jade-green paint. As we shook hands, a jolt of static electricity bit into my palm.

"Deal," she said.

Her hand rippled again as she pulled away, the Perkins disguise firmly back in place.

She stashed the contract in her case and pulled out a short stack of papers. They looked like a recipe for eyestrain, covered in dense blocks of minuscule type and festooned with date stamps in faded blue ink.

"Um," I said, reading, "I think this is the incorporation paperwork for your restaurant."

"They said to bring 'legal paperwork' to conceal the ritual. That's the only legal paperwork I had. If someone's vexing me, I don't *sue* them. I just...invite them over for dinner."

I held the papers at arm's length and squinted. They'd pass for legit at a casual glance. Under the first page was a sheet of loose-leaf notebook paper and Bentley's familiar, cramped handwriting. His transcription of the ritual I needed. I had to smile. Just like Bentley to spend an hour copying lines by longhand rather than risk cracking a book's precious spine on a photocopier.

"Is it what you required?" Naavarasi asked me.

"It's perfect."

When she spoke again, rising from her chair, she did it in Perkins's used-car-salesman patter. "A pleasure doing business, then! I'm looking forward to seeing you again, *very* soon."

She knocked on the glass door, and a guard came to let us out. He eyed the papers in my hand and I folded them protectively.

"*Privileged* communication," I said.

Back in the hive, with the papers stashed under my cot, I found Jake and Westie milling around down on the crowded open floor. The sluggish air hung humid, choked with the stench of nervous sweat.

"Okay," I told them, "here's where it gets weird. I'm going to need you to do some things that might not make a lot of sense."

"Brother," Jake said, "I'm pretty sure things have already *been* weird."

"Touché. Okay, correct me if I'm wrong. They'll be storing Paul's body on-site, until his relatives claim him, right?"

"Yeah, or they'll just bury him in the potter's field if nobody steps up," Westie said, "but...his *body*? What's that got to do with anything?"

I ignored the question. "And the morgue, is it close to the infirmary?"

"Spitting distance," Jake said.

"The doctor on call, what's his name?"

"Valentino. Guy's all right."

"What do I have to do to see him?" I asked. "If I tell the guards I've got a stomachache, that good enough?"

Westie snorted. "He ain't the school nurse, friend. If you're not bleedin', the guards couldn't care less."

I was afraid of that.

"All right," I said. "In that case, I need a razor blade."

*   *   *

Whatever Emerson expected from the beginning of his shift that day, it probably wasn't the sight of me rushing up to him with upraised, bloody hands, looking like something out of a zombie flick.

"You gotta help, man," I groaned, clasping one hand to the side of my shirt. Blood soaked through at the hip, staining the beige fabric mahogany-dark.

"*Whoa*," he said, taking a quick step back and pointing at me. "Do *not* get any of that on me. Why are you bleeding? What happened?"

I wheezed the words out like it took an effort to breathe. "Don't know. Was just...just coming in from the yard, in a crowd of people, and suddenly I felt this horrible pain. Think somebody stabbed me."

"Okay, c'mon." He unclipped the radio from his belt and raised it to his lips. "Central? This is Emerson, bringing an injured prisoner to the infirmary. Need a guard to cover my shift at point C-1 for about fifteen minutes, over."

I limped alongside him as he hustled me out of the hive and through the maze of corridors. All the while, sucking air through my gritted teeth and letting out the occasional moan.

It wasn't a *complete* exaggeration. My injury burned like a row of wasp stings. Back in the hive, it hadn't taken long for Jake to score a contraband blade from a buddy of his. Then it was time to suck in a deep breath and take one for the team.

Most people have some degree of love handles. I was in pretty good shape, but I had a little padding there myself. Padding that came in handy when picking a safe place to cut.

Usually, on the rare occasions I cut myself, I'm standing in front of a pentacle and chanting in doggerel Latin. Blood magic is powerful stuff. Do it enough times and you develop a certain skill for the quick, shallow slice, the kind of cut that bleeds, but not *too* much. While Jake watched, I untucked my shirt and pulled it up, took a deep breath, and raked the blade across my pale skin. It took a second for the pain to hit, an electric burn that slammed home as a four-inch line of scarlet welled up and began to pour.

"Jesus," Jake said, taking the blade from my trembling fingers, "you're gonna need stitches for that."

"Trust me, I've done this before. I mean, it's usually my fingertips, but still. It looks a lot worse than it is."

I pressed my palms to the cut, smearing them together, getting blood all over my hip. My shirt was next. I bent to one side, patting the fabric against the open wound. When I'd finally finished spreading the red around, I looked like a proper stabbing victim.

By the time we reached the infirmary door, I was pretty sure the cut was already clotting. Still, I played it up and clutched my wound with grim resolve as Emerson ushered me inside.

The infirmary looked like any other doctor's exam room, albeit with cheap, shabby fixtures and an industrial-sized lock on every cabinet and drawer. The cold eye of a security camera watched from the corner of the room as Valentino, a middle-aged man with a thick black mustache and a white lab coat, waved me toward a padded bench. I eased myself up onto the cracked tan vinyl.

"Got a bleeder here," Emerson told the doctor. "Sounds like it's pretty bad."

Valentino fished in his coat pocket for a heavy ring of keys and fumbled through them one at a time, finally getting a cabinet unlocked. I was glad I wasn't really dying. He slipped on a pair of disposable rubber gloves, then set a bottle of rubbing alcohol and a cardboard box of gauze pads on the counter.

"Let's have a look, then," he said and nodded to Emerson. "Thank you. I'll take it from here."

My attention was on the swinging door with the narrow, tall wire-reinforced window off to my left. On the other side, I could see a wall of stainless steel honeycombed with square doors. Morgue lockers. Bingo.

Emerson left and Valentino pulled up a stool. "Lift your shirt for me, please."

I obliged. He soaked a gauze pad in alcohol and patted at the cut. My breath hitched at the sudden sting.

"Could have been much worse," he murmured as he prodded at me. "This'll heal up nicely. You're a very lucky man."

"That's what everyone tells me," I said.

I glanced at the clock on the wall, a sterile white face under a dusty plastic bubble: 10:04. He'd be calling a guard to take me back to my cell at any minute, and I'd lose my only chance.

Then the door opened with a faint knock. Zap, the trustee, stood on the threshold wringing his hands. He looked at me before he looked at Valentino.

Right on schedule.

25.

ack in the hive, before my self-inflicted injury, I'd gone over my "shopping list" with Jake and Westie.

"Twine, or thick string," Jake repeated. "Sure, that's doable. And...a pack of cigarettes? I thought you didn't smoke."

"They're not for me. Now, I don't suppose either of you has an 'in' with Brisco's little trustee buddy?"

"Zap?" Westie asked. "We're not exactly close, but we're not on bad terms neither."

"What would it take to get a favor out of him if it won't put him out too much?"

"Eh, he's pretty laid-back," Jake said. "As long as it won't risk his trustee job, he'll probably help out for a few bucks on his commissary account."

I craned my neck, glancing at a clock set above the door to the yard.

"Okay, I'm going to be inside the infirmary at ten sharp. At five minutes after, *precisely*, I need Zap to deliver a message."

* * *

"Message from the front office," Zap said, sounding breathless. "You've got a phone call."

Valentino glanced at the counter behind him where an old beige phone sat quiet and neglected. "They couldn't transfer it to me?"

Zap shook his head. "Interoffice lines are dead again."

"Fourth time this month." The doctor sighed. "Did they take a message?"

"No, that's the thing," he said, then looked my way again. "Um, could I speak to you privately real quick? It's...it's about your wife. There's been an accident."

The doctor spun around, wide-eyed, the tail of his open lab coat swinging in his wake. The moment I'd been waiting for. I leaned forward, my fingers dipping into his oversized coat pocket and latching onto his key ring. The ring slid out effortlessly as he strode for the door, and I clasped the keys against my palm to muffle them.

Valentino joined the trustee out in the hall, keeping one foot in the door as they conversed in hushed tones. I didn't need to listen in. I'd written Zap's script.

St. Edna's, the small hospital in Aberdeen, was calling with an urgent message about the good doctor's wife and her involvement in a car crash. At least, that was what Zap was telling him. Valentino poked his head in.

"Stay *right here*," he told me. "I'll be back."

Then he was off to the races, with Zap in tow. Leaving the wolf in the henhouse.

It was understandable. Everything was locked down tighter than a submarine door, and the camera in the corner was there to ensure good behavior. Of course, that assumed anyone was actively watching the screen, one of dozens if not hundreds all across the prison.

I wasn't planning any mischief in here, anyway. My business was in the room next door.

I jumped up from the padded bench, ignoring a sudden twinge from my cut, and darted to the swinging door. The air dropped ten degrees on the other side. The chemical-lemon scent of antiseptic clung to every surface, sticking in the back of my throat.

Two examination tables stood on a water-stained granite floor, with a drainage vent between them. Both had an occupant draped under ivory sheets.

160

I pulled back the sheet on the first body. Not Paul, but I instantly recognized him from the flowery neck tattoo that read *Emilie*. It was the con I'd come in with, riding side by side on the prison bus. The one Jablonski had truncheon-whipped.

He had more than a head wound, now. His face looked like he'd gone ten rounds with a meat tenderizer, one eyelid a puffy mound and the other caved in over an empty socket. I wasn't sure if that had killed him or the savage rents that peppered his chest, leaving his flesh torn and ribs cracked.

Jesus, I thought, *what happened to him?*

I had a sneaking suspicion that whatever he'd gone through, it had happened in Hive B.

All the more motivation to get the hell out before it could happen to us, too. I replaced the sheet, stepped to the second table, and pulled back the other one. Paul could have been sleeping, if not for the ash-gray skin and the crumpled ruin where his heart used to be.

I figured, given the distance between the infirmary and the front office, I had fifteen minutes at most. Enough time for Dr. Valentino to get up there and find nothing but a dead phone line. Then he'd call St. Edna's; they'd have to search for his wife's name and ultimately tell him there was no such patient. If I were really lucky, he'd call his wife to make sure she was okay, and they'd chat for a while.

As far as Zap went, he'd just claim he got duped by a prank caller. Happens to the best of us.

A rack of mortician's tools hung on the wall, secured in a wire cage—bone saws and rib spreaders and hooks and hoses. A padlock dangled from the hasp of the cage door.

I felt the minutes ticking away as I tried one key, then another and another, fumbling my way through the ring until one made a hollow *click*. The wire cage opened with a rusty groan.

The Hand of Glory was old-school sorcery, dating back to the eighteenth century. One of the earliest attempts at an invisibility spell, or at least one of the earliest that actually worked. Sort of.

Right now, it was exactly what I needed to secure our escape plan. I was familiar with the spell, but I'd never actually used it, because it was so hard to find the key ingredient these days.

The severed left hand of an executed murderer.

"On the bright side," I told Paul's corpse, "in a way, you're still breaking out with us."

Then I surveyed the rack of tools and picked up a bone saw.

I may have committed a tiny little murder, Paul had told me when he signed on for the escape plan. One requirement down. As far as the other part, well, he'd been shot by a prison guard. If Jablonski didn't go down for killing him—and he wouldn't—that made it, by default, a legal execution.

I cheat at magic.

I took the sheet covering Paul and tucked one end into my shirt, wearing it like an oversized bib. Dead bodies don't bleed, but they do leak. I stretched his left arm out on the slab, turning his palm facedown, and fired up the bone saw. The circular blade screamed like a dentist's drill forged in hell.

It chewed through his wrist, spitting a stream of brown and red flecks that drifted down to the concrete floor along with a trickle of blood that had pooled in the base of his arm. The air filled with a stench like rotting meat mixed with burnt microwave popcorn. I just held the saw steady, careful, cutting as clean as I could until the last sinew sliced apart and the severed hand pulled free.

I tucked Paul's arm against his side and covered him back up. All I could see was the clock, the minutes counting down like seconds as I ran to a washbasin and gave the blade a quick rinse in cold water. Far from perfect, but it looked clean enough at a distance. Valentino would discover Paul's missing hand before he discovered the tool that did the deed.

And by then, we'd be long gone. Assuming I wasn't about to get caught in the act.

I locked up the tool cage, slipped Paul's severed hand under my shirt, and hustled back into the infirmary. I poked my head out the door. Just as planned, Westie was right outside with his trusty mop and bucket, taking his time as he swabbed the grimy floor.

He slid the bucket toward me with his foot, and I tossed Paul's hand into the water. It made a tiny splash and bobbed in the soap-suds.

"Jesus Christ," Westie said, his horrified gaze snapping from the bucket to me. "What the hell did you *do* in there?"

"I told you: here's where it gets weird. Head back to the hive and meet me outside the bathrooms on tier three."

He covered the hand with his mop and rolled the bucket away, muttering obscenities under his breath.

I'd barely gotten back to the bench, sitting innocently and catching my breath, when Valentino stalked into the room.

"Your wife okay?" I asked.

"Some people," he seethed, "have nothing better to do than—yes, she's *fine*, thank you. Now let's see how that cut's clearing up."

I lifted my shirt and he rubbed the cut with rubbing alcohol again, mopping away the dried blood. The alcohol felt freezing and hot at the same time, with a sting like whiskey going down my throat.

"Hm, doesn't need stitches, I don't think. Might have a hairline scar, but it should heal clean."

He turned on his stool, reaching for the cardboard box of gauze pads he'd taken down earlier. As he leaned to one side, I gently slipped the key ring back into the pocket of his lab coat.

I held a pad in place as he taped it along the edges, covering the cut under a fluffy white blanket. "Just keep that in place for a couple of days," he told me, "and let me know if it seeps through."

"Thanks, Doc," I said, "you're a real lifesaver."

I hoped so, anyway. My little adventure in the infirmary had yielded the key ingredient for a Hand of Glory. Now came the hard part: making it work.

26.

Jake and Westie waited for me outside the tier-three bathrooms, where I'd had my run-in with Mister Kim. I needed an hour with privacy, no guards and no cameras, and that grimy hellhole was my best bet.

Jake handed me a plastic bag. "Everything you asked for."

Westie just slid his mop and bucket my way. His usually ruddy cheeks were as pale as Paul's.

"All right," I said, "you guys stay out here and stand guard. Don't let *anybody* come in after me."

"Mind telling us what you're gonna be doing in there?" Jake asked.

I smiled. "That'd spoil the surprise."

Inside, I checked the stalls and made sure I was alone. Then I fished Paul's soggy hand out of the bucket, tearing off fistfuls of toilet paper and patting it dry. I tossed the damp wads of paper into the closest sink.

I knelt down, the filthy tile hard and cold against my knees, and unfolded Bentley's instructions before checking the bag Jake had handed me. Everything I needed. Well, almost.

My hacker buddy Pixie had once asked me to explain magic. I'd tried to put it in terms she'd understand and told her magic was the cheat codes for the universe. You carried out the right gestures, the right phrases, made the right sacrifices, and suddenly things that shouldn't have happened, happened.

That was the simplified version. There was more to it, the

foundations every sorcerer had to learn: visualization, breathing, how to raise and channel raw power without giving yourself a heart attack or burning your brain into a charcoal briquette. I could talk to a Taoist alchemist from Hong Kong, a Senegalese medicine man, or a blood witch from the backwoods of Kentucky, and up to a certain point we would all be speaking the same language. Working with the same primal cosmic forces, even if we gave them different names.

The deeper you went into a given tradition of magic, the stranger stuff got. Could I explain why offering the blood of a white dove over graveyard dirt on a Saturday at midnight could help break a family curse? Nope. But I'd been paid to do it, and I knew it worked. That was why, when you were working with somebody else's spells—especially the really old, really esoteric stuff—it paid to steer as close to the original as possible. You never knew when one tiny change might yank out a metaphysical load-bearing wall and make the whole ritual come crashing down.

I was making a *lot* of tiny changes here.

Instead of a meditative circle of candles, I had a filth-smeared floor and broken toilets. Instead of a murderer's hand pickled in brine, it'd been marinating in soapy mop water. And *technically*, the murderer was supposed to have been not just executed, but specifically hanged.

The last execution by hanging in the United States was in 1996. You can't always get what you want.

I laid the hand before me and rested my hands on my knees, palms up. My breath slowed, my pulse slowing with it. The stench and the outside clamor faded away, and so did the light, my world eclipsed in a glowing darkness.

I could hear my heartbeat in my ears. Glacial now, like distant rumbling thunder. A drumbeat for a dirge.

Bentley's cramped handwriting glowed like blue neon. I felt the words more than read them, the half-Latin, half-English chant rolling off my tongue in a sibilant whisper. As the chant hastened, my pitch deepening, my upturned fingers clenching at shadows, a lance of fire burned up my spine. Power from the dark, raw and eager to be used.

Sleep, now sleep. Silent in my wake. Be as the dead for this dead man's sake.

I bent back the rigor-clenched fingers, one by one. The fire in my spine arced across my arms, from my fingertips to the hand's. Then came the twine, and the final ingredient.

Traditionally, a Hand of Glory's light burns from white candles, candles rendered from a human corpse. I didn't have those. What I had was a suspicion that what really mattered wasn't the candle, or even the flame: it was the smoke.

I unwrapped the cellophane from a pack of Marlboros and shook out five cigarettes.

The chant unceasing, my voice and my hands working in unison, I lashed a cigarette to each of Paul's fingers with twine. They stood like tiny smokestacks at the end of each bloodless fingernail. I held the hand high above my head, energy coursing into it. The grimy bathroom mirrors rattled in their steel frames, and my ears filled with an electric hum.

"Sleep, now sleep," I hissed at the climax of the spell, "silent in my wake. *Be as the dead for this dead man's sake.*"

With a faint *crump*, the cigarettes ignited.

Their tips glowed vivid orange, like alien suns, and sent up wispy streamers of silver smoke. The streamers wrapped around me like tinsel garlands as I rose with my prize clutched in both hands.

Outside the bathroom, Jake and Westie's energetic conversation suddenly fell silent as the enchantment washed over their senses. They stood there, slack-jawed and empty eyed, toys with their batteries yanked. I walked past them, and the silver smoke trailed behind me. As I climbed down the metal stairs to the hive floor, an oppressive silence spread in all directions.

Heads drooped. Shoulders sagged. Men stood like broken statues, lost in opium dreams. Where I walked, no one saw me. Where I walked, no one saw anything at all.

Ahead, the ultimate test: the ring of red paint around the base of the central guard tower and the sign reading "NO WARNING SHOTS WILL BE FIRED." I steeled myself, took a deep breath, and stepped over the line.

No shots rang out, and the silver smoke swirled as I strode toward the tower door.

"No lock deters the Hand of Glory," I whispered, focusing on the key-card reader beside the steel door. "No secrets shall I be denied."

The red light above the reader flickered and turned green. The door handle clicked. I let myself in.

As I climbed the stairs, weaving past stupefied and slumbering guards, my heartbeat quickened. I had a new problem, and I wasn't sure how to fix it. My version of the Hand worked just how it was supposed to, despite my substitutions and corner-cutting, but it wasn't built to last.

A proper Hand was supposed to endure for hours. My improvised cigarette "candles" had already burned halfway down. I had just enough time, if I was lucky, to snag the night-vision goggles and get them back to my cell before the cigarettes burned out and shattered my spell.

The original idea had been to hide the Hand, take it along to help with the raid on the motor pool, and use it to get the prison gates open once we'd secured our rides home. Now I was jogging up the steps two at a time, just to make sure I could get the *first* part of my plan done.

No Hand, no open gates. The shining road to freedom was turning into a great big electrified roadblock.

Focus, I thought, swallowing down a surge of sudden panic. *Worry about that later. We'll find another way.*

Another part of me, the part that squirmed in the back of my brain like a cornered rat, wanted to run. Run for the front offices, steal some clothes, and get out. If I were fast, I'd have just enough time to reach the open highway. Hitch a ride to Aberdeen—jack a car if I had to—and figure it out from there.

I couldn't do it. I'd given my word to Jake and Westie. I could escape alone, right here and now, but I wouldn't like how I'd feel about myself when the deed was done. Then there was Buddy. If any part of that craziness his twin had shown me was real, the fate of the world might hang on his "message" getting to the right ears.

And I was the only person who could make that happen.

Jablonski sat in a chair overlooking the hive floor, stupefied, sniper rifle cradled in his arms like a newborn son. I resisted the urge to pitch him through the window headfirst. It wasn't a sense of mercy, just the knowledge that a mysteriously dead guard would lead to the entire prison getting locked down tighter than a bank vault. I turned my gaze to a rack of equipment and monitors along the back wall. There they were: four pairs of black rubber binocular-style scopes with head straps and icy winter-green lenses. I helped myself to a couple and hustled back downstairs.

The cigarettes burned low as I pounded up the steps to my tier, racing for my cell, and flecks of hot ash spilled down onto my hands. I made it just as the first light burned out. The wreath of silver smoke convulsed around me, fraying as if slashed with invisible knives. Then the other four cigarettes burned out one after another, and the magic died.

I stashed the now-useless severed hand under my mattress. *Have fun coming up with a reasonable explanation for that*, I thought. The image pleased me, until I realized they'd probably assume I was a necrophiliac.

Outside the cell, life was back to normal. Cons milling around and shooting the breeze, guards on the catwalks. Nobody noticed the lost minutes. *And there's Emerson again*, I thought, glancing up, *keeping tabs on the other guards and doing a crap job of being subtle about it.*

I met Jake and Westie outside the bathroom. Westie did a double take, while Jake pushed open the door and peered inside.

"How the hell did you get out of there without us seeing you?" Jake asked.

"Magic. Hey, out of curiosity, if the guards found a severed hand under an escaped prisoner's bunk, what would they think?"

"Necrophiliac," Westie said.

"*Major* necrophiliac," Jake agreed.

Okay, so there might be some embarrassing newspaper articles in my near future. I'd live with it.

"Changing the subject," I said, "we might have a little hitch in the plan. Don't worry about it, though. I'm working on it."

The confidence in my voice was a dirty lie. Without a working Hand of Glory, I had no idea how I was going to get those gates open. With every night in this place bringing the risk of a one-way trip to Hive B, though—and my cell number next on the hit list—we'd never get a better chance than now.

"So," Jake said, "we good to go? We really doin' this?"

I spread my hands and smiled.

"Gentlemen," I said, "let's break out of prison."

27.

I met Westie back at my cell. He rolled his bucket past, pushing it by the mop handle, whistling tunelessly. He glanced
both ways and pulled out the mop, kicking the empty bucket into
my cell. I stopped it with my foot, dropped in the two pairs of
night-vision goggles and the knife, and sent it rolling back toward
him. He caught it, covered the contraband with the mop, and
strolled away as if nothing had happened.

Buddy's cell was my next stop. He sat on the edge of his bunk,
hands clasped in his lap, fidgeting. His mouth moved like he was
having a conversation, but no words came out. I knocked softly
on his open door. He jumped.

"I'm sorry," he said.

"For what?"

He just gave me a sad-eyed smile.

"Listen close, okay?" I said. "This is really, really important.
Soon a guard's going to come get you and say you have a visitor."

His eyes lit up. "I have a visitor?"

"No. I mean, yes, but...just follow the guard. You'll see me
there, too. Just stay behind me, okay? Right behind me, the whole
time."

"It's good if we leave soon," Buddy said. "It's not safe here."

"Is that what your, uh, sister says?"

His shoulders sagged.

"My sister is dead. Something ate her. It's okay. I have lots of
other voices to keep me company."

Jake met me on the way back to my cell, falling into step, speaking fast and low.

"On my way to my work shift," he said. "It's all set up. Expect three guards, four max—one or two in the booth, two down on the floor."

"And the distraction?"

"A fire. Small one, something we can put out fast before it sets off the smoke alarms, but it'll get their attention. I soaked a rag in gasoline last night and stashed it."

"What about the other prisoners on your shift?"

"Five, tops," he said. "Could be trouble. We can't take 'em with, not enough room in the buggies, and they aren't gonna like that."

I shrugged. "So we corral them with the guards if they get feisty. Just keep an eye on the clock; your timing has to be *perfect*."

"It will be." He thumped my shoulder with his fist. "Mexico, brother. Nothin' to it, but to do it. I'll see you at the big show."

I sat in my cell and waited.

Mostly, I looked for a way to get those gates open. And I wasn't finding one.

I couldn't see the outside sky, couldn't imagine the slow descent of the sun, but I could feel it in my bones. Just like I felt the tension simmering in my gut, that old feeling of nervous energy before taking a score. Normally I'd have a pre-job drink to settle my nerves. With the only options being prison wine or another dose of Buddy's nauseating pink glop, I figured I'd do this one on an empty stomach.

A guard sauntered by, rattling cell bars with the business end of his truncheon. He glared at me behind beige-tinted sunglasses, his thin lips twitching at the corners.

"Faust! Visitor."

Our next stop was Buddy's cell. He fell right in line, shadowing my heels like a puppy. The guard—*Vasquez*, said his nametag—waved us ahead of him. He escorted us past the first gate and through the metal detector, a bulky old warhorse that would have been right at home in a 1970s airport. It didn't make a peep.

My mental map of the prison unfurled behind my eyes as we walked toward the visitor center. *Here*, I thought, as we prepared to round a bend to the left. *This is the place.*

The next stretch of hall ran about fifty feet, with arrows and big block letters stenciled on the wall pointing the way to the visitor center, the front offices, and the motor pool.

No cameras. Just a pair of convex security mirrors perched high in a corner at each end, like you might see in a convenience store. As close to privacy as we would get.

And here was Westie, still whistling as he rolled his bucket along, strolling toward us from the other direction.

I'd hoped to hit Vasquez from behind. That would have been the easy way. He wasn't having any of it, though, forcing Buddy and me to walk directly in front of him. The bucket rolled closer, time running out fast.

I dropped to one knee, quickly tugging at my shoelace. The knot unfurled, falling free. "Hey," Vasquez said, looming over me. "On your feet."

I gestured to my shoe. "Laces came untied. Give me a second, huh?"

Westie saw my play. He changed his angle of approach, moving closer to the middle of the hall. Vasquez didn't give him a second glance. He was too busy standing over me with his hands on his hips, glaring like I'd personally ruined his day.

Funny, that was the next thing on my agenda.

I finished reknotting my shoelace as Westie passed, bringing the bucket right next to me. Without a word he yanked the mop from the bucket, twirled it in his hands, and hit Vasquez like a battering ram, pinning him against the wall with the mop handle bracing his shoulders. I snatched the knife from the bucket, spinning it in my grip. Vasquez already had his gun out by the time I lunged. He pressed the barrel into Westie's belly, and I pressed the blade to Vasquez's neck.

"Pull that trigger," I hissed, "and your wife's a widow."

He froze.

"Listen to me." I pressed the knife harder. Not hard enough to cut, just hard enough to make him feel the blade every time he took a breath. "I don't want to kill you. And you don't want to die. So I'm going to take your gun now, and you're going to let me. Understood?"

His eyes narrowed in disgust, but he nodded as much as he dared. I clamped my free hand over the barrel of his pistol and gave it a tug. His fingers went limp as I pulled the gun away.

"Turn around," I said. "Get moving. Nice and easy."

I passed the knife to Westie. He kept it close to his hip. As we walked by the bucket, he crouched down, grabbed the two night-vision goggles, and handed them to Buddy.

"Do I put these on now?" Buddy asked.

"You guys," Vasquez snarled, "are morons. Nobody's ever escaped Eisenberg. *Nobody*. And more people have tried than you think."

"I'm an overachiever," I told him.

"You're all dead men. Dead, or you're heading straight for Hive B."

I jabbed the small of his back with the gun barrel. "What's in Hive B?"

"Go fuck yourself."

"Aren't you a ray of sunshine," I said. "Take a left up here."

"Motor Pool" read the black block letters on the wall, with an arrow pointing the way. At the end of the corridor, a barred access gate blocked our path. And behind that stood the tall steel double doors leading to our final destination.

"When we get up to the gate," I said softly into Vasquez's ear, "you need to get us through. If you warn your buddy, if you stall, if you do *anything* that doesn't result in that gate opening with zero delay, I'll put a bullet in your spine. I said I don't want to kill you. Doesn't mean I won't."

"The garage?" Vasquez replied. "Oh, yeah, nobody's *ever* tried escaping that way before. Real good plan you've got there. Slick."

We approached the gate. On the opposite side, a doughy-faced guard who looked barely a day out of high school sat at a stool behind a small bank of controls. I kept the gun easy in my hand, making sure Vasquez could feel it pressed to his back.

"Three coming through," he told the guard through the bars.

He shook his head. "You sure? Work detail's almost over."

A tiny trickle of sweat beaded on Vasquez's forehead.

"Positive. C'mon, I'm late for my dinner break."

"Sure, sure," the gate guard said. He turned a key in the console and pushed a button. The gate rattled open on electric tracks. As we walked through, he glanced at the empty holster on Vasquez's belt.

"Hey," he said, "where's your gun?"

"Here," I replied and pressed the barrel to his forehead. Westie stepped in fast and got the knife back against Vasquez's throat. Everybody turned into statues.

"What's your name?" I asked.

"Mc—McGuiness," he stammered.

"You get the same deal he gets," I said, nodding toward Vasquez. "You stay cool, you get to go home to your family tonight. Can you stay cool, McGuiness?"

He nodded like a bobblehead doll.

"Good man," I said and took the gun off his belt. I passed it over to Westie and got McGuiness on his feet. "What time is it?"

McGuiness raised his trembling hand just enough to glance down at his cheap Timex. "Four minutes after six."

Right on schedule. We pushed the guards through the double doors ahead of us just as Jake's distraction fired off. I had the space of a heartbeat to take it all in: the cavernous garage, bay doors open to a violet Nevada sunset, and harsh white light pouring down from stark steel fixtures high above. The transfer bus parked on one end of the repair bay, buggies on the other, and a handful of sweaty, shirtless cons doing a wash-and-wax job on a couple of guards' personal cars. Booth in the back at the top of a short flight of corrugated metal stairs, two guards sitting snug behind bulletproof glass. A third guard pacing the floor, his back turning as a flash of hot orange flared under one of the parked cars.

"*Fire*," Jake shouted, scrambling around the car. That got the booth guards moving; they came thundering down the steps, one with a fire extinguisher. Westie and I shoved our hostages to the floor. The guard by the cars spun, saw us, and froze; between the fire and the guns, it was one crisis too many for his brain to handle. He got his priorities right and reached for his pistol just in time to catch Jake's granite fist across his jaw. He dropped, out cold, and Jake grabbed his piece.

We kept our guns on the booth guards. The fire extinguisher fell, clanging as it bounced down the metal steps. One of the guards gave a shifty look toward the door and wavered on his feet, like he was thinking about running back to the booth and locking himself inside.

"This bullet can fly twenty-five hundred feet in one second," I told him. "Can you run faster than that?"

He stayed put.

"Jake," I barked, "get that fire out before it sets off the smoke detectors. Westie, disarm the booth guards. I'll keep you covered. Buddy, lock the doors behind us."

The motor pool was ours. No alarms, no blood, nice and clean. All I could think about, though, were the prison gates that stood between us and freedom.

The hard part wasn't over. It hadn't even started yet.

28.

We patted the guards down, took their belts and their radios, and had them kneel in the corner of the garage. "Yo," one of the cons on the work shift called out, "we gettin' out of here?"

"*We* are," Westie said. "You can do whatever the hell you want. Just stay out of our way."

The two Wildcats stood sleek, polished and ready, scooped-back steel skeletons painted desert tan. There wasn't much to them but fat wheels, two rumble seats, and an engine built for speed. Jake trundled over with two scarlet plastic gas cans, and I held them steady while he strapped them onto the first buggy with bungee cords.

"This much gas should get us to civilization at least." He nodded toward the open bay doors. Wispy clouds streaked a pearly violet sky as the last rays of sunlight escaped from the oncoming night. "Right across that tarmac, we take a hard left, and it's a straight shot to the prison gates."

The gates I couldn't open.

I jogged up the stairs to the booth. A hard plastic box hung on the back wall, lined with tarnished keys tied to little paper tags. As I looked down through the bulletproof glass, the answer came to me. I just didn't like it.

The transfer bus. Heavy-duty and reinforced with cold steel to keep prisoners in and would-be rescuers out. A machine like that, at full speed...sure, it could crash those gates and carve a hole for the Wildcats to blaze through. It'd also set off alarms from here to the Aberdeen Police Department thirty miles away. They'd have choppers in the sky, roadblocks waiting up ahead, and hard-eyed cops with itchy trigger fingers and orders to shoot to kill.

One person could crash the gates. And that person wasn't going home. Not tonight.

Westie or Jake? Not a chance they'd throw away their shot at escape to save the rest of us. They weren't the altruistic type. The other cons on the work detail? They weren't that dumb; a fast car might have a shot on the open road, pinned between the prison guards and Aberdeen's finest, but the bus was a lumbering target just waiting to get taken down.

Buddy? Buddy would do it. Set him in the driver's seat, tell him what pedal to push, and point him toward the gate. He was so lost in his world of voices, he probably wouldn't even ask me why.

The perfect answer. But I couldn't do it.

Putting aside the vision, putting aside the possibility that the salvation of the world was resting in Buddy's hands, he was...innocent. A genuine innocent. The fact that he'd never suspect a betrayal was exactly why I *couldn't* betray him. Not if I wanted to live with myself.

"Ruthless," I muttered, remembering Naavarasi's words. "Just not ruthless enough. Damn it."

I rummaged through the plastic box, checking tags and took the keys for the Wildcats. And the key for the bus.

I jogged down the steps and tossed a key to Westie, underhand. He caught it with a grin. "We're ready to roll. Buggies are loaded and fueled. So how are you gonna get those gates open for us?"

"The hard way," I said, waving Jake and Buddy over. "My original plan fell through, so here's how we're gonna do this. Jake, Westie, each of you take one buggy and a pair of night-vision goggles. Buddy, ride shotgun with Jake. I'll be in that transfer bus, about a hundred feet ahead of you. I crash the gates; you blast right on by. Take a hard right the second you clear the second gate, point the buggies southeast and don't stop for anything."

Jake's brow furrowed as I tossed him the other key. "What about you? We've got a spare seat. We'll stop for you—"

"Look, once I hit those gates they'll have a chopper in the sky within two minutes, with more on the way. If you get caught in a searchlight, it's all over. And if you take the time to stop for me, you *will* get caught. I'll keep the bus moving as long as I can, to try and draw their attention away."

Westie shook his head. "They'll stop you eventually, friend. And they won't be gentle about it neither."

"I told you I'd get you out of here," I said. "Don't get caught and make a liar out of me."

"Damn, man." Jake looked down at the key in his hands like it was a million-dollar bill. "Thanks. Don't know what else to say."

"My help isn't free. First, make sure Winslow knows my debt is squared." I pointed at Buddy. "Second, you get this guy wherever he needs to go, no questions asked. If he's gotta talk to somebody at the bottom of the ocean, you make sure his ass gets on a submarine."

"It's not that far," Buddy murmured. Then he frowned. "I don't *think* it's that far."

"Deal," Jake said, and he clasped my hand in a vice grip.

I shook with Westie next. He let out a nervous chuckle. "You're one weird bastard, but I'm glad to know you. If you make it out of this alive, first round of drinks is on me."

"I'll hold you to that," I said.

I turned to Buddy. "This is why," he told me.

"Why what?"

"This is why I told you I was sorry, back in my cell," he said. "I saw when I closed my eyes. Saw the buggies. Three seats, not four."

"It's fine," I said. "Just get out of here and do whatever you need to do, all right?"

He wrung his hands, shifting from foot to foot, his eyes darting around the garage. Everywhere but on me.

"There's something else," I said. "What is it?"

"The voices told me something. They say it's really important, that you have to hear it. But it's bad news and I don't want to say."

"I can take bad news, Buddy. Give it to me straight."

He scrunched up his face and tilted his head, listening.

"They say...you're going to die here. They say you *have* to die here."

"Tell your voices," I said. "I don't believe in fate, prophecies, *or* dying young. I'll make it out of here. Just not tonight."

"I just deliver the news," he said in a small voice.

Outside the garage bay, the purple sky faded to black. Stars twinkled in the distance, as far away from here as I wanted to be. I patted Buddy on the shoulder and walked away.

"All right," I called out, "remember, stay about a hundred feet behind me. Once you're through, hit the desert and don't stop. No looking back."

"Hey," shouted one of the other prisoners on Jake's detail. "What about us?"

I paused, my hand on the bus door, and shrugged. I looked at the two cars between us, freshly washed and waxed.

"You've got two choices," I said. "You can stay right here, turn yourself in peacefully, and maybe get some good-behavior time knocked off your sentence. Or you can grab the keys to those cars and follow us out. Odds are you get rammed off the road or gunned down before you reach I-80, and nobody's ever gotten farther than that, but hey, maybe you'll be the first. Somebody's gotta win the lottery, right?"

I climbed onto the bus while they scrambled for the key box, falling over each other in their desperation. I wasn't surprised. Grimly amused, maybe, but not surprised.

I sat in the stiff vinyl driver's seat and buckled up. The engine fired to life with a throaty growl and the hood rattled like it had a stallion underneath trying to kick its way out. The cabin filled with the acrid smell of diesel and gunpowder.

As I stomped on the clutch and wrestled the cracked plastic shift knob into first gear, I couldn't help but smile. *Corman always told me learning to drive stick would come in handy,* I thought, *but this probably wasn't the situation he had in mind when he taught me how.*

The headlights clicked on, halogens blazing against the night. I took one deep breath, steeling my nerves, and started to roll. The bus rumbled out of the bay and onto the tarmac outside, and I hauled the wheel around to make a sharp left turn. I saw the Wildcats in the rear-view mirror, swinging into position behind me.

There they were, about a thousand feet ahead: the prison gates, one just after the other, standing silent and tall and strong.

I punched the gas.

The bus rolled, picking up speed, my arm aching as I wrenched my way up through the gears as fast as the clutch would let me. Halfway there, a spotlight hit my windshield and blinded me in a wash of white light. A few seconds later, alarms began to howl.

I couldn't see, but I didn't need to. I held the wheel steady and braced for impact.

29.

The bus rammed the first gate at fifty miles an hour, and the world turned into a blur of shrieking metal and hot light. I jolted against the nylon seat belt, my head lurching forward and a searing pain lancing down the back of my neck. I fought to keep the wheel steady, my foot clamped down on the gas like it was the only thing standing between life and death.

Have to keep my speed up, I thought, frantic. *If I can't bust through the second gate, we're all dead.*

The spotlight's beam slipped off the cracked windshield just in time for me to see the gate coming. Gray smoke spit from the bus's crumpled hood in heavy plumes—and beyond it, looming in my blurry vision, the oncoming wall of steel.

Sparks exploded as the bus thundered through, tearing down the second gate, the windshield exploding in my face. I threw up an arm to cover my eyes, shoulder wrenching as the second impact jolted me hard enough for the seat belt to bruise my chest, and the wheel slipped from my grasp. It spun hard, the bus careening left, rising up on two wheels before slamming back down again. A tire blew with a crack like a gunshot, rubber shredding and the rim screeching against the asphalt.

The bus shot off-road, rumbling across the desert flats. A thorny cactus went down under the hood. Smoke gushed from the engine and billowed in through the broken windshield. The smoke clogged in my throat, and I coughed myself hoarse with one hand on the wheel and one clamped over my mouth and nose.

Just get it back on the road, I thought. *I can do this. I can—*

Then I was weightless, just for a heartbeat, as the right wheels jolted up on an uneven ridge and the bus keeled onto its side.

The world turned black and white, and all I could hear was a distant clamoring bell. I moved like a man sinking in quicksand.

The seat belt clicked. It boomed like a cannon in the warbling silence. I pushed myself up, or sideways, trying to orient myself in the capsized bus. My entire world was shattered glass and smoke and pain. I could move, though. Nothing broken. Everything bruised. Shallow cuts decorated my body like tribal tattoos, seeping.

The exit yawned above my head, accordion door hanging open and limp from a twisted swing arm. Using the side of the driver's seat as a step stool, I climbed. Reaching up, taking hold of the door's edge, groaning as I pulled myself out one agonizing inch at a time. Finally out, I flopped down on the ruined bus's side, rolled over and stared up at the stars. Letting the frigid air of a desert night wash over me.

It was strangely peaceful.

Blinding light flooded my vision, and the shrill rotors of a helicopter ripped away the silence. Strobing lights painted the desert in blue and red, and I heard voices now, shouting at me from behind their car doors as the chopper above whipped up a dusty whirlwind. I ignored them. I just lay there.

Eventually, they came and got me.

* * *

New voices were arguing about me under angry fluorescent lights. I heard words like "Ad Seg" and "concussion." Then calloused hands shoved me into a small, dark room and left me there.

I slept, I think.

My senses returned and brought pain with them. I flexed my muscles one at a time, moving slowly, taking an inventory of the damage. Fingers, wrists, elbows, shoulders, counting pulled muscles and bruises. They'd stripped my clothes off, and the faint bar of light that shone under my cell door let me see the aftermath of the bus crash. Angry purple splotches spread across my skin like birthmarks painted by Salvador Dali.

I slept some more. Woke up sharper, but with a faint ringing in my ears. Waves of nausea washed over me, coming and going without warning.

The cell was smaller than a walk-in closet. In the shadows, when I managed to stand up at all, I could make out a concrete slab with a paper-thin mattress, no pillow, and a stainless-steel toilet against the back wall. A sluice drain sat in the middle of the concrete floor. With no clothes, there was nowhere I could sit that didn't press at least some of my naked skin against cold, damp stone. If I stood, the soles of my feet froze. I stood anyway, walking in place, forcing my body to move over my muscles' protests. I had to stay in motion, and keep as limber as I could.

A narrow slot in the middle of the door rattled open. I recognized the piggish eyes leering through at me. Jablonski.

"Hey, Faust," he said, "shower time."

Finally, I thought with a wave of relief. A chance to see light, to clean the dried blood and feel human again—

His face moved away, and I had just a second to recognize what took its place—the brass nozzle of a fire hose—before the water blasted in. The eruption hit me square in the chest with the force of a prizefighter's fist, knocking me to the floor. The ice-cold water rained over me, Jablonski's laughter drowning out the hiss of the hose, and I scrambled on hands and knees to take cover behind the bunk. I crouched there, curled into a fetal ball with my eyes squeezed shut, and waited for it to end.

The hose turned off. The slot slammed shut. I shivered, my teeth rattling and jaw clenched, freezing in the darkness.

* * *

Time passed. Two weeks? A month? The cold burned my skin and turned seconds into hours. The slot rattled open and I hid, scurrying for cover behind the bunk like a roach fleeing the kitchen light.

Sometimes, when the slot opened, it was the hose again.

Sometimes it was a tray of food. I couldn't tell—there wasn't any rhyme or reason to it. This time it was the tray. I snatched it, scrambling back to my hiding place in the corner. Squatting down and digging into the food with my fingers. The meal was always the same, some kind of processed putrid loaf of random glop blended together. I was hungry, so I ate.

The next time the slot opened, I saw a face. Not Jablonski's but I hid anyway. The light hurt my eyes.

"Faust," a voice hissed. "Can you hear me?"

I knew the voice. Emerson. Would he hurt me? I wasn't sure. I peered over the edge of the bunk, cautious.

"Hurry," he whispered. "We're between a shift change, so I don't have long. I've got to talk to you. I can help you. Come closer."

I frowned. It sounded like a trick. Still, I crept closer to the light. A tiny spark burned deep in my heart. It felt something like hope.

"I can get you out of here, but I need your help," he said. I got closer to the slot, our eyes meeting. My vision blurred, stinging from the light.

"How long?" I croaked. My voice sounded strange, like it belonged to somebody else.

"What?"

"How long have I been in here?"

"Four days," Emerson said.

My world tilted sideways. I shook my head.

"N-no, that's not possible. Longer than that. Two weeks at least."

"You're disoriented, and your perceptions are skewed. Solitary...does things to people's heads. Look, I've got a way to get you out, but you've got to help me. Faust? Can you hear me?"

I could hear him. As my senses slowly returned, as I remembered how to think like a man—not the feral beast four days in the dark and wet and freezing cold had made me into—I recognized that burning in my heart for what it really was.

It wasn't hope.

It was rage.

And inside my mind, the beast and the man shook hands and agreed to work together.

"Tell me," I growled.

"I'm undercover," Emerson told me. "I'm an investigator for the Nevada Department of Corrections. We know something's wrong here, something *very* wrong, but Rehabilitation Dynamics has deep pockets; every time we've tried to schedule a full inspection, we get sandbagged from higher up the food chain."

"So you got a job as a guard. Figured you'd investigate from the inside, on your own."

"Exactly. Look, Eisenberg Correctional has one of the highest inmate death rates in the *nation*. It doesn't get reported because the deaths are almost always people with no family, no outside ties, and life sentences. People who nobody will miss. Statistically, it just doesn't work."

"Let me guess," I said. "Most of those dead men were tenants of Hive B."

"Exactly. And Hive B is hermetically sealed. The guards here have a fraternity; they're *tight* with each other, too tight for me to infiltrate. You don't get assigned to a shift in Hive B until they trust you like a brother."

"Which isn't you. Meaning you can't get in to find out what's really happening in there."

"Right," Emerson said, "but you can. And you will. I just saw the paperwork: you're being transferred tomorrow."

30.

A t that moment, I didn't care. I didn't care about Hive B or what horrors might be waiting behind those sealed doors. Anywhere was better than here. I swallowed hard. My mouth was dry, and a fresh wave of nausea washed over me.

"All right," I told Emerson. "What's the plan?"

"When they take you out of solitary, I'll give you a new uniform. Inside the pocket, you'll find a miniature video camera. Whatever's going on in there, I want footage. As much evidence as you can document."

"From what I hear, a trip to Hive B is a one-way ticket. How am I supposed to deliver the goods?"

Emerson passed a sheet of paper through the slot. I held it up to the thin band of light and squinted. It was a partial map of the prison, photocopied from the original blueprints.

"Right there." Emerson's finger wagged through the slot. "See the circled spot, in yellow highlighter? That's an access passage adjacent to Hive B. You'll need to get there, somehow. Given how far your last escape attempt got, I'm figuring you're clever enough to handle it."

"Speaking of," I said, letting the question hang in the air.

"Your buddies in the dune buggies? Vanished without a trace. If they didn't get themselves killed off-roading in the desert, they're probably halfway to the border by now."

I closed my eyes for a second, breath gusting out in a sigh. At least I'd done something right.

"So I get to the passage," I said, "then what?"

"There's a floor panel providing access to the maintenance tunnels. Normally it's locked down tight. I'll make sure it won't be. Follow the passage, and about fifty yards in I'll leave a cell phone with my number on it. Call me and I'll slip you out."

"You're gonna help me break out of prison?"

"Not exactly," Emerson said. "I'm going to take you straight to the DOC, where you'll present your footage and eyewitness testimony."

"And what do I get out of the deal?"

"I can't get time taken off your sentence, but I *can* have you transferred to the facility of your choice. You can do your time in a minimum-security country club."

"One of those places for white-collar criminals, where they've got tennis courts and cable TV?" I asked. "And you're pretty much on the honor system not to run away?"

"Exactly."

I liked the sound of that. I'd have to come up with a brand-new escape plan, but this time it'd stick.

"So you'll slip the camera in with my clothes," I mused. "Can you smuggle me anything else?"

"You'll go through a metal detector on your way in, so no weapons. Don't worry, the camera's smaller than your palm and it's ninety-nine percent plastic. I've already walked it through a few of the detectors myself, just to make sure it won't set any alarms off."

I thought fast. Time was running out, and I'd only have one shot to bring in something I could use.

"I'm going to give you a phone number," I told him, "for a man named Bentley. Call him and tell him everything."

"This is a confidential operati—"

"Tell him *everything*, or no deal." I recited Bentley's number, waiting for Emerson to scribble it down. "And tell him I need some alchemist's clay, pronto. He'll give you a location to meet up with him."

"Alchemist's...clay? What is that?"

"It's a special kind of clay," I said.

"And it won't set off the metal detectors?"

I stared at him through the slot.

"No," I said. "Because it's *clay*."

"I'll see what I can do." His eyes darted left. "Shit, incoming. I have to go. We have a deal?"

I didn't have much of a choice. At least with Emerson's help I had something I didn't have ten minutes ago: a fighting chance.

"Deal," I said and passed the photocopy back to him. I'd etched it all down on my mental map.

Then he ratcheted the slot door shut and left me in the darkness.

I didn't sink into a stupor this time. The wet and the cold just woke me up. I welcomed the pain and the bruises. And when Jablonski returned a few hours later, giggling as he unleashed the hose and plunged me into another freezing hell, I silently thanked him. He'd given me a gift. The gift of hatred.

Because whatever was waiting for me in Hive B, now I had to survive long enough to see Jablonski dead.

* * *

When they came for me, I was ready.

The door swung open, flooding the tiny cell with piercing light. I squinted, eyes tearing up. Three guards stood outside: two I didn't recognize, and Emerson, holding a bundle of clothes in his arm. A fresh prison uniform.

"Get dressed," the guard on the left barked. "You're being transferred."

Emerson handed me the clothes, carefully passing the bundle so that I could feel something small and hard against my palm. I turned to one side as I pulled on the tan trousers, subtly glancing to make sure I wasn't showing any suspicious bulges in my pocket. If I got searched now, Emerson and I were *both* screwed.

"We'll take it from here," the other guard told Emerson once I'd finished buttoning up my shirt. I left it untucked, the tails drooping over my pockets for a little extra camouflage. As I smoothed my shirt my fingers dipped into my right pants pocket, just long enough to brush against a square of smooth plastic and a tiny, grainy lump of clay the size of a gumball.

Perfect.

As they shackled my wrists to a padlocked waist-belt, I felt like Houdini getting ready for an escape act. It must have shown on my face. One of the guards gave me the side-eye. "What are you smiling about?"

"Just happy to be stretching my legs a little."

"Don't get used to it," he said and gave my shoulder a shove.

As we marched through the labyrinthine corridors, I watched the walls and made notes. The arrows pointing the way to "Central Security" caught my interest. If I judged right, the name was literal—it was right at the center of the underground passages, between the three hives.

When we came to the spot marked on Emerson's blueprint, I recognized it at once. A short stretch of hallway festooned with exposed piping and water valves rising up from the floor and running along the brick at chest level. My shoes clanged over a corrugated metal hatch, a trapdoor on new-looking hinges. That was my exit, then; wherever they took me, whatever happened next, all I needed to do was escape to this spot and slip through the trapdoor without anyone spotting me.

Easy enough. I hoped.

It didn't take long for my hopes to hit the rocks, as the guards led me past a metal detector, another gate checkpoint, and into Hive B.

Instead of the raucous noise and milling bodies of the other hive, I was greeted by an empty gallery floor leading up to a central guard tower. Instead of tier after tier of bars, I looked up at stark iron doors. Hundreds of them.

The entire hive, all seven stories of it, had been converted into cells for solitary detention.

They walked me up to the fourth tier. We passed cell after cell where a narrow slot stood open, the occupants' only window to the outside world. In some cells, cowering figures huddled in corners, hiding their faces from the light. In others, eyes stared back out at me. Hard eyes. Distant eyes. Mad eyes. I stopped looking.

My new cell was identical to the one they'd just pulled me out of, with one exception: on the back wall, a frosted panel under a wire-frame cage glowed with soft light. There wasn't anything to look at, but at least I wouldn't go blind in the meantime.

They took off my shackles and waved me inside. As soon as the door swung shut, clanging behind me and sealing me in, I fought a surge of claustrophobic terror. Was this the great mystery of Hive B? That they were keeping everyone in permanent solitary?

It made a sick kind of sense. Eisenberg Correctional only cared about minimizing expenses and maximizing profits; rehabilitation wasn't on the menu. Providing recreation cost money, and so did hiring enough guards to watch all the prisoners. Medical care and patching up cons after the occasional brawl cost money too. So much easier to toss every prisoner into his own personal tomb and let him rot.

All the convicts I'd been told about, the ones who had been snatched in the night and transferred to Hive B, had violent records—or in Simms's case, attacked other inmates. Exactly the kind of prisoners who gave the administration a headache. And then there were the ones who wouldn't ever be getting out and squawking about this to the press: the ones on life sentences, with no parole.

Like me.

I paced the seven-by-seven prison cell. Possibly my new home, for the rest of my life.

No, I thought. *There's no such thing as an unsolvable problem, and there's no such thing as an impossible escape.*

I did push-ups against the wall, ignoring the twinge from my tortured muscles. Working my body helped to work my brain and get the ideas flowing.

What I didn't know then—what I wouldn't find out until later that night—was that I was working the wrong problem. I thought I'd solved the puzzle of Hive B. I hadn't.

The truth was so much worse.

31.

First, I heard the sounds. Murmuring voices, echoing foot-falls, rising up from the gallery floor far below my cell. Like they'd opened all the doors and let the inmates out for some recre-ation time. I felt a spark of hope; maybe the situation wasn't as bad as I'd imagined.

Then the guards came for me.

One had a checklist on a clipboard, lined with names and cell numbers. The other two had a fresh pair of shackles for me. They marched me out onto the tier under dimmed-down lights. As we rounded the stairs, headed down, I got a look at what waited below.

Mahogany tables and candlelight. White-tuxedoed waiters with towels draped over their sleeves, ferrying drinks from a rolling wet bar. The gallery floor, surrounded by iron doors and standing in the shadow of the guard tower, had been turned into a bizarre imitation of an upscale nightclub.

"What the hell is this?" I said, hesitating. A guard's fist jabbed into my kidney, sending me stumbling.

"You'll find out. Shut up and do what you're told."

I wasn't the first prisoner down on the floor. Four others stood in a silent, grim line off to one side of the "nightclub." I recognized one of them. Simms looked different from when we'd tussled back in my cell. A long scar ran along one puffy eye, sealed with a row of black stitches.

I kept my mouth shut and my eyes open, trying to get a read

on the situation. The waiters set out more tables and chairs, light-ing elegant candles. Two men in black tuxes rolled in a baby grand piano and opened a sleek black case, taking out a polished bass. Soon the jaunty strains of a jazz duo filled the air.

The guests arrived in pairs and foursomes, dressed for a night on the red carpet. Perfect hair and designer suits, *haute couture* and diamond necklaces. They mingled and laughed and ordered cock-tails from the bar, as if finding a swank lounge in the heart of a prison was perfectly ordinary.

I risked a whisper, glancing sidelong at the convict next to me. "Hey. What's going on here?"

He gave a timid shake of his head and muttered, "Don't talk. Just don't react to anything. Safer that way."

Given the look of the guards patrolling the floor—and the Tasers they openly carried—I took his word for it.

Still, I knew an opportunity when I saw one. My shackles had just enough give to let me reach my pocket. My fingers dipped in, scooping out the tiny plastic square of the video camera, and I palmed it like a playing card. My pinky slid across a textured switch, clicking it on. As I surveyed the room, I swiveled my wrist from side to side, furtively filming as much as I could.

I caught some familiar faces in the growing crowd. Not anyone I knew personally, faces from television. A famous golf pro, with a woman who definitely wasn't his wife, shared drinks with an actress I'd seen in some summer action-movie blockbuster. A political pundit wore a huge lantern-jawed grin as he crossed the floor, rendezvousing with Warden Lancaster.

"Uh-oh," Lancaster chortled, "the media's here! Not gonna blow the whistle on us, are ya?"

The pundit laughed and raised his glass. "What, don't you watch my show? I always say we should be tougher on crime."

Lancaster handed him a glossy pamphlet. "On that note, here's tonight's program. Enjoy, enjoy."

I didn't like the sound of that.

A few more prisoners came down from the tiers, filling out

the line beside me, while Lancaster greeted his other guests and passed out more pamphlets. Two of the new arrivals headed our way. The woman, in a pink sundress and a floppy hat, I vaguely recognized from TV. She was some kind of socialite reality-show star, famous for being famous. The man at her side, a hunk of muscle in a tailored jacket, I didn't know. They walked up and down the line, glancing from us to their pamphlets. I slipped the camera back into my pocket before they got too close.

"Ooh, this one," she said, pointing at me. "Definitely this one. Did you read this? He's a former *assassin*, sweetie. Isn't that just the *coolest?*"

The man rolled his eyes. "Sure, if it's cool to throw your father's money away. Never bet on a first-timer. How many times do I have to tell you that?"

"Longer odds." She held the pamphlet in his face and rapped her fingernail against it. "Bigger prizes."

"You did this exact same thing at the Kentucky Derby last May. Do you even know how statistics work? Have you ever taken a *class?*"

They carried their argument back to the wet bar, leaving me to stew in silence and wonder what the hell was going on here.

Lights from the guard tower flickered, strobing behind the smoky glass. Conversation hushed. The prisoner on my left tensed up, manacles rattling as his hands clenched into fists. I palmed the camera again and started filming.

Warden Lancaster took the floor with a microphone in his fist. When he spoke, speakers crackled and his sonorous voice echoed throughout the gallery.

"Ladies and gentlemen, how fine it is to welcome you to another grand event. We've got quite the show planned for you tonight, and a delightful time indeed. But first...I'm afraid we have a bit of unpleasant side business to take care of."

Jablonski and another guard hauled a limp prisoner in front of the crowd, chained at the wrists and ankles with a burlap sack over his head. They ripped off the hood, and the breath caught in my throat.

Emerson squinted, dazed, through swollen eyes. His face was a mask of bruises and freshly dried blood.

"We had a bit of a...weasel in the henhouse, it appears," Lancaster told the crowd. "This man is an undercover informant. Now, now, don't fret. He never set foot in this hallowed hall—well, not until *now*, anyway."

"Please," Emerson gasped, his lips purple and puffy. "You can't do this. This is wrong—"

Lancaster talked over him, leaning into the microphone. "Fortunately, he was *not* very good at his job."

That drew a ripple of laughter from the audience.

"I highlight this incident," Lancaster said, "simply to reassure you that your safety and your privacy is of utmost importance to myself and my staff. We found the problem, and we'll fix the problem."

He reached into his jacket. His hand came out, slow and smooth, with a long-barreled .45 revolver. The gun gleamed in the candlelight as he held it aloft for the audience's approval. Someone in the back let out an eager hoot.

I gritted my teeth and kept the camera steady.

"Please," Emerson begged, "I won't tell anyone. I won't—"

"I know you won't, son," Lancaster said.

Then he put the barrel to Emerson's forehead and pulled the trigger.

The revolver boomed like a thunderclap as the bullet tore a hole through Emerson's skull, sending him tumbling to the concrete in a haze of blood mist and shattered bone. Polite applause rippled through the crowd along with a chorus of clinking glasses, as Jablonski and the other guard dragged Emerson's body away by his ankles.

The cavalry wasn't coming to my rescue. The cavalry was dead.

"We're just about ready to begin," Lancaster told the crowd, "so get those bets in. Odds are printed in your program guides, and we're happy to cover all requests...minus the house's customary ten percent, of course."

Another ripple of laughter. I stared down at the concrete floor, at the bloody smear where Emerson had fallen.

Working in pairs, the waiters rolled out something new: a pair of tall wire frames festooned with hooks, like tool racks in a mechanic's workshop. Tools hung on the display: hammers, drills, chisels.

A bloodstained machete. A chainsaw. And a baseball bat wrapped with coils of barbed wire.

"Ladies and gentlemen," Lancaster said, the crowd falling into an excited murmur. "It is my great honor to welcome you to tonight's entertainment."

He spread one arm wide, taking in the room, and flashed pearly teeth like a game-show host.

"Welcome," he said, "to the Killing Floor."

32.

I got the idea, fast, when the guards dragged two prisoners out of the lineup. They stood them front and center before the audience, unshackling them while Lancaster worked the room. They kept a ten-foot buffer between the open floor where the prisoners stood and the first rows of tables. A buffer thick with old, dried stains on the concrete.

"Diego Antunez," Lancaster boomed, "a triggerman for the Cinco Calles, with an estimated seven kills to his name on the outside. Of course, he eliminated his enemies with a gun and by surprise, so take that for what it's worth."

Laughter from the crowd. Clinking glasses. My stomach clenched.

"And Russell Finch. Stick-up man. No kills on the outside, *two* on this very floor. He's smaller, but is he faster on the draw? Betting closes in thirty seconds, ladies and gents, so make your choices now!"

Slips of paper, some pink and some green, flew like a ticker-tape parade. The audience shoved them in fistfuls at the waiters and piled them on serving trays.

Lancaster stepped aside and nodded to the guards. They made their selections from the wire racks: a short-hafted sledgehammer, and a Black and Decker chainsaw with a fourteen-inch blade. The weapons went sliding across the smooth, hard floor, skidding to a stop near the convicts' feet.

Antunez and Finch stared at each other, bodies tensed, knees bent and ready. Frozen in time. Then a klaxon rang out from the guard tower—one short, sharp air-horn burst. They scrambled for the weapons, snatched them up and jumped back, trying to get some fighting room. Finch hefted the chainsaw. He pulled the cord to start the engine. Nothing happened.

Antunez saw his chance and charged, whipping the sledge-hammer down for a killing blow. Finch darted out of the way, frantically tugging the cord, wearing his terror on his face. Antunez overshot, stumbling, almost tripping over the hammer as he tried to recover.

On the fifth pull, the chainsaw sputtered to life, deadly teeth whirring with a screech like nails on a blackboard.

Antunez spun with another wild, desperate swing for Finch's head. Finch brought up the chainsaw; its teeth chewed into the hammer's handle, the sudden kickback sending them both staggering, fighting to keep a grip on their weapons. Finch screamed, shrill as the saw in his double-handed grip, and charged with the blade pointed straight for Antunez's belly.

Antunez backpedaled, raising the hammer high, and brought it down on the saw. The chainsaw jolted from Finch's grip, hitting the floor, kicking up hot orange sparks as the blade chewed into concrete. Stunned, Finch needed a second to recover. Antunez didn't.

The iron head of the sledgehammer slammed against Finch's skull like the grill of a freight train, buckling his head back and snapping his neck. Finch might have still been alive when he hit the floor. Antunez wasn't taking any chances. He dropped the hammer and grabbed the now-silent chainsaw, revving it back to life with one brutal yank on the cord.

He pressed the grinding blade to Finch's throat, wet gore spattering his face as he sawed what was left of the man's head from his body, and the crowd went wild. I looked away from the carnage, but what I saw in the audience only made me feel sicker. They hooted and cheered, pumping their fists in the air like frat boys at a strip club. One couple, shadowed in candlelight, were wrapped tight in each other's arms. Making out while a man was chainsawed to death for their entertainment.

The teeth chewed into Finch's spine, got caught in the bone, sputtered again, and died. Antunez left the blade half-buried in his victim's neck and staggered back, panting. His eyes were as glassy and dead as his victim's. The guards quickly shackled him again, leading him away while the audience hammered their tables and screamed for more.

Warden Lancaster took center stage, laughing, waving the crowd into silence while his staff cleaned up the mess behind him.

"Now, how was that for an appetizer? Do we not deliver, ladies and gents? *Do we not deliver?*"

Under a fresh torrent of applause, the guards came back to our lineup. One grabbed Simms. Jablonski grabbed me.

"Time to pop your cherry," he said, grinning like a hyena as he clamped his hand around my elbow.

"Hey," I said, "Jablonski."

He paused. Our eyes met.

"Just so you know, I'm going to kill you."

He snorted. "Better do it fast. I'm betting you've got about three minutes left to live. Got a chunk of my next paycheck riding on it, as a matter of fact."

They stood us in front of the crowd, side by side, and unlocked our shackles. I felt the heat of the audience's eyes, a gang of hungry raptors eager for their next meal. They sized me up like I was a piece of meat in a butcher-shop window.

"Leroy Simms," the warden announced with a flourish. "Stick-up man, extortionist, arsonist. One-time winner—and what a fight that was! Can't go wrong betting on this big bruiser."

He gestured toward me now, his smile bright.

"Or can you? We've got a new contender tonight: Daniel Faust, former hit man for a Vegas crime syndicate. This one's a wild card, ladies and gents, with long-shot odds to match! Thirty seconds to go, so get those bets in now."

He looked on as the tickets flew and the waiters scrambled to collect the bids. "Warden," I said.

Lancaster turned, eyebrows raised. Like he was surprised I had a voice.

"Why are you doing this?" I asked. "This is...this is *sick*. You have to know that. These are human beings."

He cupped his palm over the microphone and shook his head.

"Son, you stopped being a human being the second you came into my prison. You're a *commodity*. Think about it: you ain't never gonna see the outside one way or another. Civilized society wants you *gone*. Locked up 'til you rot. So why shouldn't I capitalize on that? You oughta thank me. I'm making your death mean something."

He gestured to the guards by the weapon racks. As he walked off to the sidelines, he glanced back at me over his shoulder.

"Besides," he drawled, "I got a retirement fund and a brand-new Cadillac to pay for."

I turned to Simms. He wasn't the same man who'd tried to shake me down my first day behind bars. His one good eye had a thousand-yard stare and he twitched like a caged animal, over two hundred pounds of muscle and barely constrained rage.

I hadn't stood a chance against him the first time we fought. And this time, if he got me on the floor, no guards were coming to my rescue. *So don't let him*, I thought. *No matter what happens, can't let him turn this into a ground fight.*

His right eye, that was the key. Whatever had happened in his debut fight, that ragged line of stitches meant he was good as blind on one side. If I could get on his right and stay there, I might have a fighting chance.

The guards picked out our weapons for the bout. A baseball bat came rolling toward me, jolting to a stop against my shoe. Barbed wire wrapped the length of the stout wooden shaft, spikes caked with dried blood.

Simms got a machete.

The air horn blared and the crowd cheered, and I snatched up the bat. Simms barreled at me, roaring like a bull, swinging the machete wild and fast. I darted left, aiming for his blind spot, and brought up the bat with both hands to knock the blade aside. His beefy fist cracked against my cheekbone like a pile driver, sending me crashing to the concrete and seeing stars. No time to recover: I rolled, fast, as the machete swooped down and chopped into the floor with a thundering *clang*.

I came up in a crouch on his blind side, pulled back, and swung the bat two-handed with everything I had. Simms howled as his kneecap shattered like a porcelain plate. He fell as I rose. No time for thought, no hesitation, I just gritted my teeth and whipped the bat around and slammed it against the back of his skull.

Simms lay sprawled at my feet, face to the concrete. Panting, spent, I unclenched my fingers. The bat tumbled from my hand and clattered onto the killing floor. Applause and cheers washed over me, but I could barely hear it over the ringing in my ears. Everything was a million miles away. Everything but Simms.

Lancaster frowned and nodded to a guard. The guard crouched at Simms's side, putting his fingers to the big man's neck. He shook his head at Lancaster and stepped back.

"Ladies and gentlemen," the warden announced, "the fight's not over yet! Our friend Simms is still breathing. What weapon will Faust use for his finishing move? Will he make it fast, or slow? C'mon, give him some encouragement, folks!"

I stood transfixed by the frenzied cheering. Paralyzed. Cold blood trickled down my cheek from a stinging gash. I could barely remember how I'd gotten it.

"Fight's not done until only one man's breathing," Lancaster told me, growling into the microphone. "Time for the money shot, Faust. Give these people what they paid for. How many people have you killed? This is just one more body."

"No," I said, and the crowd fell into a confused hush.

I looked to the audience, seething.

"Forget it," I shouted. "I don't kill for fun. I'm sure as hell not going to kill for *your* fun. You want him dead? Do it yourself."

Now the applause turned into scattered boos and jeering. The warden calmed them down with a reassuring wave of his hand.

"Folks, folks, it's all good. Our new contender just doesn't know how this works yet. Lemme clarify for him."

Lancaster raised his hand high and snapped his fingers. I followed his gaze down to my chest.

A neon-green pinpoint hovered over my heart.

"The rules are, kill or be killed," Lancaster told me, "no exceptions. You've got thirty seconds. If Mr. Simms is not dead at the end of those thirty seconds, well...I'm afraid my sniper in the guard tower will have to invoke the 'sudden death' playoff rule."

He glanced at his watch.

"And the clock starts...now."

33.

You can go your entire life believing you have principles. Believing there are lines you'd never cross, deeds you'd never commit, even at the cost of your own life. And if you're lucky, nobody will ever put those principles to the test.

I picked up the bat.

Lancaster was right. I had plenty of blood on my hands, and while I'd love to pretend I'd only pulled the trigger in self-defense, that'd be a dirty lie. All these years, though, I'd held myself up by one fragile string, one solitary rule I kept sacred: I'd never killed anybody who didn't have it coming to them. Criminals like me and monsters like me, sure, they were fair game. People who willingly lived the life and knew the risks. But not civilians. And never innocents.

Simms might not be what most people would call "innocent," but in my book he was. He hadn't asked to be a part of this, hadn't signed up for these bastards' sick game. They'd put a weapon in his hand and forced him to fight, and only the luck of the draw put him facedown on the blood-slick concrete instead of me.

"Twenty seconds," Lancaster said, eyeing his watch.

When you don't adhere to many principles in life, you guard the ones you do have. They're the only things that let you look yourself in the mirror in the morning, that let you pretend, every once in a while, that you're a good person deep down inside.

"Fifteen seconds," Lancaster purred into the microphone. "Son, you'd best get to it."

When I decided, I decided in a heartbeat. It wasn't hard. It wasn't a debate at all.

I wanted to live more than I wanted to feel like a good person.

I raised the bat with both hands and brought it down on Simms's head, gritting my teeth as the wood cracked and the handle snapped, sending a jolt up my arms. He didn't die. He spasmed, arms and legs flopping like a fish drowning on dry land. I left the broken bat embedded in the back of his skull, splintered wood and barbed wire matted in crushed flesh and bloody bone.

"Seven seconds," Lancaster said.

I snatched up the fallen machete. The first chop went halfway into Simms's neck, snapping his spine. He still wouldn't die. He let out a rattling, wheezing gasp as he convulsed. I wrenched the blade free and raised it one more time.

The second chop, the one that drained the last of my strength from my aching muscles, the one that left me standing slump-shouldered in front of the roaring crowd—that one killed him. One more step past the line of damnation.

"Now you might call that beginner's luck," Lancaster told the audience, "but every once in a while, a long shot wins."

I stood, limp, while the waist-belt and wrist shackles went back on. The guards led me away, already forgotten by the blood-hungry audience, as the warden announced the next bout.

* * *

"You know," I said to Valentino. I sat on his vinyl exam bench, my cheek ice numb from a local anesthetic while he sewed the gash in my cheek shut.

"Only two stitches," the prison doctor murmured, leaning close and studying my face under a penlight. "That should heal up nicely."

"You know what's going on in Hive B," I said. "You have to know."

"You've also got a mild concussion," he said, shining the penlight in my eyes. "Probably from your escape attempt—I heard about the bus crash—though tonight certainly didn't help matters. I'll give you some acetaminophen."

"Yeah, let's talk about *tonight*," I said.

He shot a furtive glance toward the infirmary door.

"I can't," he said softly.

"The hell you can't. You're an accessory to this, *doctor*. You still have to take the Hippocratic Oath when you get your degree, right? Maybe that doesn't mean anything to you, but—"

"They'll kill my family."

He bit his bottom lip, turned, and put his surgical thread in a drawer. When he looked back at me, his eyes were moist.

"I have a wife and a daughter," he said. "They told me...if I even think about blowing the whistle, if I *don't* help...they'll be on stage at the next event."

"So take them and run. Go to the feds. They'll put you in protective custody."

"You don't understand." Valentino shook his head. "You think some prison warden and a gang of corrupt guards could pull this off all by themselves? Lancaster is *protected*. He has relatives in high places, old money, *very* old money. There's nowhere they couldn't get at us."

"It's all right," I said, holding up one hand. "We'll find a way. Nobody's going to hurt your family."

In the quiet of the infirmary, away from the chaos and the fear of the fight, I took a deep breath and sorted my mind out. Time to take inventory and figure out what I had to work with.

The footage from the fight? Damning evidence, and Valentino could smuggle it out, get it to the cops or the media—but there was no telling how Lancaster and his goons would react. They might run for the hills, or they might try to cover their tracks by going from cell to cell and putting a bullet in every last one of us. No. Too unpredictable, too risky. For now, the camera stayed with me.

Emerson wasn't coming to the rescue, but the plan he'd put in place before he died—the unlocked hatch and the cell phone stashed in the maintenance tunnels—was still waiting for me. I could use that.

And I could use Valentino.

"When's the next big event?" I asked him.

"Wednesday night." He shook his head. "I'm sorry. I guarantee you'll be fighting again. When a long shot wins like you did tonight, everybody wants to see an encore. More bets means more money for the warden."

"What if I told you I had a way to bring this whole place crashing down?"

He let out a nervous chuckle. "I'd say you should have already done it."

"I need your help."

"Are you not listening?" he said. "They will *kill* my *family*. I'm sorry, I'm genuinely sorry, but I'm not going to—"

"Hold up. It's something they can never connect back to you. No risk on your part whatsoever. If I succeed, you and your family are free. If I fail, nobody will ever know you had anything to do with it."

He wavered on his feet, chewing his lip, and glanced to the door again. When he looked back at me, his voice was soft.

"What do I have to do?"

"It's easy," I told him. "You need to tell the guards, tomorrow morning, that you have to see me for a follow-up exam."

"Impossible. We don't do follow-up care. My instructions, when it comes to the Hive B prisoners, are to patch you up and send you back in the best shape I can manage. Most of the time, the second visit is the one that ends, well"—he nodded toward the door to the morgue—"in there."

"You said they'll want to see me fight again, right? And the more bets that get placed, the bigger a commission Lancaster rakes in. So I'm worth money to him, win or lose."

"That's right."

I tapped the side of my head. "Not if I *can't* fight. You said I've got a concussion. Tell him it could be worse than it looks, and if you're not careful, it could kill me before the next event."

Valentino rubbed his chin. "That...could work, actually. All right, and then what?"

"Then nothing. The rest is on my shoulders."

*   *   *

Back in my cell, alone with my thoughts, I tossed and turned under the stark fluorescent light. The tiny plastic square never turned off, not even after midnight, glowing under its wire cage and flooding the room. It buzzed endlessly, a low-grade hum that set my teeth on edge.

The escort to the infirmary would take me right past the access hatchway. My one and only shot at getting out of here. All I needed was a plan to go with it. The maintenance tunnels could take me anywhere but *out*; no matter where I came up, I'd still have to deal with the exact same problems as my first escape attempt. Even if I could steal some civilian clothes, jack a car, and get out of the prison, they'd be onto me long before I reached Aberdeen. Once the alarm went up and the highway patrol sealed off I-80, I'd be sunk.

I lost track of the hours. Then a slot at the bottom of my door rattled open, and a plastic tray slid through. Breakfast was a cardboard carton of warm milk and half a bowl of greasy, cold oatmeal. I thought back to the prison cafeteria, asking the line cook how the inmates in Hive B got fed. *Lockdown means all the meals get delivered to their cells,* he'd told me. *We cook 'em up and send them all over on rolling carts for the guards to pass out.*

As I slowly stirred the oatmeal with a plastic spoon, a wave of nausea washed over me. Not from the food either, considering how my vision blurred in time with the queasiness. I tried to remember anything I could about concussions—specifically, how fast they could kill you—but I drew a blank. I needed real medical treatment, and fast.

I kept staring at the plastic tray. The food service was the only line of direct communication between Hive B and the rest of the prison...but only in one direction. Still, there had to be a way I could use that.

As my cell door rattled and swung open, the answer hit me.

I wasn't going to break out today.

I was going to break in.

34.

I stood up slow, eyeing the guard on the threshold. Red rims lined his baggy eyes, and he walked with a lethargic shuffle in his step. *Somebody's a little hungover from last night's festivities*, I thought. *Perfect.*

"Infirmary," he said. "The doc needs to check you out."

I knew the routine by now. I presented my wrists and waited patiently while he fumbled with the shackles. My eyes were on his belt. Pepper spray, pistol, key ring. I walked just ahead of him, a little slower than I needed to.

Once we passed the checkpoint gate, my fingers dipped into my pocket. They closed over the marble-sized lump of alchemist's clay that Emerson had smuggled in for me. One of Bentley's specialties. I scooped it up and rolled it into my palm, pinning the clay in place with my thumb.

"Let me ask you something."

"Shut up," the guard said. "Keep walking."

"I'm just wondering how you live with yourself, being an accessory to all this."

We rounded a corner. Just ahead, my eyes followed the pipes running at chest height along the wall, where they bent at a sharp angle and disappeared into the floor. The corrugated metal hatch stood alongside the pipes, about four feet across.

"You scumbags are getting exactly what you deserve." The guard punctuated his words with a shove, sending me stumbling.

"Why *shouldn't* we make a little money and have some fun while we're at it?"

"I am so glad you said that," I told him.

I kindled the clay with a tiny spark of power, the energy lancing from my palm and turning the marble into a smoldering furnace.

"Huh?" he said. "Why?"

I took a deep breath, held it, and hurled the marble to the ground. The clay burst and billowed, gushing a cloud of vomit-green smoke, faster and thicker than the spray from a fire extinguisher. The guard got a big lungful, choking and sputtering behind me as I knelt down and pulled on the hatch ring.

The trapdoor lifted, easy and smooth. Behind me, the guard was a convulsing shadow in the fog. My eyes burned like I'd rubbed them with fresh-cut onions, but I could see well enough to do what came next.

I drove both fists into his gut, grabbed him by the neck, then threw him down through the trapdoor. Head first.

He landed on his stomach, hitting the concrete seven feet down. I jumped in after him, stomping down hard on his spine with both feet, and dropped to one knee. Then I slipped my shackled wrists over his head, the short, stout length of chain between them biting against his neck, and heaved back as hard as I could.

"I'm glad you said that," I hissed in his ear, "because I feel bad about the last guy I had to kill. You? I *won't.*"

His feet hammered the ground, his eyes bulging. I heard the faintest crackling sound from his neck. He let out one last, rattling wheeze. Then nothing at all.

My arms shook and my teary eyes burned, but I didn't have a second to rest. I fished on his belt for the keys, unshackled myself, and scrambled back up the ladder. The smoke had cleared, and the hallway still stood empty. Nobody had seen a thing. I closed the hatch on my way back down and latched it behind me.

The tunnels hummed, lined with fat iron pipes and rattling

old access panels. Faint yellow light glowed from bulbs in wire cages, spaced out every twenty feet or so along the cramped walkway. Judging from the cobwebs and the dust, so thick I could taste it in the back of my throat, maintenance crews didn't come down here often.

I scouted ahead, squinting. I found what I needed in a blot of shadow, halfway between the lights: a tiny nook along the left-hand wall, next to a throbbing metal cabinet dripping with condensation dewdrops. I grabbed the dead guard by the wrists, gritting my teeth as I dragged him down the tunnel. Then came the laborious work of squeezing his body into the nook, folding his arms and legs and shoving with my feet.

It wasn't the best way of hiding a body, but assuming nobody checked down here, or if they just didn't look too hard, there was a good chance he'd stay hidden for a few days. Eventually he'd stink up the place and *somebody* would have to notice, but hopefully by then it'd be a moot point.

I found my prize, Emerson's last gift, sitting on a ledge about fifty feet further down. A cell phone, sealed up safe in a ziplock baggie. I dialed by memory as I prowled the tunnels, looking for exits and trying to get the lay of the land.

"It's me," I said fast. "I'm alive. Banged up and then some, but I'm alive."

"What happened out there?" Bentley asked. "The escape's been all over the news, and we thought you'd made it out, but you never came home. Then this prison guard contacted me and—"

His voice washed out in a blur of static, then silence. I took the next right and jogged along the tunnel, watching the phone's screen and waiting until a single reception bar lit up.

"Sorry," I said once I redialed, "hit a dead zone. I'm down in the prison maintenance tunnels."

"Can you get out from there?"

I paused, looking up at a short ladder to another hatch just above my head.

"No," I said. "Not on my own, but I've got a plan."

"Name it," Bentley said.

"Wednesday night. I need a car. A service van would be better, something with no windows in the back so I can stay out of sight. Thing is, you'll probably be taking it out through a roadblock; the papers and plates have to be legit."

"The vehicle shouldn't be a problem, but that's well after visiting hours. How do we get inside the prison?"

"You don't," I said. "Just get as close as you can and wait for my signal. Trust me, you'll know when it happens."

Then I told him the rest of the plan. He was silent for a moment when I finished, contemplating all the angles.

"It *could* work," he mused. "Dangerous, though."

"If you've got a better idea, I'm all ears."

He sighed. "Alas, I do not. All right. I'll make the phone calls."

As I came to a tunnel junction, craning my neck to look in each direction, a fresh wave of nausea hit me. I squeezed my eyes shut until it passed.

"Do me a favor," I said, "and have Doc Savoy on standby. I've gotten the shit kicked out of me this week, and I have a feeling things are gonna get worse before they get better."

"Be safe, Daniel. We'll see you Wednesday night."

After I hung up, I flipped the phone over, fished out the SIM card, and snapped it in half. If my whole plan went sideways, I didn't want Lancaster and his thugs tracing anything back to Bentley and Corman's doorstep. Then I tossed the phone into a dark, dusty shadow under a rattling iron pipe.

Time was running out. With every passing minute, the odds of someone noticing that a guard and one of the Hive B prisoners had gone missing became more and more inevitable. I started carefully poking my head up through access hatches as I passed them, using half-inch glimpses of the world above and my mental map of the prison to navigate.

That was how I ended up back in Hive C, standing in front of Brisco's card table on the gallery floor. He and his buddies stared at me like they'd seen a ghost.

"Need to talk," I told him, "the bathrooms on tier three. Right now."

He spit out the toothpick he'd been chewing.

"The grapevine said you got killed trying to bust outta here," he said. "Then I heard you were in Ad Seg. Then you were just *gone*."

"I'm alive and well, and right now I'm just another uniform in the crowd, but if any of these guards look too close and realize who I am, we're *both* dead men. So please, pretty please, get up and come with me."

His entourage looked between us, uncertain. Brisco sighed and tossed his cards on the table.

"Play without me," he told them.

Alone in the bathroom, under the eye of a dead surveillance camera, I took Emerson's video camera from my pocket.

"Convicts work the prison cafeteria, right? You got juice with any of 'em?"

"With the whites, sure," he said. "I could get double servings at dinner if I wanted. I just *don't*. What's going on, Faust?"

"Hive B. They're running death matches for rich sickos to gamble on. Warden Lancaster and the guards are all in on it. That's why nobody ever comes back from Hive B. They're not on lockdown, Brisco. They're *dead*."

Under two days of stubble, Brisco's cheeks turned pale.

"Jesus," he breathed. "You're serious."

"It gets worse. I've seen their 'shopping list,' the roster of who they're gonna grab next." I looked him dead in the eye. "You're on it. Two weeks from tonight, they'll be coming for you."

He bought it. Brisco put his palms against a grimy sink and leaned in, taking a deep breath.

"We've gotta—we've gotta *do* something."

"And we will," I told him. "I've got a plan to blow this whole place wide open, but I need your help. Your influence."

"Name it, man. Anything you need. *Anything*."

"First," I said, holding out the tiny camera. "Hold onto this, and guard it with your life. It's evidence. I'm going to be captured in...about five minutes, I'm guessing, and I can't risk them finding it on me. I'll come get it from you later."

He took the camera, holding it like a stick of nitroglycerin.

"If you're gonna be captured, how can you—"

I held up my hand. "Second. I need some things smuggled to me in my cell. Use the food service: have your guys in the cafeteria claim I need a special diet for medical reasons. Dr. Valentino's on our side; if anyone asks, he'll back the story up."

I gave him the list of what I needed. Brisco squinted at me.

"How is *that* gonna help?"

"Didn't you ever watch *MacGyver*? That guy could make bombs out of paper clips and chewing gum."

"Yeah, but...*you* aren't MacGyver."

I shook my head. "Oh ye of little faith. Just make sure I get everything on that list, and fast. Otherwise I'm a dead man—and you're next."

Outside the bathroom door, a klaxon wound up, screaming like a tornado siren.

"*This is a security lockdown,*" boomed a voice over a loud-speaker. "*Return to your cells immediately for counting and inspection. This is a security lockdown.*"

"You better go," I said. "I think that's my cue."

As prisoners scattered, rushing back to their cells, I took a leisurely stroll down to the gallery floor.

Just ahead, five black-masked riot guards moved in, closing in a semicircle. Tasers and batons at the ready, and one brandishing a Plexiglas shield.

I smiled and showed them my open hands.

"I believe you gentlemen are looking for me," I said, lacing my fingers behind my neck and sinking to my knees.

As rough, gloved hands wrenched my wrists back, cold shackles locking tight, I felt a moment of strange satisfaction. Sure, the odds were long. My first escape attempt had been a disaster and this one was likely to land me in an unmarked grave, but the situation wasn't all bad. At least I was able to cross one thing off my bucket list.

You know all those movies where the bad guy gets captured, but it turns out that was the key to his master plan all along?

Not gonna lie. I'd always wanted to do that.

35.

"**W**here is he?" Lancaster asked. He sat behind his desk, imperious, the office door closed and locked. I couldn't have jumped him if I wanted to, not with both wrists handcuffed to my chair. And not with Jablonski pacing the carpet behind me, openly carrying his pistol in a too-tight grip.

"Who?"

"O'Neill," Jablonski snapped.

"I'll repeat my question. Who?"

"The guard," Lancaster said, "who was supposed to escort you to the infirmary. An appointment you never arrived for. The guard who *vanished*."

"Oh," I said. "You mean the guard who said he'd smuggle me out of here, then weaseled out on the deal."

Jablonski was on me like a shot, pressing the barrel of his gun to my temple.

"You lyin' sack! O'Neill is a buddy of mine. He'd never do that!"

I inhaled through gritted teeth, fighting to keep my cool. The muzzle of the gun felt like ice against my skin, trembling in his grip.

"Check the visitor logs," I said. "My lawyer came to see me a few days ago. Brought me some paperwork."

"What of it?" Lancaster frowned.

"That was just a cover. He smuggled in cash for me. Twenty

grand in large bills, unmarked and nonsequential. Clean as fresh linen sheets."

The muzzle pressed harder, my head tilted so far to the side that my neck ached. I could feel Jablonski's finger tightening on the trigger.

"You're full of shit. You got strip-searched before you landed in Ad Seg. No way you were hiding twenty grand on you."

"Because it *wasn't* on me," I said. "It was hidden in Hive C, in the third-tier bathrooms. You know, where the surveillance camera has been busted for weeks."

Lancaster looked to Jablonski. "Is that true?"

He shrugged one shoulder. "I...I mean..."

"Is. That. True? Is there *another* broken camera on the grid that you haven't bothered reporting?"

"Yeah." Jablonski sagged. "Just haven't gotten around to fixing it yet, that's all. But that doesn't mean—"

Lancaster waved his hand, shooing him back. Slowly, reluctantly, the gun barrel fell away from my temple. I straightened up in my chair.

"It was sealed in a plastic bag," I told Lancaster, "and taped under the water-tank lid on one of the broken toilets. See, the first time I tried to break out of here, I didn't have time to retrieve it. I told O'Neill about the cash. He talked a good game, then he screwed me."

"Meaning?"

"He took me to Hive C, on a route that avoided most of the cameras. The *working* ones, anyway. I gave him the money, and he told me to wait there, hiding in plain sight with all the other cons. Said he'd come right back with a spare guard uniform and smuggle me out of the prison. Next thing I know, the alarm's going off and he's long gone."

Jablonski paced, frustrated, trying to break my story.

"But O'Neill didn't clock out!"

I squinted at him. "Why would he?"

Lancaster looked to Jablonski. "Did you check the employee lot? Is his car still here?"

"I think he carpools with somebody."

The warden slouched in his chair and stared up at the ceiling.

"Find out who, maybe? And pull security footage, see if we can spot a glimpse of him sneaking out."

"Boss, he's lying." The pistol swung in Jablonski's frustrated grip. "You know he's—"

Lancaster slammed his fist down on the desk.

"Goddamnit, Jablonski, stop waving that gun around! And use your head. Buddy of yours or not, twenty thousand dollars can induce a man to some ill-advised life choices. Believe you me, I've seen that before." He looked my way. "Now what *are* we gonna do with you?"

I shrugged.

"Well," I said, "the way I see it, you've got two options. You can let Jablonski here put a bullet in my head, or you can...I don't know, force me to compete in some kind of illegal prison gladiator fight? One way, you get money. The other, you get jack. I know what I'd pick if I was in your shoes."

Lancaster steepled his fingers, thinking it over. Then he chuckled and wagged his finger at me.

"Y'know, son, you gave us a pretty good show last night. Real David-and-Goliath action. The audience eats that stuff up. Too bad you pussied out at the end."

"I'll let you in on a little secret. Killing somebody yourself, with your own two hands, is a little harder than standing back and making somebody else do it at gunpoint. But you wouldn't know what that's like."

The warden's eyes narrowed.

"You might be surprised what I know and what I've done," he said.

I spread my open hands as far as the cuffs would let me and smiled.

"Well, hell, sounds like a challenge in the making! What do

you say, Warden? You and me, on the killing floor. Toe to toe. I'll even let you pick the weapons."

He snorted. "I don't think so, son. See, I've got this...beast of a man, two hundred and fifty pounds of solid muscle, and he's been cooling his heels in solitary for four months now. He was crazy when he went in, and he doesn't have a whole lot going on in his noggin anymore, but put a butcher knife in his hands and he turns into a world-class hibachi chef. Your ass is the steak, in case my metaphor ain't entirely clear."

"Sounds a little one-sided."

"Well, that depends on you," Lancaster said. "Do your time like a good boy and don't give my men any more trouble, and I'll send you onto the floor with an oiled-up chainsaw. Piss me off one more time? You get a butter knife."

"I think we understand each other," I said.

"Good." He turned to Jablonski. "Take him back to his cell. *In one piece*, too, no 'accidents' along the way. Mr. Faust here is gonna make us some money."

* * *

Back in solitary, I sat on the edge of my bunk. Waiting, hoping Brisco had held up his end of the deal. If he hadn't, I was good as dead.

I jumped up as my cell door rattled and the bottom slot opened. A plastic tray slid halfway in. I stopped it with the side of my foot.

"Supposed to be a special meal for me," I called out. "I have allergies."

Another slot slid open at chest height. Hard eyes, so dark brown they were nearly black, stared in at me.

"Nobody gets special meals in here," he grunted.

I clenched my hands at my sides. If Brisco couldn't follow through—

"*Check*," I said. "Dr. Valentino's orders. If I eat the wrong food, I'll be dead of anaphylactic shock by morning. Which means I can't fight. Which means Warden Lancaster's gonna lose a bundle of cash, and that'll be on *your* head."

The slot slammed shut. I waited, holding my breath.

The first tray pulled back under the door, replaced by a new one—dull orange plastic instead of brown.

I pulled the tray in, hustling to my bunk and resting it on my lap. My meal was a plastic single-serving cup of vanilla yogurt, a hunk of bread a little smaller than a billiard ball, and a carton of milk. I pinched the top of the bread and gave it a gentle pull.

It gave way. The chunk of bread was nothing but a hollow shell of crust, its innards scooped out to make a perfect hiding place. Inside, a small tuft of steel wool and a nine-volt battery were waiting for me. I snatched my treasures and stashed them under the bunk.

Once I'd eaten, I kept the yogurt container too, along with its carefully peeled foil lid. When I passed the empty tray back through the slot, the guard either didn't notice or didn't care.

The convicts in Hive B only got one meal a day. Maybe out of petty sadism, probably just to save money. Either way, twenty-four hours with nothing but some yogurt and a crust of bread had my stomach growling. The next day brought the same meal but a different special delivery inside the hollowed-out bread: a razor blade, and two tiny travel-size bottles of baby oil. I stashed the goods and devoured the rest.

The hours dragged on, and on, and on. The light in my cell never turned off, not for an instant, and the only way to tell the time was the delivery of my next meal. I attacked the bread crusts like a rabid dog; after four days, my stomach was tied in knots.

Trying to pass the time with exercise ended fast when a string of energetic sit-ups pummeled me with a blossoming headache and a wave of nausea that sent me running for the stainless-steel toilet. I figured rest had to be good for a concussion. So I rested. I lay on the bunk, and sometimes I stared at the eggshell-white ceiling and sometimes I closed my eyes. When I was exhausted, I slept. When I wasn't, I hungered.

On the fifth day, like the fourth, a fistful of tiny yellow salt packets from the cafeteria filled the hollow crust. That and a little bundle of twine, like the kind the prisoners in Hive C used to kite messages from cell to cell.

I had everything I needed.

And I only had a few hours left before they'd call me back down to the killing floor.

Now I welcomed the hunger. I let the want, the empty ache, course through my bruised and aching muscles and flood my bone marrow with its bitter pangs. I sat down with the razor blade and the twine, slicing the coarse thread into small, even pieces.

I finished my preparations. Then I took off one shoe, wore it over my hand, and smashed its rubber sole against the light as hard as I could. The wire cage rattled but held fast. Another hit and it started to buckle.

By the sixth hit, the wire was dented and deformed, pressed right up against the square of light. I reached back, turning my face away from the glow, and threw another punch. The light broke with a sound like a china plate shattering on concrete, and plunged my cell into pitch darkness.

36.

The chest-height slot in my cell door slid open. Piggish eyes peered in at me, the guard's face silhouetted by the light outside.

"You gotta be kidding me," Jablonski said.

"Light just went out," I said, crouching in the dark.

He shook his head. "You think I'm *that* stupid? Oh, sure, lemme just walk into a dark cell and get jumped. You think you're the first con to try and pull that trick?"

"Wow," I said. "Guess you're just too smart for me."

"Forget you. You can sit in the dark and rot. You're gonna die tonight anyway."

The slot slammed shut, bathing me in perfect darkness. I stayed crouched, counting down slow from twenty, making sure he wasn't coming back. Then I felt my way around the cell. I'd trained myself with my eyes closed, rehearsing how to retrieve my hidden contraband by touch alone.

Showtime.

* * *

Jablonski came back a few hours later with another guard in tow.

"Come up to the door," he barked through the slot. "Lace your hands behind your head. Warden says I can't kill you, but I've got fifty thousand volts for your ass if you try anything stupid."

I obliged. In fact, I all but jumped out to join them the second the door swung open.

"Hey, guys!" I gushed, beaming. "Is it time to fight now? Can I? Can I, huh?"

They both looked at me like I'd grown a second head, but I kept up the patter while Jablonski's partner shackled me.

"C'mon, buddy," I said, "hurry up, will ya? I've been looking forward to this all week. I've got some brand-new moves and everything!"

"Solitary," Jablonski said to his buddy, twirling his finger next to his ear and rolling his eyes. I hummed the tune to "Eye of the Tiger" and bounced as we walked.

We paused halfway down the stairs as Jablonski corralled another guard. I recognized this one: Vasquez, one of the guards we'd taken hostage on our first escape attempt. From the scowl on his face, he recognized me too.

"Hey," Jablonski said, "get up to cell four-forty-six and fix the light. This asshole smashed it."

Vasquez put his hands on his hips. "So? Let him sit in the dark."

"It ain't *for* him. It's for the next prisoner who gets put in there, after this guy bites it tonight." Jablonski shot me a glare. "I've lost enough money on you already."

"That's because you bet against me last time." I gave him a cheerful smile. "Don't make that mistake tonight. I might just surprise you."

A jaunty jazz tune rose up from the floor below as the piano and bass duo started to swing. We walked down the corrugated metal steps while waiters flitted from table to table and lit votive candles in ornate glass sconces. A tiny sea of pinprick lights at the edge of the killing floor. They'd rolled out the wet bar, and the first guests were already arriving, dressed for a five-star evening, arm in arm and sharing soft laughter.

I lined up with the other ragged-looking prisoners. A pair of socialites strolled past, sizing us up, discussing their brochures for the night's festivities. They talked about us like you might talk about a horse in a race or a pedigree show dog. Not like human beings.

My hatred and my hunger became one, simmering in my gut. I wasn't a man anymore. I was a shark on two legs, and I smelled blood.

"Warden," I said as Lancaster strolled past. He paused in the middle of glad-handing one of his guests and came my way.

"Faust. Nice to see you made it five days without another escape attempt."

I stared at his throat.

"Does that mean I get the chainsaw tonight?"

His brow furrowed. "You seem...eager."

"Well," I said, "I've had *all week* to think about killing someone. I can't wait. Put me in the first fight?"

He took a half step back. He knew something was wrong, I could see it in his eyes, but he didn't have a clue what it was or where to start looking.

"Maybe," he said and turned on his heel. More new arrivals to greet.

The seats filled in, and the champagne flowed. I stared into the crowd, marking faces, burning the ones I didn't recognize from television or the news into my memory. All the while, a hot and nervous tingle grew in the pit of my stomach. It was the anticipation of violence, the feeling of staring down a cocked fist or a loaded gun. That queasy sensation that came from knowing blood was about to spill.

Lights from the guard tower strobed behind the smoky glass, signaling it was time to begin. The sound system crackled and hummed as Lancaster took up his microphone.

"Ladies, gentlemen, welcome! We have a great show for you tonight. A banquet of thrills and excitement you just can't get anywhere else. Well...anywhere *legal*, anyway."

He paused, wrapped in a smug smile, as the audience tittered. Then he gestured toward me. Jablonski grabbed my shoulder, tugging me out in front of the crowd. Behind us, waiters rolled the weapon racks into place, teasing the crowd with promises of the carnage to come.

"Our first fighter tonight," Lancaster said, "is last week's returning long shot, Daniel Faust. Can this one-time winner beat the odds and survive another night on the killing floor?"

Jablonski unlocked my shackles. I slowly flexed my freed wrists, staring him in the eye. As applause rippled through the room, Lancaster cupped his palm over his microphone and leaned in to murmur in my ear.

"You just remember, son: I've got two men up in that tower, ready and willing to put a high-velocity round right through you. Don't try anything dumb. Give us a good show and you *might* live another week or two."

He started to move away, thought about it, and leaned in once more.

"And if by some remote chance you actually win this match? Do me a favor: make the kill good and messy this time. That's what these people paid to see."

"That's a promise," I told him.

Jablonski walked over to fetch my opponent from the lineup, while the warden strolled back and forth in front of the crowd.

"If you thought last week was a one-sided matchup, you ain't seen nothing yet. Let's meet Faust's opponent. He's racked up a legendary five wins, and that's nothing compared to his kill count before he came to—"

"I've got an announcement to make," I called out.

Lancaster paused, almost stumbling as I threw him off his patter. He glared over his shoulder at me.

"Hey, it's good news," I told him, then turned to the crowd. "The warden's right. It's going to be a great show tonight. Let me ask you people, do you like violence?"

A scattering of catcalls. So many eager, smiling faces in the candlelight. I grinned and spread my arms, playing the showman.

"I knew it. And how about blood? Do you like *blood?*"

Applause now, and someone in the back hooted. Lancaster

held the microphone, mute, as if he wasn't sure if he should interrupt me or not.

"I can't hear you, people! Make some noise if you want a good show. How about *death?* Do you wanna see lots and *lots* of death tonight?"

I took in the applause, the hollering, the hammering feet, basking in it.

Then my arm shot up, pointing one finger to the ceiling.

The guard-tower window exploded.

A man plummeted from the tower, slamming on the concrete floor behind me with a *splat* like someone stomping on a tomato. He'd been torn open from throat to groin, his chest a ragged ruin of splintered, wrenched-back ribs and mangled organs. His dead eyes were still open, jaw wrenched wide in terror.

Then came the rain. The second sniper, one piece at a time. Hands. Feet. Arms, wrenched off at the elbows. His severed head bounced like a basketball as it hit the concrete, rolling across the floor and coming to a stop next to Warden Lancaster's Italian leather shoe.

A horrified silence fell across the room. The guards looked at one another, uncertain, hands on their guns but not sure if they should draw. Lancaster stared down at the severed head, frozen like a deer in the headlights.

"Well," I said, "you're about to get everything you asked for. What do you think, Warden? Is this good and messy enough for you? Wouldn't want you to think I 'pussied out' again."

His gaze snapped toward me. He took a halting step back, away from the carnage. "How? How did you—"

A third body dove from the shattered window. Not in a guard's uniform, but a billowing white leather coat. She landed as graceful as a raptor, absorbing the impact with one knee and the outstretched fingers of a single hand, and slowly rose to her full willowy height. Her eyes blazed like molten copper, as radiant as her twist of scarlet hair.

"If anyone in this room believes themselves to be a righteous soul," Caitlin said, "I suggest you kneel down and pray. If nobody answers...then you belong to *me*."

37.

H ours earlier, alone in the dark, I had set about my work.
I needed candles, and cigarettes wouldn't do this time.
So I crafted my own. The disposable yogurt cups made a fine sub-
stitute; instead of wax, I filled each one—five in all—with baby oil.
Lengths of oil-dipped twine made crude but workable wicks, and I
carefully replaced the plastic cups' foil covers before punching a
tiny hole and running the twine down the middle.

I didn't have matches or a lighter, but I had a little steel wool
from the kitchens and a nine-volt battery. I knelt down on the
cold cell floor, rubbing the wool against the battery's terminals
like a Boy Scout trying to make fire with sticks. The steel wool
glowed Halloween orange in the dark. With a spark, the first can-
dlewick caught fire.

Soon there were five dancing lights, the candles laid out on the
floor of my cell in the shape of a five-pointed star. Next came the
salt, poured in a thin but unbroken circle. I painted glyphs in salt,
twisted signs and seals I knew by heart.

"I invoke and conjure you by sigil and name," I whispered. "I
conjure by the ministers of the Tartarean seat, by fallen powers
and principalities, by broken thrones and dominions. I speak with
the authority of the kings in the outer dark. My words will be
heard; my words will be heeded."

The circle and seals glowed in my second sight, rippling with a
cold blue fire. I extended a finger over the salt, gripping the razor
blade in my other hand. One quick shallow slice, one jolt of burn-

ing pain, and my fingertip turned scarlet. Blood dripped down, slow and steady, splashing onto the concrete.

"The elements are overthrown," I hissed, rocking forward and back on my knees as my blood fed the hungry magic. "The air is fire; the sea is dust. At the end of all things, I call to you. In the last of all places, I call to you. I conjure you by your name: *Caitl-leanabruadi!*"

The air erupted in a silent shock wave that hit me like a fist, knocking me flat. It was a sonic boom with no sound, a blinding flash of hot black light that killed the flickering candles. I sat up, rubbing my eyes.

In the center of the bloody circle, a figure rose. Slowly melting up from the floor, it twisted and writhed in the shadows. I made out arms ending in clutching iron claws. The horns of a ram. A guttural voice boomed from the dark.

"Who has disturbed my slumber?"

I had just enough time to panic, to realize I'd botched the ritual somehow, before the figure launched itself at me.

I blinked, lying sprawled on my back. Caitlin perched on top of me, human, grinning. She rubbed the tip of her nose against mine.

"Gotcha," she said.

Then she kissed me, long and slow, the pounding drumbeat of my heart melting from anxiety to raw heat.

"I'm looking for a damsel in distress," she said. "Seen any around?"

I wriggled my fingers. "Right here."

She took my hand, her warm fingers twining around mine, and pulled me up.

"I have to say," she observed, "I've been summoned under strange circumstances...but I've never been *tactically* summoned."

"I wish you could do that to me. Would have made breaking out of here so much easier."

My hands slid around the slick waist of her white leather coat.

One of hers closed on my shoulder, the other stroking the back of my neck as she pulled me close.

"True," she murmured in my ear, "but this way is much more fun. So what are we up against? Bentley just gave me the abridged version. And Naavarasi's been leaving voicemails for me, crowing about how you owe her a favor. That doesn't please me."

"The feeling's mutual. Long story short, the warden and his staff are lining their pockets by running gladiator games for the amusement of the idle rich, and I'm on tonight's fight ticket."

"Hrm. Think I would have known about something like this happening in my father's territory. None of my kind are involved?"

I shook my head. "Nope, and I haven't picked up on a glimmer of magical power. No demons, no mages, just garden-variety criminals with big ambitions. And big guns, including a sniper's nest or two. They won't go down without a fight."

"If they did, I'd be bored. But how did this happen in the first place? Bentley and Corman barely made sense. You were arrested the night I left, but everyone thought you were in prison for months?"

"That's where it gets complicated," I said. "The Chicago Outfit got me arrested in the first place; it's a frame job, to get me out of the way while they make their bid for Vegas."

"I heard." She frowned. "Nicky's a fugitive, and nobody's seen the twins either...not that anybody is looking for them. We've all been searching for Jennifer, but nobody has any idea where she's gone."

"I know, I think she's in big trouble. There's a guy in here, a Calles banger named Raymundo—I think he knows where she is, but he wouldn't tell me."

"No worries," she said. "He *will* tell me."

I held her, keeping her close, savoring every second of her warmth and the scent of her musky perfume. Her eyes glowed faintly in the dark, swirling with motes of copper light.

"Anyway," I said, "the Outfit's not our biggest problem."

I walked her through it, from the curse that left everyone with memories of a trial that never happened, to my hallucination in Buddy's cell of a ravaged Las Vegas.

"So this Fleiss woman..." Caitlin's voice trailed off as she thought it over.

"She orchestrated it for her boss: this 'Enemy,' the man with the Cheshire smile, whoever he is. *Whatever* he is. As far as I can tell, this scam wasn't about me at all. They just needed a patsy who they could swap into the 'Thief's' place, so someone else would die in here instead of him. I was on their radar because I'd just pulled that heist in Chicago for them. Once they heard I'd been arrested, well, you couldn't ask for a better stooge. They needed somebody behind bars, and there I was."

"They rewrote people's memories on a massive scale, Daniel. Like some sort of...mental contagion. I don't know anyone who can *do* that." Her voice, already soft, dropped to a whisper. "I don't even think my *father* can do that."

"And it sounds like they're just getting warmed up. At least I got Buddy out of here. If he can deliver his message to the right person, they've got a shot at stopping whatever the Enemy's got planned." I shook my head. "His twin sister told me I shouldn't get in the way. Seems I'm not 'the chosen one,' so I don't have a chance of standing up to this guy."

Caitlin's fingertips trailed along the nape of my neck. She studied me, eyes glittering.

"Oh? And what do *you* say?"

"Sweetheart, in the last two weeks I've been abducted, cut off from everyone I love, and left to rot in a prison cell. I've been beaten, tortured, starved, and I've got bruises in places I didn't think you could *get* bruises, all so the Enemy could hand somebody a get-out-of-jail-free card."

I leaned in. Our lips brushed. As I pulled away, her rising smile mirrored my own.

"*Fuck* being the chosen one," I said. "I say we track this asshole down and wreck his world."

"The Enemy," Caitlin mused. "He chose his name well. If he intends to wreak destruction upon my prince's territory—*my territory*—then he's made himself an enemy of humanity and hell alike. We should teach him the consequences of hubris."

"Good idea. Let's rescue Jennifer, push the Outfit out of Vegas, and then we can go hunting."

Caitlin glanced back toward the cell door.

"First, though," she said, "we do have the slight matter of your escape to attend to. Which reminds me: Bentley sent along a present for you."

She held up a deck of cards. Cherry-red Bicycle dragon backs, my usual brand, glistening with enchantment and the residue of exotic oils. I opened my palm. The cards leaped through the air in a stream, riffling into my hand, eager to play.

I slipped the deck up my sleeve.

"Perfect," I said. "Bentley and Corman should be on their way with a getaway van. I don't see any way of slipping out of here quietly, so assume we'll be setting off a few alarms on our way out. That means we'll have to deal with roadblocks on I-80. Don't worry, I've got a plan for that. Think you can take care of our sniper problem?"

She cracked her knuckles and smiled.

"Just one thing," I said, "Warden Lancaster. *Don't* kill him. I assume he'll run for it when the blood starts to spill, and that's good. Let him think he got away."

"*Don't* kill him?" she echoed. "Why on earth not?"

In the dark, I stared grimly over Caitlin's shoulder. Toward the door.

"Because I've got a plan for him, too. And he's not getting off that easy."

38.

My eagerness, when the guards came to get me, was a smoke screen. I didn't want them looking too deep into my cell, noticing the woman crouched in the farthest, darkest corner. Waiting, patient as a cobra.

When they brought me down to the arena floor, lining me up with the other prisoners, I had a pretty good view up toward my cell. I got to see Vasquez trundling over with a toolbox, opening the door—and the hand that clamped over his wrist, hauling him into the darkness before he could scream for help.

Not long after, I glimpsed the spidery shadow that skittered across the ceiling of the hive high above our heads. Clinging to the concrete, making her way toward the guard tower.

Soon the bodies rained down, terrifying the crowd into a petrified, confused silence. And then Caitlin joined the party.

I'd been running the numbers. Seven guards spaced out along the gallery floor, plus Lancaster with his long-barreled .45. Maybe fifty people in the audience, and more than a few bodyguard types with conspicuous bulges under their tailored jackets. Lousy odds, and I knew I should be worried.

But as time stood still, like the arc of a roller coaster as it crests that first hill and gets ready to plunge, a strange, giddy elation washed over me.

"Lover," Caitlin said.

I looked to her. She threw back one side of her coat, like a gunslinger at high noon. Her fingers traced the brass handle of the coiled black bullwhip on her belt.

Then she smiled, and whispered, "*Dance with me*."

A guard went for his weapon while the deck of cards dropped from my sleeve. Two cards whipped through the air as his pistol boomed. One flew between him and Caitlin, catching a bullet in its heart, and the other sliced open his throat from ear to ear.

Caitlin's bullwhip lashed down upon the concrete, rippling with hellfire, and the crowd—screaming now, realizing this wasn't part of the show—knocked over tables and fell over each other scrambling to get away. I hit the ground, rolling, a stray bullet whining over my head, and snatched up the dead guard's piece. Jablonski was right next to him, swinging his gun around to drop a bead on me. I jumped up from a crouch, grabbed his gun's muzzle, put my barrel up against his wrist, and pulled the trigger.

Jablonski shrieked as his wrist blew apart, shattered bones jutting through a ragged, gushing hole. I kept hold of the muzzle as I turned, using him as a human shield, and emptied my clip into the closest guard. Then I dropped the gun, yanked his away, and used that one instead, cracking off two quick shots at a bodyguard who felt like playing hero. I missed, but he hunkered down behind a flipped-over table, pinned down for a second.

One of the spectators I recognized—the golf pro—went sliding past me. He was on the ground, Caitlin's whip coiled around his throat and his body engulfed in devouring flames as she reeled him in like a prize fish.

Rule number one in a gunfight: stop moving and you're dead. I ran straight for the tables, snapping off wild shots on the go, and jumped. My shoe hit the edge of the capsized cocktail table, sending me up and over, and I put three rounds into the bodyguard's panicked face. I landed hard on the other side, bullets chipping into the wood behind me and chewing away the improvised cover one chunk at a time.

I pulled the trigger again, hammer slapping down on an empty chamber, and threw the empty gun aside. The bodyguard's piece, still clutched in his cold hand, was a sleek nine-millimeter in blue chrome. I snatched it up and sprang out of hiding before the guards could flank me. Too slow: ten feet away, one of Jablonski's buddies had me dead to rights, sighting me down his barrel like a pro target shooter. Then Caitlin's free hand flung up and a silver dagger, long and thin and gleaming like a needle, whistled through the air and buried itself four inches in his ear.

Another guard burst from the guard tower door, smart enough to go for the big guns. He clutched a pump-action shotgun, aiming it for Caitlin's back. I sent a handful of cards flying. The shotgun roared and the cards dropped, taking the hit for her. She spun, crouching, and her whip cracked as it coiled around his ankle and yanked him off his feet just before his flesh ignited.

Over the screams, over the crackling of flames and gunfire, Caitlin's delighted laughter rang out. Her wild grin mirrored mine as we went back-to-back, picking off the last of Lancaster's men. The audience had fled, a screaming mob headed for the security gates, desperate to escape.

At last, silence.

Corpses littered the killing floor, sprawled across overturned tables and chairs, some riddled with bullets and some charred black. Caitlin casually flicked her wrist, calling her whip back and quenching the flames, then coiled it around her bent elbow. I leaned against her, and she nuzzled my shoulder as we both caught our breaths.

"We should do this more often," she murmured.

Strained whimpers caught my ear. I turned. Jablonski knelt in a pool of his own blood, clutching the ruin of his wrist.

"Oh, we're not finished just yet," I told her.

I walked over and nudged Jablonski with my shoe.

"Hey. Asshole. Get up."

He looked up at me, tears streaming from his squinting eyes. "Just kill me already. Just *do* it."

"Changed my mind. I'm not gonna kill you," I said. "Not if you do everything I say. I need you. I have to get back into Hive C. What's the best way to do that?"

"Th-the whole place is gonna be locked down by now. Automatic fail-safe if the alarms go off."

I pressed the barrel of my gun to his forehead.

"And that fail-safe can be deactivated by..."

"Central—central security. They've got overrides for the entire prison."

"Do they have eyes on this place? Security cameras?"

"No, they're blind when it comes to Hive B. The warden puts most of the new guards in there, the ones we aren't sure we can trust yet. All they'll know is a riot alarm went off and they should call for help from the highway patrol."

"Good. On your feet. You're gonna take us there."

Klaxons droned through the deserted halls, every loudspeaker blaring a warning. Jablonski stumbled ahead of us, squeezing his wrist to try and stop the bleeding as he led the way. The stampede of escaping spectators had left us an open path.

"They'll be buttoned up in there," he whined. "It's like a panic room; nobody gets in or out when the alarms sound."

"Let me worry about that," Caitlin told him.

The door to central security looked like solid steel, the only opening a tiny window laced with reinforced wire. Caitlin waved us back, out of sight. Then she ran to the door and hammered on it, twisting her face into a mask of raw panic.

"Help," she cried, "I'm all alone out here. You have to let me in!"

I heard a muffled refusal from the other side.

"There are prisoners everywhere," Caitlin begged. "You can't let them get me, you can't! *Please!*"

After a moment's hesitation, the lock clicked.

Caitlin barged in. I was right behind her, shoving Jablonski and using him for a shield, one hand on his collar and one on the gun. On the other side, one guard lay on the thin blue carpet, knocked flat by the swinging door. Another two stood by a bank of controls and security monitors that ran the length of the far wall.

One went for his pistol. I put mine to Jablonski's head.

"Uh-uh. You do, he dies."

He was loyal enough, or dumb enough, to freeze. Caitlin moved fast, stripping the three guards' weapons and herding them into one corner of the room. I studied the grainy black-and-white monitor feeds, trying to get eyes on Raymundo.

"A few days ago," I said, "there was a riot in the yard. A few Calles bangers got sent to solitary. They still in there?"

"I...I think so," one of the guards said. "I'm not sure."

"And how do I get in there?"

"Y-you can't. Not from here, I mean. Ad Seg is all manual. They never updated the cell doors."

"Okay," I said, taking a step back and rubbing my chin. "So what you're telling me is all the *other* cell doors *can* be controlled from here?"

Nobody answered. I put my thumb on the hammer of my gun and cocked it back. A meaningless gesture on most modern pistols, but thanks to Hollywood it got the point across.

"I've got four hostages here, and I only need *one*. If I don't have an answer in five seconds, we start making staff cuts."

"There are overrides for evacuation," one said, "in case of a fire. We can open up everything from here. The security gates, individual cells, everything."

"Well then," I told him, "you'd best get to it."

He approached the console like a zookeeper walking into a lion's cage. His fingers trembled as they touched the keys.

"Go on," I said.

Ten seconds of rattling keys, the flip of a switch, and the wall of monitors flickered to life. All across the prison, locks disengaged and doors glided open as one. I saw tilted heads and curious faces peeping from their cells, and nervous-looking guards walking fast as they chattered into walkie-talkies.

"You're crazy," Jablonski breathed. "Do you even know what you just did?"

I gestured to a microphone at the end of the console. "Is that a PA system? Turn it on. I want to make a prison-wide broadcast."

The guard obliged. I cleared my throat and leaned in over the mic. As I spoke, I heard a popping squeal and my own voice echoing back from loudspeakers outside.

"Good evening, Eisenberg Correctional. This is your new warden speaking. You may have noticed that every single door in the prison has just opened. This is in keeping with our new 'leave whenever you want' policy. We fully encourage you to explore this exciting new option! Also, for your information, the guards have been complicit in a scheme to orchestrate inmates' deaths for profit, and you outnumber them by about fifty to one."

I clicked off the intercom and looked at Jablonski.

"No, *that's* crazy."

39.

"**W**ait," one of the guards said, looking from me to Jablonski. "*Deaths?* What the hell?"

"No time to explain." I grabbed Jablonski's collar and dragged him backward. "But I suggest you gentlemen barricade yourselves in here. And don't open the door for *anybody* until the highway patrol moves in."

Caitlin took one of the purloined guns and aimed at the console. Bullets blasted metal and chewed wiring, round after round until she'd emptied the clip. Now they wouldn't be locking the place back up once we left. She gave the pistol a disdainful glance and tossed it to the floor.

"C'mon," Jablonski said, "let me stay in here with them. I did what you wanted!"

"Not done with you just yet," I told him. "Besides, that wrist looks pretty bad, and you're awfully pale. If I left you in here, you'd probably die from blood loss before help came. What kind of a guy would I be if I let that happen? *Move.*"

As we approached the doors to Hive C, walking past access gate after open, abandoned access gate, I heard the muffled sounds of war whoops and gunfire. Freed from their cages, the locals seemed more interested in tearing the prison down and settling old scores than trying to escape.

The unlocked double doors opened onto pandemonium. Corpses littered the floor, some guards but mostly prisoners, the first casualties of the riot. The gallery floor was a free-for-all, shiv-swinging inmates tearing at each other in a brutal melee while others tried to hammer down the watchtower doors. The guards in the tower treated the hive like a shooting gallery, crowded up in their perch and raining down fire as fast as they could reload. The air stank of fresh blood and gun smoke.

We kept to the sidelines, moving low and fast, trying to stay out of the snipers' sight. I hoped they might hold back if they saw Jablonski, but I didn't want to test that theory. As we hustled for the stairs, a skinhead launched from an open cell door and threw himself onto Caitlin.

She didn't give him time to regret it. Looking vaguely annoyed, like she'd just found a mosquito on her arm, she shot out her hand. Her index and middle finger punched into his eye sockets, two knuckles deep. She flung him to the concrete, striding past his shrieking, thrashing body without a second glance and flicking blood from her fingertips.

Jablonski stared back over his shoulder as I nudged him along. His eyes bulged.

"How the hell...who *are* you people?"

"She's the right hand of a demon prince," I told him, "and I'm her boyfriend. Probably should have found that out before you blasted me with a fire hose, huh?"

"He did *what?*" Caitlin said.

"Aw, it's okay." I gave Jablonski a shove, getting him moving up the corrugated metal stairs. "I can let bygones be bygones. Besides, I promised I wouldn't kill him if he did what I told him to."

We found Brisco a couple of tiers up, surrounded by his boys and with his T-shirt and uniform slacks drenched in blood. Most of it, except for a nasty-looking gash across one beefy bicep, wasn't his. Judging from the trail of bodies he'd left in his wake, most of them tattooed with Calles ink, the guards had gotten that race war they wanted after all.

"Nutty thought," I said, "but maybe you should think about getting out of here while you can."

He shrugged. "Where am I gonna go?"

"Fair enough. You didn't happen to see Raymundo, did you? I need a word with him."

"Nah," Brisco glanced over his shoulder. "He's still in the hole. At least until me and the boys pay him a little visit."

"Me first. You got my camera?"

He slapped it into my palm. A little worse for wear, a little sticky, but the memory card was intact.

"What about him?" one of Brisco's entourage asked, glaring at Jablonski. They *all* were, actually. He wasn't a popular man.

I pretended to think about it.

"Well, here's the thing. I promised I wouldn't kill him if he did everything I told him to, and he did." I patted Jablonski on the back. "So I guess here's where we part ways. Nice seeing ya, buddy."

"Wait," Jablonski said, his head on a swivel as he backed up against the guardrail. "You can't leave me here!"

"Sure I can. Look, all you have to do is make it from here to the exit by yourself. It's not like you went out of your way to give every man in here a reason to hate you, right? What do you think, Brisco? What are his odds?"

Brisco slapped his fist into his open palm.

"Not good."

Jablonski tried to run. He made it two, maybe three steps before they fell on him. Then it was all fists and feet and strangled pleading, and we left Brisco and his boys to their revenge.

As we hustled down the stairs, Caitlin took her phone from her coat pocket.

"Yes," she said, then fell silent for a moment. "*I'm* breaking Daniel out of prison, Emma. What are *you* doing? And I'm hoping the answer is 'the quarterly financial reports' because they were due last Thursday."

She looked sidelong at me as we ran, listening to the quick, almost frantic chatter on the other end of the line, and mouthed "*unbelievable.*"

"Oh. *Oh*. Well, that is useful information. Thank you, dear. Yes, yes, you're terribly thoughtful and I couldn't have a better best friend. Yes, we'll have to do a—"

A con with a bloody spike in his grip charged at us, shrieking like a madman. Caitlin's free hand clamped down over his face. She wrenched his head sideways, his neck breaking with a sharp *snap*, and let his corpse drop to the concrete.

"—a girls' night out when I get back," she said. "But right now I really need to focus on the task at hand. I'll call you."

"Problem?" I asked as she slipped the phone back into her coat.

"You could say that. Apparently somebody had a bit more political pull than we anticipated. They're not sending the highway patrol." She kicked open a swinging door, leading us out of the hive, away from the chaos. "The governor has just deployed the national guard."

"Tell me you're kidding."

"Emma's watching the live news coverage," she said, "which spread impossibly fast. They're selling this riot as an organized terrorist attack, carried out by prisoners with extremist Muslim sympathies. Allegedly the guards have been rounded up and their captors—who have a bomb—have been calling all the cable networks to issue demands."

I shook my head. "That's insane. There's nothing remotely like that going on here. Who's making the phone calls?"

"Well-paid actors, I'd imagine. We're witnessing a contingency plan in action, Daniel. This isn't Rehabilitation Dynamics protecting their investment; this is Warden Lancaster, or one of his celebrity guests, covering their tracks. I guarantee that 'bomb' is going to go off in Hive B, just as the military prepares to roll in."

"Wiping out the evidence," I said. "Since we opened all the doors, I can't imagine any of the prisoners in there are still hanging around, but nobody will believe them. It'll be their word against Lancaster and his staff."

"We need to leave. Now. No telling how much time we have before the Guard arrives."

We paused at a junction in the corridor. The alarm screamed over a loudspeaker, reverberating with my throbbing head.

"We can't," I said, "not yet. Jennifer's in trouble out there, and Raymundo's the best lead we have. We *have* to get the truth out of him."

Caitlin wrinkled her nose, but she didn't argue. The Ad Seg wing wasn't far, just down a short flight of concrete steps painted with a long yellow line. The air in solitary was dank and cold, smelling like old mothballs. A duty log at an abandoned guard station told us which faceless cell was Raymundo's, and they'd been kind enough to leave their keys behind.

The door rattled, swinging open onto darkness. Raymundo had been getting the same treatment I had: he huddled, naked and shivering, in a puddle of frigid water.

"I don't have a lot of time," I told him, "and I'm a lot more interested in saving my own neck than getting payback, so I'll make this real easy. Tell us where Jennifer is, and we'll leave you alone. Hell, I'll even leave the door open behind me and give you a shot at escaping. *Talk.*"

He spat something in Spanish, and it didn't sound like the information I wanted.

"Time is real short here," I said, "and soon I'm gonna have to stop asking nice. Look, just cooperate and we can both win today."

"JJ's probably dead by now," he said, leering in the dark. "Yeah, that *puta* is dead and buried in a shallow ditch—"

Caitlin brushed past me without a word. She grabbed Raymundo by the throat and slammed him up against the wall.

"I'm going to torture you now," she said and snapped his index finger.

She didn't ask questions. She just pinned him in place and kept breaking bones, one joint at a time, his finger crackling like a broken wineglass under his shrill screams. Then she stopped.

"You have ten seconds," she said, "before the pain resumes. This is your window of opportunity to speak. Once the pain resumes, however, it will not stop until another finger is crushed. You will then be allowed another ten seconds' grace to reconsider before I move on to the third finger. We will continue in this fashion until you have told us where our friend is, or your hand is irreversibly mutilated. Daniel?"

I blinked.

"My phone," she said with a nod, "is vibrating. Answer that, would you?"

I reached into her pocket and took the phone. I decided to answer it outside. As I crossed the threshold, stepping out into the light, I heard Caitlin say, "Ten."

Then the screaming started. I cupped my hand over the phone.

"Caitlin's a little busy right now."

"Daniel!" Bentley said. "Oh, thank heavens you're all right. The riot is all over the news—"

"Yeah, don't worry, there's no terrorists and no bomb. That whole story's bogus."

"The National Guard response, however, is not. Cormie and I are on our way. We, er, 'acquired' a local news van. We're about ten minutes away, and the first Guard trucks are *five* minutes behind us. I have no idea how they mobilized so quickly. I-80's already been shut down in both directions, and there's no way out of Aberdeen without a full-vehicle search."

Behind me, the screaming devolved into broken sobs.

"We'll be ready for you," I said.

"Oh good. Do be prompt, please. We're trying to get you out of prison, not all land *inside* one."

I hung up, went back into the cell, and gave Caitlin her phone back. She stood over Raymundo, arms folded and looking pleased with herself. He huddled in the corner and let out a ragged whimper, his tear-streaked face turned away from the light coming in through the open doorway.

"I got creative while you were out," Caitlin said. "Fingers just weren't getting the message across."

"Please," Raymundo sobbed, "just keep her away from me. I'll tell you whatever you want to know."

"That was fast," I said.

Caitlin shrugged. "I can be *very* creative."

40.

"It was all Cesar's idea," Raymundo said. "See, this whole alliance between the Calles and JJ? That was Gabriel, our boss. Cesar, he's second on the totem pole. He figured our cut was way too small, said that bitch should have been working *for* us, not as an equal partner."

"Call my friend a bitch," I told him, "*one* more time."

He flinched.

"Few weeks ago, Cesar's shooting dice with a guy who knows a guy, and they get to talking. I guess these heavy dudes from Chicago have been putting out feelers, trying to move into Vegas, and they were looking for friendly faces."

"So Cesar figured he'd sell out Jennifer, stab Gabriel in the back, and join forces with the Chicago Outfit," I said.

"First time we talked in the yard, man, I was tellin' the truth. All I knew was she'd gone missing. Then Cesar called me and filled me in. He's got a whole crew of Calles who are sick of Gabriel's crap. They're all gonna jump ship and throw in with Chicago."

"And Jennifer?" Caitlin asked. "Where is she?"

"I don't know."

Caitlin uncrossed her arms.

"I *swear*," Raymundo said, pressing his back to the wall. "All I know is she's got all kinds of shit locked up in her head. Like where all her grow houses are at, all the people on her payroll, and she's got, like, stacks of cash stashed in a Cayman Island bank account, but only she knows the account number and the pass-code. Cesar wants *all* of it before they cap her."

My jaw clenched. They wouldn't be getting that information out of her by asking politely.

"If they've hurt one hair on her head—" I started. Raymundo shook his head, panicked.

"No, no, man, it ain't that easy. You—you know. You can't make that *chica* bleed, man. Shit gets freaky when she's around blood. Her own or anybody else's." He crossed himself with his good hand. "That shit's *el diablo*. Ain't nobody with any sense gonna take a razor to her. She'll just laugh and spit poison at you. So Cesar talked to these Chicago guys, and they got a solution."

"Which is?"

He fell silent. His gaze flickered between Caitlin's cold eyes and the floor.

"Do I need to start counting to ten?" she asked him.

"All right, all right!" He winced. "Chicago's got this guy, they call him the Doctor. Pure fuckin' evil, man. Used to be CIA or something. They say he can get anything out of anybody, no prob-lem. Like he just looks in your eyes and *knows* how to break you. Cesar warned 'em about the blood thing, and they said it wasn't no big deal; the Doctor's got a hundred ways of hurting somebody without leaving a single mark."

"And this 'Doctor,' he's..." My hands curled into fists at my sides.

"He's on his way. I paid off one of the guards to smuggle a burner into solitary for me. Fucking thing shorted out when Jablonski gave me the fire-hose treatment, but I talked to Cesar last night. He said the Doctor and a bunch of Chicago heavies were getting in a car and driving out here for a meet-up. See, they can't fly with, uh, his...equipment. They'll be in Vegas any day now."

"And this meeting?" Caitlin asked. "Where will it be?"

"I don't know. God's honest truth, there's tons of places it could go down."

"This Cesar," I said, "he got a last name?"

"Gallegos. Cesar Gallegos. That's all I know. Swear to God, that's all I know."

Caitlin and I shared a glance.

"Shall I?" she asked.

"Nah," I said, "I think he's had enough for one day. Let's get moving. Time's not on our side here. Congrats, Raymundo, you get to live."

He had the most hopeful look on his face, right up until the moment I slammed the cell door behind me and locked it.

"But you're also staying in prison. And we'll make sure to let all your old Calles buddies know how you stabbed them in the back."

"Hey," he shouted from the other side. The stout door rattled. "Hey, you can't do me like that! *Hey!*"

"I think we just did," I said.

Caitlin nodded in agreement and gestured to the stairs. "Shall we?"

The front offices were a wasteland of overturned furniture and smashed windows, with the occasional body—inmate, guard, or too blood-soaked to tell the color of his uniform—littering the walkway. We headed out the same way I'd come in on my first day in prison, through the processing wing. All I could see was Jennifer's face.

We had a chance to save her. How slim, I didn't know, but we had a chance.

The stars shone down on a deserted tarmac. Floodlights from abandoned watchtowers cast random, desolate pools of light. The mass exodus of Warden Lancaster's "guests" and his smarter henchmen was long over; nobody wanted to go down with this ship. We stayed low as we ran, just in case, keeping to the shadows, but nobody stood in our way as we made our escape through wide-open gates.

A tinny horn beeped. Up ahead, a van parked by the roadside fired up its engine and cast headlight beams across the desert flats.

The side door, emblazoned with a Channel Five Eyewitness News logo, swooped open as we jogged up. Bentley waved us on board, while Corman looked back from the driver's seat.

"Cuttin' it close, kiddo," he said as he threw the van into gear.

I pulled Bentley into a hug with one arm, reaching out to squeeze Corman's shoulder with the other. I didn't have words just then. Bentley patted my back.

"We were unavoidably delayed," Caitlin said, glancing around the back of the van. It was windowless, lined with steel bins for storing camera equipment. She crouched down, perching on the raised wheel well, while I helped Bentley into the passenger seat up front.

"Yeah," I said, "good news is we have a lead on finding Jennifer. Bad news is, she's in deep trouble. We've gotta move, and fast."

As we drove, I filled them in on the details. We'd only gone a couple of miles down the road before blinding high beams washed across the van window. National Guard trucks, draped in camouflage green, roaring in the opposite direction. I counted five in all, followed by a parade of highway patrol cruisers painting the desert in red and blue light.

Nobody tried to stop us. All the same, I held my breath until we'd passed them.

"I-80's gonna be locked up tighter than Fort Knox," I said. "You're sure you can get this thing through a checkpoint?"

"Our press credentials are immaculate," Bentley said. "As is the vehicle registration. Paolo does exceptional work."

Aberdeen was thirty miles south, a sleepy little burg that more or less existed to give the prison staff a place to live and buy groceries. It was all trailer parks, churches, and bars with blue neon lights advertising longneck bottles of Budweiser long into the night. We navigated along a string of back roads, while I squinted at faded street signs.

"Up here," I said. "I think this is my stop."

Bentley handed me a grocery bag from Vons. A couple of plastic water bottles nestled inside, along with three slim energy bars in bright orange foil.

"It's not the gourmet meal you should have for a proper homecoming," he said, "but it'll tide you over."

"Not home yet." I hauled open the side door as the van rolled to a stop. "But I'll be there soon. Just have one last loose end to tie up."

Caitlin rose, and her fingers trailed down my shoulder.

"Be swift," she said.

"I will. And while I'm gone, do me a favor: get in touch with Pixie. We'll need her tech toys for this job. Tell her it's for Jennifer. Pix was a little freaked out in Chicago, and I don't think I earned any favors when I made her go home before we went after Damien Ecko, but I don't think she'll refuse if she knows Jen's in danger."

I squeezed the doorframe, wincing as a sharp wave of nausea hit me. It passed as suddenly as it arrived.

"Dan?" Corman asked, eyeing my grimace.

"And get Doc Savoy on standby," I said. "I'm fine. Don't worry. Just...better safe than sorry, right?"

They pretended to believe me, which was nice. I jumped out and scurried into the shadows, disappearing into the bushes behind a quiet ranch house.

41.

The sun rose over the sleepy streets of Aberdeen, warm light washing away the sirens and the chaos of the long and terrible night. Sitting behind an old walnut-stained desk in the back room of his house, Warden Lancaster sipped from a mug of coffee that read "World's Greatest Grandpa" on the side and pecked at his keyboard.

"Working from home today?" I asked, casually leaning against the doorframe.

He jumped. One hand shot under the desk.

"Looking for this?"

I showed him the long-barreled revolver in my hand. His fingers pulled out slow from under his desk, away from the empty holster.

"Now, now, son," he said, holding up his hands, "let's not do anything rash here. We can work this out."

"Can we?" I strolled toward him, keeping the gun aimed at his chest. "After what you did to me, do you really think we can 'work this out'? Because if you've got any ideas, I'd love to hear 'em. You must figure I want *something*. If I was just here to kill you, I'd have done it hours ago."

He blinked. "H-hours ago?"

"It's all about the great quandary. The reason nobody's ever escaped the Iceberg. Desert's a natural barrier, and by the time anybody passes through Aberdeen, the highway patrol will already be on high alert and have I-80 barricaded in both direc-tions. Everyone told me you can't get out that way."

I loomed over him, wearing a grim smile.

"So I didn't. The way to defeat a roadblock isn't to sneak through it; it's to *outlast* it. All I had to do was let myself into your house—the last place anybody would be looking for me—and wait until morning. Now? Roadblock's gone. I can just drive on out of here."

"You were...*here?*"

"I was hiding under your bed. All night long," I told him. "Lis-tening to you *snore*. You sleep like an innocent man, Warden. Me? I didn't sleep at all."

Lancaster shrank into his high-backed leather chair.

"Look, son, I...I know you must be upset—"

"Upset? You forced me to kill a man."

"You killed *plenty*," he snapped, the fear on his face turning into an angry, pinched scowl. "You killed plenty of men before you came into my prison, and you killed plenty on your way out. You're a murderer, Faust, plain and simple. What's one more body on the pile, huh?"

I felt my finger tighten against the trigger. I had to take a deep breath and force it to unclench.

"I never killed anybody who didn't deserve it," I told him.

Lancaster snorted. "And who decides that? *You?* Who died and made you God? If you get to decide who lives and who dies, so do I. You're no different from me."

I paced the floor in front of his desk. I didn't want to think about it. Maybe I was afraid that if I thought about it too much, he might start making sense.

"Look." He reached for his inside pocket. I spun, sticking the gun in his face, and he froze. "Easy, easy now! This is something you'll want to see."

His fingers trembled as he tugged out a business card, resting it gingerly on the desk between us. Gold-leaf letters in neat cursive swirled over creamy-white parchment. "Weishaupt and Associates," it read, "Attorneys at Law."

"I know what you are," Lancaster told me. "You and that woman. I know what I saw. You're sorcerers, ain't ya?"

I sent out psychic feelers, squirming invisibly across the room, brushing over the skin of Lancaster's mind. Not a spark of magic there.

The card, though, was another story. It glowed ultraviolet in my second sight, seething with absorbed power like a nugget of enriched uranium.

"You know what that is, right?" He tapped the card. "That's a *golden ticket*. A genuine, authentic golden ticket. And you can have it."

"Unless you're about to introduce me to Willy Wonka," I said, "I don't know what the hell you're talking about. Something tells me we move in different social circles."

He waved off the question. "Doesn't matter. All you need to know is you take that card, call that number, and tell 'em I gave it to you."

"And then?"

He laughed. "And then you get whatever you want, that's what! You want money? Girls? Boys? One of those fancy Italian sports cars? They can make it happen. They *will* make it happen to show their gratitude for you letting bygones be bygones."

"And who are 'they,' exactly?"

"Friends of my family. We go way back. Now, there's a flip side to all this largesse. You decide to pull that trigger instead, and there's no place on earth you'll be able to hide from them. They'll find you in Timbuktu. And you won't die easy, or quick. Make the right choice, son. Take the golden ticket."

I didn't know if the offer—or the threat—was legit, but I knew one thing: *he* believed it. Lancaster's fingers stroked that card like it was a magical talisman that could turn him bulletproof.

"You can promise me the sun and the moon," I told him, "but right now there's only one thing I really want. You're filing the official reports, I assume. Your version of what went down last night."

"My little contingency plan." He smirked. "All tracks covered, all hands clean, and we can start the show all over again as soon as the reconstruction's finished. It's easy to control the narrative when everybody who knows the truth is locked up or on board. Are...you on board, son?"

He nudged the card an inch closer to my side of the desk.

"That card won't do me any good if I get caught and sent right back to prison." I nodded at his computer. "I need you to amend the official story."

I'd been thinking, long and hard, about Buddy's last words to me. The message from the voices in his head.

"Well, sure," Lancaster looked uncertain. "What do you need?"

"Daniel Faust," I told him, "died in the riot. Confirmed kill, body cremated."

They say...you're going to die here, Buddy had told me. *They say you have to die here.*

It wasn't a prophecy. It was a plan.

I walked around the desk, keeping the gun on him, to watch over his shoulder as he worked. Lancaster pulled up his reports, the account of the riot and its aftermath, and the lists of the dead.

"Now just so you understand," he said as he added my name to the list, "I can't do nothin' about your fingerprints and such. You've got a ViCAP file now. That's a federal database. So if you ever get arrested again and they run your prints, your boat is sunk. Your mugshot's on file, too."

"Then I guess I'd better not get arrested again. You let me worry about that."

He rattled a few more keys and sat back, resting his hands on the desk.

"All right," he said, "done is done, and it's all official. As far as the entire world is concerned, you died last night. Only you and me know different. Don't you worry, long as we've got a truce, I'll keep your secret."

I chuckled. "Yeah, okay."

He relaxed, sinking back in his chair, mirroring my smile.

"But you know the old saying," I told him.

His brow furrowed. "What old saying?"

"Two people can keep a secret," I said, "if one of them is dead."

He barely had time for the shock to register on his face as I grabbed his wrist and yanked up his right hand. I pressed the muzzle to his temple and his hand to the barrel. "*No*," he gasped, just before I pulled the trigger and painted his desk cherry red.

I let go. His corpse slumped sideways in the chair. I headed for his kitchen.

I came back with a terrycloth dishrag and wiped down the gun. Then, carefully, I worked it into his limp fingers, making sure to press his fingertips in to leave solid prints. I had put his hand to the barrel as I fired to make sure it'd be covered in plenty of juicy particles in case the coroner ran a gunshot residue test. A world-class CSI would know the blast pattern was all wrong and figure out he wasn't the one who pulled the trigger, but prison bosses in blue-collar towns didn't *get* world-class CSIs.

On a surface-level examination—which was exactly what Warden Lancaster's corpse would undergo—he was a textbook suicide.

I opened a text file on his desktop and whipped up a quick note, something for the first responders to find: "*I can no longer live with the monstrous things I have done. May God forgive me.*" I figured brevity was best.

I took Emerson's tiny camera from my hip pocket and weighed it in my hand. Then I opened it up, slid out the storage card, and slotted it into Lancaster's computer. The footage was all there, blurry and jumpy but unmistakable: Emerson's murder at Lancaster's hands, the fights to the death, even a few clear glimpses of the audience.

Those glimpses were the key. I counted five minor celebrities—actors, athletes, cable pundits—whose faces and voices were unmistakable. If the video went public, they'd go down as accessories to murder.

I nestled the camera in my palm and drummed my fingers against it, thinking.

At least five celebrities, and any or all of them would pay to keep this quiet. And *keep* paying as if their lives depended on it. Because they did. Blackmail wasn't my usual game, but I could turn this video into solid gold.

If I did that, nobody would ever know the truth. The dead prisoners, Emerson's murder, all of it would be swept under the rug and forgotten. And that would be on my shoulders. The only person who could bring a little justice to this whole sorry mess was me. That was my choice: justice, or a lifetime supply of cold, hard cash.

I leaned over the keyboard, sighing as I typed. "Sometimes," I muttered to the empty room, "doing the right thing *sucks*."

Most of my business was secrets and lies. Every once in a while, though, I could inflict more damage with the truth. I opened Lancaster's email client and attached the video file. With a single click, it went to the newsrooms at CNN, MSNBC, Fox, and CBS. What Emerson had given me wasn't a camera after all; it was a hand grenade, and I'd just pulled the pin and lobbed it at the world.

I think he would have appreciated that.

The golden ticket sat on Lancaster's desk, but now the gold was flecked with scarlet stains, one corner soaked in drying blood. I picked it up and eyed it thoughtfully. Even if anything the warden had told me was true, his "friends" at Weishaupt and Associates wouldn't be coming after me; they wouldn't even know there was a murder to avenge. Good. I didn't need any more enemies.

Still, I had to wonder how much juice they really had. Could they kill a scandal before it hit the nightly news? I laughed when the solution came to me.

Then I opened a YouTube account in Lancaster's name and

threw the raw footage up on the Internet under the title "*Celebrities and Murder in Prison Scandal—Explicit Violence!*"

By the time I wiped down the keyboard, the door handles, and everything else I might have touched, erasing my tracks, it already had over three thousand views.

I pocketed the golden ticket, out of curiosity more than anything else, and traded my prison uniform for one of Lancaster's suits. He was bigger and broader shouldered than me, so it fit like a tent, but it was better than nothing. The uniform didn't have a name or number stitched to it, nothing to identify me as the one who'd worn it, so I shoved that in a plastic bag and buried it deep in the garbage cans behind the house.

I found around three hundred bucks in his top dresser drawer, a little rainy-day stash. Not much, but it would get me where I was going.

Home.

42.

I'd come to Eisenberg Correctional in a bus, and I left the same way. A Greyhound this time, barreling down a long, dry desert highway. No dust, no diesel fumes, just clear blue sky and sunlight. I got off in Salt Lake City and grabbed lunch at a McDonald's while I waited for my next bus. A two-dollar cheeseburger tasted like filet mignon. I sat there, savoring every bite, looking at the people around me and marveling. Because I could.

I didn't know what freedom was worth until I lost it. I would never, I quietly vowed to myself, lose it again. Never.

The waiting lounge at the bus terminal had a television set mounted on brackets high in one corner of the room. I paused for a moment. The video was already headline news, the story of the day, and two pundits behind a curved desk were spinning up a storm.

"—our beloved colleague found dead in his home, allegedly of a self-inflicted gunshot wound just like—as we learned twenty minutes ago—Warden Lancaster himself. Now even if that wasn't his face and voice on the recording, and frankly our in-studio experts have serious questions about that, clearly he believed he'd already been tried in the court of public opinion—"

"And that's exactly it. That's exactly it. We're hearing reports of *dozens* of indictments being handed down this afternoon. Was he even named? Isn't it far more likely that instead of being a patron of this 'fight club,' he was reporting undercover and planning to expose it? And why isn't anyone asking the *real* question:

why isn't this graphic, violent footage, which could be seen by children, being erased from the Internet immediately? Doesn't the attorney general *care* about children? That's where we should be focusing all our attention right now."

I smiled, shook my head, and moved on. Some things never changed.

The next bus ride was a straight shot down I-15, all the way to Las Vegas. Six and a half hours on the road, and I moved closer to the edge of my seat with every passing mile. My seatmate made small talk now and then, in between naps; he was an airplane-parts salesman. I didn't know anything about that, so I asked him some questions I didn't care about the answers to and let him ramble, responding with nods and "hmms" here and there. It was good background noise.

The sky turned gold; then it turned black. No stars shone above us. The city ahead, looming large in the dusty bus window, had put them out of business. My Vegas, sacred lady of halogen and neon. The spotlight from the Karnak pyramid touched a white-hot beckoning finger to the sky.

"Think you're gonna win big?" my seatmate asked.

The bus wheezed as it pulled into the terminal. Hard light flowed in through the window, washing over me like a baptism.

"I'll give it my best shot," I told him.

Caitlin waited for me out in the parking lot, leaning against the hood of her snow-white Audi Quattro. She'd traded in her coat and her weapons for a gray silk jersey dress, and she curled her arms around my neck to pull me close.

"I've been watching the news all day," she murmured once our lips parted. "Nicely played. You know, those celebrities...you *could* have blackmailed them."

"I know. I decided to be the good guy for a change."

She arched an eyebrow. "Oh? Did you like it?"

"Not enough to make a habit out of it. It's *really* expensive and kind of exhausting. Have we heard from Pixie?"

"She's on board." Caitlin plucked at the shoulder of my oversized jacket. "*This* needs to be fixed. You look like a vaudeville comedian."

"I'll steal clothes from a smaller guy next time I break out of prison."

"I'm taking you shopping," she said. "But first, you have a much-overdue doctor's appointment."

*　*　*

"For a dead man," Doc Savoy murmured, "you sure are spry."

I sat on the edge of a cold steel mortuary slab, following the movements of his penlight as he shone it in one eye, then the other, swiveling the light from side to side. The doc's "office" was the quiet mortuary behind the Rosewood Funeral Home; he'd sometimes joke that if he ever lost a patient, coffin-fitting was just fifty feet away.

He didn't lose many patients though. Doc was pushing seventy, and his eyes were rheumy behind his wire-rimmed glasses, but everybody in the Vegas underground knew he was the best off-the-books sawbones in the business. If you took a gunshot wound or anything else you didn't want the authorities asking questions about, he'd patch you up good as new—and more importantly, he'd keep his lips sealed.

I didn't mind that he was really a veterinarian. Decades of experience had to count for *something*, right?

Caitlin stood behind him, arms crossed, eyeing my shirtless chest. There was nothing lascivious in her look: my skin was a tapestry of fading blotches, the ugly coat of bruises finally starting to heal. I was getting around all right now—the headaches and nausea notwithstanding—but every once in a while I'd move the wrong way and wince at a sudden muscle twinge.

"I'm just experimenting with being dead as a fashion statement," I told him.

He snickered at my suit, folded neatly on the slab beside me. "I thought *that* was a fashion statement."

"First man to ever escape from Eisenberg Correctional, and I get no respect."

"Aw, you weren't even the first," the Doc said. "Didn't you hear? Couple of guys on ATVs busted out the day before you did, clear across the desert. You should have hitched a ride with them, would've saved you a whole mess of trouble. *They* had the right idea."

He checked my eyes once more and took a step back.

"Hm. Well, no doubt about it, you took a hit to the noggin. Good news is, with plenty of rest—I'm gonna say ten days, minimum—you should be right as rain. Go home, go to bed, and stay there."

I shook my head. "No can do. Can't you give me some medication or something?"

"For a concussion?" he said. "Sure. Tylenol. It'll help with the headaches. Past that, there's no way around it: you've *got* to rest. No physical exertion, no mental exertion, no booze—"

"Wait a second. I just broke out of prison, and I can't even have a drink to celebrate?"

He beamed, rubbing his hands against his old butcher's smock. "Sure you can! In ten days. *After* you come in for a follow-up and I give you a clean bill of health."

"This isn't working for me," I said.

"Does permanent brain damage work for you? 'Cause that's what you're risking if you go running around acting crazy out there. You take *one* more solid hit to that thick head of yours, you could end up with internal bleeding, maybe even second-impact syndrome. Makes your brain swell up 'til there's no more room in your skull and then, well, that's all she wrote. Lousy way to die, my friend."

"He *will* rest," Caitlin said, locking eyes with me.

"By the by," Doc said, "you know my stance on doctor-patient privilege. That's something I don't break—"

"Which I appreciate," I told him.

"—but *that said*, I can speak in the vaguest of generalities. Something's brewing out there, Dan, and it sure isn't good."

"Brewing how?"

"My business is brisk these last few days. *Too* brisk." Doc Savoy nodded toward the door. "I'm selling bandages and caskets like they were going out of style. Lots of street kids coming in all messed up, lots more than just the usual bloody faces and scuffed-up knuckles."

"More gang fights than usual?"

"Looks to me like a few alliances, both the explicit and the formerly presumed kind, are breaking down out there. Nicky Agnelli was no saint, but he held this city together. Now that he's gone..."

He spread his hands. I got the message, loud and clear. The Vegas underworld worked because Nicky ran the city like a seasoned CEO. Sometimes he was a tyrant, sometimes a dealmaker, usually a little of both. Whatever he needed to be to keep the pot from boiling over. That worked great until the feds finally got the "evidence" they needed—courtesy of the Chicago Outfit—to put him away for good.

With the King of Vegas on the run, nobody had any incentive to play nice. And *everybody* would have their eyes on Nicky's throne.

"If you ask me," Doc said, "somebody needs to find Nicky and *make* him come back. That or find a darn good replacement, and pronto. Otherwise things are bound to get a whole lot worse."

*   *   *

We had one last stop before getting down to business: Crystals. A shopping mall nestled in the heart of the Las Vegas strip, Crystals was sprawling and sleek and aimed squarely at catering to the lifestyles of the rich and famous. Caitlin and I walked along the polished tan floors past marquee after glowing marquee. Bottega Veneta, Porsche Design, Versace...I cleared my throat, keeping my head down.

"Uh, Cait," I murmured, "I usually can't afford to shop here on a *good* week, and when I got busted...well, almost everything I owned was in my wallet or my car, and the cops took both. I can't afford to breathe the air in here."

"What? Don't be silly. I'm expensing it."

She flashed her credit card at me. It was a Corporate Platinum AmEx, and the block letters at the bottom read "*Caitlin Brody / Southern Tropics Import/Export Company.*"

"Wait a second. How can you possibly justify buying me clothes as a business expense?"

She sniffed at me. "Simple. You are my consort. If you look poorly, it reflects badly on me. And if I look bad, it makes my prince look bad. Therefore, by buying you clothes, I'm serving my prince. Quite easily done."

"That's...devious."

"Thank you." She steered me by the shoulder, guiding me through a gleaming arch and into a store on the left. "Yes. Brunello Cucinelli. A good place to begin, I think."

If I thought Doc Savoy had poked and prodded me, that was nothing compared to the attentions of a staff of tailors and fashion experts. Caitlin perused the racks of imported Italian styles while every part of my body was tape-measured and double tape-measured.

"He'll need a sport coat," Caitlin told one clerk, who followed her like a puppy dog. "Blazer style, I think. Two buttons, something slimming."

He draped a length of black fabric over one arm, holding it out for her to touch.

"Ultralight twill," he said as she ran her fingertips down his arm. "It's a silk blend, durable but thin as a whisper, perfect for the climate."

"Very nice. Do you have it in black or navy?"

"Both," he said.

"Then we'll take both."

"And shirts?" he offered her another length of fabric. "May I recommend cotton poplin?"

"Cait," I called over, "how much is this going to cost?"

Sudden silence. Every eye in the room fell upon me, cold as winter ice.

"Right," I said, holding up a hand. "I'm just gonna maybe shut up now."

It took a while, but we made it to the end. Caitlin tugged my hand and steered me over to a full-length mirror.

The battered, bedraggled convict in prison beige was gone. The man in the mirror was sleek in midnight black and ivory, from his narrow silk tie down to the tips of his polished Italian shoes.

"I think I'm back," I said. "Do I look okay?"

"I think," Caitlin said, curling her arms around me from behind and beaming at our shared reflection, "you look like a man who's ready to do some serious damage."

43.

I t was long after closing hour, but soft lights still burned behind the window of the Scrivener's Nook. The Dickensian clutter of a bookshop was an odd place for a late-night clandestine rendezvous, but it was an easy place to rally the troops. As Caitlin and I arrived, Bentley hustled us into the shop and locked the door behind us.

"It's my fault," Mama Margaux said, pulling me into a rib-squeezing hug. "I should have been keeping better watch over her."

"Not your job," I told her. "Jennifer got bushwhacked, that's all. Happens to the best of us. The important thing is, for now, she's alive."

Pixie gave me a nod from the counter, where she'd set up her laptop, but didn't say a word. I wasn't sure if we were on speaking terms or not. The rest of us congregated in the middle of the shop, making a ragged circle.

"Here's the situation," I said. "We know Jennifer's being held by traitors inside the Cinco Calles, led by a man named Cesar Gallegos. Cesar's the right hand of Gabriel, the Calles' top dog; looks like he's tired of waiting for Gabriel to retire, so he's making a side deal with the Chicago Outfit. We don't know how many men he's got on his side. Could be a handful, could be half the gang."

Caitlin looked to Pixie. "They're smart enough not to make Jennifer bleed, but they very much want to interrogate her. To that end, Chicago is loaning them a torture specialist."

"How much time do we have?" Pixie asked her.

"Precious little."

"We've got two jobs," I said. "First, track down Cesar Gallegos and make him give Jennifer back. Second, find the Chicago delegation and take them out."

Bentley raised a frail finger.

"Dealing with one problem," he said, "will easily solve the other. If Cesar is already planning to meet with these outsiders, he'll know where they're going to be. An ambush would be simple enough."

I nodded. "Agreed, so let's focus on Gallegos."

"Gabriel would know where to find him, right?" Pixie asked. "I mean, if we went and told him that his right-hand man's a traitor, wouldn't he help us?"

"The problem there," I said, "is we don't know who *else* in the Calles is dirty. Jen converted an entire tenement by the airport into an urban fortress. If we walk in there, we might not walk out again if we say the wrong thing to the wrong person. And no matter what, word would get back to Cesar that the jig is up. He might kill Jennifer before we can get to him."

"Could we catch Gabriel alone somewhere and talk to him in private?"

"The guy runs one of the biggest street gangs in Las Vegas. I guarantee he's *never* alone. And if his number-two man's turned traitor on him, it's possible his bodyguards have turned too." I paused, a thought occurring to me. I snapped my fingers. "But I think I know someone, someone *outside* the Calles, who might be able to tell us where Cesar hangs out. I'll be back in half an hour."

"And in the meantime?" Corman asked.

"Just sit tight for now. I need to see this guy alone. He's going to be hard to deal with." I paused, looking around the room, suddenly sheepish. "And, uh, could I borrow somebody's car? Mine's impounded and I can't reclaim it because I'm kinda legally dead right now."

"Take a taxi." Caitlin handed me a couple of twenty-dollar bills. "No driving until the doctor says otherwise."

Pixie followed me to the door, keeping a safe distance. She didn't speak up until we were both out on the sidewalk, wrapped in a cool night breeze.

"Hey," she said.

I paused and looked back at her.

"Hey yourself."

"I was really mad at you." She crossed her arms over her chest and looked down at the sidewalk. "When you wouldn't let me help, going after Damien Ecko. I mean I was really, *really* mad."

"You had every right to be."

She looked up at me, frowning.

"That was some patronizing bullshit, you know that? I'm a grown woman. I don't need to be protected from the consequences of my own decisions."

I shrugged. "True."

Pixie stubbed the toe of her sneaker against the sidewalk. She sighed.

"Then, on the flight home, I kept thinking about what you said to me. About not getting blood on my hands if I didn't have to. About how once you go down that road, you can't come back. And...I think you're right. I *don't* want to be like you. I don't ever want it to be easy to hurt somebody."

I didn't answer. She needed to talk. I just needed to listen.

"I left town for a few days. Went to the coast, just to get my head clear. I sat on the beach. Thought about staying there, just...never coming back. But I kept thinking about Coop. Margaux said you took down Stanwyck, but Ecko got away."

"Yeah, well," I said, "we did our best. We didn't figure he had a warehouse filled with living mummies in crates. In retrospect, probably should have seen that coming. But look, Pix, nobody's giving up. Ecko's the most wanted man in the western United States right now. When he pokes his head out of hiding—and he will, eventually—I'm going after him with everything I've got."

"And that's why I came back," Pixie said.

"For Damien Ecko?"

"For Coop. Because he was my friend, and until Ecko pays for what he—what he *did* to him, I can't rest. I'm not asking to be in on the kill, Faust. You're right, I don't need blood on my hands. I don't want it. But when it comes to the *hunt*? You call me."

I gave her a tired smile.

"I wouldn't call anybody else."

"Good." She nodded. "Now let's get Jennifer back, huh?"

"On it," I told her. "I just have to pay a visit to an old friend."

* * *

"Friend" was probably the wrong choice of words. At least that'd be my guess given the look on his face when Gary Kemper, Las Vegas Metro detective, walked through the door of his studio apartment and found me sitting on his couch.

"No," he said, clutching the grocery bags in his arms, "no, no, *no*. This can't be fucking happening."

His backup piece, a .22 I'd found hidden in his nightstand, dangled easy in my hand. I didn't point it at him; it was just there to keep the conversation civil.

"Oh, yeah," I said. "It's happening."

I'd met Gary Kemper when Harmony Black's all-star task force set me in their sights. He was Agent Black's local liaison, a superstar in the gang-crimes unit. He was also a member of the Redemption Choir, a pack of cambion terrorists. *And* he had been working for Lauren Carmichael.

They say a man can't serve two masters, let alone three, so I simplified his life for him. Thanks to a little bit of blackmail, soon he only had one boss to worry about. Me.

"You son of a bitch," he seethed. "You made me think Harmony and Lars were dead!"

"I needed you to get me close to my targets, and frankly, you aren't that good of an actor. You had to *believe* it. If Sullivan smelled a lie on you, he would have killed us both."

Kemper's shoulders slumped. He kicked the door closed

behind him, walked into the kitchen nook, and set his grocery bags down on the counter between us. I watched to see if he'd go for the gun on his hip. He didn't even bother.

"Yeah, well, maybe. I spent a week in this crack den of a 'safe house' in Los Angeles. Word got back that Sullivan was dead, and everybody just...drifted off. The end of the Redemption Choir."

"You wanted out of the Choir. I got you out. A little gratitude wouldn't hurt anybody."

He mustered a tired glare as he unpacked his groceries. Bananas, a six-pack of Sam Adams, a stack of microwave dinners, another six-pack.

"I heard you got sent to Eisenberg Correctional," he said. "Then today I heard you were dead. Either of those true?"

The last of his groceries was a tiny chocolate cake under a plastic dome, dipped in fudge, sized for one.

"Both, sort of. Hey." I nodded at the cake. "What's with the fancy dessert? Are you...are you *celebrating* my death?"

He wrinkled his nose. "It's my birthday tomorrow, smartass. I'm down for a twelve-hour shift, so maybe I'm gonna want a little cake and a beer afterward. Nothing wrong with that."

"Twelve hours. Yeah, I can imagine, with all the gang violence now that Nicky's gone."

He twisted the cap off a bottle of beer and tossed back a swig.

"Clusterfuck. Unmitigated clusterfuck. We were supposed to take down Nicky *and* his entire organization in one big sweep. Sparkly clean Vegas streets and nice big headlines. Now? It's total chaos out there. The task force is over, too. Lars went on disability leave from the DEA, and Harmony...hell, that's just a pile of weird."

"How do you mean?"

"She left." He took a long pull from the bottle. "I figured back to the Seattle FBI office, right? But no, turns out she got reassigned to the 'critical incident response group,' whatever the hell that is. So I poke around, find out she's supposedly running field investigations for a higher-up named Walburgh."

He stepped around the counter and leaned against it, eyeing his bottle.

"I got a pal in the Bureau, and I asked him to get me in touch. Thinking hey, I never really got to say a proper goodbye before Harmony left town, and I'd like to give her a call. Well, wherever she is, she can't be reached. And this Walburgh guy? As far as we can tell, he *doesn't exist*. He's a voicemail box in an empty office. There's some shady shit going down in the Bureau, and Harmony's neck-deep in it."

I wished I could say I was surprised, but Agent Black had intimated that her connections in Washington ran deeper—and to far stranger corners—than anyone would have guessed. Whatever she was into, I just wanted to keep under her radar and out of her way.

And as long as Daniel Faust stayed dead and buried, I had a pretty good shot.

"Whatever it is you're here for," Gary told me, "say it and get out. You can't blackmail me anymore. Sullivan and Lauren are both six feet under."

"Technically he's about fifteen feet under," I said, "but that's arguing semantics. I'm here to ask for your help."

He blinked. "Help *you?* Why the hell would I do that?"

"Because," I said, "you and me are gonna save some lives together."

44.

"You're seeing the violence in the streets," I told Gary, "everyone fighting to fill the vacuum now that Nicky's on the run, but you aren't seeing the hand behind it all. And if you think it's bad now, just wait a few more days."

Gary's frown dropped a couple more notches.

"The Chicago mob," I said, "is about to make a move on Vegas. That murder that landed me behind bars and sent Nicky running? Frame job, from start to finish. They've got a shape-shifter on their payroll. He set the whole thing up."

"Shape-shifter?" he snorted. "No such thing."

I leaned back on his couch and tilted my head at him.

"Gary?" I said. "You've got demon blood. You know I'm a sorcerer and that magic is real. Are you *really* gonna take the 'no such thing' angle with me?"

He glanced down, biting his lip.

"Yeah, okay," he said. "Fair point."

"Their whole plan was to destabilize the Vegas underworld. As you've seen, mission accomplished. But that's just the prelude. The Outfit's gonna roll in here, guns blazing. In fact, I know they're sending a delegation to hook up with some of the locals. The Cinco Calles are about to get ripped right down the middle."

Gary finished his beer. He stared at the bottle for a moment, shaking his head. Then he uncapped another one.

"What are you talking about? Some kind of civil war?"

"A big and messy one," I said, "and I guarantee there *will* be civilians stuck in the cross fire."

"What's your angle in all this?"

"The splinter faction, the one who wants to sign up with the Outfit, has a friend of mine. They're holding her hostage."

"So file a police report," Gary said, "and let Metro handle it. That's what we do."

"All due respect, this isn't a job for the cops. You go in all heavy-footed and she'll end up dead. This is a job for *my* people. If you help me out, though, I can stop the civil war, and I can help push the Outfit out of Vegas. No civilian casualties. You've got my word on that."

He studied my face like he was trying to read a book in Sanskrit. I could hear his mind turning, weighing his options, deciding how much he believed me.

"What *exactly* would you need from me?" he finally asked.

I set his purloined gun down on the coffee table. It didn't look like I was going to need it.

"I need to find a high-level Calles banger, a guy named Cesar Gallegos. I figure you work gang crimes, so you might know of him."

Gary flashed a bitter smile. "Know *of* him? I've busted him twice, personally. Guy's a real piece of work. What are you gonna do when you find him?"

"Resolve the situation."

"In other words, you're gonna put a bullet in him."

I shrugged. "I didn't say that."

"Faust, do you even understand what you're doing? You're asking a Metro detective to set up a goddamn assassination. That is so wrong I don't even know where to start *explaining* how wrong it is."

"Come on," I told him, "you were involved in dirtier business than that when you were on the Redemption Choir's payroll. Besides, you need to look at the end, not the means. Way I see it, there are only two possible outcomes here."

"Yeah? And those are?"

I ticked them off on my fingers. "One, the Calles turn on each other, with one side playing the welcome wagon for the Chicago Outfit. If you think you've got problems now, just wait. We're looking at a full-on gang war in the streets with military-grade firepower. Two, you help me and I resolve the problem quickly, quietly, and outside the city limits. Nobody gets hurt but the bad guys."

He paced the floor, half-drained bottle swinging limply in his hand. I let him think it over. He stopped in midstride, then looked my way.

"*No* civilian casualties." Half question and half command.

"Not one."

He nodded to himself, slow, and slipped a business card from his pocket. I rose from the couch and took the card from his outstretched hand.

"I've got seven guys under me," Gary said. "Come sunrise, their number-one business is gonna be tracking down Cesar Gallegos. The Calles have hangouts all over the city, but if we spread out, we should get eyes on him pretty quick."

"You're making the right call," I told him.

He watched me as I strolled to his apartment door.

"Faust," he said.

My hand rested on the doorknob. "Yeah?"

"Something just occurred to me. It'd really suck for you if anybody found out you were still alive, wouldn't it?"

I shrugged. "Fair to say."

"It's just funny." He let out a little chuckle. "Now I've got something to hold over *your* head."

*   *   *

Back at the Scrivener's Nook, I laid out the game plan.

"Once Gary and his team find Cesar," I said, "we'll keep our distance and put him under surveillance. Pixie, can you get some gear together? Maybe a parabolic microphone or something?"

"Done and done."

"Then what?" Corman asked. "Follow him to wherever he's keeping Jennifer?"

I shook my head. "Only if we have to. If we get lucky spying on him, maybe we can find out where the meet's going to be and get there *first*. Then we can set up an ambush. For now, let's all get a few hours of sleep. Tomorrow's gonna be a long day."

Caitlin hooked her arm around mine, steering me toward the door.

"I know you're welcome on Bentley and Corman's couch," she said, "but given you've spent the last couple of weeks sleeping on a prison cot, I think you're entitled to a *real* bed tonight."

Music to my ears. Back in her penthouse at the Taipei Tower—an expanse of polished hardwood, black leather, and chrome with decor out of an '80s music video—she led me into the bedroom. She undressed me, slow, her fingers unbuttoning my shirt with feathery grace. Her dress tumbled to the floor in the dark, a pool of shadow around her feet.

We sank under the storm-gray comforter together, sliding across warm satin sheets. I leaned in and brushed my lips across the curve of her bare shoulder.

Her fingernails, five little spear points, rested over my heart.

"Daniel," she said. "What are you doing?"

I blinked.

"Uh, I thought, I mean...I thought we were going to—"

"You have a concussion."

I couldn't quite parse that.

"And?"

"And," she said, gently pushing me onto my back, "the doctor's orders were quite clear. *No* unnecessary physical exertion."

"He didn't mean sex."

"I'm quite certain he did."

"He could not possibly," I said, "have meant sex."

She rolled onto her side, facing me, and flipped her hair back with a toss of her head.

"Daniel," she said. "Are you claiming that having sex with me is *not* physically exerting?"

She had me there.

"I've been in *prison*," I said, trying a different tack. "All those long, lonely nights. I have needs, you know."

"You were in prison for two weeks, not two years, and *I* need you to *not die*. In ten days, once the doctor says you're in the clear, we will have a very lovely—and vigorous—evening. Now get some sleep."

Somehow, I managed. For a fleeting handful of hours, anyway, before the alarm clock flipped to 6:00 a.m. and a shrill electronic whine hit me like a mustang kick to the skull. Aching, coasting on a wave of nausea, I trudged to the bathroom and tried to make myself pass for a functional human being.

Back at the Scrivener's Nook, Pixie was ready for action and lugging a hard black plastic case about the size of a bowling-ball bag. As I walked in, she passed me a slim Samsung phone.

"Here," she said, "figured you'd need a fresh burner."

I did. The first number I called was the one on Detective Kemper's business card. Gary picked up on the second ring.

"It's me," I said. "Any word?"

"My guys are canvassing the streets. This a good number?"

"Good for now," I told him.

He hung up. We weren't waiting for long. Maybe fifteen minutes later, the phone buzzed and lit up in my hand.

"Got him," Gary said. "You know the taqueria on South Decatur? He's at a table in the back with some of his homeboys. What now?"

"We're on our way. Hang back, okay? We don't want to spook him."

He let out a disgusted-sounding snort. "I'm not *leaving*, if that's what you want. If you break your word and start shooting up the place, I'll be on you in two seconds flat."

I hung up the phone. A minute later he sent me a grainy photo, snapped from under a nearby table in the restaurant. Five guys hung out at a corner booth, laughing, openly flashing Calles ink on their arms and rocking yellow and brown bandannas. "*Gallegos is the skinny one, second from the left*," read a follow-up text.

"All right," I said, "we need to keep a low profile for this. Pix, it's you and me. Everybody else, stay by your phones and be ready to move fast."

*　*　*

Caitlin lent us the keys to her Audi. Well, she lent Pixie the keys, pointedly telling her not to let me drive.

"He's had a head injury," she said.

Pixie gave me a sidelong glance. "That explains *so much*."

Even with Pixie at the wheel, we broke speed records getting across town. The taqueria was styled like an old Spanish mission on the outside, with white stucco walls and clay shingles the color of fresh salmon. As we cruised by, I spotted Cesar and his boys in the back booth. Spotted Gary Kemper, too, passing for a casual diner with a low-slung ball cap and keeping a sharp eye on the place.

"What'd you bring?" My hands rested on the black case on my lap. "A microphone?"

"Even better," she said.

Pixie pulled the car around the side of the restaurant, squinted, then kept going. We ended up around back, pulling in next to an overstuffed Dumpster.

"Getting a little close there, aren't you?" I said as the front bumper nearly brushed dirty stucco. "This *is* Caitlin's car, remember."

"Limited range. We need to be within ten meters. I think this is just about right."

I handed her the case. She clicked open the plastic hasps. Inside, another black box rested on a fuzzy felt tray. It was about the size of a claymore mine, and she handled it just as gingerly as she closed the case, set the box upright on the lid, and swiveled up a stubby antenna. A red light flickered on the side, then turned blue.

"Hold this," she said, handing me the box, "and keep it steady." Then she reached into the backseat and grabbed her laptop, booting it up.

"What *is* it?"

"That," she said as a waterfall of luminous blue text flooded her screen, "is called a femtocell. It's basically a miniature cell phone tower in a box. Short range but very, very nifty. Hand me that burner I gave you."

She studied my phone for a minute, keying in digits with her right hand while she typed on the laptop with her left.

"Cell phones are designed to connect to the closest tower," she explained. "Which, for every phone within ten meters, is now *this* one. There's no permission request, no warning. You can't even tell it's happening. Which is fine, assuming the femtocell hasn't been, say, compromised by a creative hacker."

"And this one has?" I asked.

By way of response, she handed the phone back to me and tapped on the screen. I had a text message waiting. Well, *I* didn't.

"Just stopping to get a bite. Did you call the babysitter about tonight?"

"Every piece of network traffic that passes through our little cell tower—incoming and outgoing—is now being copied to your phone," Pixie said. "Pretty cool, huh?"

"Hold up," I said. "So you can take this thing and spy on *anyone's* cell phone? *Anywhere?* And it's that easy?"

"Yep. As long as they're within ten meters, no biggie."

I peered at the box in my lap. "So this is like, super-secret tech, right? Like some kind of stolen military prototype?"

"Two hundred bucks over the counter, totally legal, no questions asked. Like I said, I've done some tinkering with mine, but it wasn't too hard."

I watched messages scroll across the screen, fleeting glimpses into the lives of complete strangers.

"Sometimes, Pix," I told her, "I think you're scarier than I am."

45.

I solating Cesar's phone amid the digital noise was a problem. Every piece of data that passed through the femtocell had a number attached, but we couldn't tell which one was his; people didn't usually sign their names to text messages.

"If we could only *make* him call somebody," Pixie said.

I grinned as an idea hit me. "We can. Can I make an outgoing call on this thing?"

She rapped a few keys on her laptop.

"Go for it."

I rang up Detective Kemper. His voice was low, furtive.

"You coming or what?"

"Already there," I said. "Question for you: you ever rumble these guys? Just throw your weight around a little and let them know you've got your eye on them?"

"Sure, all the time. Easiest way to clear 'em off a street corner."

"I need you to rattle Cesar's cage. Go over there and tell him Gabriel's in custody, and that he's already talking about making a deal."

"I thought you *didn't* want me to spook these guys."

"This is the right kind of spooky," I said. "Trust me."

To his credit, he didn't laugh. I hung up the phone and waited.

Sure enough, barely five minutes had passed before a flurry of text messages hit my screen. All in Spanish, though. I gave Pixie a helpless look.

"I took two years in high school," she said. "Lemme see. Yep, that's him! Cesar's trying to get ahold of Gabriel and find out if he's really in jail. And...there's Gabriel, telling him not to be so gullible and—whoa. Those are some words I did *not* learn in class. Hold on, now that we know which phone is his, I'm isolating the feed and digging up his number."

I tilted my head at her while she typed up a storm. "We have his number," I said, tapping the phone.

"Not his phone number. Every phone also has an ESN—an electronic serial number—that interfaces with the network. Be quiet a second. I'm busy being awesome."

I waited, as patiently as I could, while she did what looked like backward calculus on her laptop.

"Boom, *headshot*," she suddenly chirped, pumping a fist. "We can turn off the femtocell now. Don't need it anymore."

"Why not?"

"Cesar's phone. I cloned that sucker. As far as the network is concerned, your phone *is* his phone. Everything that comes into his phone comes into yours too, and everything that goes *out* from your phone looks like it's coming from his number. Gets billed to his account, too."

Before long, a new message pinged across, this time in English.

"*Writing to confirm tonight's appointment. The Doctor is eager to meet his patient.*"

I squeezed the phone until my knuckles turned white.

"*Seven pm,*" came Cesar's response. "*Rockahoola.*"

"Rockahoola?" Pixie said. "That's...not Spanish, I'm pretty sure."

I glanced at the time. It was five minutes past eleven. We had just under eight hours to save Jennifer's life.

* * *

"Rock-A-Hoola," Bentley said, leaning against the counter at the Scrivener's Nook. "Now there's a name I haven't heard in a while. Remember, Cormie? It was called Lake Dolores, back in the day."

"Yep," Corman said. "Stupidest damn thing I ever saw."

Bentley looked my way. "It was a water park, just off Interstate 15, between here and Los Angeles."

"I-15 goes through the Mojave," I said.

"Correct."

Pixie squinted at him. "Somebody built a freakin' water park in the middle of the desert?"

"That's what I said the first time I saw it," Corman told her.

"It was first built in the fifties," Bentley said. "Then it closed. Reopened. Closed again. Last time it shut its doors was...ten years ago, perhaps? It's just a ruin now, sitting dry in the Mojave."

"In the middle of nowhere," I mused. "The perfect place for what they've got planned. All right. We've got a few hours. Jennifer's safe until the Outfit's thugs get there. Which means we need to make sure they *don't* get there. Pix, you said any call from this phone will look like it's coming from Cesar?"

"As far as the network is concerned, it *is* coming from him."

"I think we need to bring in a little backup," I said.

We didn't just have the Chicago liaison's number; thanks to Gary putting a scare into Cesar, we had Gabriel's number too. He answered his phone with a rapid-fire stream of irritated Spanish.

"Gabriel," I said, "my name is Daniel Faust. I'm a friend of Jennifer's. Do not react strongly to anything I say. You may be in danger."

No answer for a moment. Then he said, "Yeah. Okay."

"Are you alone?"

"Nope," he replied.

"We've found Jennifer. She's being held hostage by one of your men. You've been betrayed, and it's possible your own bodyguards are in on it. They're planning to kill her, and they're coming for you next."

A long stretch of silence. I could hear footsteps and faint thumping bass from a distant room.

"Aw, man," he said as casual as if he were discussing the weather. Still, I could hear his voice tighten. "That...that sucks. Real sorry to hear that."

"Can we meet, in private? Until this gets sorted out, you can't trust *anybody* in your crew."

"Yeah, that's a—that's an interesting proposal you got there. I'd like to hear more."

"Come to Our Lady of Consolation in half an hour," I said. "I'll be in a pew on the right-hand side of the church, alone and unarmed."

"Yeah, a'ight. Sounds good."

He hung up the phone.

"Alone and unarmed?" Caitlin frowned at me.

"For all he knows, I'm leading him into a trap. He'd be dumb not to be wary."

"Well," she said, "he certainly won't notice the woman sitting by herself in the back of the church, keeping an eye on you. Let's go."

* * *

I didn't know why I'd picked Our Lady of Consolation when I needed a spur-of-the-moment meeting spot. It wasn't odd to hold a low-profile meeting in a church—I'd done it once or twice myself—but that *particular* church had history for me. That was where I'd met a priest named Alvarez, a man hunted by feral half-demons.

Turned out Father Alvarez, who I risked my neck and my home to protect, was a spy working for the Court of Night-Blooming Flowers. I was normally a good judge of character, but that was not one of my shining moments.

Nothing had changed since the last time I set foot inside. Same old weathered and splintered pews, same anemic wreaths and shimmering votive candles in dusty red glass. Desolate, except for an elderly man with a bad comb-over slumped in the last pew, snoring loud as a vacuum cleaner. And Caitlin sitting across from him, waiting patiently, a trapdoor spider.

I took a seat right up front and waited.

I shifted in the pew. Rapped my fingers on my knee. Checked Cesar's phone for the fiftieth time. I picked up a hymnal and leafed through it, though I wasn't sure why. There were beautiful words inside, words of comfort and hope, but they weren't written for me. I felt like a trespasser, so I closed the book and put it back.

Out of the corner of my eye I saw Gabriel kneel down, cross himself, and slide into the pew behind me. He was hard to miss, built like a linebacker after a three-steak meal, with a sculpted and pencil-thin goatee.

"I know your name," he said softly, leaning forward in his seat. His voice didn't match his girth; it was high-pitched, smooth, almost musical. "JJ's talked about you."

"All good things, I hope."

"Says you're solid, but I dunno. You talked some crazy shit back there. And why's my caller ID say you've got Cesar's phone?"

"Magic," I said. "And Cesar's the one to watch. He stabbed you in the back. He ambushed Jennifer, and once he gets every last bit of info out of her—her grow houses, her bank account codes—he's going to kill her. Then he'll be gunning for *your* head."

"You got proof?"

I showed him the phone, calling up the texts from the Chicago liaison. Even as I did it, I knew what what his answer would be.

"Pretty flimsy, *ese*. Doesn't even say her name. That could be about anyone."

"Look, this guy he's texting with? He's representing Chicago. The mob wants to muscle in on Vegas, and they made Cesar an offer. He's gonna take his boys and jump ship."

Gabriel folded his thick arms.

"Anybody can tell a story."

I was losing him. I needed to take a chance. While he watched, I tapped out a new message, directing it at the Chicago contact.

"*After we ice JJ,*" I wrote, "*might need help taking down Gabriel. Can you lend some firepower?*"

The answer came back in thirty seconds.

"*We'll discuss it at the meet. Not on the phone, please.*"

Storm clouds brewed behind Gabriel's eyes as he leaned forward in his pew, reading over my shoulder.

"When's this all supposed to go down?" he asked.

"Tonight at seven."

"Hold on."

He took out his own phone and launched into fast Spanish patter, pausing now and again. Asking questions. And from the way his eyes narrowed, he wasn't liking the answers.

"Well," he said, hanging up. "What do ya know. I just asked some of the guys if they wanna hang out tonight, around seven. Turns out Cesar has stuff to do. So do about five other guys. *Everybody's* got stuff to do."

"They're meeting in the desert, about two hours along I-15. That means they'll have to leave by five."

"Yeah? So?"

"So," I said, "at a quarter after five, call your *entire* set. Anybody who shows up is still loyal to you."

"And anybody else," he muttered, frowning, "anybody out in the desert, like that backstabber Cesar, is gonna get *buried* out there. I think we're all gonna have to take a nice drive and see what's what. Drop in on our homies unexpected."

"Take it easy," I told him. "They've got Jennifer, and if you go in hard, they might kill her."

"You got a better solution?"

"I might." I turned the phone over in my palm, weighing it along with my options. "Can we work together on this? Give me a chance to get her out safe before you curb-stomp these guys?"

"Hey, she's a friend of mine too. If you got any ideas for getting her back in one piece, I'm down. Just say when and where I gotta be."

He reached his hand over the pew. I half turned, and we shook on it. His grip felt like granite.

"So what about these fools from Chicago?" he added.

"We need to take them out before they get to the meet. Fewer bodies and less guns in the mix that way."

Gabriel nodded.

"You know where they're at?" he asked. "If you've got an address, let's ride. I'll round up some soldiers and we'll light their asses up."

Tempting, but brute force didn't feel like the right play. This was our chance to send a serious message back to the Outfit, letting them know we were ready to dance. Bullet-riddled bodies were a message, all right, but they were also *easy*. There had to be a way to outclass them, to show we had more than guns on our side.

"I'll take care of that part," I told Gabriel, an idea forming. "Just one thing...can you get me some pot, real fast?"

He patted his shirt pocket. "Sure, like what, a dime bag?"

"Oh," I said, "I need a *little* more than that."

46.

"Problem," I texted the Outfit contact, *"Rockahoola is hot, cops sniffing around. Gotta move the meet."*

"When and where?" came the reply.

I put some thought into that. Nicky Agnelli owned a half-built and vacant subdivision out in Eldorado, in North Vegas. Eventually he'd been planning to flip the lots and make a bundle on legitimate real estate, but for the time being he mostly used the display homes as kill-houses and body dumps.

Someday, some suburban pioneer was going to dig out a swimming pool in the wrong spot and unearth a whole bunch of nasty secrets.

"Eldorado," I typed and gave him the address. *"Let's do this ASAP, don't wanna wait until tonight."*

"On our way," he replied.

Two model homes stood at the tail end of the subdivision, gathering dust in the autumn heat. Caitlin and I crouched on pristine carpet the color of desert sand, watching through the window in an empty living room.

A black Mercedes with tinted windows and Illinois plates rolled up slow. It pulled into the driveway across the street.

Four men got out of the car. I couldn't tell which one was supposed to be the "Doctor." I knew muscle when I saw it though, all hard eyes and bulges under their tailored pinstripe jackets. They marched up the walk and the man in the lead, a wispy blond, rapped his knuckles on the front door.

It swung open under his fist.

Terse conversation. Two of them drew pistols, holding their guns close to their chests as they peered inside. The blond took out his phone and sent a quick text.

"*Where are you?*" flashed across my phone.

"*I've got her in the basement,*" I replied. "*Come on in when you get here, I can't hear the front door from down here.*"

Across the street, the blond shrugged and tucked his phone back in his jacket pocket. He followed the others inside and shut the door behind him.

That was my cue. I bolted out the front door just as Bentley's silver Cadillac rumbled down the street. As I ran past his open window, he passed me a pair of latex gloves, a rubber doorstop, and a long, slender metal rod with a cherry-red tip. I felt like an Olympic sprinter in a baton race as I ran up on the Mercedes, keeping low and watching the house. I'd have five minutes—*maybe*—to get this done, and no room for mistakes.

I tugged on the gloves and studied the driver's-side door, thinking fast. The sedan was an older model, but it came standard with automatic locks. I could work with that. I jammed the thin end of the doorstop into the top of the door, rocking it back and forth, working it into place one centimeter at a time. The door bulged, buckling on its frame. After a minute of work I'd opened a hair-thin crack.

Next step, the metal rod. I slid it through the opening, biting my bottom lip as I fumbled the tip back and forth, feeling for the lock-release button. A new wave of nausea hit and I fought through it, struggling to keep my focus. After three near misses, and a harrowing second where the rod nearly slipped from my fingers, the lock released with a gratifying *click*.

I let myself in and pulled the release for the rear trunk. Bentley and Corman were already on the move behind me. They had the Caddy's trunk open too, and they were busy unloading half of Gabriel's present: two thick bales of marijuana, pressed into fat bricks and sealed in plastic wrap. We loaded the goods into the Mercedes's trunk and shut the lid.

I passed the break-in tools to Corman and waved them off. They jumped back into the Cadillac and pulled a U-turn while I sprinted back across the street and into the other model home. I met up with Caitlin in the living room, hunkering down behind the plate-glass window, just in time to hear the sirens.

Fifteen minutes ago, I'd made a quick call to Gary.

"This is a friendly anonymous tip," I told him. "I just saw a bunch of guys, probably carrying unlicensed firearms, making a drug deal in an empty model house out in Eldorado."

"Is that so?" he said.

"Yeah. You should probably check their trunk. And you might find another twenty or thirty pounds of pot down in the basement, too. Move fast."

Fun fact: getting caught with that much marijuana constitutes the intent to distribute, which moves the crime from a minor misdemeanor to a class-five felony.

The Outfit thugs figured out what was up, about thirty seconds too late. They bolted out the front door just as four squad cars came screaming up the street, screeching to a stop outside the model house. The thugs froze, grabbing air as their guns clattered to the sidewalk.

"As frame jobs go," I said to Caitlin, "this was pretty quick and dirty. Charges might or might not stick, and in any case I can guarantee they'll be bonded out by morning."

She frowned at me. "Then why do it? Why not just kill them?"

I watched as the wispy blond went down hard against the hood of one cruiser, his hands wrenched behind his back as the cuffs slapped on. I couldn't help but smile.

"Beyond the satisfaction of doing unto others as was done unto to me? It's all about sending a message. Chicago thinks that with Nicky gone, the Vegas underworld's in chaos."

"It *is*."

"Yeah, but four of their boys just got set up and rolled by

Vegas's finest. It's gonna *look* like we've got the cops in our pocket."

"Making the city appear to be a harder target than it really is," Caitlin said, putting it together. "Or that perhaps Nicky isn't really missing after all."

"And hopefully providing food for thought." Across the street, the cops popped the Mercedes's trunk, one holding up a brick of pot like it was a hunting trophy. "That thought ideally being, 'Let's find a different city to pick on.'"

"Do you think they will?"

My shoulders sagged. "Realistically? No. This war is coming. Doesn't mean we have to make it *easy* for 'em, though, and the more misinformation and confusion we can hit them with, the better."

Eventually the cops finished their search, bundled the thugs into backseats, and headed out. As the last cruiser rumbled down the street, I gave a salute through the window.

"Happy birthday, Detective Kemper," I said. "Enjoy your cake."

Caitlin glanced down at the slim platinum Chanel watch on her wrist. "Four o'clock, pet. Cesar will be expecting that delegation's arrival in three hours."

"I've been thinking about that. Let's head back to the Nook and rally the troops."

The Mercedes sat abandoned across the street, waiting for a police tow to haul it to the impound lot.

"But first," I said, "give me a hand. I want those license plates."

* * *

Pixie had aerial maps of Rock-a-Hoola up on her laptop screen. As we walked into the bookstore, the door chime jingling, she and Margaux were shaking their heads at each other.

"You're right," Margaux said, "there's no way."

"There's always a way," I replied, locking the door behind us. "But what specific impossibility are we talking about?"

"Getting in there without getting, well, shot." Pixie turned her laptop to show me the screen, gesturing with the cap of a pen. "Look: the way in from every direction is completely open. No cover, no way to sneak in. If they put sentries here, here, and *especially* here, up on top of this old water slide, they can cover every possible approach to the park."

"We *do* have the Calles on our side now," Bentley said, emerging from the back room with Corman in tow. "And that Gabriel gentleman sounded quite eager to settle scores. If we let them attack first and supplement their firepower with a bit of subtle magic..."

"And then Cesar shoots Jennifer." I held up an open hand. In my other, I cradled the two license plates we'd stolen off the Mercedes. "No. The bullets don't start flying until *after* she's secure."

"But we can't get to her," Margaux said.

"I've been thinking about that." I showed them the Illinois plates. "Look, I've only been to Jennifer's fortress once. So the Calles might know my name, but only a few of them have ever seen me, and they've got no reason to remember my face. And I *know* Cesar doesn't know me."

Corman's brow furrowed. "I don't like where you're going with this, kiddo."

"They're expecting the mob's torture specialist to show up, and they've got no idea the guy just got busted. If I roll in and take his place, they'll lead me straight to Jennifer. All I have to do is take out Cesar and anybody standing watch and set her loose. The two of us can hunker down and hold out while Gabriel and the Calles blitz the park."

Caitlin curled her lip. "When the doctor told you 'no unnecessary physical activity,' which of those words was unclear?"

"It's the definition of necessary. Look. Margaux, Bentley, Corman—you're the best at what you do, but this *isn't* what you do. The only person here more qualified than me for this job is Caitlin, and she can't do it either."

She put a hand on her hip. "And why not?"

"Because the Outfit is old-school organized crime, and old

school means all the macho bullshit that goes with it. Unlike Nicky's organization, they *don't* hire women, period. No chance Cesar would believe you. Me, though? I can waltz right in."

The room fell into a pensive silence.

"It's a two-hour drive to the park, guys," I said. "Clock's ticking."

"I hate to say it," Pixie sighed, "believe me, I really hate to say it, but he's right."

"We'll be directly behind you," Bentley said, "parked just off the highway, in case anything goes wrong."

It was a nice gesture, and I knew he meant well, but I also knew "just off the highway" was going to be too damn far to do anything if this job went sideways. Two lives were lives resting on my shoulders tonight—Jennifer's and mine—and if I made a single mistake, they were both forfeit.

"Let's call Gabriel," I said. "We're burning daylight."

47.

We slapped the Illinois plates onto Bentley's Cadillac. He curled his hand around mine as he pressed the keys into my palm.

"Be *careful*."

I pulled him into a quick hug, squeezing his frail shoulders. There wasn't anything left to talk about, and we were running out of time.

I cruised out of the city on I-15, bound southwest and chasing a neon-orange sunset. I knew my family was behind me, dots in the rearview, but I couldn't have felt more alone. The Caddy jolted over a rough patch of road and sent my stomach lurching. A quick flood of nausea passed over me like an ocean wave, there and gone again in the space of a breath.

Just don't get hit in the head again, I thought, smiling grimly at the road ahead. *Easy*.

The last rays of sunlight guided me to the outskirts of Rock-a-Hoola. The corpse of the water park had gone to rot a decade ago, and now nothing remained but its rusting bones. Stripped girders and crumbling graffiti-plastered walls gathered dust, abandoned to the desert. The spiral of a broken-down water slide still stood; atop it, a man with a pair of binoculars and a rifle slung over one shoulder stood watch.

Two bangers wearing Calles colors, yellow and brown, waved me down the open front drive. I cruised in slow, an easy five miles an hour, as the Caddy's wheels thumped over broken pavement.

I kept both hands on the wheel.

The water park's builders—or rebuilders, one of the times it closed and reopened—had a thing for '50s kitsch. The buildings that still stood were all angled art deco huts painted in neon oranges, blues, and greens. Even faded by weather and time, their colors shone against the gathering dark.

The road ended at Cesar. He stood in front of a ticket booth, flanked by five of his men. His shoulders went back as my headlights washed over him, his chin raised, putting up a front for his buddies. Every one of them was packing, either carrying their steel in shoulder holsters or openly in their hands.

I killed the engine and got out of the car. I didn't have a gun. Instead, I carried a simple black plastic box. I'd borrowed Pixie's femtocell case, but I'd swapped out her gadget for one of my own.

"We were expecting more men," Cesar called out. I stood beside the Cadillac. He stood by the ticket hut. Neither of us closed the distance.

"You only need one," I told him. "They call me the Doctor."

He nodded at my case. "What's in there?"

I gave him the creepiest smile I could muster.

"Tools. For my...examination."

"They told you the deal, right? No blood. Do whatever you gotta do to make her talk, but you can't cut on her. Not one drop."

"That won't be a problem," I said. "Is my patient ready?"

I walked along with Cesar, and his entourage followed. Not good. I was prepared to take out one target. Six, not so much.

I counted heads as we strolled through the desolate park. Flashlights glimmered on the other side of sagging palm trees. A cluster of men crouched in the remnants of a cafeteria, faces lit by the glow of a battery-powered lamp, throwing dice across the broken ceramic tiles and waving fistfuls of cash at each other. All in all, I figured Cesar had convinced about thirty of the Calles to turn traitor, not counting the wolf pack that surrounded us as we walked.

Cesar led the way along a broken path framed by beds of yellow scraggly weeds and dirt. Fat brown roaches swarmed around our feet, and a bloated insect hummed as it winged past my ear. Up ahead stood the park's old video arcade, painted in Day-Glo purple. Three rolling aluminum doors, like loading bays for trucks, barred the way inside, but the one on the left stood open. Faint electric light glowed from within.

I knew she was in there before I even set eyes on her. I didn't have to see her. I could *feel* her and the seething cloud of occult energy that hovered over the arcade like a toxic storm cloud. She'd been weaving a spell, maybe for days, feeding her power and her rage into it one drop at a time. It hovered on the edge of climax, a heartbeat from eruption, like the pressure in your sinuses one split second before a sneeze.

I knew exactly what she was waiting for, and what I needed to do.

That's my girl, I thought when I saw her. They'd bound her by the wrists, a rope looped over a girder pulling her hands taut above her head, leaving her to stand on wobbly tiptoes. There wasn't one glimmer of fear in Jennifer's eyes, though. No, I knew that look. It was pure, unadulterated fury.

For a moment, when she saw me step into the room, I thought she might give the game away. I should have known better. The glimmer of relief on her face vanished in a heartbeat, and she turned her scowl on Cesar.

"What's wrong?" she drawled. "You finally realize you're not man enough to kill me yourself? Had to bring in some outside help?"

"Oh, we ain't gonna kill you, *chica*." Cesar waved me forward. "Not *yet*. This guy's gonna ask you a whole lot of questions first. And you *are* gonna answer him."

I scoped the room fast. All the old arcade games, except for a busted and lonely Space Invaders console going to seed in the back corner, had been hauled off or sold for scrap ages ago. The arcade was more or less a concrete box with only one way in or out. They'd set up a card table near Jennifer's side and a single folding chair.

"Sorry, what was that?" Jennifer asked. "Couldn't understand you. I don't speak pencil-dick."

"You oughta take this seriously." Cesar's nostrils flared. "You're about to be in a whole world of pain, bitch."

Jennifer rolled her eyes at him. "Jumpin' Jesus on a pogo stick. I'm in a world of pain every time I gotta look at your ugly-ass face."

I walked to the table and set down my plastic box. Nestled in my pocket, my phone buzzed twice, then fell silent. Two rings and a hang-up was the signal that Gabriel and the loyal Calles were ready to roll.

Now it was all on me.

"You," I said to Cesar, "obviously need to stay. As for your friends, I don't work in front of an audience."

Cesar locked eyes with me. Trying to read me. He hesitated a moment, then pointed at two of his men.

"You two, guard the door. Everybody else clear out."

They moved to guard the door, all right. On the inside, flanking the open bay door and standing where they could get a good view of the show. So much for getting Cesar alone.

At least now it was one against three, instead of one against six. Those were almost survivable odds.

"All right." My fingertips rested lightly on the rough, corrugated face of the plastic box. "What would you like to know first?"

"Her bank account in the Caymans," Cesar said. "Number and passcode."

"As you wish." I unclipped the hasps on the box and looked to Jennifer. "Are you ready to begin?"

She bared her teeth in a feral grin.

"Do your worst."

My hand reached into the box and closed over a curve of bright orange plastic. As I lifted it, Cesar—standing about five feet away and trying to look over my shoulder—leaned in.

"Hey, what is that?" he asked.

"Flare gun," I said and swung it toward the thugs by the door. Not at them, between them, toward the open door and angled high. The gun ignited with a crackling *whoosh* as I pulled the trigger, and the arcade erupted with a flash of blinding light. The flare screamed from the muzzle, firing out into the darkness.

The surprise bought me two seconds. One to toss the empty gun. One for a pair of aces to drop from my sleeves. I caught the cards in my fingertips, whipped my arms up, and sent them flying. One thug took it dead on: he dropped, gurgling, the ace of diamonds buried halfway into his throat. The other card went wide, slicing alongside his buddy's neck and ripping open his jugular. Blood guttered through his fingers as he slumped against the wall, hands clamped over his torn flesh as if he thought he could press himself back together.

A third ace jumped from my jacket pocket as I dropped low and spun on my heel toward Cesar. The card flew like a hornet, but it barely touched him; instead it winged along his bicep and hit the back wall, leaving a thread-thin trickle of blood no deeper than a paper cut.

Cesar grinned and raised his pistol.

"You missed."

"Nah, sugar," Jennifer told him. "Danny just knew I'd wanna kill you myself."

Then she spat a single word. A long, guttural, twisting word that evoked frozen Germanic winters. The trigger to the spell she'd been weaving for days. The toxic miasma above our heads exploded with a peal of thunder and her spite-fueled power crashed down on Cesar, one man alone in a torrent of death.

The paper cut on his bicep ripped open, as if someone had taken pliers to his skin and given it one brutal, wrenching tug. Blood gushed from the wound as he screamed, flowing faster than it should have, and even faster by the second. He collapsed to his knees, shrieking, and a scarlet torrent blasted from the wound like the spray from a fire hose and splashed across the arcade wall.

His skin turned ashen and taut, his fingers and toes curling, crumpling. Bones cracked as his limbs folded in on themselves and the flesh on his skull stretched taut like a mummified corpse. Jennifer's death curse slowly crushed his body like a juice box, squeezing every drop of blood from every last ragged vein.

What collapsed to the floor when the spell was done, gray and bloodless and small as a child, didn't look human anymore.

"That's what you *get* for fuckin' with a witch," Jennifer said. "My momma taught me that trick."

I worked at the ropes binding her wrists, getting her down as the night erupted with the crackle of gunfire. Engines revved in the distance, roaring over the staccato pops and thudding shotgun booms.

"What's going on out there?" Jennifer asked me, wincing as she rubbed her wrists.

"Your buddy Gabriel and the cavalry are here. That flare wasn't just a distraction; it was the signal that I had you and they were safe to move in."

"You telling me they started the party without us?"

Jennifer scooped up Cesar's fallen pistol. Then, after a moment's deliberation, she grabbed one of his thugs' guns too. She checked the loads fast and sighted down each barrel.

"Seriously?" I said. "You don't want to maybe take a breather or something? You've just been through a lot."

"Hon, this moment is all I've been thinking about for *days*. Not a chance I'm missing the fun." She leaned in and kissed me on the cheek. "And thanks for the rescue. Now grab a piece and let's *go* already! There's a whole lot of backstabbers who need lead tombstones out there, and you're slowin' me down."

I sighed, prying a pistol from the other fallen thug's cold fingers, trying to ignore a sudden twinge in my back.

"I think I'm getting too old for this," I told her.

Jennifer stood silhouetted in the open bay door, a pistol cocked and ready in each hand.

"Less whinin', more shootin'," she said. Then she was gone, charging into the dark.

I followed her into the fight. Of course I did. That's what friends do.

48.

The Flamenco was one of the older hotels on the Strip, a relic of Old Vegas. They'd remodeled the place a few times over the decades, but you could still imagine Frankie and the Rat Pack strutting through the halls on their way to play the grand showroom.

I walked under the flaming marquee of light, flared and cherry red, shaped to resemble a showgirl's headdress. The packed bar drew my eye, but the best I could do was grit my teeth as I walked on by. It had been almost a week since the showdown in the desert, which meant five more days before I could finally have a stiff drink. The headaches and nausea were coming less frequently now, but they hadn't gone away.

Up an escalator, down an access hallway, a meeting room waited behind ivory double doors. It would have fit into a corporate tower anywhere in the world, sporting a long oval table surrounded by high-backed chairs and a crisp hotel notepad and pen placed neatly at each seat. Pixie was already there, wearing bulky headphones and sweeping the room with a gadget that looked like a stage magician's wand.

"They drafted you too, huh?" she said.

I held up a hand. "Security."

"Ditto. You think this is gonna work?"

"Maybe. I don't see an alternative to *trying*, anyway."

When Jennifer arrived, I almost didn't recognize her. She'd traded in her usual T-shirt and jeans for a pressed olive pantsuit, her hair coiffed. She always clipped her nails short, but they didn't usually show the gleam of a fresh manicure.

"This room is certified bug-free," Pixie announced, giving Jennifer a wave. "I'm gonna get to work on the hallway."

Jennifer took my hand and gave it a nervous squeeze.

"Thanks for helping out," she said. "Means the world to me."

"Hey, I wouldn't miss it. You feeling confident?"

"Nope." She grinned. "Public speakin' ain't exactly my forte. And there's all kinds of ways this could go real, real bad."

"Then we'll just have to handle it, won't we?"

The rest of the security team wasn't far behind her, a handful of Gabriel's men. They'd traded in their gang colors for rented suits.

"You two," I said, divvying up the jobs, "I want on the door. You, cover the hallway entrance on the lobby side. Nobody who's not on the guest list gets past you, and that includes employees. If the hotel staff make a stink about it, send 'em to me. Now who's got the sharpest eyes in this bunch? You? Okay, you're on lobby detail. Just watch the hotel entrance and radio ahead when you see our guests show up, or if you spot anything hinky..."

Somehow, with an effort akin to herding cats, I whipped up a reasonable security detail. Soon the guests started to arrive. Gabriel was first on the scene, and the big man gave me a nod in the hallway.

"Thanks for the assist out there, *ese*. Anything you need, you just say it."

"All I ask is that you hear Jennifer out and try to keep the peace today."

He laughed. "Hell, I won't blast any fools if they don't *make* me blast 'em."

Winslow came next. He wasn't inclined to take off his black leather vest, the one with the screaming skeletal eagle on the back, but at least he'd worn a shirt under it for a change. He took my hand in a vice grip.

"Heard from Jake and Westie," he said. "They're raisin' hell down in Tijuana, free and clear. Gotta say, I had my doubts about you, Faust. But you manned up and delivered. Far as I'm concerned, your debt's wiped. Hey, how's that Barracuda treating you? She still running right?"

I gritted my teeth.

"The, uh, cops impounded it when they arrested me. And the gun, too."

Winslow barked out a raspy laugh. "Hell, son, this just hasn't been your month, has it? If you're looking for another ride, stop by the garage sometime. I'll set you up. But I *will* need cash up front this time."

"Hey," I said, "did Jake and Westie mention another prisoner who escaped with them? A guy named Buddy?"

He rubbed the gray stubble on his chin, thinking.

"Yeah." Winslow nodded. "Said they had a guy with 'em, but they parted ways halfway to the border. Said he had someplace important to go."

So Buddy had made it. He had a shot at delivering his message, at least. And next...well, I didn't have time to think about next at the moment, not with the guest list filling out by the minute. There was Eddie Stone from the Bishops, looking flashy in a peacock-blue three-piece suit, Little Shawn from the Playboy Killers, even a hard-eyed delegate from the Fine Upstanding Crew. Guys who had no reason to sit down at the same table—and every reason to shoot each other on sight.

Everybody stayed cool, for now. And even though every single one of them had ignored the "no guns" request, the chrome stayed holstered and out of sight.

Pixie sidled up next to me as I patrolled the hall, keeping tabs on five things at once. "Faust, this is getting weird fast."

"Long as it's not getting murderous fast, that's fine by me."

"That guy in the black silk suit and half a missing pinky finger coming up the hall," she whispered. "Is he from the freaking *yakuza?*"

"*Inagawa-kai*," I murmured back. "They're actually based out of Yokohama, but they've got investments in Vegas. And here comes the rep from the Fourteen-K Triad. Smile and be friendly."

One of the last arrivals wasn't on the guest list. Emma Loomis came striding up the hall, dressed for business and carrying a crocodile-skin attaché case.

"Emma?" I said. "How did you even—"

"Protecting my prince's interests. This is more my area of expertise than Caitlin's."

"Yeah, but did Jennifer send you an invite?"

"She must have forgotten. An understandable oversight." Emma leaned close, tiny flashes of copper sparkling in her eyes. "But nobody is denying Prince Sitri a seat at *this* table."

She had a point. I let her pass.

As the last guest arrived, taking his seat at the oval table, we closed the conference room doors. Jennifer beckoned me to the front of the room to stand at her shoulder. Voices murmured, gazes darting across the table, old enmities smoldering.

"War is coming," Jennifer's voice rang out. The murmuring fell silent.

She paused a moment, holding their attention, then spoke again.

"The Chicago Outfit is on the move. They've already driven Nicky Agnelli out of town. Spread confusion and dissent. Recruited traitors within our very ranks. And they're just gettin' started."

Eddie Stone flashed a gold-toothed smile. "Seems to me like running Nicky out of town was good news for all of us."

"Good for now," I told him, "but divided, at each other's throats? Chicago is going to *steamroll* this town. And if you didn't like the old boss, you're sure as hell not gonna like the new boss."

Winslow slouched in his chair, one weathered arm on the table. "You got a better idea?"

"Damn straight," Jennifer told him. "Look, let's get one thing clear. Nicky's gone and he ain't coming back. He held this city together. Mediated between us. Yeah, he threw his weight around a little too much, we can all agree on that, but right now we're just a bunch of lone targets waitin' to get picked off."

The Triad delegate, an elderly man with the sharp blue eyes of a twenty-year-old, waved a hand.

"And you would take his place? Don't waste our time, girl."

"Nope. Not take his place. I got something better in mind. What did Nicky really bring to the table? He minded the borders. Kept everybody talking instead of shooting, most of the time anyhow. But Nicky's job was all done before, and it was all done better."

She raised her hands, taking in the room.

"I picked this place 'cause it's got history. Meyer Lansky, Bugsy Siegel, Moe Dalitz—they all met in this very room. Back in the days of the Commission, people like us knew how to work together without a single strongman at the top."

"Sure," Winslow said, "'til the feds ran the mob's ass out of town and the corporations moved in."

Jennifer rested her fingers on the table. She smiled.

"But the feds ain't here now, are they? Like I said, alone, we're just waiting to get picked off one by one. But think about what we've got. Look around this room. I reckon the folks at this table control seventy, seventy-five percent of all the action in this city. We've got the rackets. We've got the influence. We've got our eyes on every truck that comes outta McCarran Airport and our fingers in every heist. When it comes to the streets, we've got over two *thousand* hardcore soldiers flying our colors, ready to fight back and kick the Outfit's ass so hard they'll wish they'd never *heard* of Las Vegas."

Palms pressed to the table, she leaned in, taking a long, slow look across the room. Meeting every gaze with eyes of steel.

"Ladies and gentlemen," Jennifer said, "let's get *organized.*"

Epilogue

The towers of Dubai blazed against the night, a sea of white-hot diamonds on the edge of the Persian Gulf. One of those towers had acquired a parasite.

The man in the black leather bodysuit clung to the skyscraper like a barnacle, scaling his way up one careful inch at a time with suction cups the size of dinner plates strapped to his forearms and calves. The bustling nightlife and tangled traffic were distant blurry lights, over seventy stories below.

Cold wind ruffled his wavy chestnut hair. His eyes, safe behind tempered goggles, narrowed in concentration. His muscles burned like wildfire now, three hours after he'd begun his ascent, but his goal wasn't far away. Clamped onto a smoky window, he gripped a carbide-wheel glass cutter and got to work.

The restful sound of the wind shattered. A Beach Boys song blared in his left ear, Carl Wilson crooning "Good Vibrations." With an annoyed grunt, he tapped the earpiece and took the call.

"Little busy right now," he said, his voice tinged with a French accent.

"Marcel, my friend," the Smile said. "Where are you?"

"Seventy-two floors up the side of Princess Tower. Where did you *think* I'd be?"

"Hm. Don't look down."

"I never look down, and I never look back," Marcel replied. A circle of glass the size of a manhole cover separated cleanly from the window. Gripping it with another suction-cup handle, he carefully pushed it inward and laid it down on the floor inside.

He pulled himself through the hole, bending like a contortionist, lowering himself onto a polished Italian marble floor.

"Is that your catchphrase?" the Smile asked. "It's cute. I'm calling with good news: we've just gotten the official confirmation. Daniel Faust is dead."

The room beyond the window was a private art gallery. Rows of glass cases stretched into the darkness, divided by runners of red velvet carpet. Marcel's gaze went to the corner of the room, where a scarlet light blinked on the gray plastic shell of a motion detector. Keeping his back pressed to the window, just out of its range, he drew a tiny prong-shaped pistol.

A dart streaked out when he pulled the trigger, fired on a puff of air from a pneumatic cylinder. The dart hit the motion detector's case, cracked it, and let out an electric hiss. The flashing light flickered from red to green.

"Should that name mean something to me?" He threw himself into a roll, dodging beneath an infrared eye, and came up in a crouch.

"Your sacrificial lamb, who nobly gave his life to die in your stead. Congratulations, Marcel. The cycle is broken. You aren't the Thief anymore."

Marcel tapped the side of his goggles. They flipped into night-vision mode and turned his world into a wash of green light. Artifacts from around the world filled the glass cases, golden conquistador crosses sitting side by side with jade from the Ming dynasty.

"So this Faust," Marcel said. "He's the Thief now?"

"Was. For all of five minutes before he was killed in a prison riot. Just don't *die* again. Your soul will be pulled right back into the cycle and you'll ruin all my hard work. Fortunately, seeing as you're not doomed anymore, that shouldn't be a problem for you. Do you have eyes on the target?"

Marcel crouched in front of a case, his eyes wide behind his goggles. On the other side of the glass, his prize nestled on a bed of black velvet: a bowl of turquoise, its sides inlaid with swirling Aztec symbols. The basin of the bowl still held a dark stain, the memory of heart's blood shed centuries ago.

"You held up your end of the bargain," Marcel replied, "and I'll hold up mine."

* * *

Half a world away, dingy gray clouds roiled from smokestacks and painted the sky over Gary, Indiana, with oily smears. Angelo Mancuso wrinkled his nose as he stepped out of his sleek white limousine. A long cashmere overcoat draped his athletic frame.

"Does it always stink like this?" He glanced at Sal, his body-guard. The big man shrugged.

"It's from the steel mill."

Angelo looked around, taking in the run-down street, the broken windows shrouded by tacked-up bedsheets. He knocked on the driver's window. His chauffeur rolled it down and poked his head out.

"Yeah, boss?"

"We'll be out in ten minutes," Angelo said. "Do me a favor. If anybody comes near the car who ain't us? Just shoot 'em. I don't think the locals are gonna mind."

Sal put his hands on his hips, shaking his head. "I don't think the locals are gonna *notice*."

The tenement awaited, the stagnant halls reeking of rotting trash and sweat. Angelo's wing tips crunched on broken glass, disturbing the uncanny silence.

Sal glanced over his shoulder, one hand buried inside his jacket pocket. "You sure we got the right place?"

A sigil adorned the door at the end of the hall, painted in rust red. It resembled the Egyptian Eye of Horus, with a ragged X daubed over the pupil.

"Yeah," Angelo said, sounding as wary as Sal looked. "This is definitely him."

The door swung open at a touch. The apartment beyond,

lights doused and the windows plastered over with sheets of brown butcher paper, was a forest of dangling bones. *Tiny bones*, Angelo thought, *birds and squirrels*. The dirty bone mobiles hung bound together by strips of twine, configured into stars and cubes and strange spiral ladders. He dodged around them as they stepped inside, his shoulder bumping one ornate design and making it spin in the stifling, humid air.

"Boss," Sal whispered and nudged his back. Angelo followed his gaze. A naked corpse lay upon the kitchen table, butchered almost beyond recognition. Mason jars piled up in a miniature pyramid at its side, each one filled with a few inches of congealed blood.

A tired voice sounded from the open bedroom doorway.

"There was an instrument once, the Black Eye, forged by a cult of silence. They say that if you wore it, the gods themselves were blinded to your presence. My version is...impermanent. Needs cambion blood to feed the sigil. Caught a cambion, but as you can see, I used him up."

Sal gave Angelo a leery glance. Angelo cleared his throat and turned to face the doorway.

"My name is Angelo Mancuso. I represent a very distinguished organization based out of Chicago—"

"I know who you are."

A ragged shadow moved in the dark, shambling closer.

"We're about to embark on a business project," Angelo said. "And I'm looking for recruits. I need...skilled hands. Specialists."

As the figure stepped into sight, his funeral suit hanging loose on his malnourished frame, he reached up to adjust his dusty bow tie.

"I believe you mean," Damien Ecko hissed, "*freaks*."

Angelo held up his hands, pinned by Ecko's mad gaze.

"I mean no disrespect."

Ecko's lips pulled back in a death's-head grin.

"*Disrespect?*" he said. "And how could I, surrounded by such luxury, living such a life of grand indulgence, possibly feel disrespected by anyone? I am simply on top of the world. The butler should be around shortly, with caviar for everyone."

"I heard a little about what happened," Angelo said. "Pack of crooks from Vegas hit your house, right? They didn't just rob you; they burned you down. Didn't leave you with a pot to piss in."

Ecko chuckled, a rasping sound that sent a chill down Angelo's spine.

"Oh, they did far worse than that. I'm a hunted man. But as long as I stay behind my sigils, they can't find me. You...don't have any cambion blood, do you?"

"Come work for me," Angelo said. "We're taking a little road trip, and we're gonna hit Vegas *hard*. You want payback against the people who stuck you in this shithole? Sign up with me, I guarantee you'll get it."

Ecko wavered on his feet, eyes gleaming. He let out a tittering laugh.

"*Faust*," he whispered. He grinned at Angelo. "Yes. I would be delighted to aid your...amusing little dreams of conquest. I'll merely need one thing from you first."

"Name it."

"Access to a city morgue," Ecko replied. "If we're taking a road trip, I want to bring *lots* of new friends along."

Afterword

And there we pause the story for now, as Vegas and Chicago rally their forces for battle, and the man with the Cheshire smile...does whatever it is he's doing. All I'll say is, if you're anywhere near Las Vegas, you might want to invest in a bulletproof vest. And a bomb shelter. And maybe a one-way ticket to anywhere *but* Chicago.

As always, thanks to my awesome team: Kira Rubenthaler on editing (a.k.a., making my drivel readable), James T. Egan on cover design (a.k.a., making my drivel pretty), and Maggie Faid. And thank *you*!

Want to get the advance scoop on new books and projects? Head over to http://www.craigschaeferbooks.com/mailing-list/ and hop onto my mailing list. Once-a-month newsletters, zero spam. Want to reach out? You can find me on Facebook at http://www.facebook.com/CraigSchaeferBooks, on Twitter as @craig_schaefer, or just drop me an email at craig@craigschaeferbooks.com. I always love hearing from my readers.

Daniel Faust will return in 2016. In the meantime, watch for the launch of the Harmony Black spin-off series coming from 47North Publishing in January, where you'll get an all-new perspective on Daniel Faust's world...and maybe see a few familiar faces along the way.

26275755R00205

Made in the USA
Middletown, DE
23 November 2015